THE
NIGHT
STAGES

THE
NIGHT
STAGES

JANE URQUHART

FARRAR, STRAUS AND GIROUX   NEW YORK

Farrar, Straus and Giroux
18 West 18th Street, New York 10011

Copyright © 2015 by Jane Urquhart
All rights reserved
Printed in the United States of America
Originally published in 2015 by McClelland & Stewart, Canada
Published in the United States by Farrar, Straus and Giroux
First American edition, 2015

The poem on page 230 that begins "Humble Anchorites" is from *Skelligside* (1990),
copyright © Estate of Michael Kirby and The Lilliput Press. Reprinted by kind
permission of The Lilliput Press of Dublin, Ireland.

Farrar, Straus and Giroux books may be purchased for educational, business,
or promotional use. For information on bulk purchases, please contact the
Macmillan Corporate and Premium Sales Department at 1-800-221-7945,
extension 5442, or write to specialmarkets@macmillan.com.

www.fsgbooks.com
www.twitter.com/fsgbooks • www.facebook.com/fsgbooks

1   3   5   7   9   10   8   6   4   2

Frontispiece: Photograph of the passenger terminal at Gander International Airport
in Newfoundland at night. Photograph by Tootoon's Photography.

For Michael Phillips,
with thanks

—

In memory of artist Kenneth Lochhead,
poet Michael Kirby,
and aviator Vi Milstead Warren

As if I were the ghost of the fog

—

EUGENE O'NEILL
Long Day's Journey into Night

CONTENTS

I   Leica   3

Iveragh   6

Commission   50

Truancy   56

Rage   75

The Critic   84

The Purple Hornet   94

Concrete   117

Mosel   139

The Mountains   146

II   Search   167

Gentleman   199

The Essential   222

Halls of Departure   247

America   273

Source   284

The Corner That She Turned   315

Belleek   338

The Rás   349

Morning   380

Acknowledgements   399

I

—

LEICA

There is a black-and-white photograph of Kenneth standing in sunlight beside a prairie railway station. He is loose-limbed and smiling, happy maybe, or at least unconcerned about the journey he seems poised to take. Slim, fresh-faced, all dressed up, he appears to be just a kid really, possibly leaving home for the first time. But nothing about his posture, or the atmosphere around him, suggests anxiety. He wants to get going, this young man, but he is not at all unhappy with, or uncurious about, the place where he stands. His shadow falls behind him, but the gesture painted by it is one of eagerness. He will never lose this alertness, this aura of keenness.

The station's platform is dry and clean: there have not been any recent bouts of snow. But Kenneth's overcoat, and his gloves and scarf, suggest that it is cold. There is also a winter clarity of sunlight and crispness of shadow on the cement under his feet, a full sun in a clear sky above him. And then there is this anticipation – that eagerness.

A cable telegraph sign is just behind his left shoulder: it could be he has sent or has received some sort of message, a declaration or a summons. Perhaps he will be gone from the place where he stands, and quite soon. Everything around him in this picture – shadows, the raised arms of the railway signal, the sky and the station – speaks of a departure to places larger and more complicated, a drift toward relationships more sophisticated than those unfolding in the town or village beyond the edges of the picture. An entrance into commerce, perhaps, or maybe sudden fame. It is not at all hard to imagine Kenneth gone, the quay empty, and the photographer, who-ever he or she may be, turning away, walking back into a town that has already begun to fade.

But Kenneth is older than he looks in this image: he has already taken and abandoned several points of view. He has been to Paris, Milan, Madrid. He has been educated by museums and instructed by teachers. He has met – briefly – certain celebrated artists. He has visited important monu-ments and gazed at significant landmarks. He has gathered all of this together and has brought it with him to this stark place, along with a wife and two children. Yes, he is married and has children.

There is a grain elevator in the distance on the other side of the tracks. Some sort of field, far away, is almost hidden by Kenneth's left elbow. He is not a prairie boy, but he has chosen this sky, this platform, and everything beyond it as a background to his daily life, and he has become familiar with returning to such a landscape after completing projects in the outer world. In spite of how things may look, this is a photo of arrival, one taken just after disembarkation, when the airport mural was still bright and alive in his mind, the paint on it hardly dry.

If he were to close his eyes now, the figures he has created would stare back at him – a questioning congregation – wondering where he has gone. His back is turned to the distances suggested by the converging lines of the railway tracks. The sky is utterly empty. Kenneth's shadow is a thin ghost on the quay. But there are thousands and thousands of miles inside him.

IVERAGH

——

Just after midnight she walks out the door, steps over frost-stiffened grass, and approaches the grey shape of the Vauxhall. She slings her suitcase into the back seat, slams the door, then opens the driver's side, sits behind the wheel, pulls the door toward her. She turns the key in the ignition, places her palm on the cool, vibrating knob of the gear shift, and allows herself one moment of hesitation. Her white cottage, an unlit rectangle against a sky busy with stars, is as grey as the car. The turf shed is grey as well, squatting at the back of the yard. There is a moon somewhere, but she refuses to look for it. She flicks on the lights. She shifts into reverse.

The grass of her own lane flattens under the wheels; then, when she turns the car, an ill-repaired road with a ribbon of similar grass at its centre appears in her windscreen. Three miles of hedgerows accompany her to the crossroads at Killeen Leacht, with its single tavern, dark and empty, and its wide, slow river. Salmon are gently turning in their sleep under that shining water. Salmon and the long green hands of water weeds, shaken by the current.

Soon she is deep in the Kerry Mountains, disturbing flocks of sheep drowsing near potholes, and birds probably huddled in hidden nests. The car's lights bounce on the stone bridges of Coomaclarig and Dromalonburt, then illuminate the trunks of last standing oaks of Glencar. She wants the constellation tilting in the rear-view mirror to be Orion, and when it follows her for some time along the hip of the mountain called Knocknacusha, she concludes that it is. Climbing to the Oisin Pass, she thinks about the ancient warrior Niall had spoken of, the one who had searched from that height for lost companions but not found them. He'd been gone for three hundred years, Niall said, but the woman he was with made him believe it was only three nights. He had lost everything, Niall insisted, for three nights with a woman.

She descends to the plain. Lough Acoose, still and dim under faintly lit clouds, slips into her side window. On the opposite shore the hem of a shadowy mountain touches the water. Ten minutes later there is the town of Killorglin, and then the Laune River, oiled by moonlight.

Goodbye, she thinks, to all that. Goodbye to the four flashing strands of the Iveragh Peninsula, to the bright path of surf in St. Finian's Bay, the Skellig Islands freighted by history, the shoulders of mountains called Macgillicuddy's Reeks. Goodbye to her own adopted townland, Cloomcartha, to the kitchens that had welcomed her, and to dogs whose names she had known. Goodbye to her own small drama — that and the futile, single-minded tenaciousness that had almost maintained it. The changing weather patterns, the gestures, the theatrical light.

An hour and a half later she reaches the smoother roads and quieter hills of neighbouring County Limerick. She accelerates, and as she does, she begins to visualize the abandoned peninsula unfurling like a scarf in the wind, gradually unwinding, then letting go, mountains and pastures scattering behind her on the road. "Iveragh," she says out loud, perhaps for the last time. The landscape, she knows, will forget her. Just as Niall will forget her. What she will forget remains to be seen. She imagines her phone ringing on the table and no one there to answer it. This provides a twinge of pleasure until it occurs to her that it might not ring at all.

She leaves the car in the airport parking lot, knowing it will be towed, stolen, or junked when it becomes apparent that no one is coming back to claim it. The sky, overcast now, is a solid black, echoed by greasy black macadam. It begins to rain in a half-hearted way as she walks with her suitcase toward the lights of the terminal, leaving, she hopes, such full preoccupation and terrible necessity. She is leaving the peninsula. Leaving Niall.

Ten hours later, the airliner on which she is travelling shudders, preparing to descend. The window is an oval, the shape of a mirror that once hung on a mother's bedroom wall. A mother, she thinks, and a mother's bedroom wall. What she sees through this oval is the blurred circle of the propellers, then a broken coastline, froth at the edges and rocks moving inland as if bulldozed by the force of the sea. Now and then an ebony ocean emerges between long arms of altostratus clouds trailing intermittent rain. *Altostratus.* One of the words Niall has slipped into her vocabulary, along with *geomagnetism, cyclonic, convective, penultimate. Ultimate.*

All night the hum of the engines has remained constant, but reaching this shore the sound changes, the Constellation banks, and the seascape below tilts to the left. There are caves and inlets, and the curve of a sudden beach like a new moon near dark water. The noise diminishes and the cliffs move nearer until she can see the ragged cut of the bitten periphery, then the uninterrupted northern forest, moving inland.

She searches in her handbag, finds a cigarette, and lights it while staring at the blue flame near the propeller, which for a moment echoes the reflected orange flame of her lighter. While she smokes, the roar of the aircraft intensifies, then diminishes again, like an argument. One silver wing dips toward the sea, and she sees a freighter half a mile or so beyond the rocks of the coast. She believes the ship is fully lit and of a great size, waves cascading over its long deck, pale castles of ice on the bow in the full dark of a late December afternoon. But it is autumn, not winter, and the day is opening, not closing.

She cannot visualize the cockpit of this very domestic plane, this padded and upholstered airborne parlour called a Constellation. More than fifteen years have passed since the war, the Air Transport Auxiliary, and the intense relationship with aircraft that filled her then-vivid life. The young pilot she had been then, the young woman behind the controls, would have been disdainful of what she has become: a sombre person with the bright centre of her life hidden, her days unfolding in the pause that seems to define this half-point of the twentieth century. *Fuselage*, she thinks, *instrument panel*. These terms are still known to her, but she has, beyond her facile drawings of aircraft, no real relationship with them. She has become unknowable, and very likely uninteresting. She has blamed Niall for this, and for much else, though she knows it has been her own acquiescence that has caused her to become, in every possible way, a passenger.

Her younger self would have been disdainful of the clutter of what passes for comfort in this airborne interior: the seats that become beds, the blankets, the linens and tableware. She can remember evenings when, after a day of ferrying war-planes, the moon would sit complacently over the dark airfield and the makeshift bunkhouses where she and her flight companions would sleep. She can recall whispered confidences and bursts of laughter, the sense of guardianship, inclusion. And now, more than a decade and a half later, she is being flown into nothing but personal scarcity. She leans her head against the curved frame of the window, trying to bring the communal engagement of the war years back into her heart. But when she closes her eyes, the memory of a map falls into her mind.

Because it was drawn on a narrow slice of paper, she had believed Niall had placed a drawing of a river in her hand. Then she had looked at it more closely and had seen there was only one shoreline moving down the sheet, defining thumb-sized spots of blue. Bays, he had told her, the beginnings of open water in a cold climate. Whoever made it must have been working on the deck of a ship that was following the coast, he had said. It was one of the few gifts he had ever given her, and she cannot now recall the occasion that had prompted it: only that it had moved her, and she had not told him how much. She would never, now, be able to tell him how much.

She opens her eyes, turns back to the oval.

What she sees below is not quite arctic, is a mirror image instead of the sea cliffs that were visible after the takeoff from Shannon, except there are far too many trees now to mistake this country for Ireland. The cliffs appear to be wilder, though the surf breaks around them in the same familiar way. As the plane lowers more purposefully, making its final approach into Gander, Newfoundland, the pine forest approaches. Sea, rock, then acres and acres of forest. Like all transatlantic flights, the aircraft would refuel in this bleak, obscure place. The passengers would disembark for an hour or two.

Tam recalls the bright new American aircraft she had sometimes been instructed to pick up at Prestwick in Scotland: Mosquitos often, or Lancasters. Those planes had set out for the transatlantic part of the journey from the place that is now directly below her, as Ferry Command had been situated at Gander. She had always wanted to pilot a transatlantic flight, but it was understood that no woman would ever be invited to do so, regardless of her skills or accomplishments, so the idea of Gander had remained a vague point of intersection to her, situated between one important shore and another. Soon her boots will be on Gander's transient ground, however: all these years later. You bide your time in a temporary place like this, she thinks. You make no commitment. This is the geography of Purgatory and the aircraft is about to touch down.

She had always enjoyed "touching down," noise and power and forward momentum lightly brushing the ground, then settling in, becoming calmer, silencing. She recalls the satisfaction of a completed mission, the pleasure of performance. But now she believes that when she lands it will be as if an idea, something tonal – a full weather pattern, Niall would say – will have closed up behind her, and she will be in the final stages of leaving him.

In the mountains of the Iveragh, he had told her, there would always be times of scarcity. But the old people of the Iveragh knew the difference between scarcity and famine. There is hope in scarcity, the old people had said. She had heard them say it. They had said it to her.

There was no hope in her. Not anymore. From now on she would starve.

Niall had been born in a market town on the Iveragh Peninsula of County Kerry – the Kingdome, he called it – and except for university and a handful of years working for the Meteorology Service in Dublin, he had never lived anywhere else. Sometimes he would recite the ancient names of the peninsula's townlands and mountains when she complained, as she occasionally did, of his silence, until, laughing, she would ask him to stop. Those names were tumbling around in her mind now, mixed with the sounds of the engines. *Raheen, Coomavoher, Cloonaughlin, Killeen Leacht, Ballaghbeama, Gloragh.* Beautiful places, as she had come to know, though diminished by the previous century's famine and then by ongoing, unstoppable emigration.

Niall's direct antecedents had survived the famine. Probably by their wits, he'd said. They had not perished in the mountains, he told her, but had made a life for themselves instead in the town. Nor had they later run up the slopes of mountains during uprisings or in the tragedy of the civil war, as those in the rural parishes had done. He had shown her the memorial plaques that were scattered here and there around the countryside at the places where rebels had been shot or beaten to death. He had had a sentimental, if not a political, sympathy for those desperate boys and the songs that were sung about them. "'We'll give them a hot reception,'" he had sung to her more than once, "'on the heathery slopes of Garrane.'"

No one in the family had taken the boats from Tralee either, he'd told her. There were none of them in London or New York. Not until his younger brother, Kieran, of course. Kieran, who had been the first of the tribe to go.

Goodbye to Niall and his impossible, lost brother. Goodbye to the heathery slopes of Garrane.

Niall had himself once made the journey to America, seeking his brother. He had bought a ticket to New York and spent his holidays tramping through the streets of that city, from flophouse to flophouse. After this, he stayed away from her for more than a month, and his phone calls – the few times he made them – were brief and tense. When she did see him, he would not describe his life to her in any kind of detail. It was during periods like that, when he went silent, that she knew he associated her with everything that was dark and wrong. She was a mistake he had made or, worse, a crime he had committed. She was misdirection, shame, something for the confessional, though he never went to confession. At times like that she would begin to suspect that he had taken a vow against her.

So Niall too would have spent some time in this airport. She thinks about this as she descends the lowered steps that lead to the ground. He would have heard the hollow sound of his footsteps on these aluminum stairs, the slap of his shoes on this damp tarmac.

Now she is entering a cool room filled with yellow-and-orange leatherette benches, the tiles beneath them polished, light from the large windows mirrored on the floor like long silver pools. Certain details surface in the room, this waiting room: the four clocks announcing the time in distant cities, the acidic green of the plastic plants placed among the banquettes, hallways leading to washrooms and restaurants, and at one of these entrances, a sign with the black silhouettes of a man and a woman, lit from behind.

She walks down the corridor and pushes open the door of the women's washroom. Inside she finds herself in a pink-tiled antechamber. There is a series of mirrors above a counter in front of which a number of stools are bolted to the floor. She sits on one of the stools and becomes slowly aware of her face in the mirror. By habit she takes lipstick out of her handbag and paints her mouth. She had sometimes felt that beauty was the one, perhaps the only, gift she could give him. She looks for a moment at her wan skin, her own exhausted eyes. Then she reaches for a tissue and angrily removes the colour from her lips.

Minutes later she stands at the end of the hall outside the washroom and gazes across the passenger lounge toward a colourful wall, only a part of which is visible from this vantage point. She wonders if what she sees is a large map, but as she walks into the room itself it becomes clear to her that she is looking at an enormous painting: oranges and greens and blues. It holds her attention for several seconds before she turns toward the window where the dark shape of the airliner can be seen, along with the fuel truck that is connected to it by a thick hose. A soft rain is falling now, but there is no hint of wind, no storm. The low light and the rain obscure the fir trees that had been so clearly visible at the end of the runway. The plane is lit from within. The line of yellow oval windows looks faintly yet ominously militaristic in the weak light, much more so, oddly, than any of the warplanes she had flown in the past. She turns away from the window, back to the mural.

There are children of various sizes, placed here and there across the painted surface. Some of them are toylike – not dolls exactly, more wooden and brightly coloured than dolls. They resemble nutcrackers, she decides, remembering the ballet she had been taken to as a child. In spite of their fixed expressions, they seem to be filled with an anxious, almost terrible, anticipation, as if they sense they are about to fall into a sudden departure from childhood. All around them velocity dominates the cluttered air. Missile-shaped birds tear the sky apart, and everything is moving away from the centre. How strangely sad, she thinks, that children should be affected by such abrupt arrivals, such swift departures. And their stance, the way they stare out and away from the frantic activity surrounding them, is resisting this. It is a kind of defiance. She turns back to the room, walks to an orange banquette, and sits down, facing the mural. But she is no longer looking at it because she is once again thinking of Niall.

Her Kerry kitchen had been closer to the earth than the rest of the house: two steps leading down into it from the parlour. She is seeing Niall now, sitting on the first of these steps early in the morning after one of their few full nights together. Behind him the morning sunlight was a path into the parlour. But he was turned toward where she stood, in the darker morning kitchen. How strange they were then, still tentative in their reunion after months apart. She recalls how she had walked over to him and pulled his head toward her hip, her hands in his hair, and how his arms were warm around the backs of her thighs. He was still stunned by sleep and it seemed to her that they had remained in this embrace for a long time. She couldn't remember disengaging, or when exactly they had broken out of that moment. She couldn't remember how they had moved through the remainder of the morning.

She glances at the clock, under which the phrase GANDER, CROSSROADS OF THE WORLD is printed in large red letters, then out the window toward the airliner. It is almost eleven a.m. The rain, intermittent upon landing, has settled in, and a dull shadow has darkened the fuselage and dimmed the lights of the plane. "A common greyness silvers everything": that one line comes into her mind, Niall saying it in relation to literature and weather. Shelley, or was it Browning? He had told her that silver was the colour most often, and inaccurately, associated with weather, something about climate theory that, even when he explained it in detail, she had not quite grasped.

The plane is blurred, the runway has vanished.

There is no argument with fog. In its own vague stubbornness, it wields more power than wind, rain, snow, even ice. During the war, just a hint of it cancelled all plans, all manoeuvres. Having no access to radar, she and the other ferry pilots in the Air Transport Auxiliary had flown beneath the clouds, following roads and rivers, sometimes even a seam of limestone, from airfield to airfield. Once she had flown along Hadrian's great wall in a wounded Hurricane that had coughed as it plowed through the air, a dangerous situation, but one not impossible to manage. Fog was impossible. There was no avoiding it, no manoeuvring around it. The flight here in Gander would be delayed.

All the children in the mural accept this. They do not intercede on behalf of themselves or anyone else. Neither their defiance nor their anxiety has anything to do with the world outside the painted landscape where they live. They themselves would never change, and are uninterested, therefore, in a world undergoing constant revision.

Whenever anyone asked her about her childhood, she would always reply with one word: *temporary*. No one had ever taken the conversation further, until Niall. "Isn't everyone's," he had said, the words meant as a regretful statement of fact rather than a challenge. He did not ask for an explanation, which may be why she had provided one. "I felt trapped in it," she said to him, "trapped in my body, which wasn't aging fast enough to please me. I wanted out."

"Of your body?" He laughed.

"No, I just wanted that to grow. I wanted out of my childhood."

"I ran with a brilliant pack of boys all over the hill behind the town," he said. "We'd only go home if the midges came out, and even then reluctantly, and only after the tenth bite." He told her he still saw some of these boys – men now – in the Fisherman's Bar in the evenings. They were labourers, he said. A few had gone to London or New York, work in the parish being so scarce. A distance had developed between him and those who had either returned or remained, something to do with the stability of his own employment, he thought. His brother, Kieran, however, had neither returned nor remained.

There were things, she told him, that had made her childhood more livable. A dog, belonging to a boy she played with and whose house was connected to the walls that surrounded her father's property, the little village her father essentially owned. She didn't mention the boy himself, though he had made her happier than she knew. Later it had been the nearby airfield. She had hated it at first, this airfield. The whole village had been destroyed to build it. Compulsory purchase. Expropriation. Miles of Cornish dry-stone walls were bulldozed, she'd told Niall, ancient fields, and, yes, the whole village. It had felt to her as if some of her childhood had been destroyed at the same time because she had always believed that the good part of it had taken place *outside*, not inside, her father's walls. "Since I was a toddler," she said, "I'm certain I preferred to believe this."

Niall had particularly liked her descriptions of her early life among a gang of village boys – the men's club, her mother had called them. As she had grown older and other girls her age began to go to dances and house parties in the company of just one boy, the tomboy in her had remained stubbornly emplaced. She and the boys had on occasion tracked down couples parked in cars, interrupting their intimacies by jumping up and down on the rear bumper, chanting insults, then running away.

"Football with 'The Boys of Barr na Sráide,' the Upper
Street," Niall, the athlete, had said. He mentioned that there
was a poem, one that had quickly become a song. "Back in
the hills where my brother lived," he added, "almost every
story, even a simple anecdote, turned into a song."

She remembers now that she had never heard the song
about the Upper Street, "Barr na Sráide."

A room full of leaf shadows and the two of them talking,
explaining themselves: what had they looked like during their
hesitant, first conversations? Very early in the morning,
because it was often Saturday, when he had the afternoon
free, a diagram of the day's forecast would have been chalked
up by him in the weather station near the town where he
lived. He had spoken about this, as if he were embarrassed
about the way he spent his days. "I am a meteorologist," he
said, almost shyly, "and in these parts that means I spend
most of my time measuring rain."

She told him about her war. Day after day she would
have departed to fly somewhere with only a map and the predictions of the meteorologists to guide her. Likely she would
have had an instruction manual in her hand as well, for the
Mosquito or Spitfire or any of the other half-dozen aircraft
she and the others might have been required to ferry on that
particular day. "Forty-seven aircraft, I flew four dozen different kinds of planes during the war." She added that there had
been a number of women pilots, all quite young. On the final
run of the day, one or the other of these girls would fly from
airfield to airfield picking up the others who had delivered

planes to different military locations or to factories. Once, returning to the base, seven or eight of them were seated in the back on the floor of an Avro Anson, knitting.

He had been entranced by this. "Was he any good, then, your weatherman? Had he predicted fine weather for the knitting?" She could feel his body shaking with laughter.

"No," she said, smiling.

"But you trusted him, I expect, took his advice."

"No, I did not."

There was a good chance that the day's weather had already been telegraphed from the Kerry Station by Niall's boss, McWilliams, or by his own father, as bad weather arrived in the west of Ireland first. "It bursts in from the Atlantic," Niall said to her, "like the front line of an army aching for a battle." He opened his arms expansively. And then there was his laugh.

Aching for a battle, she thinks now.

There had been sun moving on the wall as they spoke, and now and then, when the wind shook the fronds of the sallies on the lane, it travelled across the pillow and into his hair, gold and red, so that when she thrust her hands into it, it was warm.

"Why was it you didn't trust him?"

It had taken a moment to remember that they had been talking about her war-time meteorologist. "Because our weather person was a woman," she told him. "And, yes, I trusted *her* completely." He laughed again, his face opening with delight, when she told him that the woman's nickname was Wendy Weather.

She walked outside with him that day into the dampness of the late afternoon. Two fields away toward the mountain, they had seen a heron rise from the marshlands, then fly purposefully in the direction of the lake. "He will have a nest there, Tamara," Niall said, "or she will."

She preferred the single syllable of Tam. But the sound of her full name carried by his voice, the formality of that, drew her to him in a way that surprised her.

Sitting now in the airport, looking at the Constellation cloaked in mist, then back toward the sun yellows and night colours of the mural, she thought about his and her own resistance. She had always run away. But after the fact of him, what they were to each other, she had come to an uneasy sort of rest. "I've nothing to make you want to stay," he had said to her, more than once. "Nothing but trouble. You could step into desperate trouble from something like this." When early on she had asked about his children, he explained that it hadn't been possible or, at least, that it had never happened. "Sometimes," he said, "it is as if he was my child and I somehow lost him." When she asked, he was astonished that she hadn't known he had been speaking about his younger brother.

The house where Niall's brother had been raised still stood near the heathery slopes of Garrane, looking as if it had grown out of the rough pasture. Beside it, one of the Iveragh's disordered burial grounds tumbled down the hill toward the bog below. The brother had lived there in his later childhood, and into young manhood under the care of the country woman that Niall would refer to as Kieran's Other Mother, and was happy there, Niall had said, in a way he had never been in his own home. Niall had shown her a newspaper clipping concerning his brother, and two black-and-white photos, one with the brother astride a bicycle, grinning. Kieran was a chancer, Niall said. You never knew what he was going to do.

"Dead?" she asked gently, having noted his use of the past tense.

"I hope not," he said, not looking at her. "I don't think so. In England or maybe America, for a long time now. He just vanished in the night. Working, or so they say, on building sites or perhaps the motorways."

Later he would begin to look for his brother in the most desperate of ways. It was my fault, he said. My fault.

It is even darker outside the window now, as if the fog is trying to cancel the struggling light.

NIALL'S BROTHER, KIERAN, HAD BEEN SO FIERCE IN his entry into the world that their mother's pelvis was broken by the birth. "Who could ever completely forget, or be able to bear the memory of such a night?" Niall had said. The whole house, the street outside the door, the empty butcher shop, the rain pounding down on the estuary, even the stars above the church had seemed to be in agony. Pain was everywhere.

But Niall's mother had resisted even a loss of consciousness. As if pain were a relationship she was refusing to leave. As if she had married it. During the lengthy ordeal, Niall had looked through the partly open door for as long as he could manage. The tendons of his mother's neck were visible, he told Tam, as taut as strings on a musical instrument. For some reason this had horrified him even more than the unearthly noises she was making. She had been almost singing the anguish, verse after verse after verse of it.

In the farthest corner of the room, Niall's father, a man who as county meteorologist would have foreseen and explained all manner of extreme systems, was swaying back and forth, his hands over his ears. His lips were moving, but he was not able to endure the full sound of his wife's pain even long enough to pull the rosary from his pocket, as the feverishly praying midwife had done. It was the first time, Niall said, that he had witnessed a grown man's weakness. He would never forget it.

In his boy's mind he felt that he had disappeared, could not even be recalled. There would have been nothing he could say, no amount of sound that he could have made that would cause him to be noticed, so he remained quiet. He was walking back and forth in the hall, his bare feet moving soundlessly from one red triangle on the carpet to another, draughts made by winds outside the walls moving up his pyjama legs. He was nine years old.

The doctor had finally swung around. He crossed the room and grabbed the father by his upraised wrists, shaking him into attention. "For God's sake, man," he said, "go wake the chemist. Tell him to bring morphine. Now!" Niall remembered him saying this. "Now," he repeated to Tam, his fist slamming into the palm of the opposite hand.

"Have you none in your bag?" Outside the door, Niall heard his father ask this question, his voice querulous and childlike, filled with tears.

"Would I be asking you if I did?"

A scream had torn the air in half. Niall could feel the muscles in his back and down his arms clench. He stepped from one red triangle to another, moving back and forth between the walls of the hall. Then, he admitted to Tam, he had begun at last to cry.

The doctor pushed his father out the bedroom door. "Throw a rock through the man's bedroom window if you have to."

His father had thundered down the stairs, moving straight past his quiet son, who stood entirely still now in the hall. There was an electric lamp on the hall table and behind it a glass bell that covered an arrangement of stuffed dead birds. Niall had thought that he had become completely invisible until he saw that his own limbs were elongated in the reflection on the curved glass, his face smeared, and then he believed that the horrors of the night had left him distorted and askew. He was unrecognizable, and his father was running frantically into the night, as if caught in the midst of burglary.

He could hear his mother moaning in response, he half believed, to the sound of the closing door. The dim light in the hall looked to the boy like smoke, the colour of pain. Even the carpets on the floors and the faded birds behind the glass were drawn into this dusk, this sound. He discovered he could no longer remain upright so he crouched on the floor, listening to the doctor's voice but not to what he was saying. Abruptly his mother began to shout as if calling out to someone in anger. The silence that followed the shouting filled the boy with dread. But then the smoke cleared, became absence.

"Jesus," the doctor finally said, "you little bugger."

And Niall heard the baby's cry. He was furious with the baby. It was an intruder, an outrage. How dare it cry? It was damage and torment. It had been trying to kill his mother.

Some minutes later the tall man who was the town chemist walked in the front door with Niall's father. His night clothes were drenched with rain and he held two bottles, one in each hand. Though he looked up at the landing as he climbed the stairs, Niall knew he did not see him. He believed now it was the baby that had cancelled him out. His father was sitting on the bottom step, deflated, as if he were one of his own weather balloons damaged by storm.

In the room, the boy followed the tall man to his mother's bedside, not even looking at the despised, dangerous baby or the midwife who held it. The doctor thrust a syringe into one of the bottles. He turned then and plunged the needle into the mother's arm. Her mouth was a circle of pain: there was neither breath nor voice in it, but her eyes were bright and open, alive with suffering. The noise of the newborn was everywhere, shrill, demanding. Niall was certain that the baby had stolen his mother's voice.

The baby quieted and something in the room changed. Kneeling by the bed, the chemist picked up one of his mother's clenched fists, which he held in both of his hands for several moments while looking down at her face on the pillow. Then he bent toward her. "Not too much longer now and the pain will be moving away," he whispered into his mother's ear, and as he said these words, the silent howl began slowly to melt from her mouth.

She was broken. Rags and bones tossed on a bloody bed. Her loose hair shone with sweat and her thighs and knees, still open, were smeared with crimson. But she turned her face toward the whisperer.

Niall would always remember the way the man uncurled his mother's fingers, one at a time, the left hand and then the right, and the way he smoothed those hands, with the palms of his own, into the wrinkled sheets of the ruined bed.

"Who are you?" she asked, and the question was one long exhalation of breath.

They had known each other two years before Niall had spoken to Tam about his mother. By the time he finished, he was pale, exhausted, and the bottle on the table between them was empty.

"Was that how she died?" Tam wanted to know.

"No," he said, "not like that."

—

The way she was pulled back to being with him, the way she submitted to the force of his personality during their times together, astonished her over and over. As the years passed there were times when she suspected that he walked unwillingly to a meeting knowing there could no longer be anything new for her to bring to him: the same room, the same caresses. Had not everything already been said, touched? Sometimes he would appear at her door like a bewildered pilgrim, one who had travelled too far, much too far for this small spate of comfort, the brief awakening, if it could be called an awakening, to pleasure. Sometimes, if it was winter, he would have to remove a coat, a hat, and these he would place gently on the arm or the seat of a chair, and while he did this, he would comment on the weather in the most ordinary of ways as if he had no scientific knowledge whatsoever concerning the rain he had shaken from his sleeves.

There was always that one moment she waited for when he would place his forehead at the intersection of her neck and shoulder and she would feel his body relax against hers, a full stop, an ending to everything outside of them. The rest of her life without him vanished; then language, then geography until there was only the white rectangle of the bed and how they moved there. There was the soft zone beneath his ribs at the place where his waist met his hips, and her own waist twisting in his hands, his breath entering her throat.

Goodbye to all that, she thinks now, looking at the entranced children in the mural here in the passenger lounge.

They are not interested. There is no active drama left in them.

—

Niall's boss, McWilliams — he of the much-admired encyclopedic mind — was someone he cared about and quoted. McWilliams might have told him something new about the weather in Croisset during the week that Flaubert was completing page 216 of his *Bovary*, or the effect of fog on Victor

Hugo's thirty-second chapter of *Les Misérables*. There was a much-told story concerning the path of Halley's Comet on the day of Mark Twain's birth, and its reappearance the day before the same author's death. He might have rhymed off some of the meteorological questions put by God to Job. *Hast thou entered into the storehouses of the snow*; or *hast thou beheld the treasures of the hail* are the only two she remembers. There were parhelia and fogbows, famous gales and bog bursts. A shower of orange snow, the village of Sneem upside down in the sky. There were Sun Dogs – even Moon Dogs. He could chart the history of a snowflake through the structure of its crystals. He was very fond of meteor showers, international date lines, undersea ridges, and the kind of low pressure systems that determined the outcome of battles.

Sometimes she ventured her own opinions about weather, even about literature, but Niall would barely register these, was more interested in the segments of her life that he considered to have been truly hers. Her memories of her English childhood fascinated him, he having limited first-hand knowledge of that country beyond a series of weather patterns. What did she remember of butlers, he, a P. G. Wodehouse fan, wanted to know, or of Hardy country, or of Constable's cloud studies, which he had heard about from McWilliams? They would see these things together, she had told him, knowing, even as she spoke, that this would never come to pass.

"And the two of you?" she had asked once, about the brother. "What happened?"

"There was the living apart," he eventually told her. "And then a kind of betrayal."

He told her that Kieran had moved in full-time, or at least as close to full-time as he could manage, with their house-keeper, the other mother, Gerry-Annie. "He was impossible for my father to control at home," he said, "and knowing where he was, more or less, my father let him go to her." Kieran soon had a bicycle – where he got it his family never knew – and had sped around the parish and finally the whole county on it.

"He had the gift or the curse of charm, though no one but Gerry-Annie knew this in the beginning. But when she made such observations, she spoke them in Irish, and in such a declarative way! So we didn't really understand whether they were good or bad, which was what she wanted, I imagine.

"A sort of Irish Nelly Dean," he said then, adding that *Wuthering Heights* was one of McWilliams' favourite books because of the weather in it. She was their maid, came in from the country daily to help look after them when Kieran was small. Her name was due to the way country people of the parish occasionally identified a woman. "There would be many Annies, many Marys," he said. "And most of them were either O'Connells or O'Sullivans. This particular Annie had been married to Gerry O'Connell: hence Gerry-Annie."

When Kieran went off to school, Gerry-Annie had come down to clean only two or three times a month. But after their mother died, she was, again, regularly in the house. Niall had liked her well enough, but Kieran took to her wonderfully.

So, a year or so after their mother was gone, off he went with Gerry-Annie into the mountains. "It was only five or six miles," Niall had explained, "but a completely different world, and Kieran became a part of that."

Descriptions of Tam's tomboy childhood always made him laugh – the runaway in her, and her fascination with planes. Sometimes she felt she was performing for him, but she carried on, eager to make him happy. He would offer accounts of Gaelic football victories, and all the training that took place in every imaginable kind of weather. He had been a sort of local hero, he admitted. There were cups and trophies and the townspeople caught up in a number of victorious homecomings. She'd pictured him riding on the shoulders of cattle drovers and shop clerks and recalled for him the beginning of a poem concerning an athlete dying young. "Who wrote that?" she asked.

"Housman," he'd said. He never would have known about this, he confessed, were it not for McWilliams. "On Wenlock Edge" was a particular favourite. "''Tis the old wind in the old anger,'" he quoted. Then, after reciting these words, he had taken her open hand and had placed it over the left side of his face, as if instructing her to silence him.

He had read science at university in Dublin, and after graduate work in meteorology, he had accepted a position at the Dublin Weather Office. A few years later there was an opening at the weather station where his father worked, and he'd come home for that. "And to get married," he said.

He measured rain, the movements of the magnetic North Pole, and the fluctuations of solar wind. His father launched the daily weather balloons. "Every day," Niall said, "right on time. He did this every day until he retired." He mentioned that his father, who could have afforded to send him to school in England, did not.

Except for the artificial wind, created, she believes, by the rendered velocity, the mural she is looking at is oddly without weather. It is all oranges and yellows and reds, the colour of sun, the colour of heat and fire. Parts of it are blue. But no ocean, and no weather. There is full grey now beyond the window glass, and full silence. Calm and erasure. She is thinking about the fog in these terms. But when she whispers the words *calm and erasure*, the sound is like that of a wave pulling up a golden Kerry strand and then withdrawing.

She is remembering a winter afternoon, the fire banked high, the wind pushing rain against the glass of the west-facing windows, and Niall speaking in surprising detail about his lost brother's life as a child. He was establishing the actuality of Kieran, what he had been, what he still might be. She was moved by this, by the fact of his giving her, through the brother, at least this one path into his past. She hadn't seen the pain yet. That would come later.

"There is a natural secretiveness in my family" — he had lifted his hand, making a point — "that is to say, a natural discretion." He looked at her then and smiled, his face flushed. She had loved this in him, his shyness.

But in Kieran there had been a level of fearfulness added to this. "It was as if," Niall said, "having found what he wanted, he felt anyone would try to take it from him."

Niall had been preparing to leave and was standing, reaching for the jacket he had placed on the back of a chair when he had entered the cottage. Two empty glasses rested side by side near a half-finished bottle. She would drink the wine later, alone, after he had gone.

"He was out in the bog and up in those mountains in all seasons, any kind of weather. He afforded himself no protection."

Niall had bent over and reached for Tam's hand across the table.

"The girl I married had no links at all to a life like the one lived out in the country," he said. "The smell of the turf and the animals would have put her off, I think. There was nothing in her life like that."

"I'm glad you became a cyclist," she said, looking at the bicycle that he had, as always, brought into her house and that he would soon walk to the door. She did not want to talk about his wife.

He had joined the Dublin Cycling Club on a whim while he was at university, he told her, and it had stuck. He had liked the long stretches of training, how there would sometimes be a full day of it, unlike the football practices that would often be over in a couple of hours. "I was, I still am, the opposite of my father, never fully took to quiet times in the house." He reddened again, as if suddenly realizing the irony of what he had said and where he had said it.

KIERAN HAD GONE QUITE WILLINGLY TO SCHOOL IN the beginning, walking solemnly beside his older brother, under the shadow of the large church, past several pubs, the bank, the food stores, the hardware store. Other boys drifted down from the High Street and joined them at the tower house, so named because of its round wall and curved windows. He was able to see himself in the glass of those windows, the uniform too large for him and his socks crumpled at the ankles. Girls passed them as they moved toward the school, dressed in their own uniforms, heading for the convent at the opposite end of the town. His brother, Niall, so much taller, older, would turn toward the Upper School, leaving him alone but filled already with a clear knowledge of his differences.

He learned to read quickly, and with considerable enthusiasm – he was delighted by anything that included a story. Early mathematics, for example, that involved children with a limited amount of money being sent to a shop to buy a specific number of apples. These children were, to him, rich with the all-frightening and wonderful possibilities of drama, and how that drama would move through their lives – even at that early age he was aware of the branching of narrative. There would have been a house of many rooms attached to each of the children who set off for the shop, and in those rooms there would be barely understood conversations taking place among adults wielding unequal degrees of power. He thought of the different voices his mother used when she spoke. How sometimes he couldn't break through her preoccupation no matter what he said, and how that preoccupation was centred on something he felt he would never find. He knew that she had been a child once, and that there had been a whole lived childhood when she hadn't known his father, hadn't known his brother, Niall, or him. This fascinated and disturbed him.

The early years of his childhood had passed in a fairly orderly and ordinary manner. He formed friendships with a couple of other boys; the relationships mostly revolving around board games. He liked the progression of the men along the straight lines of the board, the suggestion of a journey being taken, and how the arbitrarily chosen card could change the course of things, the place where a marker stood. But he was indifferent about winning and confused by the disappointment he saw in others when they didn't win a game. Group sports didn't interest him at all. Out of doors he preferred to be alone, or to walk through the streets in the company of one silent dog that did not belong to him and whose name he did not know but who was almost always present and available.

He was contented enough. He and the dog had discovered that the streets of the town led to roads in the mountains, and he imagined that these roads led to other roads, other worlds. Inside his home or at the school it was always warm and dry. The prospect of his own discomfort had not yet occurred to him, though he sensed the disquiet in his mother and, at certain times, in the way his father looked at his mother when she was sealed behind the wall of that unknowable preoccupation.

What is it, Deirdre? his father would ask softly. But she would shake her head and look away from him. She would not answer. No one in the house had ever heard her complain.

One day when he was about eight, Kieran had walked alone into the house after school. He had removed his wet shoes and had gone silently down the tiled hall, stopping by the parlour door when he heard a male voice that was only faintly familiar. Looking into the room he saw the profile of the town chemist outlined by the low afternoon light coming through the bay window. His mother sat in a chair near the window, one arm falling across her lap, the other bent, and her forehead resting in her open palm. The air of the room was liquid with dusk and both his mother and the chemist were caught in it, perhaps drowning. No one had lit a lamp. It was only when his mother spoke that the boy knew she had been weeping, was perhaps still weeping. "I know," his mother said, "I know."

"And it will always be so," the man said. "And we can do nothing."

The boy instinctively withdrew, walked backwards to the front door, opened it and closed it noisily, then waited for his mother to call to him as he knew she would. "Niall, Kieran," she sang, "come into the parlour. Mr. Keating is here and he has brought your father's Christmas gift . . . a new electric razor. But you mustn't tell him."

"It's only me," Kieran called back. "Niall's at the football." Then he ran over to the stairs and up to his room. There was something about the brass rods that fixed the carpet runner to the groin of each step that he would always remember in relation to this, and it put him off brass in any form, for life. He did not come down until dinnertime, when there was no one in the parlour at all.

After that he was aware of secrets and distances in the house. There was that thick, impenetrable air, and his father rarely talking but watching his mother closely.

His mother had become like an ocean to the boy, vast and unknowable, with faraway shorelines he could never see, could not even imagine from where he stood but that he nevertheless sensed were vivid and real. He could read his father's helplessness yet nothing at all in his mother but an ocean, then waiting and indifference. When he was older, and she had been gone for many years, he would wonder if she had been waiting for her life to pass.

He had his first tantrum two weeks later in the midst of a class devoted to arithmetic. The children who had gone to the shops to buy a specific number of apples with a limited amount of money had been banished from the blackboard and from the page for a couple of years at this point and he had missed them, finding he had been unable to force himself to care about the empty numbers that replaced them. When he asked about the disappearance of the stories, one of the Brothers who taught him had laughed out loud and had told him that he had discovered the difference between pure and applied mathematics. "You're a right little philosopher, you are," the man had said. But this compliment made no difference to Kieran. He could not find it in himself to care about addition and subtraction when it was detached and free-floating and only about itself. Soon he began to fall behind and there was no more laughter in the classroom.

One afternoon, while staring at a column he had made himself in his notebook, he felt something large and dark moving inside him, as if he had swallowed a sizable animal that was struggling to burst out of his body. Soon he found himself wondering where the noise was coming from, why his books were on the floor, his chair overturned, and his arms and legs moving in an aggressive manner. With his eyes closed he saw a collection of piercing beams almost exactly like the swords of blinding light that made him squint and turn away from the sea on a clear January day. He was small for his age and easily overtaken by the strength of the Brother, and in no time he found himself panting in the hall where he was told to stand for the remainder of the morning. An outburst, the Brother called it, and indeed Kieran himself was terrified by what had happened, what had burst out of him.

All that winter the house seemed to fold in on itself while the dark and the rain pressed up against the windows. Niall, who was now seventeen, had gone mad for Gaelic football and was often not there after school, busy instead on a drenched field, in the company of a group of noisy teenaged boys of his own age and height. When he came home, it was as if he brought the fresh sea wind with him. This energized their father, who would talk then about the tournaments of times past in places as far away as Clare or even Donegal. This talk sometimes set off a tantrum in Kieran, though he wouldn't have been able to say why. But even when he was at his worst, his mother would remain in her chair so that her husband and Niall, if he was home, would be required to deal with him.

Still, sometimes, on a Saturday or a Wednesday afternoon when there was no school, he would walk quietly beside his mother in the town so that he could help her carry whatever she bought at the food store or the butcher shop. Once or twice they went to the chemist to buy seltzers for his father's indigestion or plasters for Niall, whose knees were often a mess because of the football. The man Kieran had seen in the parlour was courteous but unsmiling. Behind him was a collection of small wooden drawers, each one bearing an unpronounceable name, *Plumb Acet, Capcisi, Ichthyoc.* Will that be all, Mrs. Riordan? he would say, solid in his white coat, handing a white paper bag to her over the counter. His mother said nothing. She put the payment beside the cash register, placed the package in Kieran's hands, then turned toward the door. Once, the chemist had run after them, shouting, and Kieran's heart had become huge and demanding in his chest, but the man had only wanted to give them change for the punt note his mother had left behind. The boy saw the coins dropping from the man's naked, freckled hand into his mother's gloved palm. "Deirdre," the chemist began, but she took Kieran by the shoulders, pointed him in the direction of home, and they both began to walk. He could hear the sound of the man's footsteps then, becoming fainter and fainter, moving in the opposite direction.

Later his mother had prepared the evening meal in silence and had eaten next to none of it herself. His father and Niall discussed football. Kieran left his chair, went to his mother's side, and placed his hand on her arm. Then, when she didn't react, he tugged at her sleeve, which was silken and inert. Niall stopped talking to their father in mid-sentence and sent a hard look across the table to his younger brother. "Leave her," he said. "Don't pester her." The whole room became silent, as if it had filled with water during the few moments the boy had been touching his mother. Kieran returned to his place and ate and drank everything he could in order to stun or drown the dark animal he could feel squirming inside him. He succeeded more or less. But, as he was nearing sleep, the foreign-looking names on the chemist's drawers floated through his mind. The tantrum was pacing at the periphery of the rooms he walked through, and while he was sleeping it attached itself to a nightmare that catapulted him from his bed in the middle of the night.

Kieran had been to Valentia Island only once on a class expedition with Father O'Sullivan. The old bus on which he and the other children rode had lumbered onto the ferry at Reenard Point a few miles out of the town and then had been driven sedately onto the island shore only ten minutes later. He had been delighted by the brief journey over the water and, released for a few moments from the bus, had run with the other boys back and forth across the deck.

Once they were on the island, the old priest had wanted the children to understand the geography they were passing through and the historical and religious significance of the spot they would be visiting. "One of the most westerly points of land in Europe," he told them, swaying beside the driver at the front of the bouncing vehicle, "and St. Brendan himself departing from there in his skin boat. Glanleam," he said vaguely, naming the places they passed by. "Gortgower, Coarha Beg." The yellow wins were being replaced by bursts of hawthorn in the hedgerows. Now and then there was the startling pink of a rhododendron.

Each child had a relic to place at the Holy Well, where they would stop to pray, a saint's medal from Lourdes or a small plastic statue of the Virgin. Kieran had only two coins in his pocket, his mother having forgotten to give him anything else, but he had seen the money pilgrims had left at grottos and he hoped that no one would notice his shame when he placed coins rather than tokens at the rim of the well.

The day was fine and the priest asked the driver to stop by the side of the road so that the company could walk the mile or two of green road heading for the coast. An almost indistinguishable ancient trackway crossed their path at one point, one made so long ago the priest couldn't say just when. Among the fields there were three or four abandoned houses with the thatch on them ruined and sagging and the glass in their windows gone altogether. "Off to America, I suppose," the priest said, though no one had asked him. "Couldn't make a go of it."

After they had climbed over a stile at the end of the road, three stone crosses came into view, and the slabs surrounding the Holy Well beside them. The land tilted up from the spot, making a clean line against the sky and giving the impression that the earth was faintly unbalanced, awry.

Kieran couldn't see the ocean from where he stood, but the sound of it was loud and constant in his ears. Several of the boys were preparing to run to the edge of the cliffs, but the priest put an end to it. "Too much danger in it," he said, "we'll stop where we are." There followed a lengthy sermon on the voyages of Brendan. "But how did he get into the sea, Father," one of the boys wanted to know, "it being so dangerous?" "It was God's pleasure that he do so," the old man replied. "It would be God guiding him." And then, relenting, he told them they would go a little farther so that they might glimpse the very sea that Brendan had sailed toward the west. The priest's few remaining strands and the thick young hair of the boys was moving in the wind. The grass bent under the force of it. It was a brisk wind but not strong enough to cause discomfort.

When they had walked for five minutes, Kieran spotted a jet of white water rising like an energetic fountain above the land and pointed to it. The priest explained that there was a long, narrow crack in the cliff into which the sea pressed with a force so great it exploded above the land. "Culloo Rock," he said. "Very dangerous!" The boys regarded the rising column of water with collective curiosity, drawn to the danger.

"There are those who have been lost there," the priest added sombrely, with no suggestion in his voice that he was likely to pursue the topic in any satisfactory kind of way.

On the returning bus Kieran put his hand in his pocket and touched the two coins he had not left behind. There had been a scrum of boys at the moment of presentation and no one had noticed his own hand being absent from those at the edge of the well. The following day he spent the money on four jelly doughnuts, eating three and saving one for his brother, for this was during a time when he worshipped Niall, who mostly ignored him but was never unkind.

That had been two years before, in advance of his mother's long withdrawal and before the tantrums had taken up residence in him. But he recalled the jet of water and the Holy Well on the May afternoon when he walked into the house and heard the words *Culloo Rock* being spoken in a stranger's voice. "Didn't his own father go off the end of Culloo Rock," the voice was saying. "And now this."

His mother had been missing for two days. She had slipped out of the house on an autumn afternoon when her husband was at work and the boys at school. That first night no one had eaten supper, waiting instead for her to reappear. At eleven o'clock their father had gone to the telephone to call the guards, then had wandered from room to room extinguishing all the lights except the one in the front bay window and the one that shone above the door. He stood in the gloom with his head bowed as if he were filled with a terrible sense of shame. "Go to bed, boys," he eventually said, "she'll very likely be here when you wake in the morning."

But she was not there in the morning; not then, nor on the morning that followed that one. There was the rain and wind outside and a bleak calm indoors. Even Gerry-Annie, who came in from the hills to help with the housework, was silent and grim. She stayed to prepare the meals and slept on the parlour sofa now, and Kieran heard her weeping and praying in the dark. But she made the boys go to school the following day and packed the lunches they would take with them.

Kieran had awakened on these two mornings exhausted by dreams he could not remember and longing to stay in the vicinity of Annie. But he stepped out the door with Niall when she told him to do so. Neither he nor his brother spoke on the walk to the corner, where his brother would turn away to head up the hill to the Upper School while he, Kieran, proceeded toward the Lower School, where there were no more stories attached to numbers.

And then he was home again and a stranger's voice was saying, "Didn't his own father go off Culloo Rock?" When he stood in the doorway that led to the parlour he saw the men gathered there: the priest, the coast guard man, a couple of the guards, and a few of his father's friends. And then from above him came the sound of his father's heavy footsteps on the stairs. He was dressed for the outdoors and had his hat in his hands. If he noticed Kieran he showed no sign of this but waited quietly in the hall until the man from the coast guard, the two guards, and the priest joined him. They paused for a moment. Then they all walked out into the wind.

Kieran looked out the front bay window and watched the men depart. Just after they had opened and closed the wrought-iron gate, Niall appeared on the sidewalk, and the father fell weeping into his arms. The other men moved as a group respectfully to one side. Kieran could tell from the way his brother's shoulders were moving that he was weeping as well, and it was only then that he himself began to cry, recognizing as he did so that the sounds he was making came from the same faraway part of him where the tantrums lived.

It would be years before he found out what had happened. He was living in London by then and had stopped for an evening drink at a pub near the worksite where he was employed. As he ordered his pint, an older man at the bar turned abruptly to look at him. "You're from Kerry," the man said, "it's in your voice." Kieran named the town where he was born. "Yes," said the man, "it's as I thought. You are one of the Riordan boys. I was at your house that afternoon. I was in the guards then, though I gave it up later to come here."

Kieran knew the afternoon the man was referring to but remained silent, focusing on the wood grain of the bar.

"A terrible thing that," the ex-guard continued. "I suppose you don't know when you start something like that how it will take you. And him with everything so close at hand, so tempting like. They say she began to use it after a difficult childbirth. We found some needles near the rock."

Kieran put his hand on the man's arm, worried he would remove himself without explaining.

"You don't know then," the man said, surprise and embarrassment all over his face. "Sorry, I wouldn't have said except I thought that you knew."

"No, I didn't," Kieran said, remembering the words in the guard's mouth that afternoon.

"The chemist's own father went off Culloo Rock, you know, twenty years before. But it wasn't the drugs with him. And it wasn't love. Just despair." The man was silent for a while. Then he sighed and said, "It's the way the apple pulls the earth toward it, I suppose."

Kieran thought about this sentence while he worked on the latest London office block. Four and five storeys up, walking the criss-crossed tightropes of the girders, he thought about it. He thought about it later when he went north for employment on the motorways they were building there. While he operated the machine that scraped the landscape clean of its vegetation and its history, he ran the sentence through his mind, the apple pulling the earth toward it.

It came to him then that it might not be the tragedy itself, but rather the intensity of reaction to the tragedy that mattered. Was his reaction supposed to have been measured or immeasurable? He had no answer for this.

He knew about magnetic force, though, and the apple's helplessness in the grips of it. He knew about love, all right, the way it pulled you toward it until nothing about you was predictable, even to yourself. How afterwards you could never return to anything like the reliable neutrality of your previous life. And he knew he was still angry.

COMMISSION

—

The Gander Airport commission would be a godsend, and Kenneth had known this from the beginning.

He had been living for three years with his wife and young children in the small prairie town on the edge of the small prairie city. He had built a studio and his paintings had sold reasonably well. But the going was tough and he wondered, sometimes, if he could continue to manage. A part-time teaching job in the prairie city – the reason he had come to this province in the first place – helped, but it took time and concentration away from what he wanted to do, away from the making of art. Normally he was a prolific painter; canvas after canvas appeared as if by magic at the end of his brushes. Then they were stacked against the studio wall and every now and then sent out to a dealer or patron. The job slowed his output, but it didn't stop him. He worked in the early mornings. And he worked at night.

He, whose most intense periods of growth had unfolded in

the vicinity of hills, rivers, and trees, then later on the streets of cities, was often out of step with the apparently limitless horizons and exaggerated weather of the prairie. But he was moved by the openness around him as well, particularly at night in winter when starlight alone would occasionally provide sufficient ambient light for him to walk by. Sometimes he circled the unlit house, knowing those he loved slept inside the walls. Sometimes he followed the line of the railway away from the safety of domestic buildings and toward the howl of wolves, coyotes. These long, collective announcements from distant animals astonished and delighted him: he could feel the seductive pull of that wildness, and then the resistance, the refusal in him. And he was grateful, both for the pull and for the refusal. When he passed the railway station, the stillness and the sound of his footsteps in snow made him remember that Tolstoy had died in such a place.

In spring and summer he often sketched the same tracks he had followed in winter, softened now by weeds at the edge, and leading toward the rest of the world. For these drawings he used the toughest grain of pencil, creating slender lines, wanting to emphasize the delicacy of prairie grasses flourishing near steel. And then the narrowing lines of perspective, the thrust toward everything that existed beyond the picture plane and the place where he stood.

Kenneth worked throughout the winter on sketches for the submission. The mural was to adorn a wall of the passenger lounge in a new air terminal being built by the federal government in Gander, Newfoundland, where almost all transatlantic flights stopped to refuel. "Crossroads of the World," as the announcement of the competition had put it. He made dozens of watercolours, keeping the composition miniature, yet fully rendered, both in his mind and on the pieces of paper – some not much larger than a bookmark – on which he worked. He was developing a visual metaphor for flight, one that would not be specific to flying machines – there was to be no reference to Leonardo or the Wright Brothers and those who followed them, and he avoided even thinking about Icarus. He was drawn to more natural modes of flight, but he didn't want untransformed birds to dominate. Increasingly, however, when he attempted to fuse bird, machine, and myth, almost everything resembled a missile or a bomb.

He was not unhappy with this, but he also wanted to depict paradise, wanted the tale being told to unfold in an Edenic setting. He would choose this rural landscape he now inhabited, and was coming to know, as the setting. But it would be torn by departures, ripped apart by entrances, exits. *Flight and Its Allegories* is what he would call the mural, were his submission to be chosen, though he knew the title bordered on pretension. It was the phrase that most often came to him when he was in the planning stages, and he sensed it would appeal to the panel in Ottawa.

The characters emerged slowly, working their way out of the basic shapes and colours he had chosen, as if each human being were an animal revealed by firelight on the uneven wall of a cave. The birds arrived more swiftly, their flight made evident from the beginning by the sharp angles his pencil drew, and the left-to-right motion implied by the long dimensions of the mural itself, so the eyes of the on-looker would be swept from one side of it to the other. The flight of the birds that occupied the better part of the central panels was the gesture of the piece, the forward momentum.

As the months passed and intermittent skeins of snow were blown by the wind across the glass of the studio's win-dows, he thought about the various human emotions con-nected to flight. There was the burst of freedom. But there might also be a fearful backward look, a sense of pursuit. He sketched one figure opening his arms to new experience, and then another, a fugitive with a hunted look. Children seemed to want to be in the picture. He drew one boy holding the bluebird of hope, and another juggling apples in a tribute to chance, skill, and gravity. There would be a suggestion of memory attached to the adults in the scene. Almost all of them would be based on people he had observed during his own earlier travels, men and women he had not known well – in many cases he had not known them at all – but whose arrivals and departures had struck him as poignant, heart-wrenching, or sometimes abrupt and cruel. He knew that the backward look could also be filled with longing or regret, and some-times a desire to recover the past.

All of this was to be executed in egg tempera. Combining the pigment with the egg yolk each time he used a new colour would make the project protracted and complicated from a technical point of view. But there was something about the busy velocity of the subject – all that speed and change – that drew him toward a medium that was painstaking. He estimated that it would take him ten full days to prepare the ground and prime the panels – thirty-six in all, each four by six feet. It would also take a considerable amount of time simply to assemble the materials: plywood, pigment powders, various brushes, eggs. He knew he would need carton after carton of eggs to do the job. He fervently hoped that there was a great quantity of chickens in Newfoundland.

It wasn't until he had completed several dozen preparatory drawings that he realized that it was the sensibility of his own past he was attempting to recover, the sharpness of that post-adolescent vision that had been so available and clear when he had been moving from place to place without plans or obligations. Occasionally, when he was working on the maquette, this sensibility came so palpably near he felt he could almost reach out and touch the time that had engendered them.

On a frigid pre-dawn morning in late March, Kenneth left his house and studio and walked through the town to the train station with the letter from the committee in the pocket of his long grey overcoat and only one suitcase in his hand – his crated art supplies and a trunk filled with personal items had been delivered to the quay the previous afternoon. The station itself was hidden behind mountainous banks of plowed snow, but as he turned onto the short street that led to the tracks, he saw the veil of yellow light that rose from the facade's windows. The door of a pickup truck slammed, startling, in what had up until then been total, glacial silence. Then he heard the train, and though he knew it was still a long way off, he quickened his pace.

TRUANCY

—

The first thing Tam sees when she wakens in the dim morning light is the flat grey fog framed by one of the large windows of the terminal. Wrapped in her coat, with her handbag for a pillow, she has managed to achieve a few hours of sleep by lying down on the banquette. As she lifts herself into a semi-upright position, she regards the neutral greyness behind the glass. She is nowhere, and she feels nothing but a sense of disorientation. And then she recalls the journey in the car, the flight over the ocean, and the particular weather pattern, emotional and actual, that has resulted in her waking in this place. Niall walks into her mind, and the pain sets in; familiar, dogged, unavoidable. She rises quickly to her feet.

She thinks about making inquiries at the Airlines desk, as she had on several occasions the previous evening and after-noon. But the answer to the question she would ask the two uniformed attendants is so obvious in the face of the blurred images beyond the glass, she decides against this and returns to the banquette. Other passengers have awakened now and are either making their way toward the washrooms or are sitting in their wrinkled clothing, stunned and defeated-looking, staring at the floor. Some had tried to engage her in conversation the previous day, hoping, she assumed, to pass the time. But there is no talk in her, nothing beyond a long train of memories and an inner annulment.

There is a small fool in this mural, she thinks, as the painting comes into focus; a fool disguised as a child. The fool wears a tri-cornered hat and is positioned at ground level, almost but not quite at the centre of the picture, one of several children placed in a row. The figure is genderless, though fools were traditionally male, were they not? As far as she knew, no woman had embraced this particular vocation, at least not as a performer. Niall might know or, if not, his boss McWilliams. There was more than likely something Shakespearean about fools and weather that both men would be happy to quote. Puck, maybe, but was Puck a fool?

Her first husband was a fool of sorts, she decides, but essentially blameless, though thoroughly irritating in his foolishness. Her father is a different kind of fool. Opinionated, sometimes blind to the suffering of others, and always opportunistic, he is the kind of fool who preys on the foolishness of others. But perhaps she is being too hard. Her parents were kind enough people really, at least until her father entered the commercial world. Before the war they had been rich in a courteous manner, presiding over their village and the tenants in it in a vague, good-natured, almost listless way, following a system of life that they believed had always been, and would therefore continue to be, in effect. The idea that there might be some other system that would be more just had simply never occurred to them. Tam had tried to convince herself that she had run away because, even as a child, she could understand injustice and wanted no part of it. But she has to admit now that this was not the case, not when she was a child and not later either, when the village was gone and her father had become a successful industrialist, using the family name for his construction company: Edgeworth Enterprises. She hadn't even run from that, not really. She had run because she could never make a viable agreement with structure, and what the structure was attached to made no real difference, even though, there near the mountains, among those country people, with Niall circling her life, she had been sometimes happy in a way that almost made her believe she would remain so forever.

The small dry goods shop, at the west end of her childhood village of St. Derwent, was attached to the shopkeeper's home. A curtain hung at the back of the shop, beyond which one could glimpse a dark hallway that led into the mysterious domestic interior. This had fascinated her as a young child. But the shop itself had fascinated her as well: she had been intrigued by bright objects in battered wooden bins, or wrapped packages placed on long shelves on either side of narrow aisles. She was always told to remain on a high stool near the counter while her nanny gossiped with the shopkeeper. Mrs. Bentley, she thinks, or Mrs. Benchley. It was there, at the age of six, that she had learned that the following autumn, after her seventh birthday, she was to be sent away to school. There will be no governess for her, her nan had said, and no job for me either. She had loved her nan, whom she had never seen again, and loved her still in some buried, deep way, often dreaming about her very early in the morning so that she would wake with the comforting feeling that this uncomplicated, affectionate woman was sleeping in the next room.

She glances at the large, welcoming woman on the far right of the mural. Her nan, sort of. Yes, a bit like her. Some of the painted children are gathered around this woman, though they seem to be paying no attention to her.

It was the anticipated loss of her nan that had made her slip from the stool, at a moment when the adults had changed the topic to a story concerning the drinking habits of the grocer, and pass quietly beyond the curtain. Here was a dark, transitory space with a door at one end leading to a long, tapering, under-the-stairs broom closet, the contents of which she could barely make out in the gloom, though she recognized the shape of a wooden stepladder and crawled under it. Soon she had wrapped herself up in an old rug she found. Her feet faced the closed door, and her head was under the first of what would have been the house stairs. She had always liked lying on the floor of a room, imagining what it would be like to walk on the ceiling, and the inverted stairs were challenging enough in this fantasy to distract her. She determined to stay there for a long period of time. This she had done, all through her nan's hysterics which had erupted not long after her disappearance, and all through the stillness, later, after the shop had gone quiet. She stayed when she heard voices once again: policemen questioning the shopkeepers, and even when she heard the husband tell his wife that the village pond would be dragged. This news frightened her enough that she wondered if she could ever leave the spot to appear in front of her sometimes explosively bad-tempered father. She finally emerged, however, the next morning, after a fairly good sleep under the rug, and walked into the kitchen of the house. The shopkeeper had screamed and then rang Tam's father. "I'm hungry" were the first words she had said. And she was.

When she went away to school, and in spite of what she had told Niall about her childhood, she had, for a while, loved the order of the day and of the surroundings, the desks arranged in rows, the bells that marked out the time for each activity, how numbers ran up and down in columns and words marched along in a straight line. And she kept close to her heart the fact that art classes were held three times a week in a room full of easels and unlimited paper of every size and texture. She drew horses mostly, and the skyscrapers of New York that she had seen in magazines, because she intended to live in one of these as soon as she could arrange to do so. She was at the top or near the top of her class in every subject – she couldn't imagine laziness – but she could be wild as well in the dormitories and out of doors, often running with the older girls or taunting them from a distance when they refused to let her join in a field hockey or netball game. She knew instinctively that by the time she was old enough to be granted inclusion in such activities, she would no longer want them. All through her life, once she had gained anything she had previously desired, the thing itself would immediately lose lustre.

She had run away from the school for the first time when she was twelve, after half a year of elaborate planning, hoarding of weekly allowances, sweets, and biscuits, and a spate of cheerful cooperative behaviour that was designed to put the school authorities off the scent. Her report card from that term praised her mature demeanour and leadership qualities and insisted that she was a credit to her school; a suggestion she would have scoffed at at the time – had she known – but that merely amused her when she came across the report in a drawer years later.

She had enjoyed the school's riding lessons with all the various sides of her nature. In spite of having told Niall that her favourite time was after lights out, when she could no longer see the place, each week she would look forward to the warmth of the animals and the fleeting sense of freedom that came to her when she was able to move the horse from a canter into a gallop, which is precisely what she did the day she escaped. Except that when she reached the limits of the field, rather than turn back, she encouraged her mount to jump the fence. The fact that she was able to do so successfully seemed like a sign to her that she had taken the right decision, and she therefore encouraged the animal to jump the next fence as well, an act that placed them both firmly on a country lane where they trotted contentedly toward an unknown horizon.

She was fully happy then, as she would always be when the truant was alive in her, and she listened with satisfaction to the sound of hooves on gravel mixed with the faint jingling and crackling of the pocket money and wrapped sweets in her backpack. How perfectly simple escape was – there had never been anything holding her back – and she wondered why people didn't do it all the time, why they departed each day at a time arranged by others in order to sit in shops and offices and classrooms they despised. She was also certain that her costume – breeches, jacket, riding cap, and boots – did not identify her as a schoolgirl the way her daily uniform did. (This was naive on her part, as she would eventually discover.) In her backpack there was also a brassiere, stolen from one of the senior dormitories, and a pair of mittens, brought along not because she thought she might be cold but because, the following morning, she intended to ball up the mittens and stuff them into the brassiere. She believed that the whole contraption, combined with her unusual tallness, would immediately make her eighteen years old and unrecognizable as a child to any onlooker. She had also stolen a few carrots and an apple from the school kitchens so that she could feed the horse.

She slept outdoors for two nights, which she had enjoyed, or so she told Niall. But in spite of the false breasts, she was apprehended on the High Street of a village as she rummaged through a garbage pail looking for food. The sweets had run out and, anyway, had soon lost their charm. Everyone appeared to know who she was. No one mistook her for an eighteen-year-old. It seemed that she had been travelling toward and not away from the school to which, in no time at all, she was unceremoniously driven by the local constable. Her father, who had been of course already called, motored over, and in the midst of a conference with the headmistress, it was decided Tamara should return home for a few weeks in order to cool down. In any case, it was very near the Easter holidays. Once situated in the old nursery at the oddly named Edgeworth Hall, a place haunted by her vanished nan, she announced she would bolt again were she ever forced to return to the school.

As it turned out, her upper-crust parents had been considering the almost unheard-of notion of sending her to the local school anyway, for diplomatic and social reasons. Secret negotiations for the upcoming airfield were underway, and her father, who since the First World War had harboured a militaristic mindset (never mind that as a senior officer he had seen precious little live action), was intrigued by the idea of having such a large and aggressive toy right at his doorstep, and that, combined with a seat in the House of Lords, made him a key player in these negotiations. Furthermore, he had taken to investing in concrete and almost fully owned the company that would become Edgeworth Enterprises. After the war the business flourished to such an extent that in spite of its being primarily concerned with the various motorways that were being constructed, there would be few projects in which E.E. did not play at least some part. His nickname, among thousands of labourers he would never meet, would be "Concrete Charley."

"They demolished the village," she had told Niall. "Absolutely everything went."

He thought she was exaggerating. "Not the whole village," he said.

"No, everything," she assured him. Absolutely everything was gone except for the church and the gardener's cottage, which was near the entrance gate. "My parents honestly believed that by sending me to the village school it would seem as if they too were experiencing a loss when that school was knocked down."

She told him that when her mother had inquired, not unreasonably, about what was to become of the tenantry, her father had said confidently that she should not be concerned. The younger men would all soon be in uniform anyway, and the rest would have several months to make other arrangements.

During the year she attended the soon-to-be-destroyed village school, a boy called Teddy O'Brien – the owner of the dog beyond the walls – became her weekend and after-class friend. His father was the estate gardener of Edgeworth Hall and the cottage they lived in hugged the outer walls and would, as such, survive the demolition that would soon obliterate the pubs and shops and homes a half a mile down the road. As a younger child Tam had played marbles in the dust of the road with Teddy, dismissing the game itself and instead giving the tiny round objects names and making up stories about them. A set of small vehicles, buses, lorries that Teddy had in his possession was called into service, and extreme dramas came into imaginary being among them – wrecks, sometimes even a love affair between an omnibus and a lorry, sometimes murders. Moving so close to him and to the ground they hovered over, Tam came to know the details of his hands and face and his bare knees so well that, years later, she could recall that pattern of his freckles and the shape of his fingernails, the tawny colour of his skin. He was a pleaser, always giving her access to his toys, his tools, his dog, and accepting as law all suggestions she made as to how their activities should progress.

Back in the St. Derwent playground on schooldays, she betrayed him utterly, making it clear to him that she preferred to try to curry favour with the kind of boys who most often ignored them both. The power of exclusion would always draw her toward certain events and people, at least until the war, when everything, including her barely formed character, changed. Teddy had a quiet air, somehow, which probably accounted for his dismissal by the pack. And he had, in summer, vague allergies that visited him in the form of a leaking nose. But during the summer she was thirteen years old, it was this boy who had taken her to the far side of the airfield, where she could see the airplanes, which up until then had dwelt only in the skies, hum sedately down toward the earth or lift off with an unimaginable amount of noise. And it was he who had shown her how to scramble unnoticed through shrubbery and under the wire fence so that they could get dangerously close to these magical machines.

She accepted as rightfully hers all that Teddy revealed to her when they were together in those days, but, as she later realized, she never once gave him credit for the astonishing gift he was giving her. Once she was there, the experience of the airfield swept from her mind all credit for Teddy's role as her guide.

She let Teddy lead the way to further adventures, never venturing forth alone. By the next summer they were not only braver but able to stay out later, and dusk sometimes found them cross-legged beneath the undercarriage of a Bristol Blenheim or, stunningly, on one occasion, a visiting Hawker Hurricane.

Eventually, the inevitable happened. By now they had become so bold as to stroll around in the gathering shadows, lounging casually against the fuselage of one airplane or another in a proprietary fashion, even moving a propeller or two. She was hanging on to a blade with both hands trying to budge it by swinging her body weight back and forth when she was caught around the waist by a pair of adult arms. "Run," Teddy had yelled, preparing to do just that himself. But it was useless, and in no time he too was intercepted by another official-looking figure, and the two of them were marched back in the direction of the fence, each man holding a child's arm in his hand.

"What the hell are you two doing?" one of the men was asking.

"Guess you like it here," the other said. "How about you stay a spell longer?"

"Cannot," said Teddy, recognizing an adult trick. "I have to be home by half-nine."

"He has to be home by nine-thirty," the tallest man repeated. "How about that? And what about you, young lady, do you have to be home by nine-thirty? I think we'd like to keep the both of you out all night, that's what I think."

This was not what Tam had been expecting. A reprimand, maybe, but not an incarceration. The night was deepening; she suddenly and uncharacteristically wanted to go home to her parents. The planes seemed to be grinning at her, their windscreen-eyes dark except for one or two pinpricks of light, the lamps of the quiet airfield. She could hear Teddy sniffling and felt disdainful, even when she remembered the allergies. "Are you going to put us in jail?" she asked the man who was holding her shirt.

He laughed then and called to his companion, "Will we put them in jail?"

"Not sure," the other man said. They were all standing close together now. Tam could smell the alcohol and smoke on the breath of this smaller man. "Can you climb?" he asked.

"Yes," she said.

"I wasn't asking you, actually." He jerked his head in the direction of Teddy, who had stopped sniffling and was paying attention. "I want to know if *he* can climb."

Suddenly Tam realized that these were men much younger than her father, and the fact of this calmed her considerably. They obviously had no idea where she came from.

"I can," said Teddy in a surprisingly clear voice. "And so can she," he added, wanting to be fair to her in everything.

"That's the ticket then." The taller man looked at the watch on the hand that was not holding Teddy's arm. "If you can get over that fence, that one, over there" — he motioned toward the farthest side of the airfield — "if you can get over that fence and out of our sight in less than two minutes, you win. If not, we win."

Both Teddy and Tam squirmed at the end of the men's grasp. "Not so fast," said the shorter of the two men. "There is something else. There is no school these days, correct?"

Tam wondered if she should disclose this information, but Teddy nodded.

"*If* and only if you get over that fence in two minutes, we will not call the coppers. And if we don't call the coppers, we want you to come back tomorrow morning early and climb back in using that exact piece of fence. If you don't appear, the police will come to your house to get you."

Tam wanted to point out that it was far easier for them to crawl *under* the fence but doubted that facility of entrance and exit was what the man had in mind.

"You don't know where we live," she said.

"Ah, but we have ways of finding out," one of the men said. "Isn't that right, Teddy?"

This knowledge of her friend's name genuinely interested her.

"Isn't that right, Teddy?" the man repeated. Tam recognized his accent as being one not unlike her own, and one entirely different from Teddy's. In the distance she could hear the sound of revelry by night, coming from a long, lit Quonset hut in the distance, one she had not paid attention to until that minute. It was a phrase she liked, the sound of revelry by night, but she wished she had noticed this revelry earlier.

"Right," said Teddy softly.

Suddenly they were both running, she without any real memory of being released. They hit the fence at full speed and tore their way up the clanging chainlink, vaulted over the top, then fell into the weedy ditch on the other side. To get back to the road that led to Teddy's cottage and the entrance to Edgeworth Hall, they had to run the full length of the airfield in the opposite direction. She didn't look to see if the men were watching, but as they turned the corner she heard a masculine voice call out, "Nine o'clock tomorrow morning. Or the law. Your choice!" and then a lot of laughter, which made her realize that this might well have all been a joke. But, just in case it wasn't, she ran faster and for longer than she ever had before.

Several minutes later they slowed to a trot. When she could speak again, Tam asked him who the men were and how they knew his name. Was he known to the police? Had he a secret life of crime? Was that why he knew how to sneak onto the airfield? Teddy had suddenly become more appealing to her.

"My sister's used-to-be boyfriend," Teddy wheezed. He stopped, leaned against a tree, and pulled out the handkerchief for which Tam had always had nothing but disgust – couldn't he just hork and spit like the older boys at school whose attention she coveted? – and coughed into it once or twice before folding it neatly and putting it back in his pocket. But she was too intrigued by this mention of romance to think long about the handkerchief or to take into consideration that Teddy was on the edge of a full-blown attack of asthma.

"Who is he exactly? Why was he there?"

"A heartbreaker," Teddy said, "that's what my mother told my aunt. When he didn't come to our house anymore, my sister locked herself in her room and played the radio and cried. My father says he's a good-for-nothing toff, a real bad character. Rubbish, is what he said."

Tam digested this information.

"He flies planes," Teddy went on. "And I think he's part of some university flying club or something. Or he might be in the Air Force. They have dances there at the airfield sometimes with boys who fly planes. That's where my sister first . . ."

Tam was filled with astonishment. No wonder the sister locked herself up in that room and cried. "Did he take your sister up in a plane?" she interjected. Teddy nodded, though Tam would later realize that this was highly unlikely. But at this moment she felt that there could be no real life after having, and then losing, access to flight. And yet, she had seen his sister recently; so she was out of her room. She had a new permanent hairdo, and she seemed serene, if a little vacant. The world of older girls was still mystifying to her. They were nearing Teddy's cottage now. All the lights were on, as if there might be trouble. "I better go in," he said.

"If we don't go back tomorrow," Tam said, "I don't know. Your father told you he's a real bad sort." And then, "Do you think he's a bad sort?"

"Yes . . . well, no. But tonight . . . he would have called the coppers for sure."

"I'm going back," said Tam. "You're going to come with me as well, because I am going to make that one take us up in a plane."

"Yes." Teddy wheezed. "I suppose so." She knew he thought there wasn't much that she couldn't accomplish.

She turned to go, but he caught her arm. "Tam," he said. "What?"

"Oh nothing." His nose was running. He reached for his handkerchief.

"What's his name, by the way?" she suddenly asked.

"Reginald." Teddy was looking nervously at his own door. "My sister called him Reggie."

Tam married Reggie three years later, the summer she turned seventeen, he having been deemed suitable by her parents because of Cambridge, the Air Force, and certain Byzantine and ancient family connections stretching back to the Wars of the Roses. By then the village of St. Derwent was completely gone and the airfield, being in a position to protect the Cornish coastline, was fully operational. The war was in full swing, and Reggie was a glamorous flying officer (whose squadron was sometimes stationed at St. Derwent), and she was once again languishing in the dormitory of another boarding school from which she wished to bolt. She once told Niall that the mere sight of walls covered with ivy could bring out the truant in her.

Reggie, who had been much taken with her during the holidays of the summer before, seemed to her to provide the perfect avenue for escape. She had made flying lessons a condition of their engagement, having never until then managed to get up in one of the planes, and these he had arranged for her at a nearby private field, never once, she later realized, believing that she had been serious. He found her interest in flying amusing rather than alarming, assuming it was a feminine whim, and that one experience behind the controls would frighten the wits out of her and that would be that.

"My little shrinking violet," he sometimes said to her teasingly during their intimate moments, and before she had achieved her licence and joined the Air Transport Auxiliary, "the Spitfire pilot."

REGGIE HAD PROVED TO BE UNKILLABLE DURING the war, perhaps because of his unflagging good nature that in no time had begun to wear on Tam's nerves. He was not a particularly skilful pilot but was for some reason blessed with such reliable good fortune that his mates began calling him "Lucky Lenthall." His surname, which Tam had never been fond of, was pronounced in the same manner as the beans that went into the making of a soup that she had always refused to eat. She sometimes thought of this when their leaves overlapped, or when his squadron was posted near enough to the home base of the Air Transport Auxiliary that she saw him regularly. During these spells of togetherness she would try not to be put off by the way he talked like a two-year-old while nuzzling her neck, his saluting and heel-clicking whenever she asked him to do something for her, the dandruff on the collar of his uniform. But things of this ilk would always slip into her mind the moment he suggested she remove her clothes. When he was far away, however, she could muster some fondness for him, mostly based on her completely reinventing his character to fit that of the other airmen who were regularly in her vicinity. She often thought of them in a way that she never thought of her husband. And she was thinking of them now, looking at the few figures in uniform on the mural. All the bright, handsome young men whose lives were often over in an instant, and who were at times intense in their dealings with others, at times witty and seemingly carefree, and always touching in the way they walked cheerfully toward their machines and leapt eagerly onboard.

Back on the ground at St. Derwent, Teddy had shown himself to be a gifted mechanic: as if the planes were enlarged examples of the model vehicles he, in the past, had handled with such tenderness. He was sensitive and patient with them, and they, in turn, appeared to respond to his attentions in an almost human way, their engines bursting into life, their fuselages shining in the sun.

He had been a true innocent, Tam remembers telling Niall, utterly incapable of duplicity. If he thought there was a problem – mechanical, social, or personal – he would do his best to identify it and then make an honest attempt to solve it. It was almost, she mused, as if the machines knew this. And people too. They liked him and trusted him, but nobody got stuck on him. Teddy was needed to accomplish certain tasks, and he was comforting to have about, but he did not have the knack of being emotionally essential. "Poor Teddy," she added.

"But you miss him," Niall said.

"Oh, yes," she said, turning her face from his as if ashamed. "Poor Teddy. I miss him."

RAGE

———

During the first year after his mother's death in the autumn of 1943, things had come to an impasse regarding Kieran. He had spent the previous six months avoiding school and collapsing into rages whenever anyone suggested he do anything at all. Now he no longer needed to run away from the school, as the Brothers flatly refused to take him and his tantrums back under any circumstances, including the circumstances threatened by the truant officer if one of their charges remained on the loose. Father O'Sullivan visited the house frequently and attempted to talk to the boy but found he could interest him in nothing at all beyond tales of Jaweh at his most vengeful and bloodthirsty. Any attempt at the Rosary was met with either a complete withdrawal or a tantrum, and finally the fear of the latter resulted in the priest removing himself entirely from the huge project that the boy had become.

Almost everyone in the town had a theory as to how Kieran might be trained, and few were shy about offering their advice. Shouting, strapping, confining, singing, set-dancing, Bible memorization, manual labour, and even the questionable idea of a chemistry set were suggested to his father as possible cures for his behaviour. Kieran was talked about in shops, pubs, market stalls, caravans, cottages and byres, and at the weather station, where the men spoke to his father about him metaphorically in terms of various kinds of – mostly bad – weather. Niall, who on calm days was fond of his younger brother, had taken to giving him a wide berth on weekends when he was home from the Dublin University. The knowledge of the younger boy's volatility, and the attention that was drawn to him as a result, seemed to him unbalanced and unfair. More than once he said, you're too old now, Kieran, for the temper. It looks very bad on you.

Kieran began to suffer from migraines. His gentle father could minister to him with damp cloths and soft words when he had the headaches, but the tantrums put the man's wits astray. He was heartsick for the boy and blamed himself, as he hadn't the inner fortitude to whip him, though he doubted, and likely correctly, that a beating of any kind would produce the desired results, and believed that it might in fact make things worse. With the shame and grief of his wife's death all around him, he could not commit an action for which there was no guarantee of a positive outcome. Often that meant no action at all.

And so the father of the boys became prematurely old and absent. Even Niall's repetitive triumphs on the sports fields and in the classroom could not shine through the vague, sad mist that surrounded him. Niall would later tell Tam that there were times when he felt he had simply slipped his father's mind. But, truly, there had been a kind of elderliness about the father's character as far back as anyone could remember, an adherence to schedules and habit and a love of simple comfort. He grew roses and fed birds and took the same walk each evening, past the courthouse, then up the hill to the High Street, then down Market Lane and along by the shops and pubs of Main Street until he was back at his own gate. He now took longer walks each evening, his head down and his hands clasped behind his back, contemplative, strolling with apparent calmness through the capricious variations of weather he had forecasted at the end of the previous day. And then he stepped back inside, and under a roof he kept in perfect repair against the storms he himself had predicted, he prepared to endure his son's chaotic, unpredictable anger.

Coming and going from the house more often now that there was no woman in it, Gerry-Annie watched the child's behaviour with a look of disapproval but said nothing. She had no children of her own but had come from a family of eleven. Her siblings had been far from subdued, but in her world no child could ever have stood centre stage for more than a moment unless they were sick and dying, and even then the attention from adults was, by necessity, brief. In between these emergencies, any behaviour of this nature would have been ameliorated by the fists of older brothers, and nobody would have thought any more about it.

One day, while Annie was mopping the tiles that covered the floor of the long entrance foyer, Kieran rounded the corner at the far end with a full tray of Waterford crystal in his hands, his mouth open in a howl of rage. He came to a stop when he saw her, then flung his burden in her direction. Not one shard of glass came within five feet of her person, but Annie had a temper of her own. In seconds she had the boy's collar in one fist and his hair in the other and was holding him at arm's length several inches from the floor. He kicked like an angry donkey, but although he was now almost twelve, he was still small enough that she was considerably larger than him and he was unable to extricate himself from her grip or make contact with the arms he was wheeling in her direction. But it wasn't until he began to swear energetically that Annie took extreme measures. "You've the mouth of a Black and Tan on you," she announced just before she forced his head into the pail full of brown and soapy water. When that head emerged still cursing, she plunged it in again. And when his head came back up with soapy bubbles ballooning out of his nose she threw her own head back and laughed a loud and protracted laugh, and as she did, the boy produced a tentative smile in return. "Go get a cloth," she said, prodding him with the handle of the mop. "You'll be picking up every piece of that glass, and you'll be doing that carefully. If there is one speck of it left, or if you cut yourself, that head of yours

goes right back in this water." The broom handle was explor-
ing Kieran's ear. He stuck out his tongue. Annie lifted the
mop to cuff him, but he had vanished before she could even
take serious aim.

He fetched some rags and he carefully picked up the
glass. He rolled up the collected shards in a cloth and took the
bundle to the bin. And more than once he smiled radiantly,
and not a little insolently, at Gerry-Annie, who was standing
like a sentinel in the hall. She ignored his cheekiness. It was
only cheekiness, after all.

When she returned to the house the following Friday, he
was down the stairs to meet her in an instant. Throughout
the morning as she involved herself in a number of tasks he
trailed around behind her picking up various objects and
putting them in places they didn't belong so that she would
be required to speak to him. It turned out that he liked the
sound of her voice, which was firm without being high or
sharp; there was not a trace of hysteria in it no matter what
he did. "That's enough of that," she would say, often without
even turning around, or "Put that back this instant."

He was also pleased and impressed by the ways she
described his own face to him. "You've the devil in you as
vigorous as a viper," she would say, or, "You're as anxious for
trouble as a ram in full rut." Eventually she set him to polish-
ing silver, which he did with uncommon enthusiasm, blackening his clothes in the process and bringing a wealth of
further insults down on his head. She filled the laundry tub
with water, handed him a cake of lye, and made him scrub his

own shirt. He liked the washboard, he liked the lye, he liked the way his hands felt in the warm water. Later in the day, when the shirt had gone from wet to damp, she heated an iron on the stove and showed him how to press the wrinkles out of the cotton. Then she told him he would be finishing the job by himself, and she would be calling the guards if there was one scorch mark on the garment. She made him dust the sideboard in the dining room, every picture in the house, and the stairs and banister. All this was very satisfying to him; he would do anything she said.

His father noticed the change in him. But even when a full week had gone by without a tantrum, he was still apprehensive. When three weeks passed without an incident, he nervously asked Niall, who was home from college for the weekend, what he thought accounted for the serenity in the house. Niall announced, with a smirking irony, that his brother had fallen in love with Gerry-Annie. Their father laughed for the first time in a year but had to admit that Annie had Kieran doing housework and he seemed to have taken to it.

The tantrums, however, returned in full force when Annie was unable to come to the house for two weeks because of a bad bout of bronchitis. At one point it was necessary for his father to put Kieran in the coal cellar, this being the only part of the house with a door that locked. The boy ran back and forth in that dark prison, beating his hands until they bled on the limestone walls and hurling handfuls of coal at the planks of the closed door. He was unaware at such times of anything beyond the swollen beast of the tantrum pushing a path through him, the way that overburdened lorries or flocks of animals pushed their way down the long, narrow street of the town. When his father eventually unlocked the door, Kieran ran down the hall, blackening the wallpaper with a soiled sleeve. Then he pounded up the stairs into his room where he flung himself onto the bed without removing his clothes. When she returned the following morning, Gerry-Annie would see that the sheets had been darkened by him. She would be furious and would describe his face to him once again. He thought of this just before he fell into a deep sleep.

It was Annie who made the decision. She approached the boys' father in the courteous manner that was natural to a country woman, but without a hint of deference to the fact that she was employed by him. "I'll be taking himself home with me," she said. "It's for the best." "What about school?" the father asked, though it was a rhetorical question, both of them knowing that school was lost to Kieran. "I'll get him to work around the place," Annie said. "He'll be happy enough with that."

The boy, listening at the top of the stairs, turned and walked into his room, where he packed a few belongings in his schoolbag. All that year he had carried in his mind the dimly remembered landscape near Culloo Rock, how the priest had said it was the final end of everything, the end of the known world. He recalled the other boys' hands at the verge of the well and his own hands not among them. There would always be an air of transgression somewhere near him. He could bring to mind the way the land tilted upwards toward the cliffs, and at times he could picture his mother and the chemist, two dark figures quietly making the uphill walk toward the edge, the decision taken and all tension drained from them. Even though he was a child, he knew that the tragedy they shared would not feel as lonely as his busy, muscular tantrums.

He stood for a moment at the door of his room. The stairs, the entrance hall they led to, the forward thrust of the garden walk he could see through the glass in the door, and then, across the way, Bridge Street moving down toward the harbour – all this combined to make one steep, continuous path. He felt light-headed, as if he might stumble and fall helplessly out of his childhood and into something that was not quite adulthood, something not fully human. Then he saw Gerry-Annie removing her apron and putting on her coat with the lambswool collar in the calm, ordinary way that she always had at the end of the day, and he knew he was safe from the tug of dark gravity.

That evening, before he left the house with Annie, he shook his father's hand without speaking as if he had already become a stranger to him. He could hear his mother whispering something in his mind and he was trying not to listen. His father touched his shoulder at the door. "It's only for a while," he said, "and you'll come back to me on Sundays." *Sundays*, his mother whispered from somewhere halfway up the stairs.

Kieran said nothing, but as he closed the door behind him, he could feel the tantrums separating themselves from him, as though they were insisting on remaining behind in the dim corners of the house, or as if they had tumbled down the bridge road and into the inky water that lapped at the quay.

THE CRITIC

—

Five years before he began to work on the mural, Kenneth had moved with his young family to the small community in rural Saskatchewan. He bought a simple stone house and built a frame studio in the adjacent yard, where he worked on paintings in which landscapes remained representational but figures and animals were abstract in nature. During the winter he taught at a college in the prairie city ten miles away, and in the summer he and a handful of other artists held summer classes in a recently abandoned TB sanatorium situated in a river valley one hundred miles from any kind of urban settlement.

It was at this time that his ideas about distance and migration began to solidify. He would walk out his door toward the railway tracks and stand looking at the two converging lines that seemed on certain summer days to stand upright like a giant's apple-picking ladder and, on others, particularly in winter, to be Masaccio's carefully determined lines of perspective progressing across white paper toward the vanishing point. Everything about the landscape was clear and well defined, the flat wheat fields in the foreground, and the city visible in miniature, framed on the horizon against a too-perfect sky of a ridiculously pure blue.

He had no idea how to transform such unreachable space on the canvas, so began to document the details of the place instead, attempting to capture the intimacy he had come to believe he was interested in. He drew railway cars and signals and grain elevators, coils of rope and wire and the railway station itself. The curve of tracks moving toward a siding and the great iron wheels of the cars waiting there caught his attention for a while, but the resulting drawings were, ultimately, unsatisfying on the page.

As time passed he found it impossible to ignore the extreme, unreadable, and seemingly irreproducible distances. There was some echo in all this of his remembered pre-marital travels in Europe, and the sense that, no matter how far or how fast he moved, the destination, whatever it was, would always recede. Unfulfilled potential and missed opportunities began to absorb him. In the town, he found the teaching repetitive and un-rewarding. And in the long, echoing, and still faintly medical halls of the summer school, he was haunted by thoughts of those who had lived and died there, of lives cut short or narrowed by circumstance or bad luck. He feared that his own life would be of the narrower variety, and that it would be made that way because of lack of courage, not even having the excuse of dis-ease. And then, as if by magic, an alternative narrative presented itself, for it was here, of all places, that he met the famous critic.

The man had come up from New York to the summer school almost on a whim. Intrigued by an invitation to such an out-of-the-way locale, and bemused by the whole notion of the old sanatorium, the critic agreed to give a lecture and to stay for a couple of days to speak informally with the students and teachers there. He had arrived wearing a city suit and a narrow tie and had worn that costume for the entirety of his visit. Kenneth was somewhat disappointed by the man's physiognomy, having expected someone thinner and more obviously the aesthete. This man was tired, overweight, and world-weary. Still, his reputation had preceded him, and it was this reputation that intrigued Kenneth, that and the cold voice of authority that presented itself whenever the critic began to speak.

As they sat side by side on a bench in the neglected grounds drinking a beer at the close of the second day, the critic told Kenneth that the purity and quiet of the situation was soothing to him after the noise, the commotion really, of the art scene in New York. The unselfconsciousness of the art being produced here in this prairie province, the utter lack of ego, and, in some cases, even the lack of skill was refreshing, he said, smiling, a column of smoke emerging from his mouth and dispersing in the clear air. Absolutely nothing has ever happened here, he added, which is what makes it so appealing. Nothing has been *built*, he said. Then he made a quick, insistent rectangle with his hands.

On the third day of his stay, the critic agreed to look at some of the paintings Kenneth was working on in the vacant ward that was acting as his temporary studio, and after only a glance or two, the critic announced that he believed that Kenneth had the potential for a full career beyond this half-life of part-time teaching and full-time rendering of landscape. But he must, the critic insisted, move fully into the abstract. He should look at Olitski, Pollock. He should discard subject matter – it was no longer relevant, hadn't been for some time – and concentrate on the purely plastic elements: line, shape, colour, texture. It was the only way forward, he maintained. Anything else was backward-looking, and redundant, and told us nothing new about the world.

The critic looked for some time at the diminutive, realistic egg tempera of the beautiful Qu'Appelle Valley, which Kenneth had been working on at the same time as the three landscapes in oil. "Good God!" he eventually said. "You're not seriously breaking eggs! Messing around with yolks and pigment. It is admittedly charming to think of you in this bucolic valley attempting to resurrect such an ancient medium. But it's a supreme waste of time and effort. You need to work with something fast and free; you must learn to use paint extravagantly, as if there were an unlimited supply of it gushing from a tap nearby. There's just no place anymore for the painstaking."

Kenneth immediately agreed, said that the exercise had been purely recreational anyway, and that he had never intended to show the results to anyone, anywhere.

"Look at Diebenkorn, Barney Newman," the critic continued. "They may not always achieve what they set out to do, but they would never be held hostage by technique." He lifted a double-zero-point brush in his hand. "You must throw anything smaller than two inches into the garbage," he said.

As the famous critic spoke, the magnificent subjects of European paintings faded and then withdrew from Kenneth's consciousness. Gods, landscapes, battles, shipwrecks, towns on rivers, beautiful naked women, bleeding saints, mounds made of fruit and dead rabbits, skating peasants on frozen millponds all turned and filed, obedient as schoolchildren, out of the room that had held them in his mind. The simple prairie subjects – railway tracks, farms, grain elevators, this valley – that had occupied him all year followed in suit until everything in the perceived world seemed small and banal. He found himself apologizing for his recent work, and all the work that preceded it.

"Not at all," the critic said. "I can see rumours of the abstract in some of these." He pointed to a roughly painted prairie sky in one of the oils. "Here," he said, "the brushstrokes are moving toward something a little more interesting, aren't they? And here," he said, running his fingers over a wheat field busy with wind.

Kenneth was electric with engagement, watching the plump white hands swaying over the beginnings of paintings he was now mostly embarrassed by. And he was filled with relief that the man had been able to discover even one brushstroke he approved of. He could actually see himself creating fierce, undomesticated works of art, the required muscular activity in front of the canvas, quantities of molten paint being flung by him from the end of a large, angry brush, his brain on fire.

"You are absolutely right," he said to the critic. "I can see it now. That's where I was heading."

"But don't use yellow," the critic said. "I despise yellow."

After that, the critic was persistently present in the room in his mind that had been previously occupied by Europe. Kenneth wrote long, eager letters to the New York address, explaining the current series of paintings, the choice of various colours, the prevalence of one shape or another. He waited weeks, sometimes months for a reply, a reply that often arrived in the form of a postcard with two or three lines hastily scribbled on the back. *Stop rendering*, one of these read. *It is a habit left over from the time you wasted making pictures. Nothing important can result from this, so let it go. That which is truly abstract recoils from rendition.* Some of the postcards were sent from places that made Kenneth itch with desire. *Am writing from Pollock's place in the Hamptons*, one card began breezily, *where I am walking him through some necessary changes.* Another was sent from a private gallery in New York, though the image on the front was of a slightly askew Empire State Building. *Get down here immediately*, it commanded, *and see the Jack Bush show. It goes in far too many directions, as he realized himself with a pang once I pointed this out to him. In truth, it is so uneven and spotty, I feel there would be a world of things for you to learn from it.*

Kenneth could not get down there immediately, and likely not for some time what with his family and the teaching, and he suspected the critic knew this. He replied, instead, with an invitation for the critic to return to Saskatchewan the following summer.

A card from Los Angeles arrived the following week. *Delighted to come back*, it read. *You have no idea how much I am betting on Saskatchewan as New York's only true competitor, especially after seeing the tripe here.* Then a P.S. *Take some slides of your work and send them down to me.*

The next few weeks of Kenneth's life were spent both desperately attempting to squeeze a decent fee for the critic's visit out of provincial officials and those at the university, and waiting for the perfect light to enter the studio so that he could photograph the paintings in an acceptable way. Neither was completely successful. Officials in both places were reluctant, and he was able to manage only half of the money the critic wanted. As for the light, the prairie winter produced day after day of blinding sun reflected from a pure white landscape, and in the end he simply could not put together a full set of slides that was free of glare.

He sent the package anyway, along with an explanation about the weather and the critic's proposed payment. Then he began to wait. Weeks passed. A month went by. Finally a card depicting the New York Public Library arrived. The critic had nothing to say about his reduced fee; in fact, the summer was not mentioned at all. It concerned, instead, Kenneth's paintings. *Square shape of the canvas is wrong*, the critic wrote. *Never take the shape of the canvas for granted.*

He wrote the critic another long letter, setting out what he intended to do, and asking which dates the man might want for the school. The critic did not reply, perhaps, Kenneth conjectured, because of the fee. He wrote another letter in which he suggested that the Arts Council might be able to come up with another couple of hundred dollars because of the importance of Saskatchewan art being recognized in New York. Still no response.

Reworking the now-rectangular paintings proved to be a design problem more complicated than Kenneth had anticipated, and he often laboured in the studio until one or two in the morning. His wife was beginning to feel neglected and said so during the few moments, usually at meals, that they spent together.

Finally he was able to send off a new set of slides to the critic along with a letter explaining that although the Arts Council was not able to come up with all of the funds, every man, woman, and child in Saskatchewan was hoping that the critic would return. He wondered if he should block out time for the critic now. Perhaps for the last week in August?

Kenneth heard from the critic only one more time. By then, the summer school had come and gone and the winter sun was once again blazing in through his studio windows, making him wince, and causing a glare on the rectangular paintings stacked against the wall. He had stopped painting altogether, having found himself unable to continue without word from New York. He taught in the daytime and at night he walked along the tracks as he had before abstraction entered his life, but without the attentiveness he had brought to his previous rambles. He was becoming increasingly distanced from his wife, and his marriage began to falter. Finally in midwinter an envelope with an American stamp arrived. Inside it was a single piece of paper with a typed message, one that was longer than anything he had ever received from the critic.

The opening paragraph asked after Kenneth's health and that of his family, and contained some references to people in the critic's own personal life, names that Kenneth did not know.

The second paragraph got down to the business of the paintings. *There really is nothing that I can see of any worth in the slides you sent me. Immature, unrealized work, and entirely derivative. Too much green! And the amount of rendering is insupportable and gives an unhealthy three-dimensionality to the canvases even though there is no subject matter. It would do neither your career, nor indeed my own career, any favour to exhibit these paintings in New York.*

Two years later, when he began to work on sketches for the Gander mural, Kenneth found himself placing a huge, pasty, ghostlike figure in the centre of the picture plane. Painted cylindrically, and with great bulk, the figure held a wooden decoy in one raised arm as if attempting to persuade the inanimate to take flight. His expression was pugnacious and his white costume resembled the military garb of a dictator. Almost everything around him that wasn't painted green was painted yellow.

As he moved toward a final version for his submission, however, Kenneth would paint the critic out altogether, using as a substitute a man he had seen once in Domodossola, Italy. Or, at least, what he remembered and felt about him. But, in the beginning, it had given Kenneth great pleasure to make a portrait of the critic by breaking every rule the critic had tried to enforce, making him vivid, real, ignoring pure shape, pure colour, making him speak, pretentiously.

When he replied to the letter that came a few months later offering him the commission, he wrote that he hoped that there were a lot of chickens in Newfoundland. The mural, he wrote, would be executed in egg tempera.

THE PURPLE HORNET

———

K ieran's first job at Gerry-Annie's was to fix the stone wall that ran alongside the road and kept Joe Shehan's sheep away from Annie's roses, for which they had developed a taste. He didn't mind the work, though it wasn't technically the kind of domestic chore that he had become accustomed to under Annie's supervision. It took him into the hills looking for particular stones, however, and allowed him the use of Gerry's barrow, the only object around the place that had a wheel, if you didn't count the pulley that brought the bucket up from the mysterious darkness of the well. He knew nothing about the building or the repair of dry-stone construction, but Annie said it was like a puzzle where the pieces fit together and he could use his wicked cleverness to figure it out, since God himself had already provided the stones and plenty of them. She was of the opinion that St. Padraig would have been better employed in removing the stones from the land rather than in banishing the snakes, but since there were rocks in abundance they might as well be made use of.

Though he was small, Kieran was strong enough, and he found holding on to the handles and pushing the empty barrow up a slope to be thrilling in a way he wouldn't have been able to explain. Controlling the object when it was heavy with stones and bent on a rapid descent equally absorbed him. It was his initial encounter with transportation, and with an object driven by gravity, and he was for a time obsessed by the notion that, like him, the vehicle seemed to have a mind of its own. At one point he loaded it with rocks and set it free on a particularly steep slope just to see what it would do, amused by the way its unwilling hind legs bounced awkwardly after the momentum of the wheel until the whole thing came to a halt in the bog. The barrow was unharmed, having been unable to gather much speed under the weight of its burden. But Annie had seen the whole performance and forbad further experiments of this nature. He was disappointed by this but always obeyed her in a way he had never been able to obey anything or anyone else.

The length of broken wall was fixed in three days. Kieran had discovered by himself that rocks could be made to stay in place with the help of small stones used as wedges, and all seemed to be stationary and firm. Annie had nodded three times – an indication of full approval – when she came out to the front of the house to examine the completion of the job. Still that night, when the wind came up, Kieran's sleep was disturbed by worry and his mother was whispering in his mind. The wall had become a kind of daylight home to him in the past few days, and it was as if in placing them one atop another he had come to know forever the peculiarities of each stone so that when he closed his eyes he saw patterns of lichen and granite. *Cliffs of stone*, his mother whispered. There was something in him, even at that age, that dreaded the collapse of anything he himself had completed, and he rose early and anxious for a full week, running outside in the dawn in order to assure himself that the wall still stood.

It was toward the end of that week that the bicycle appeared. There it was in the morning sun, leaning up against the road side of what both he and Gerry-Annie were now calling Kieran's wall, neither beautiful nor new but a bicycle nonetheless. Beads of moisture clung to the parts of the fenders that still had paint. The leather seat was greyed and cracked with age and the rear wheel was missing several spokes. A bent wire basket hung from the rusted handlebars, and a flat metal platform, from which several pieces of frayed rope trailed, jutted out over the back wheel. Though he had never owned one, Kieran had known bicycles all his life. The streets of the town were filled with them. His own father came and went to the weather station on such a vehicle. But the fact of this specific bicycle leaning up against the part of the wall he had built himself, placed there while he was sleeping, seemed magical to the boy, portentous.

It remained there all morning while he hauled water for Annie or bent over a small leather volume called the *Vest Pocket Library*, which contained a dictionary, a parliamentary manual, general information, a few maps and tables of numbers, and a literary guide, and which had been sent, decades ago, to Annie's family as a Christmas gift by a relative who was working in London. It would be all he needed, Annie had said, until he decided to go back to school. When he told her he was never going back, she said we'll see about that. She herself had never learned to read, nor Gerry either, she told him. They had both regretted this, she added when he did not reply. I already know how to read, he informed her. Yes, she said, but you'll keep at it every day for an hour, in case you forget.

When he pointed to the bicycle and asked if she had seen it, she replied that whoever had left it would be back for it soon. "It's nothing to do with you," she told him, "so you'll be leaving it alone."

In the afternoons, if there were no further chores, he was free to roam around the hills because, as Annie had said, boys needed to be aired. He had found a collapsed beehive hut a couple of miles from the farm and, with his new masonry skills, was trying to build it up again and finding it more difficult than his work on the wall, though even more compelling, especially after Annie had told him old stones like that were sacred and not to be meddled with. "I'm only fixing it," he told her, and she seemed to be placated by that.

When he came down to the house again in the dusk he could see that the bicycle was still there. "Could be someone after a lost sheep," Annie ventured. "Did you see anyone when you were above?"

But he had seen no one and believed the bicycle had no owner. He became more certain of this the following day when the morning light revealed it to be in the same location, untouched, leaning against the wall.

It was still there three days later. "Put it in the turf shed," Annie said. "There is some fierce weather coming in and, whoever he is, he won't want his bicycle lifted up by the gale and thrown down on the rocks."

Kieran stepped outside, went to the road side of the wall, and placed his palms on the handlebars. When he walked the bicycle toward and then into the shed it felt to him as if he were stabling a courteous and cooperative animal, one who was grateful for the attention and the shelter. He stood in the gloom near the large stack of turf, patting the old seat. Then he moved outside and closed the door. The moonlight whitened the road that lifted itself up the mountain, and something in him, something fated, wanted to slip along this silver track. He thought of roads he had known, the streets of the town, and the main road by the sea that had taken his brother, Niall, away to the university in Dublin, removing him even further from the life that he himself was living in the hills. *Long sad roads*, his mother said in his mind, and then she said it again in the voice of the wind, which was high and coming at him from all directions. He turned and headed back to the house, to the one lamp he could see in Gerry-Annie's window with the flame in it still lit.

The next morning the air was dense with what Annie called "soldiers of rain" advancing over the fields. Looking out the window, Kieran announced there was another bicycle filling the spot left vacant by the first. His voice was loud with excitement. Annie said it couldn't be so, threw the shawl over her head, and went out to the turf shed to make certain that the original vehicle was still there; that it had not been moved, somehow, in the night. But Kieran knew this was an altogether different bicycle when he went out into the weather to inspect it. This one was gleaming with fresh, unchipped purple paint and was in comparatively good repair. Not one of the spokes was missing from the wheels, there was no rust anywhere on it, and, most wonderfully, it had a bell. Outside in the weather, Kieran stood beside the new bicycle for some time, pushing the bell's small silver lever with his thumb, transfixed by the sound, as if it were the most powerful music he had ever heard. Rain fell on his head and ran down the inside of his shirt, but he hardly noticed. Finally Annie marched out to fetch him. "Put this one in the shed as well," she said. "Make no mistake. These men are booleying up in the mountain, or perhaps preparing to burn off the gorse, though how they can do so in the midst of such rain God alone knows."

Annie was astonished when Kieran said he didn't know what "booleying" meant. For a thousand years at the end of summer, she told him, the animals have been taken by their keepers to pasture for a time to the highest parts of the mountain where the grass remained green and sweet.

Two days passed. The wind finally abated, and the sun came out, changing the wall from the dark slate colour it had become under the rain to its usual soft grey. The weather was dry for the following two days and then, as if aware of Annie's theory, once the sun went down, Knocknadobar and Canuig Mountain came volcanically alive with thrilling rivers of fire.

"As I said," Annie offered, "burning gorse. They'll be down for the bicycles in a day or two, if they don't fire themselves to cinders."

She was afraid of the fires, though not of the men who lit them. "Pray to God we won't be getting a black gable," she said. Gerry himself had been trapped inside his family's cottage when he was a child, Annie told Kieran, the ground outside livid with fire and his father ready to kill the neighbour who had lit the blaze but unable to step outside to reach his intended victim.

A few nights later the mountains resumed their customary large black shapes in the evening and there was no smoke in the air. But no one came to claim the bicycles. "Men can stay on the mountain for a long time," Annie said, and when Kieran asked her why, she replied with four words: "Because they are men."

Half a week later another two bicycles were leaning against the wall. By now even Annie was becoming perplexed. She was not a woman who was used to an abundance of anything except the arrival of wind and rain and other people's babies, and she wondered out loud if perhaps there might have been a spell of sorts placed on the bicycles of the parish so that they might multiply indefinitely. As if to prove her point, three bicycles materialized the following week, four the week after that, and by the end of the summer twelve bicycles were safely housed in the turf shed out back and in an unused cow byre at the far end of the yard. Annie had taken to glaring at the mountains suspiciously. I don't like what those men are up to, she muttered repetitively, and when Kieran asked what she meant, she said that Gerry himself would still be alive if men weren't so frequently up in the mountains talking and planning things.

When Kieran was much younger, Annie had taken Niall and him to see Gerry's name written into a list on the stone of the small monument near the town library. His name was the only word she knew how to read, being unable even to print her own on a piece of paper, and she had pointed to it and said, That's my man. Kieran, being too young to understand really, had believed that the stone figure with the rifle perched atop the plinth was what Annie was referring to and after that, even when he knew better, whenever he passed the monument he thought to himself, There's Annie's man.

Once, after he had come to her house in the hills, she let him look in the little painted box where she kept her treasures: a rhinestone brooch Gerry had given her, four holy medals, including one a neighbour had brought back for her from Lourdes, an inch of frayed green ribbon attached to a small metal bar, and the twisted silver bullet the town doctor had removed from Gerry's lung just before he died. Kieran was fascinated by this small object and often begged to see it, but Annie had to be in a soft mood before she would open the lid. Once she had been so wistful she had let Kieran hold the bullet in the palm of his hand. "Bent by passing through bone," she had whispered to him, before beginning to weep. *Bone*, his mother said softly, *bone*.

Kieran thought about the bicycles all summer long. He thought about the first few bicycles, the early arrivals, in June while he helped the neighbour, Brendan Shea, cut the two small hayfields that had once belonged to Gerry but that Brendan now sowed. He thought about them in August when he went into the mountains with Brendan to move the sheep from one grazing area to another. He thought about them in the loft at night and every time he went back to work on the beehive hut. Whenever he walked out to the turf shed to collect fuel for the fire, he spent some time with the second, beautiful purple bicycle, and eventually he was able to narrow his thoughts and to think only of that one. Annie had told him to stop ringing the bell. Convinced it had only a certain number of rings trapped inside it, she was fearful, she said, that he would wear it out before the bicycle owner came down from the mountain and the dire undertakings he and his mates were planning up there. But she could not stop Kieran from looking at the vehicle and patting its seat in a proprietary fashion. He even gave it a name: the Purple Hornet.

"I've been up and down the mountains all summer, Annie," he said finally when he came back into the house after a session of communion with the Hornet, "and there were no talking men anywhere." Brendan had introduced Kieran to the Mulcahey brothers when they had come across them, some of their sheep, and two of their dogs at the summit of Knocknagantee. "But they told me their bicycles were safe at home," he said, "and there is no one else up there. I promise. Could I not ride just one of them?"

"That would be thievery," Annie told him. "Riding another man's bicycle and him not knowing about it. Did you hear anything about an uprising while you were above? Those Mulcahey boys, now, they would be talking about something like that."

Kieran had heard about nothing but sheep and about one particular ram who belonged, they said, to Padraig O'Connell and who had broken out of a field and run off and been spotted only infrequently, gallivanting around in the company of two wild female goats.

Annie snorted at this. "That could be code," she said, "for a traitor in the vicinity. Men love to fight," she added darkly.

But there had been no fight in the elderly Mulcahey brothers. They had invited Brendan and himself to their cottage for sandwiches, but the notion of the visit had been interrupted by a sighting, and then the capture, of the wayward ram.

"We caught that ram," Kieran told her. "He was real enough, and he's now in Padraig O'Connell's cow byre."

"Is he now," said Annie, "and what of those wild goats?"

There were none to be seen as far as Kieran could tell.

"As I thought," said Annie. "They were code for something else. Gerry himself was called the Red Fox on account of the colour of his hair." She was putting washed dishes onto the shelves of the dresser. "And didn't they shoot him down just like a fox in the end," she said.

One morning, while Kieran was busy with the washing up, Annie announced they would be visiting the tailor called Davey who lived on the other side of Mastergeehy, three miles away.

"Your father has given me money for a winter coat," she told him. "For you," she added, "in case you are confused about that."

Kieran's hands became motionless in the warm suds. He knew that Annie still went twice a week to clean in the house in town, but since she rarely spoke about this, it had been easy for the boy to forget. He himself went there as seldom as possible, though he was happy enough to have his father and sometimes his brother visit him at Annie's on a Sunday afternoon. Something now about his father and this intended coat made him recall the dark, formal rooms of the house, and the sense that everything there was waiting. Even now, more than two years after the worst had happened, there was this terrible waiting that greeted him if ever he stepped over the threshold. Lifting the pan out of the dry sink, he walked toward the open door and threw the greyish water into the yard. A fork and a spoon he had overlooked bounced on the grass. As he bent to pick them up he consciously shook the rooms of the house in town out of his mind.

"And so today," Annie continued as he re-entered the cottage, "we will be sorting out a coat for you."

"I don't like coats," Kieran offered, hanging the tin pan on its customary nail. He had always felt restricted by this second layer of clothing, embraced and therefore imprisoned by it. "I won't wear it."

Annie ignored this. "Your father wanted me to take you to the shop in town. But I told him that the shop had the same coat for everyone. And what was the good in that, I said to him. A coat needs to be yours through and through or it won't warm half enough and you'll be dead of a fever before January. A coat needs to know it's yours or it's a good-for-nothing piece of cloth." She gazed with fondness at her own two coats hanging on hooks Gerry had screwed into a board beside the door. The one with the lambswool collar that she wore into the town and over to the church was a source of great pride. The other, a plainer garment that she wore out to the hen house, the turf shed, and any time it was raining, was a source of great comfort. "Davey will make certain that your coat knows you. He's done that for everyone in the parish. And now you've come to be among us, you'll be needing a coat like that too."

It was dull but dry that October day. They had walked only half a mile when they found themselves confronted by a flock of Joe Shehan's sheep. Driven by dogs between the high hedgerows, the animals roiled around them. Then there was the red face of Joe himself. A conversation blossomed between the adults concerning the merits of Davey's coats, and those of his father and grandfather before him. "Almost everyone is buried in old age in the one they bought in their youth," Joe confided to the silent boy. "They are a rare protection against fever, and they never wear out."

"He'll grow out of his," said Annie. "But he is almost thirteen, so I suppose he'll only be needing one more after this."

"And that one will look fine in his coffin," Joe said while his sheep fed on the roadside grass. Two dogs danced beside the animals, eager to get them moving. Kieran knew the whole flock would be going down to the market in the town. He could hear his mother's footsteps on the road behind him and, faintly, a song she used to sing when he was much younger, before she stopped singing altogether. Then, remembering the tantrums, he allowed an inner picture of the Purple Hornet to form in his mind to encourage calm. The conversation ended and Joe Shehan blessed them both and moved on. The road, when the sheep had left it empty and his mother had faded, ached for a bicycle, Kieran thought.

"That Joe Shehan has a terrible quantity of talk in him," Annie said as they resumed walking. "He could talk the hind leg off a chair."

The road rose under them and soon Kieran could see the whole valley – from the edge of the sea in the west clear over to the Dingle Mountains in the east. Far below there was a warm, rich blanket of bog and long geometric strips where the bog had already been cut. Annie pointed to a small house situated in a little gully with the top of its gable end flush to the road. "That is the house of Eithne of the Streams," she said. "When I'm going to mass I stop there to wash my boots if the road is full of mud. She has a coat with a lambswool collar, something I have myself. Yes, she has that, but her house is full of damp because of the streams."

Kieran could hear the faint hissing of the water but he could not see it because of the thick hedges that bordered the road. By now the village of Mastergeehy was directly beneath them and they were looking down at the slate roof of Annie's church. The smell of turf smoke from cottage chimneys reached them, that and the noise of children out for recess in the National School's playground.

"That's not the school you will be going to," Annie said, "when you get over your stubbornness. All that noise! I'm thinking they teach shouting and screaming there."

Kieran said nothing. He would not respond to her humour. He would not look toward the school. He would not wear the coat. He was full of refusal.

Before they reached the tailor's house Annie stopped to pray at the grotto that marked the crossroads. Kieran stood to one side and looked toward the little Cummeragh River, which moved under a stone bridge then looped behind the white shape in the distance that Annie had told him was the tailor's house. He was suspicious of grottos, which always brought into his mind the memory of the two coins he had not offered at the side of the well four years ago.

"The Virgin says you'll wear the coat," said Annie, closing the grotto's iron gate. "She says that once you know Davey, you'll want to wear it."

Kieran didn't want to talk about the Virgin. At the bridge he stopped to look more closely at the river. Long green and brown weeds moved in it. He thought he saw a fish as well and a suggestion of the dark skirt his mother had worn the last morning he had seen her. Then Annie tugged his sleeve, bringing him back.

"Knocknagantee," she said, naming the mountain directly ahead of them. "Coomcallee." She pointed to a wall of rock to the south so huge it filled over half the sky five fields away. Kieran could see that it was busy with jumping waterfalls.

"And on this one short road, four townlands," Annie was saying. "Cushcummeragh, Namona, Cappanagroun, and Cloonaughlin." They passed by a minor hill, part of which had been removed to have gravel for the road. "The travellers sometimes come there and stay for a time," Annie said. "Then they go away again."

"Could the travellers have left the bicycles?" Kieran asked his first sentence of the morning.

Annie laughed. "No sensible traveller would leave behind something as useful as a bicycle."

There were two delicate ash trees in front of the tailor's house and between them sat a slight man on a green chair. "That's himself," said Annie as the man rose to his feet. "He is wondering who you are, as he's never seen me with a boy before."

Kieran noticed that the man had a violin in one hand and a bow in the other. He set both down carefully on the chair as they approached and came halfway down the lane to meet them. He shook their hands, Annie's first and then Kieran's.

"I said to myself," he confided to Annie, "that it wasn't Brendan O'Sullivan and it wasn't Jonnie O'Sullivan and it wasn't Sean Shea and it wasn't Micky Shea and it wasn't Cormac O'Connell and it wasn't Donald O'Connell and it wasn't Eugie O'Connell and it wasn't Niall O'Connell and it wasn't Tim O'Connell." He paused, thinking. Then he continued. "It wasn't Jimmy Curran and it wasn't Matt Curran and it certainly wasn't Des Curran. So, I said to myself, it has to be a stranger."

"It's the son of the weatherman I work for," said Annie. "He's mine now."

"Yours, is he?"

"So to speak. He's now living with me."

Davey seemed unsurprised by this. "And does he have a name?" he asked.

"He, does, Davey. He has a name and he has a temper something awful."

Kieran looked up, taken aback. Since he had left the town neither he nor Annie had spoken about the tantrums.

"Well, I like that in a child," said Davey. "It shows character — a mind of his own, like." He turned toward Kieran. "What makes you angry? Whatever it is, it's something you care about in a powerful way."

Kieran realized that he had no notion of what made him angry. The tantrums, when he had them, had been like visitors who had taken up residence inside him, not like blood relations. And not like his mother was now. "I don't know," he said.

"Come now," said Davey, "not everything can be perfect. What has disappointed you then, since you came to be with Annie?"

Kieran looked at Annie timidly. "Say it, whatever it is," she advised.

"Having many bicycles and not being able to ride any of them."

Davey turned to Annie and raised his eyebrows questioningly.

She cleared her throat. "There is the odd bicycle around the place," she admitted. "Do you remember the raid of the bicycles, Davey?" she suddenly asked. "Gerry himself once had ten or more in his possession. And they all being from the barracks in town. It was the only time all the young men in the parish had bicycles and they'd leave them by Shehan's gate when they went up the mountain to do their talking." She closed her eyes. "And to do their drilling and marching as well. They were talking and training in the mountains, Davey, as were you yourself. Do you remember?"

"Of course I remember," said the tailor, "but that was a good long time ago now, Annie."

"But not so long it couldn't happen again. It's a way men have, I suppose."

"I suppose," said Davey uncertainly. "But that was a good long time ago, and at the moment there is not much of it left in us, I'd say." He looked thoughtfully across to the distant waterfalls of Coomcallee. "Nor in the young folk either who have no work." He turned again to inspect Kieran. "What did you say his name was, Annie?"

"I didn't say, but I will now. His name is Kieran."

"That explains it." Davey picked up the fiddle and bow and began to walk toward the open door of his house. Annie and Kieran trotted behind him. For a small man, an old man, this tailor was surprisingly swift.

"St. Kieran," said Davey, ushering the woman and the boy inside, "was the son of a wagon maker. 'Tis how the wheel got into the Irish cross and stayed there." Kieran, he told them, had a lifelong love of the wheel, and all named after him would have the wheel and the love of it in them. St. Kieran had this love and he had the anger brought about by the unused wheel. "What in blazes," he was wont to say, "is the good in a wheel that is unused?" Davey motioned his guests over to the settle by the fire. "I can feel that anger in this boy," he said.

Kieran was fascinated by this but suspected his anger, or what was left of it, had little to do with wheels. He glanced upwards. The room they sat in had a high ceiling made of tongue-and-groove boards. There was no loft, but beside the fireplace there was a door that led into another room.

"It was the roundness of wheels that led St. Kieran to dwell on islands, which as we know from looking toward our own sea and the Skellig Islands in it, are round at their base." The tailor began a precisely described verbal tour of various holy islands, of the circles with which the monks began the construction of their beehive huts, of the round towers he confessed to never having seen, and of the turning wheel of the mill where St. Kieran had ground magically multiplying oats. "They'd say of St. Kieran, Columcille himself was heard to say of him, that he was anxious for the useful wheel."

While Davey was delivering this speech, three small cows walked sedately past his back window, startling black against the bright green of the grass and moving west. There was something about them that was not unlike the dark garments hanging from hooks nailed into a piece of the wooden moulding that was fixed like a plate rail around the perimeter of the room. Kieran had never before been in a room so occupied by the presence of absent others, their arms and shoulders, and occasionally their legs, outlined against the whiteness of the wall. He felt examined, as if the people for whom these garments were destined were watching him and waiting, expecting something from him. Outside the front window the light changed and the mountain called Coomcallee appeared to step two or three fields closer to the house, as if it wanted to examine him as well. He looked again out the more predictable back window, where a fourth cow had paused to graze.

"Are you looking at my cows, Kieran?" the tailor asked. "Aren't they lovely?"

Kieran, embarrassed, studied the ashes in the grate.

"On the subject of our cows," the tailor continued, unaffected by Kieran's silence. "Bo Chiarrai," he said. "Kerry Cow." Then he stood. "'In the histories they'll be making they've a right to put her name / With the horses of Troy and

Oisin's hounds and other beasts of fame/ And the painters will be painting her beneath the hawthorn bough/ Where she's grazing on the good green grass my little Kerry cow.'" He sat down again, smiling.

"Might there not still be some men in the mountains talking?" Annie asked Davey, after a respectful silence.

The tailor bent to place a piece of turf on the fire. He poked at it for a moment with an iron rod, then sat on the wooden chair he had turned toward the settle. "If two men meet in the mountains, they will of course be talking, Annie." He gazed at the clothing hanging on the wall opposite him. "But there are fewer and fewer men in our mountains nowadays. Donal is up there of course, and Tim the Sky, and Brendan Shea on occasion. But not many young ones that I know about." Motioning toward four sets of trousers hanging in a corner, he announced, "Many have not come back to collect these."

Kieran could hear his mother in the room behind the fireplace. *Have not come back*, she whispered like an echo.

"Oh, but they will, of course." Annie twisted on the settle to regard the pants. "They will wear out their trousers and then they'll be back."

"Someday. Perhaps. Which is why I keep them. When they come back, they will need one good set of trousers."

"Where have they gone?" Kieran asked. The sound of his own voice startled him.

The tailor looked surprised. "To London, of course, for work; London or America. There is none here. And no money either." He stood, opened a drawer beneath the table top, and pulled out a long brown tape. Then he turned back to his visitors. "This time we are living in, this time of scarcity, has broken the farming people of Kerry," he said with sudden vehemence. "It has pauperized them and scattered them." A silence slipped in through the door and inhabited the indoor space. Then it slipped out again. "Let's measure you up then, lad," Davey said.

"How do they get there, to London?" Kieran stood, willing now to entertain at least the abstract notion of the coat.

Davey wrapped the tape around the boy's chest and pencilled a number on a scrap of paper. The cows drifted again by the window, moving now toward the east. Kieran felt the tailor's fingers at his shoulder and then on the side of his leg. He heard the squeak of the pencil writing another number on the scrap.

Applied arithmetic, his mother whispered in the adjoining room.

"It would be brown for you," Davey said, reaching up to a shelf to remove a bolt of worsted wool. "They'd take the train in Cahersiveen, for Dublin, then the boat, I'd say. Some come a fair distance in from the mountains to catch that train. I've seen them on their bicycles heading into town. It's the one pack on their back that lets me know that will be the last of them, going over the hill."

Kieran looked quickly across the room at Annie, a thought taking him. "But what do they do with the bicycles? Do they take them with them to London?"

"Well now," said Davey, "I'd not thought of that. They'd not be able to take the bicycles to London. What would you say they'd do with those bicycles, Annie?"

She said nothing for a moment. Then she shifted her weight on the settle and replied, "They'd lean them against a wall, I'd say, somewhere in the countryside outside of the town. It would be too heartbreaking, like, to leave them at the station."

"And do you think you have some of those bicycles, Annie?"

Annie's face was stern with thinking. "I have, Davey," she eventually said.

"Well, there's a mystery solved," the tailor said. He rolled up the measuring tape and, after shaking open a reluctant drawer under the table, placed it among a jumble of mysterious objects inside, then kicked the drawer closed with his boot.

A small bird swung through the air of the open door and flew in the direction of the tailor, settled down near his chair, and bounced along the floor, turning its head quizzically from side to side. Soon it was joined by another. "Greedy little beggars," Davey said to the birds, "it's your second visit and not yet noon."

Kieran was amazed, but Annie barely gave the birds a second glance.

As he opened a biscuit tin, the tailor said to Annie, "This boy is longing for a bicycle. Surely he could ride just one of them." He tossed some crumbs to the floor. "Think how wonderful the new coat will look gliding down the hill to the church in Mastergeehy."

"Will you wear the coat then?" Annie asked the boy.

"I will," he said. "But I'm not going to the church."

"And the bicycle, it won't be stealing?" she asked the tailor.

The tailor handed a biscuit to Kieran so that he could eat some of it and share the rest with the birds. "It will be like giving life to the machine," he said. He looked at the boy's face. "You've chosen one of those bicycles already, I'd say."

"Yes, I have."

"And have you a name for it?"

"The Purple Hornet."

"It's as I thought, Kieran," said the tailor. "I knew you would have a name. And I knew it would be a good one."

CONCRETE

———

The afternoon has darkened now, as has the fog beyond the glass. This murkiness appears to be made of vapour, or even liquid, and the absence of light. It is as if there is no air outside the passenger lounge, as if she would suffocate or drown were she to step outside. She thinks about the man Niall so much admired; about McWilliams, and how he had at one point given a talk, Niall told her, about references to night vapours in Victorian literature and the science that was once used to support the theory that one should close one's windows against such evils. She can't remember the theory or the science, but recalls the word *miasma*. This fog looks the way miasma sounds: clotted, sticky, as if it might cling to the skin. If she as a girl had flown into this miasma, she would have trusted nothing and might have wandered right into the path of the war. She had heard of pilots so disoriented by fog they believed their instrument panels were intentionally lying to them. They had flown far out to sea, some of them never returning. When she told Niall this, he said that fog was the most stealthy and silent of weather phenomena. Often difficult to predict, it crept up on meteorologists while they were paying attention to an oncoming low pressure system or an approaching gale. Looking the other way, he had said.

Tam had never thought that meteorologists might be distracted, might look the other way. It was difficult to believe that they, alert to the most fractional change of wind or pressure, dogged in their attempts to be accurate, would ever step away from full engagement with their subject. They had always been the strict guardians of flight. Even during the war, one dared not even glance at an airplane without clearance from the weather office. How absurd, really, that she, a retired pilot, had found herself in love with a meteorologist more than a decade and a half after the war. And what had she wanted from him? Full engagement? Clearance? Some kind of permission?

She sees her younger self now in the mural before her, a girl with outstretched arms and a rapt expression launching out of dense foliage a black-and-white streamlined bird-form with red-and-blue markings, as if she were helping to guide it through a troubled atmosphere and into the clear air. And the girl herself is caught in this gesture of ascension. She will follow that bird. Everything about her is connected to flight. Looking at her, Tam thinks of the enormous, roaring sense of freedom on takeoff, then a sky full of stars and wind, or sun and cushioned vapour. And she recalls her own helplessness in the face of such ridiculous joy.

Each morning at the Cosford Airbase she and her room-mate, Elspeth, would place a bet on the weather that would be waiting for them on the far side of the blackout blinds. Sun, rain, snow, and, yes, fog. Most often it would have been grey in Shropshire, damp, with light rain threatening. In winter, however, a moist, penetrating chill would settle in, exacerbating the proliferation of cold germs that seemed to be ever-present in the dormitories. The girls took these colds with them into the cockpits. Nobody wanted to be grounded. Tam often won the dawn weather wager, opting for grey conditions. Elspeth was more optimistic. More innocent actually, Tam thinks now, remembering.

After collecting the half-dozen or so chits that would tell them which planes they would fly on any particular day, and which factories or airfields they would fly them to, the girls would consult with the mechanics, many of whom were women, and they would be told about the flaws and wounds of the planes they were about to climb into. Then they visited Wendy Weather in Meteorology. Wendy would have been up for hours sorting through forecasts, attempting to draw together predictions for at least a dozen itineraries criss-crossing the large island of Britain. An island surrounded by the North Atlantic Ocean. An island not known for its elemental stability.

Wendy had a maternal side – she would, in fact, go on to have five children – called the girls "love" or "dearie," in spite of being only a few years older than most of them. And she worried – about whether they had their flannels on under their uniforms, whether they had had enough sleep, about their colds, their romantic adventures. She dispensed cough lozenges with her reports, but she never suggested caution. Either she gave permission or she didn't. If permission was granted, the pilots themselves made the final call about take-off. After that, either you got through the weather or you didn't. "Take it or leave it," Elspeth would often say about the weather. You took it or you left it. "Here it is," Wendy said each flying day, "my latest attempt at defeating surprise."

Romantic weather was another thing. Young men were plentiful in the vicinity, and in spite of her marriage, Tam had had her heart injured if not broken on more than one occasion and had inflicted a few wounds of her own. (Men were both frightened out of their wits and driven mad with desire by the sight, or sometimes even the notion, of these slim young women leaping in and out of aircraft.) Still, there was no question that tearing off into the ether at the controls of one complicated machine after another was the perfect antidote to these dalliances. The earth fell away beneath the wheels – or beneath the belly of the plane once Tam was flying equipment with a retractable undercarriage – and most earthly things fell away as well. No entanglement, Tam had believed, would ever be able to compete with this intoxicating mixture of risk and joy. All of them had felt this, even innocent Elspeth.

On a typical day, Tam might have been required to taxi five other pilots in an Anson from Cosford to Prestwick, then to ferry a Dakota from Prestwick to Speke, then a Spitfire from Speke to Lynham, then a Mosquito from Lyneham to Kemble, and another Spit from Kemble to Lichfield, where an Anson would be waiting to taxi her and several others back to the base at Cosford. It was during these return flights that the knitting she would later speak to Niall about had taken place.

From the first, Tam and Elspeth had always talked after lights out, replaying their routes or revisiting childhoods that would seem so surprisingly sedate in comparison to the crazy stimulation of what had become their daily lives. They confessed their proclivities and dislikes and, never speaking above a whisper, acknowledged the strangeness of quiet and calm after a day of mechanical noise and speed. Within weeks Tam felt closer to this arbitrarily chosen roommate than any of the girls she had encountered at school. Unlike some of the others in the Ferry Pool, who were more or less of Tam's "class," Elspeth had been born in the Midlands, daughter of a free-thinking village butcher who had done what he could to help out when his daughter announced that she wanted to learn how to fly. Tam had adored the sound of Elspeth's whisper, its hint of a Midlands accent. Sometimes as they were falling asleep they would say the names of the children they intended to have. "Brian," Elspeth would say, "Sally, Rebecca."

There had been another kind of meteorological variable to contend with, one that concerned airborne balloons, though not the sort of balloons that Niall's father had so punctually launched in Kerry.

The Maps and Signals Officer was an older woman whose bouts of bad nature were famous in the Pilots' Routing Room.

Still, it was she who provided the warnings about anti-aircraft installations and practice ranges of the RAF and the Balloon Barrages that discouraged the enemy from attacking the factories, to and from which planes were delivered. Each day a new corridor was established through these balloons, which were tied to the ground by long, thin wires, so that pilots could take off and land. "Don't annoy me," Maps and Signals would say to the girls. "Pay attention to these corridors."

But sometimes there was fog. And, one piercingly bright and crisp day, Wendy Weather had said there might be fog in Stirling. Elspeth had been given a chit to fly a wounded Fairchild to Stirling for repair at the factory there. She had made the final call, she had taken the weather. Tam never saw her again.

The morning after the accident, Tam had accepted the day's weather predictions from a subdued, red-eyed Wendy. They had clasped hands for a few moments but not said anything. Maps and Signals, however, was noisy with grief and rage. "So bleeding unfair!" she shouted when she saw Tam approaching. "She was so full of life!"

Looking now into the density of the fog, Tam remembers something else. A few weeks after she had stopped the nightly weeping, she had taken a vow. If she ever had a child, she had decided, she would call it Brian or Rebecca.

Shortly after the war, the government had purchased the family's Edgeworth Hall in Cornwall, which was now bordered

by the recently decommissioned airfield, and the back acre-
age attached to it, in order to create a cattle breeding and
agricultural research station. Tam's father, who had decided
the future was in concrete and had invested accordingly, had
set up the offices of Edgeworth Enterprises on Fleet Street
and had opened a number of quarries in a half-dozen country
locations. Even a rumour of limestone in Shropshire,
Devonshire, or Yorkshire would cause him to become in-
ordinately fond of the locale, and he took more and more
trains – seemingly every two or three days – to distant parts
of the country. In the course of the phone calls he made
nightly to his tired and uninterested wife, he would enthusiastically praise the skills of his geologists and drill-core men and
carry on about the virtues of the surrounding scenery he was
about to destroy. Opening things up appealed to him. I can't
wait to see what's underneath, he announced after a lyrical
description of some valley or another. A pleasant afternoon
to him was one spent watching dynamite lift the green "over-
burden" out of a field. He liked things to be blown apart.

Perhaps that is why he chose the last standing house in
London's St. John's Park to be "home base," as he liked to
call it. Tall, wide, white (except on its east side, which had
been scorched black by the fires that had destroyed the rest of
the neighbourhood), it stood in the wreckage like a still-intact
ocean liner in a scrap yard. The views from its windows
included a fascinating jumble of beams, roof slates, collapsed
staircases, smashed glass, and the rubble of broken bricks. "A
survivor!" he announced to the confused estate agent who

had wanted to show him houses in the more undamaged parts of town. "I'll take it. They are going to need a lot of concrete in this neighbourhood. It will be a pleasure to watch it pour."

But he was rarely seen at home base, was instead chasing after limestone that lay, undisturbed since the Ice Age, all over England. He revelled in new, large discoveries, but older, smaller, and discrete pre-existing operations were of interest to him as well, and he purchased every piece of property he could. Even humble gravel pits on farms were appealing. Gravel, he was wont to say, is simply a premonition of limestone. It was obvious, as well, that gravel itself would be needed to rebuild everything that had been smashed.

After a year in the grips of extensive travel and a frenzy of mad acquisition, he came to the conclusion that swift transportation was of the utmost importance. "We'll be needing a lot of heavy equipment," he assured potential investors over port and cigars in the exclusive London club he had joined shortly after buying the house, "and we'll be needing to get that equipment rapidly to the sites. Then we'll need to get the product into the bombed cities expeditiously, and on a daily basis. You've heard, I dare say, of Hitler's Autobahns?" They had. "It will be necessary to have a lot of autobahns all over this country," he continued enthusiastically. Those autobahns, he told his new friends, would be made of gravel and concrete.

After a lunch at the club, he liked to walk back to the last standing house in St. John's Park – the only occasion when he would be indulgent with his time – because he was curious about the pattern the bombs had left in the city. There was something, he later told his bewildered wife, something poetic about it. Not in terms of human suffering and loss: he wasn't entirely indifferent to that, but it wasn't the suffering that interested him. What caught his imagination was the manner in which things were broken. Sometimes a Tudor beam from a structure that was otherwise pulverized beyond recognition would remain intact. Decorative stonework endured admirably, when simple hewn blocks, from what he could see, had not. And concrete, he was saddened to note, had apparently succumbed in a way that great slabs of old plaster, with their lathing and horse hair, had not.

He was fascinated by the walls and large shards of plaster that had survived the bombing of some of the poorer districts he strolled through. They seemed so personal, so vulnerable, with their coloured paint and floral wallpaper on display. More than once he had passed a block of bombed-out flats with the roof gone and three of the walls collapsed. It was not uncommon to see pictures of serene landscapes, and framed family photos, barely askew on the last remaining wall. This was not the case in St. John's Park. Apart from his own solid house, everything in the surroundings had been so thoroughly annihilated, not even a whisper of the personal remained.

It was to this destroyed landscape that Tam returned after leaving her husband, Reggie: there really was nowhere else to go. She arrived in August, shortly after a country house garden party during which her tolerance for Reggie's jocular behaviour completely vanished. By then her father had built walls around the house and her mother was overseeing the installation of an elaborate garden. Both parents were distracted; her father by his growing entrepreneurship and her mother by plants and garden statuary. This meant that there was little discussion of Tam's separation, much to her relief, and she was left almost entirely on her own.

In the days that followed, she would stand in the second and third storeys of the house, gazing out the windows and into the wreckage. Everything she looked at seemed to her to be a mirror of her life. She knew this notion was self-involved and not at all fair when considered in the light of others who had survived, or not survived, this war. But she had been grounded and miserable on the one hand and bored on the other. The garden was too new to be a comfort. There was often fog. Rain was constant, and once reconstruction was underway in the neighbourhood, so was noise. She missed the girls she had flown with. She missed the flying. But there was no going back to that life. It was a sad observation, she con-cluded, that war was more palatable to her than peace, but that almost seemed to be the way it was. There were parties, of course, but everything about them was to her mind retrospec-tive or pointless in nature, anecdotes of the war dominating the conversation while the rest of the evening was given over to energetic dancing, frequent passes, and no conversation at all.

One evening after an uncomfortable dinner during which she felt her father was sitting in judgment of her at the head of the table, she went out for a twilight walk in the vicinity of the rubble that she had decided was the only phenomenon on earth – animal, vegetable, or mineral – that she could understand. There was scaffolding in some spots, and some new structures were, as her father would say, beginning to be poured (it was the groaning of concrete mixers that she had wakened to each morning). But destruction was still ruled to such an extent that it was impossible to imagine what had been before.

She stood on the edge of an as-yet-unreclaimed site, looking into mud, broken stone, and fractured wood flooring. She wanted to care about the human beings who had lost all this, perhaps their lives as well, but was having trouble bringing to mind what all of that had been. A failure of character on her part, she thought, a kind of neutral vacancy. So little was left behind it was as if there had never been anything *but* debris. But still, that word *debris* wasn't right somehow. *Armageddon* wasn't quite right either, she thought; it would be brighter, bolder, would not be painted in shades of grey and brown. Then she noticed a spot of colour sitting in the midst of blackened bricks, only five feet or so beyond the wire that cordoned off the site, and she slipped between the barbed strands and saw that it was a china sugar bowl, whole and undamaged.

Everything about it was heartbreaking to her, the gold edging, the dark reds and purples of the roses painted on it, and the deep green of the thorns. The sad fact that the top, also undamaged, sat so perfectly in its place. Later she would tell Niall that she didn't know whether to celebrate or mourn, but she would not be telling him the truth. She was celebrating, utterly. She was celebrating the return of feeling, which was as painful as the return of blood to a limb to which it had been denied access.

She stood there on the broken bricks with the bottom of the sugar bowl filling the palm of her right hand, weeping like a mad fool and full of gratitude, relief.

When she returned to the house, her mother told her that Teddy had been hired to oversee the garden. She neglected to notice that her daughter was holding an empty sugar bowl.

He had been working as a casual labourer since the end of the war on various building sites, no one wanting aeronautical mechanics now that the war was over, and he had been in touch with the family, once his father had told him they had moved to London. Her mother had been delighted by this single conduit back to what had once been, to her, generations of stability, and had hired him on the spot, assuming that Teddy's father's gardening prowess had been imprinted in his son's genes. He was to live in the coach house at the back of the property, which had been only partially damaged, and was, at least at first, to spend part of his time roofing this structure and the rest digging manure and topsoil into the dank London clay.

"It's not much different," he had confessed to Tam once they began to spend time together, "than what I was doing on the sites." They had fallen back into a kind of childhood repartee in the garden, with such simple ease that she felt he might produce the toy lorries and motorcars she remembered.

"Did you hate that?" she asked. "All that digging?" It didn't occur to her to ask if he hated it now.

"Not really," he told her. "The lads I worked with were mostly Irish. We lived rough, but they were a good lot."

Irish. Until that moment she had never even thought about the Irish. She recalled, however, that they had opted for neutrality during the war. When she asked what the Irish were doing in London, he had looked at her, surprised. "No work at home," he said and then, "Don't forget, I'm Irish myself."

His name, O'Brien. But second or third generation, of course. "But not born there," she said to him.

"No, but my grandfather was. And then he came here, to England. No work at home in those days either."

Home, she thought. What an odd word for him to be using. "And why did you come to work here?" she asked. She suspected, and as it turned out correctly, that her mother wouldn't have paid him much more than the gangers.

He was silent for a bit. Then he cleared his throat and spoke, "I came for you, Tam. I had heard that Reggie was gone and that you were here."

Sleeping with him had been surprisingly easy to manage. All she had to do was slip out of the house after the evening meal, into the garden, and from there, over to the coach house.

He was timid at first, but that passed. What arrived in the wake of timidity was a shocking amount of sentiment. He was worried, he said, about her honour. When she laughed, he told her he was in love with her and always had been. She was silenced by this and concerned, being genuinely fond of him. But gradually their narrative began to make some sense to her. There was no man with whom she had been as comfortable. When placed against a life in this house – in her father's world – a life with Teddy was not unthinkable. And then there was the purity, the wholeness of him, set against the broken streetscape, the crushed, bombed streetscape beyond her father's new walls.

"What would they do?" she had asked when the idea of an escape with him had begun to solidify. "Perhaps we should go somewhere." Lying beside him, she believed she was attached to him in a cellular way, their shared past, their love of aircraft. It was odd, she realized, that they had lost both: the past and the aircraft.

"I've been left my grandmother's cottage in Kerry," he told her. "There is nothing stopping us from going there."

She had lost her compass. She had no idea which way to steer for a happy outcome. It was as if the inner aircraft she was attempting to fly at the moment was too wounded and fragile to get her where she ought to go anyway. She looked at Teddy, who was youthful in a way that neither her father nor Reggie had ever been – his open face, his long, clean limbs. There, enlarged now, were the same knees and forearms she had unconsciously memorized as a child while hovering with him over a dusty bit of earth outside her father's walls, absorbed by marbles and toy trucks. She had known his wrists and hands since childhood. "Yes," she said while attempting without success to imagine Ireland. "There is nothing to stop us."

On the boat to Dun Laoghaire and during the journey by train Teddy talked about their destination. She had been feeling tired and could find no way to enter the conversation, so she let him continue on his own. He was re-visioning a place he had visited only once or twice as a boy but remembered vividly because any kind of travel had been such a change in the ordinariness of his childhood. It was called Clooncartha, he said, and it was inland on the Iveragh Peninsula, County Kerry.

There are mountains, he told her, and quite a number of good fishing rivers and streams. He loved to fish and would bring fresh salmon and trout for their suppers. It rains a good deal, but then there is the green everywhere. The cottage came with two fields, one on each side. We could keep a cow, he said. His grandmother had left him a small amount of money as well, though God knows where she got it, he said. She had inclined toward gentility, so the cottage would be nicely fitted.

They would use some of the money to buy a battered Vauxhall in Killarney while they were staying in that town in a room above a pub. It's either that or a donkey, Teddy would say, laughing. She had never in England been near a pub that generated the kind of noise this establishment mustered in the evenings: singing and accordion music. She was unable to sleep until the National Anthem had been sung downstairs, a strange, slow, and, to her mind, dirgelike droning, only marginally redeemed by a slight crescendo near the end. Then full dark and silence and sometimes Teddy reaching for her in the gloom.

The day they arrived in the lane that led to the cottage she knew she would be happy there. There were roses in the hedges and small pink flowers in the grass beside the door. Remarking on these with delight, she recalled she had never been a person who cared about such things. Several mountains stood at discrete distances from one another, and a modest river ran behind the house. The road they had driven into the valley where the cottage stood was used so infrequently that grass and wildflowers flourished in the centre of it. No one, not even her previous self, would ever find her there.

Teddy fixed the gutters and painted the rooms. He built a hot press and installed wiring for the hot water tank and lights and an electric cooker. They were lucky to have the electrical services in place, he told her, something that had not yet happened deeper in the peninsula. Then he worked on the rusted outdoor pump until it spat clear water. Neighbours called and referred to her as Mrs. O'Brien and neither she nor Teddy corrected them. She sewed curtains and baked lamb chops. It was summer and the sun stayed in the sky until well after ten p.m. In the lowering light she looked at Teddy's smooth face and long lashes while they played board games or did crosswords in a newspaper they had bought in the small shop two miles away. He had found work, as his grandfather had years before, in the Gap of Dunloe, driving a donkey cart loaded with tourists. His grandfather had had to stay in the vicinity during the season as the eighteen miles between Clooncartha and the Gap was such a distance in those days, but Teddy could drive the Vauxhall there and back. There had been some fuss about his English accent until the grandfather had been cited and remembered. "And then," he told Tam, delighted, "it was as if I was a long-lost member of the tribe coming home."

There was a sailor's valentine framed and mounted on the bedroom wall. It was made from the tiniest delicate pastel shells, mauve, pink, and white, fashioned into the shape of a heart, and surrounded by rosettes made out of a deeper shade of pink, the whole thing under glass and bordered by worn green velvet. His grandfather had been on the ships for some time, Teddy told Tam when she asked, while he was engaged to his grandmother. It might have been Ceylon he was near, or the West Indies, some place, anyway, where you could collect such shells, and he made this for his intended bride on the long passage back. "In this family," he said, standing behind her and encircling her with his arms, "we are romantics."

Teddy was more interesting here. She was changed as well: calm and domestic, letting each day fall into her life as the rain fell outside the door. She found she could make accurate drawings of the planes she had flown during the war, and she began to do that during the long afternoons while Teddy made his way with a cartload of tourists back and forth through the Gap. She liked the results, and wondered if she might publish a book of them. Remembering a man her father had known in London who was said to be in the business of publishing, she sent a few examples in the mail after finding the address of his publishing house in the Kenmare library. He didn't reply right away, but when he eventually did he returned the drawings and wrote that there was a house in New York that he knew was putting together an encyclopedia of war aircraft. She should try them. They might very well be looking for someone to illustrate the English planes. So she sat down at the kitchen table and wrote a letter to America. When she was finished, she folded it up and put it in a brown envelope along with a drawing of a de Havilland Mosquito Mark 6, her favourite aircraft from the war.

Teddy's allergies vanished. Perhaps, he maintained, laughing, because I am in my natural habitat. He made suggestions about her drawings of aircraft. Having been involved with the smallest details of the machines, concerning himself with their well-being, they had become like family to him, and Tam agreed it was so for her as well. "A family we lost," she said.

There were no members of his human family, however, beyond the most distant of cousins, left in the Parish. Tam liked this peculiar combination of anonymity and belonging, a secure new start. She hadn't known him long, this adult Teddy, but the child she had known lived inside him. She felt they were ancient.

He found his grandfather's hip waders and some old rusty fishing gear in a little cow byre behind the cottage. The river out back, as expected, was filled with salmon. During the day it was silent and dignified, moving with slender solemnity through the fields. But at night they could hear it carrying on a conversation in the dark. Teddy could hardly wait to get at it. There was no stopping him now, he told her.

Unfortunately, because of her contact with the London publisher, her parents, and through them Reggie, had discovered her whereabouts and had begun to send letters full of questions and accusations through the post. Teddy was deemed by her mother to be ungrateful after the kindness she had shown him by giving him a job. Reggie allowed that somehow he had always known Tam was unreliable, deceptive, and unsure of her own mind, and Teddy, he wrote, was a vile seducer who would abandon her in the end. She laughed out loud reading this, remembering how Teddy's father had called Reggie a "bad sort." It was difficult to imagine Teddy in the role of a Lothario, leaving as he did each day, with his lunch in a brown bag, to drive a cart pulled by a donkey through a sylvan glen filled with rocks, emerald green grass, and falling water.

There was a letter from the American publisher as well, asking to see some more of her drawings.

Teddy drowned a year later while fishing behind the house. It had been raining for weeks and weeks and the little solemn river he waded into must have developed a strong-enough current that it had caught him offguard. When he hadn't returned for the evening meal she had gone out back of the house to call him. She thought her voice wasn't carrying because of the wind, and so when he didn't reply, she had climbed the low stone wall and headed down to the river. He was only about fifty feet downstream. Someone long ago had built a fieldstone weir there, and though not much of it was left, Teddy's body was bumping up against the stones that remained.

There had been a full Irish wake in the cottage, with whiskey and the repetitive saying of the rosary. The cart drivers and their wives embraced her and wept. People became drunk and delivered piercingly beautiful eulogies. Neighbours carried his coffin to the church. She responded with such gratitude to these rituals she felt she would never leave the place. She believed she needed nothing more.

And she had deeply mourned him, his illuminating optimism, and the way he had refined the simplicity of their life together. Everything about him had been so eager and fresh. She couldn't imagine him without his childhood looks still alive in his physical being. The appearance of one line in his brow, one grey hair, would have cancelled, somehow, who he was, had been, or so she thought, seeking consolation in the face of such a premature death.

She will often recall him standing at the window the day before he died, looking out at the rain. We're receiving a desperate drowning, he had said. He had been with the cart drivers long enough by then that some of their language had crept into his own speech, though he wouldn't have known that anymore than he would have known that the word *drowning* would have predicted his own end. The bright water of his ancestors, quick with silver fish, had reached out to claim him at his most perfect, while Tam had walked steadily on, deep into the adulthood she had always thought she wanted as a child.

Child, she thinks now, looking at the mural. There is one particularly introspective child, a young man really, who stands with his hand touching the trunk of a tree, inward-looking, dreaming, and blameless. He does not cause, would never cause, damage. Beside him stands a dark-haired woman, arms raised, palms open. Is she reaching for something or has she been sent some kind of airborne message: a passenger pigeon, perhaps, or a kite? No matter. She is filled with expectation, the way she herself had been filled with expectation.

At the opposite end of the picture there is a benign-looking man, the only figure in the painting who carries even the trace of a smile. Plump, bald, and bearded, he appears to be a chef or baker, judging by the apron he wears and the pie he carries in his hands. Behind him a tree is hung with bright blossoms. Is he delivering the pie to the swan that unfurls its wings in his line of vision? Tam thinks not. He is out of a fairy tale, a children's book. He is Simple Simon's pie man, or the baker in Pat-a-Cake.

Even the smallest children, however, ignore him. They are vagrants; they don't appear to belong to anyone. Though they gather sometimes in company, each one is alone, each one is silent. Whatever the experience is, they are unable to speak about it with her, the viewer, or with any of the larger figures in the mural. They ignore the adults, who, in turn, are indifferent to them. Nothing, no one holds them. The children of the Killeen, Tam thinks, remembering the sites here and there on the peninsula that were said to be burial grounds for unbaptized infants. No one had ever been able to say how old these places were, when they had been in use, so she's had trouble believing that the jumble of rocks and rushes she looked at were connected to personal sorrow. Too much weather had blown through, she had thought, too much unmeasured time. And yet now, here these disregarded infants are, stationary, lonely, trapped in a painted landscape and full of longing for their unlived and unremembered lives.

MOSEL

———

He enjoyed the work on the blossoming tree, the nest, the echoing nest of the old man's cupped hands, and the fruit pie he carried in them. "'A pocketful of rye,'" he sang quietly as he painted, "'four and twenty blackbirds diving in a pie.'" The tree appeared to explode from the man's head, as if a vigorous dream could no longer be contained and must now be permitted to enter the world. Around him, everything planted demanded to be harvested.

Kenneth was remembering something that had happened to him about ten years before, in the days when he had been a student and had been travelling in the vague, unfocused manner that had interested him at the time. It all seemed so long ago and yet now he found that he was placing that younger self, alert and curious, here and there in the painting.

During the months he had stayed in London he had discovered the work of J.M.W. Turner and, in particular, that artist's smaller sketches and watercolours. He had read everything he could find about the painter and had spent time in the Tate Gallery's archives, falling into the intimate drawings and practical lists contained in the pocket-sized travel notebooks with such concentration that years later he would be able to remember Turner's laundry items and the price of the hotels where the artist had stayed.

Finally, Kenneth had decided to make a pilgrimage to Germany in order to follow the river journeys Turner had twice taken in the 1830s. He spent some time on the Rhine, hitching rides up and down its shorelines, some parts of which had clearly suffered damage during the war, then moved down to Koblenz, where the secondary Mosel River, smaller and more complicated, looped away from its more celebrated parent. After wandering through the gingerbread architecture that lined the streets of the old town, he strolled down to the harbour, and at the end of one of the wharfs he stepped unnoticed onto a departing barge, where he found a seat on a convenient coil of rope. Terraced vineyards laddered the slopes of the mountains while under him the currents twisted and the river turned back on itself, changing direction over and over.

Here everything was smaller than on its doppelgänger, the Rhine. Houses, castles, churches had been placed in more discrete positions in relation to the landscape, and the cliffs shouldered less-forbidding fortresses. He was as delighted by all this as he had been by the toy towns his mother had always put under the tree at Christmas when he was a child, and he reached again and again for one of the small sketchbooks that he, like Turner, always carried with him. The landscape had not been bombed. It was impossible to believe there had ever been war here, never mind a war so recent and so hateful. He recorded this thought, as Turner might have done, on the bottom of one of his sketches. Then, remembering miniature pencil-drawn riverbanks and Mosel townscapes falling like sentences or musical scores down the pages of Turner's notebooks, he tried to reproduce exact copies with his own hand, until he remembered a story an essential teacher had told him and stopped.

He walked off the barge at Cochem, intending to hunt for the locations that had so intrigued Turner in 1835 and 1839, but it was September, and the wine harvest celebrations were in full bloom all along the shore. Vintners stood happily behind cloth-covered tables under striped tarpaulins and handed out free samples of their wine. Kenneth did not know German, so attempted to speak to them in French. Turner, he said, peintre anglais du dix-neuvième siècle. They shook their heads or simply looked confused but handed him small bright glasses filled with clear yellow liquid as a reply. In spite of its coolness, the Riesling tasted of sun and flowers, and after he had drunk a few glasses, everything around him was infused with warmth and a peculiar but not unpleasant heightened clarity, partly due to the wine but also due to the afternoon sun that bounced off the river and drenched the stone walls he passed with trembling, liquid light.

He followed a bicycle path along the river and into a neighbouring village where a smaller but no less vibrant festival was unfolding. There was a dark-haired girl there, presiding over a stall, while an old man, having succumbed to sun and wine, slumbered in a chair behind her, his chin on his chest, his white apron covering a large belly. Kenneth thought the man looked like a slumbering Bacchus and pulled his sketchbook from his pocket in order to draw him, but while he was making the first tentative strokes, the girl came to his side and put her hand over his on the page. "Nein," she had said quietly. "Mein fader." She was trying, Kenneth supposed, to protect her parent from the embarrassment of interpretation.

After he had pocketed his sketchbook, the girl gestured to one of the small tables that were set here and there on the grass by the river, and as if he had always known he would do so, Kenneth put his satchel on the ground and sat down. The autumn sun was so low that everything, even a blade of grass, stood dwarfed by its own shadow. A moment later the girl placed two full glasses on the cloth that covered the table and sat opposite him, examining his face in the rich light of late afternoon. Barges slipped by them on the river. Her dark hair seemed to blend into the bushes growing behind her, and her pale face was difficult to read. But, eventually, she took his hand and moved her thumb back and forth in his palm.

They danced that night, after the girl had brought him a sausage wrapped in pastry and a warm bowl of sauerkraut. Her revived father was playing an unidentifiable instrument as part of some kind of band and seemed unperturbed by the attentions his daughter was paying to the stranger. There were lights on and in the river, and the village on the opposite shore blazed with its own festivities. When the band paused between songs, a faint similar music could be heard travelling across the water.

Near midnight a gang of young men drew Kenneth away from the table and made clear that he should join them in the construction of a temporary bridge. Almost anything that could float was pressed into service: barrels, dismantled fences, rowboats, scrap lumber, tables, even a dead sheep, went into this frail, brief act of engineering, a large necklace strung across the neck of the river. When the chain of objects reached the opposite embankment, Kenneth found the girl and, hand in hand, laughing, they made the unsteady, hilarious journey to the other side, falling twice or three times into the river, then clamouring back onto the makeshift bridge via a floating wheelbarrow or wagon. On the far shore the dance they joined seemed simply to be a continuation of the one they had left behind. Morning found them doused by dew and sleeping in each other's arms. Kenneth pushed the girl's hair away from her face and kissed her on her lips and forehead before joining the young men who were, one by one, quietly returning home across the floating path. He had left his satchel near her father's stall. It was as he bent to pick it up that he realized, after she had requested that he stop drawing, neither he nor she had uttered another word.

A year later, just before he left Europe, he returned to the Mosel in winter, a season so estranged from the one he remembered it was as if he were visiting another country altogether. He spent one night in a small riverside hotel in Koblenz, and the following morning he once again boarded a barge that was heading downriver toward Luxembourg, delivering its store of empty, blackened wine barrels to the villages en route. The golds and lime greens of the terraced vineyards, even the fawn colour of the Roman walls that had pinned each plantation to its slope for two thousand years, had changed to the dark purples and dung browns of a time of stasis. The passing river barges hauled hills of black coal and girders of steel; the ochre coils of rope and pale yellow crates of wine that had surrounded him on his late summer journey were nowhere in evidence. The birds were larger, darker, and flew more purposefully through the cold sky along the path of the river valley. The river itself was the colour of gun metal. Half-heartedly, he looked for signs of the girl but found he could not even identify the spot where her father's stall had been situated, and he realized then that the stall, the bridge, the full architecture of that harvest night had been temporary and easily dismantled. He did not feel any sadness about this. He had been blessed, he knew, by the wholeness of the experience. It was something transitory that could nevertheless be kept intact and undamaged in his mind.

The next afternoon, back in his room in Koblenz, he opened the curtains and was met with the full brunt of the Fortress of Ehrenbreitstein lit by the low winter sun. It had been built a thousand years before, placed so firmly and permanently into the stone cliff of the opposite shore, it was difficult to see where the rock ended and architecture began, and all of it now washed with this metallic, copper radiance. Turner himself had been intrigued by the improvised bridges of the Mosel, which he had rendered with the most minimal of brushstrokes in his pictures, as if making a statement about that which was tentative and fleeting. But it was the enduring fortress that fully absorbed the nineteenth-century painter's attention, and for years he painted

Ehrenbreitstein over and over, using chalk or watercolour or oil, making it pierce, like the blade of an axe, through the mists of the two rivers that pooled and joined at its feet.

Standing by the winter river, Kenneth recalled that as he had begun to walk back to the village that summer night, while young men and old had been floating the components of the transitory night bridge back toward their own shore, he had seen the girl sitting patiently in one of the rowboats. He had waved to her and she had lifted her arm in return. Then, before he turned away, her father, back in place at the stall, had called out the words "Auf Wiedersehen" and had lifted one hand as a kind of benediction, his white apron gleaming in the morning light. Moving away Kenneth had known he would forget neither of these two figures.

He painted the girl now in the background of the scene, a cherished but almost forgotten memory, and then he painted her again seated in the foreground, with fruit in her lap. Her father was more central to the scene, his white apron glowing, his large torso dominant, birds diving into the pastry he held aloft in his hands. Kenneth rendered, as well, one of the young men who had built the miraculous makeshift bridge, placing him in the foreground. The binoculars he held in front of his eyes were focused on the far shore of future seasons. And there, in the insistent bronzes and coppers he chose for the scene, was the forceful atmosphere of Ehrenbreitstein, the bright stone of honour.

THE MOUNTAINS

—

Gerry-Annie said, "You can, of course. But not until after your hour with that book." She pulled the grey volume out from under the tea cosy where it was kept and handed it to him. "Soon I'll be demanding that you tell me everything that is written there."

Kieran had been asking about the bicycle and had no wish to be pinned to a table by a book. "I've seen too much of this book," he said.

Annie's expression became stern. "How can you say that? Did you never hear of Tomás Rua's sorrow at the loss of his books? Did no one ever sing you that song?"

No one had.

"'Amhrán na Leabhar,'" she said, "a lament for the books the poet had lost at sea. He was a schoolmaster as well, long ago now. Gerry knew that song. As do I." She began to sing quietly, a tune so beautifully mournful that Kieran became lost in the cadence and felt he could see the sinking books and feel the poet's torment about losing them.

But he would not have lamented the loss of this book. He could have recited certain pages verbatim – the instructions for writing a letter to a prospective employer, the population of Bolivia or Peru, the ports of call for the PNO line – but the possibility of the bicycle put all these facts out of his mind. "I'll give the bicycle back to the man who owns it, I promise, if he comes back," Kieran said, imagining someone who had made his fortune – a tycoon, perhaps – walking to the cottage door and demanding his bicycle.

But Annie did not answer and her look was troubled and faraway. She was pouring a kettle full of boiling water into the tub Kieran had filled for her early that morning at the pump. It was wash day and Kieran knew, because the day was fine, she would soon hang his shirts, three or four versions of himself, he thought, on the line to dry. She had sung all eleven verses of "Amhrán na Leabhar," but now there was no song. *No song*, his mother was saying in his mind. *The song is finished.*

Kieran was trying to concentrate on the list of the colonies of Great Britain, but he could not do it. There was some sorrow around Annie that came between him and the letters on the page, and he didn't believe that sorrow was about the schoolmaster and his lost books.

"You know, Kieran," Annie said slowly, "I am thinking there are men yet up in the mountains, talking." She pulled herself upright from where she was bending over the tub on the table, but her head was down and her shoulders were rounded. She appeared to be looking at her hands, which remained in the water, but there was something about the way she stood that made Kieran suspect that she had gone out of herself. And suddenly he understood: these men and their talking was something Annie actually heard in some part of her mind. The men, and Gerry among them, were whispering to Annie in the same way his mother whispered to him. It had been his suggesting that someone might come back that had put it in her mind, he thought, and that being so, he wished he had said nothing. Still, he was curious. "What are they saying, Annie?" he asked softly, the British Empire moving back to the distant parts of the world where it resided, even the bicycle dimming a bit in his mind.

Her face was pale. "They are saying there is to be fighting, that there will be killing."

Kieran rose from his seat and walked over to where Annie stood. "Annie," he said, recalling the tailor's words, "that was a good long time ago now." He put his arm across her broad back, his first physical act of premeditated kindness. Through the back door, open to the sun, he could see the shed where the bicycles were waiting. "There's no need for fighting anymore."

Annie sighed. "It's a way men have, I suppose."

"But not anymore. Not now."

"There will be no more of it?" she asked uncertainly.

"No, not now." He had seen the cross at Ballagh, commemorating Gerry and the others who were executed with him at that spot. As if it were an admission of defeat that she did not wish to acknowledge, Annie, who was so proud of the statue in the town, would walk by this marker without a glance. But though she didn't look in its direction, Kieran had never known her to continue talking when they were near the part of the road where it stood, and he himself had gone back alone many times to read the names that were engraved on its surface.

She turned back to her washing. "You may as well have the bicycle now while the weather is fine," she said to him. "Do you know how to ride it?"

For the first time the thought struck him that he was twelve years old and had no idea what to do with a bicycle once seated on it. There had been no need for a bicycle if you were a child in the town, and, anyway, once the tantrums began his father would never have allowed one. Niall had had a bicycle once, but the dramatist in him took to stunts, and he was spotted by neighbours riding the vehicle across the Valentia River railway trestle on a dare. The bicycle was confiscated and then given away, and soon football began to satisfy Niall's need for performance. After that, references to this form of transport were never again made in the house. Though his father had departed punctually each morning on a bicycle, and returned on the same at night, neither boy would have dared to touch the thing.

"No," Kieran admitted now, "I've never been on a bicycle."

Annie pulled her hands out of the water and dried them on her apron. "Well, I'll have to show you how, I suppose. Go fetch the creature."

Five minutes later, Annie was seated on the Purple Hornet, circling unsteadily while Kieran stood, full of aspiration, in the centre of the road. Finally, she dismounted and walked the bicycle over to the place where he stood, and he swung his leg over the bar and straddled the seat. His legs were quite long enough to steady himself with the bicycle upright, but Annie had to hold on to the back fender while he settled his feet on the pedals. "Look straight ahead," she advised. Then she pushed him off in the direction of town, a few miles away and almost every inch of it downhill, calling after him that he needed only to pedal backwards to slow down.

As if he had been born to it, Kieran surrendered himself to being transported, every muscle and many of his brain cells knowing instantly what to do, his spine making fractional adjustments for balance, his peripheral vision on high alert, taking in the now blurred and soon vanishing graveyard on his left, a smear of black cows and one donkey on his right, and hawthorn bushes in the hedgerows like trails of white smoke emerging from his shoulders. The speed was like an electrical current entering his bloodstream, and he recognized almost immediately his need for it, and forgot altogether Annie's instructions about slowing down. He shouted with joy as small houses, stone walls, the ruins of Ballagh Workhouse, tidy and untidy fields, staring sheep dogs, sedentary turf stacks, and two important-looking standing stones swept past him. On the flat stretch leading to the main road that would eventually enter the town, as if intuiting the boy's reluctance to cross the line into his previous life, the bike began to lose momentum. When the vehicle began to waver, Kieran jumped off prematurely. Unsure of how to dismount, and having forgotten in the ecstasy of his flying descent that there were pedals that one could use to gain speed and therefore balance, he landed, astonishingly, on his feet. Then he strolled casually back to where the bicycle lay on the road and picked it up by the handlebars, which now felt familiar in his hands. He walked the vehicle all the way back up the four miles of the hill, talking to it as if it were a horse or a dog, something animate and faithful, that had done him a great service and that should be praised and petted for its efforts.

Gerry-Annie was not on the road when he returned, but he could see his three shirts waving their arms on the line that stretched from a pole to the back wall of the house, his several selves reacting with great gladness to this wonderful transformation that had taken place inside him.

It soon became clear that the bicycle could be used as a bribe by Gerry-Annie to make the boy do things he would normally have tried to avoid, and it was in this way that Kieran was persuaded to go to school for a time, to attend mass now and then, and to visit his father in the town when his brother was home from Dublin. But his mother was able to begin her whispering in the house when both boys were there, and to plant this whispering deep enough in Kieran that it would be two or three days before he would awaken empty of her. When he told Annie then that he couldn't go back for a long time, she was wise enough not to ask why.

The school, five miles away at Derriana Lough, on the other hand, proved to be a surprising delight for the boy. He had no trouble at all with lessons in history or English, and even the mathematics lost its power to disappoint once he had novels by Dickens or Wilkie Collins to look forward to, the poetry of Yeats, and a view of a silver lake and blue and ochre mountains to turn to if the days were long. The western arm of the mountain of Knocknagantee reached out to embrace the lake on its southern side, and the play of light on the rocks, bogs, and pastures on days when there was sunshine, or the passing squalls of rain and fog on wet days, provided a carnival of stimuli, and there were times when he simply could not turn away. The mountain stood upright like a wall made entirely of rocks and vegetation, changing with the seasons from greens to yellows, from browns to purples, the colours visibly intensifying when under a coat of moisture.

The master, a mild young man not much taller than some of the bigger boys, often suggested walks to his pupils if the day was decent, and in this way Kieran discovered two green roads tucked into the seams of that mountain. It was not uncommon on these roads to find the remains of a village with a few old people still there with their sheep, two dogs, and a donkey, living a life that seemed impossible with such rough access to the outside world. How did they manage the thatch for their roofs, the turf for their fires? Kieran wanted to know but was too shy to ask such questions – in spite of the courtesy shown to the young scholars by these people, their delight in visitors, evidenced even in their prancing, welcoming dogs. And, as if put there as a deterrent to inquiry, there were also the abandoned houses of men and women who had not been able to survive the isolation, and then the low, collapsing walls of cabins that had been left empty because of death or emigration, at the time of the famine, now just over one hundred years in the past.

One old man, inviting the class in for tea, told the group that he had carried everything in the cottage up the track on his own back: the dresser, the settle, the table and chairs, which were tied to the table legs and dragged behind on the broken road, and finally the bed for his bride, a large four-poster that Kieran could not imagine the man paying for. "She died in childbirth," the man told them, "in that very bed in which I sleep each night of my life, and where she was by my side, she the flower of Coomavoher." The child, he added vaguely, was now a solicitor in Killarney.

Died, Kieran's mother whispered, but so softly he almost didn't hear. A mountain stream rampaged past the east wall of this man's house, turning one whole room, floors, ceilings, walls, green with moss, and in that room Kieran spotted a bicycle, also emerald, the spokes of its wheels furry with moss. "Ah the room of the damp," the old man said when he caught Kieran looking, "and my brother's bicycle I haven't the heart for."

And so the notion of riding his own bicycle three miles up this slippery ruined road was planted in Kieran, something he was to do almost every day from then on before the lessons began. When the winter came he pedalled in darkness, negotiating his way around unconcerned flocks, toward the two candle-lit homes and then beyond them to the empty sites of Dughile and Coomavanniha, where he stopped until he saw a light in the schoolhouse on the lower land across the lake. Then he turned the bicycle around and began the bone-rattling descent while the sheep scattered and the dawn smudged the horizon.

There were twenty-one children of all sizes in the school, almost all of whom spoke Irish, though they were admonished by the master for doing so in the classroom. Lessons were taught in English only. Still, the master, an Irish speaker himself, was from only ten miles away, and he was Republican enough to want the old legends to be alive in the children of the parish, and encouraged them to speak about them. So it was the high-pitched voice of a very small girl that told Kieran about Oisin and the Fianna, and how the pass that led out of the mountains and into the world was called Ballagh Oisin. He would always remember this child reciting the stages of a story that had been spoken for a thousand years, the music of it, and the wonder, the English words breaking apart as the rhythm of her Gaelic accent entered them, while many one-syllabled words opened in the middle to two or three different sounds as if they were being sung. Kieran listened, rapt, as she recounted the tale of the ancient warrior, seduced by Niamh, returning after three hundred years to this high place where he searched for his long-dead hunting companions in the land below him. No woman, not even Niamh, had ever been able to compete with his affection for them. Oisin

could see the whole world from there, the child said, the bays
of the sea and the headlands on either side of them, the oak
forests, and the lakes and rivers, and the fields climbing halfway up the hills, but he could not find those of whom he was
so fond because they were long dead, though he was slow to
come to know this, believing, as he did, that he had been gone
only three days. And it was St. Patrick – out of courtesy the
saint came to meet him at the summit of the pass – who told
him what the day was and the year, and tried to comfort this
old son of an old chieftain when he wept. I will instruct my
monks, Patrick said, to write down your stories and those of
your kin so they will not be lost, though your world has been
vanquished by my world and will never come back.

When the school was dismissed for the summer, Kieran asked
Gerry-Annie how far it was to the pass they called Ballagh
Oisin. She told him it was not far unless you were going there
with local sheep who knew where they belonged and had a
tendency to turn back to their own mountain pastures.
Gerry's father, she told him, had been a drover for the landlord when he was a boy, taking the landlord's flocks great
distances when they had been sold. "And he had the devil's
own time of it," she said, "those sheep belonging to
Cappanagroun and them insistent on it." If he as much as
turned his head they were gone back in the direction they had
come from, and then he would have to chase them and climb
the pass with them one more time.

"But on the bicycle?" he asked.

"No time at all," Annie said. "Though a terrible climb to get there."

But his morning training on the rough green mountain trails opposite the school made the ascent to the summit of the pass a fairly easy pedal once he went there. And when he reached the top he saw that what the child had said was true: he could see the whole world from this height, the world of the mountains where he lived and the world of the lower lands and the towns beyond it. He could see the four booming strands of the Iveragh, and the islands beyond them. He stood on the pedals of his bicycle, balancing and looking for several moments. Then he began the exhilarating descent.

During the next few years, when he wasn't busy with school or chores, Kieran cycled everywhere he could. In the beginning he rode all over the parish, visiting every road, bóithrín, and even the roughest of tracks, following the latter until they petered out, often in an upland bog. Eventually he moved farther afield, into the neighbouring peninsulas of Dingle and Beara, where the mountain roads were unfamiliar and more thrillingly daunting. He was always happiest on higher ground, where the view was extensive and the path was demanding. Often he would return to Gerry-Annie's fully drenched, wind-blown, and spattered with mud. She would scold him then, but there was no real anger in her admonitions. "You're a climber," she told him. "Always heading for the sky. No wonder you have all these collisions with wind and rain."

He liked it when she said that, savouring, as always, the way that Annie explained him. There was something about the word *collision* that was just right as well, for when he was on the bicycle, mountains, pools of rainwater, gullies, groves of trees, all of this exploded around his swiftness. As he closed his eyes just before he went to sleep, the images of the day would rush toward him, and he would collide with them, but softly, as if they were made of nothing but light.

After he had left the Derriana school, Kieran had fully ignored his father's requests that he return to town in order to study at the Upper School there, preferring to hire himself out on occasion as a temporary labourer, a *spalpeen*, to farmers needing the extra help. Sometimes there was a hiring fair in his own town, but more often he would ride as far as Killorglin or Tralee. Because of the bicycle, he was able to travel far enough that he had some kind of work more often than not, in spite of the time being one of scarcity and the fact that many young men his age were leaving Ireland to search for employment abroad.

Late one summer, he was hired on by a farmer called Donal O'Shea, who held two thousand acres of commonage in the mountains with three O'Sullivan brothers. Donal had been a particular friend of Gerry's but, as Annie said, one who had never taken to politics and was therefore still alive.

"Perhaps I was a coward, Annie," he said when this was explained to Kieran in Annie's kitchen, "for I believed in what they fought for but never fought for it myself."

But Annie disagreed. "You were too far into the mountains," she told him, "to do the necessary talking. Those men went up the mountain, all right, but they never went as far into the Reeks as your sheep are. There would be no point in that, all the fighting being in the town, or near enough to it anyway. It's why I want Kieran to work for you. He's gone sixteen, you see, and there is a man coming out in him. There will be no talking that far into the mountains. He won't end up bleeding and ruined at the side of the road, or off in some jail yard in Dublin."

"But does he want to go with me, Annie, that's the question." Donal looked doubtfully at the boy. "Does he want to go with me for the little I have to give him?" His dog, Ean — named, Annie had told Kieran, for the way the animal seemed to fly above the sheep when he was herding from one part of the mountain to another — looked doubtful as well.

"And shall I take the bicycle?"

"There'll be no need for a bicycle where we are going, no chance of that."

Kieran cast a sad glance at the shed where the Purple Hornet was waiting.

"It is only a week or so, Kieran." Annie was already packing a bag of supplies, clothing, and some food.

"And your legs will be stronger for it," said Donal. "They'll be stronger after all the climbing."

What he saw up the mountain: the chain of lakes below him that Donal said were known as the Pater Nosters, the rosary beads.

You could pray with those lakes at the end of your arm, looking at them from a distance, and the shining of them, the silvered mystery, made you want to do it. More lakes, each one with its name in Irish, and each Irish name a story that is being told less and less, Donal said, as the people moved away from the language and gathered elsewhere. Donal, silent before these bowls of water as if he had never seen them before, turned to Kieran and said, "The hardness of this life, and then the beauty."

And he saw the four rivers – Inny, Cummeragh, Caragh, and the Sneem – named for the way the water moved through the land, rising together at the top of the Teermoyle Mountains, the booleying places, places where one man died and another prospered. "You can turn your back on it or you can set your face toward it," Donal announced. Ean, who trotted beside them, who tore off and looped around straying sheep and who responded only to Irish, was less condescending with Kieran now that the boy had entered the mountains but was still not fully approachable.

"That dog doesn't have a word of English," Donal said when Kieran tried to coax or command the animal. "He doesn't trust you with those sounds in your mouth, and anyway, it's me he knows."

They climbed higher, the dog running away from them, circling the flock, then returning, filled with purpose and quivering with the joy of some private accomplishment, brushing Kieran's pant leg before hurrying off in the opposite direction. A second dog appeared. A leaping, mock-biting reunion ensued, followed by a further chase.

"Where did he come from?" Kieran asked Donal.

"That would be Scamall, the Cloud, Tim's dog," Donal said.

A few minutes later Tim himself approached and introduced himself to Kieran as Tim the Sky. "I am so named," he said, "because mine is the house highest in the mountains." He pointed to a stone cottage, hardly bigger than a turf shed. "There is no one higher living here," he added, "and I've seen things at this height that none of the others will ever see."

"He once saw three suns in one sky," Donal confided.

"And flying ships," Tim added.

"You mean airplanes," Kieran said.

"No, I mean flying ships. A full fleet of them sailing over Teermoyle. I've seen lakes turn to blood." He pointed to a small bowl of water far below and surrounded by sheer rock. "Iskanamacteery, it was, the Lake of the Wolf. And once there was a shower of grain so plentiful every blade of the grass and every bush of the gorse was covered with it like snow."

"He baked bread with that," Donal said.

"I did," Tim confirmed. "I ground it with stones and I made four fine loaves of bread."

"He's had a black gable more than once from gorse burning in the mountains," said Donal.

"Sometimes those fires were my own. Sometimes they were the fires of the valley people, fires that came up the mountain. And I've seen other fires," Tim insisted, "fires from long-ago times. I've seen armies crashing in the air."

"You mean the men talking in the mountains," Kieran said.

"No, I mean armies from so long ago, nobody could say whose armies they were. I am well above the current talking." Tim pointed toward the heavens. "I own the sky."

"There's the mountains, and then there is the rest of it down there," Donal told Kieran when they were approaching the end of a day. They looked toward the lowlands, where small white houses grew in the fields like safe flowers. "There are those who go into the mountains with sheep, and there are those who can barely leave their hearthstones," Donal said when they had moved far enough into the mountains that even the house of Tim the Sky was no longer visible. There was nothing judgmental in this remark: it was a statement of fact.

During the two weeks that Kieran was with Donal, the weather was mild and calm. After each rain there would be a full rainbow joining one mountain to another, and then the sun. Some nights were so still the stars shone as brightly in the still lakes as they did in the sky. Sometimes you could see the stars in the dog's eyes. As they bedded down at the end of the last day, Kieran heard Donal say a poem, his voice so private and quiet it was as if he were praying.

I came unto him
The sheep were gathered by him.

There were Soldiers of rain
Marching on Knocknacusha and Knockmoyle
And the great broken hill of Drung

With his sheep gathered to him
He spoke slowly of his townland
A place with its name split apart
And the remnant sounds of it
On one side or another

What he knew of travel was this
The distance he was able to plough in one day
And the distance a cow's lowing, a lamb's bleating
Can be heard on high mountains
Or a stone marker can be seen

Fainter and fainter
These frail measurements
Myself in his arms
And the rain coming down on us

Kieran sat up in his blanket. The poem went deep into him and made him alert to a kind of thrall that he suddenly knew he had always been susceptible to. It was not like the poem about the books that Annie had sung for him in Irish, then later recited in English, though he felt there was certainly a lament in it, or some sadness he couldn't name. He sensed that his mother was nearby, though he could neither hear her nor see her. He knew it wasn't her that he wanted, but something, someone, as yet undefined for him. He thought he might weep and his voice was unsteady when he asked Donal what the words meant.

It's a poem I keep in my mind, Donal told him. It was said to me long ago by a girl I loved.

She had left her home at dawn, Donal said, once when he was for the first time booleying alone. And she had climbed and walked all through the mountains until she found him, bringing food, but mostly bringing herself to him. "I remember when I saw her I said, Come here to me, and she did that. It was all I was to know of women," Donal said, "and it has been everything I have kept with me always."

"What happened to her?"

"She went to Africa with the nuns, she having taken the vow herself. And before she left, she said that poem to me."

"Could you not make her stay?"

"I could not. She had received the call."

Kieran lay down again, the thought of the girl in the mountains who had gone to Africa fierce in his mind.

As he was sliding into sleep, Donal added, "We were both very young, and yet she knew me well. And she said the poem in Irish, which made it much more beautiful. But I said it tonight in English so that you would understand."

II

—

SEARCH

——

There is no suggestion of either day or night out on the tarmac now. The interior lights of the airliner have been shut off and the shape of the fuselage is now barely discernible in the fog. It is as if this weather pattern is attempting to extinguish the length and breadth of time, to make it immeasurable. Tam looks at the clocks, wondering as she does so which hour she inhabits: the afternoon of the place she has abandoned, the early evening of her intended destination, or the midpoint of this waiting room stasis. She feels wretched, too exhausted to fight the futile and mostly painful longing, sometimes bordering on panic, that has always been a part of her involvement with Niall. No amount of thought on her part, no amount of examination or interpretation had been able to explain it, dismiss it, or satisfy it. It has followed her across the ocean and is seated beside her here on this leatherette bench. All this humiliating, helpless sorrow.

She closes her eyes and finds herself listening to the sounds around her. The couple directly behind her are arguing: she can hear the blame in their whispered exchanges. A baby begins to cry, then falls silent, comforted, Tam assumes, by food or by being held. Nearby someone is pacing: the subtle tap-tapping of their footsteps slowly increases then just as slowly decreases in volume. There is something palliating in this sedate form of advance and retreat. Her head begins to nod.

When she opens her eyes, she is drawn once again to the stories the painting tells, and notices, for the first time, that although oranges and yellows are plentiful, these are actually night scenes set against a midnight blue sky. The exception is the part on the far right of the picture, which she has now come to call the arrival zone. There the figures are bathed in theatrical morning light: the maternal woman who put her in mind of her lost nan, the bird standing guard over the two eggs in her nest. And yet the children who are gathered there are still shadowy, even under the assault of such radiance and in the midst of such an eruption of blossoms. She considers the possibility that they might be hiding.

In late May 1944, just in advance of the invasion of Normandy, Tam had been required to conceal each of the ten Spitfires she delivered from factories to a variety of airfields to protect them from being seen from above by those who would want to destroy them. She recalls now the strangeness of this; the bumpy journey of the grounded aircraft lumbering away from the smoothness of the runways toward a landscape in full flower. One Spit was placed in an orchard.

Another was squeezed between rows of poplars, its beautiful thin wings only inches away from bark. She had loved these aircraft because of the solitude of their single seat and their apparent lightness in flight. She loved their manoeuvrability. But on the ground they became less organic, more ungainly and machinelike. She abandoned them under willows, beside ancient oak trees, and once in the centre of a famously tall growth of rhododendrons. At night she dreamed anxiously that the moonlight, or even the starlight, might cause a metallic glow to emanate from them, silvering the trees and bushes from within rather than without, and alerting the enemy. But by day she would forget her night fears and set out once again on a round of deliveries, and of camouflage.

———

Niall told her it had taken him five stubborn years before he would allow himself to begin to look for his brother. Embarrassed about his need to do this, and unnerved by his sudden fear of disgrace, he said nothing to anyone: nothing about what he was thinking and nothing about what he was planning. Even when nothing of the sort was going on, he would say he had a meteorological conference or some other kind of appointment in London rather than admit to the sense of shame that prompted his search.

"Your father," Tam had said when he told her this, "your father would have known there was no conference." This insistence on secrecy and shame was confusing to her.

But his father was retired by then, he told her. After years and years of launching weather balloons and drawing up charts, he had turned away from meteorology as if it had never existed for him. He had become an older man. He sometimes worked on the *Irish Times* crossword; occasionally he went for a pint in the pub at the end of his evening walks. Now and then he would ask his son how things were going at the station, but not as often as one might think.

McWilliams, however, as chief at the station, would give help and advice at every opportunity, and in such a warm way that Niall would only realize later that the wide conversation he had with the man had been laced with instructions. Niall adored him, and would eagerly comply with anything the older man wanted him to do. He told her that McWilliams knew everything about everything, that he was animated, life-enhancing, a born teacher, a sage. As his own father greyed and withdrew, became hard of hearing and querulous, this other, more ebullient man became, for Niall, an essential guide.

Yes, McWilliams knew everything. He talked about the blue rays in the sky, how they scattered toward the earth, diverted from the direction they had intended to take. He said that Irish lakes were dark because of the molecules of peat that intercepted the path of light. He could name the date and duration of each of the most famous gales of the Iveragh going back two hundred years. He knew about fogbows, rainbows in various shades of grey made of fog, the droplets compos- ing them being too small for the spectrum of colour. He had anecdotes about ice: a French cavalry, two hundred years before, had captured the Dutch fleet brought to a halt by being deeply frozen into a bay. The only naval victory won on horseback! He knew that there were twenty thousand windmills in Germany in the mid-eighteenth century. He could list the artists who best depicted storms, and remarked how few of them could paint rain. He would conjecture the numbers of thousands of miles one wave had travelled before it broke on a Munster shore. He claimed that several of the colourful birds he kept in cages throughout his house had been blown into his hands during a gale that was the result of a hurricane in the Caribbean. "Blow-ins," Niall said to her. "Like you."

A few years later there actually was a conference. Niall, visiting her after a month apart, told her this as he was leaving her house. London, he said, in May.

She asked him if she could go with him and he was silent, thinking.

"One night," she said. "One morning. Waking up together." The tone of her voice was humiliating to her, the supplicant in it. She would not say it more than once.

Three nights, he eventually agreed. But not London, somewhere near Gloucester instead. There was a village there, he told her, where Francis Drake had lived in a large house that was now an inn. McWilliams had told him it was rumoured that Drake had not written his *The World Encompassed* there because that book had been assembled by his great-nephew, another Francis Drake, thereby leading to centuries of confusion. "The old slave driver," Niall had added, though whether in reference to the elder or the younger she wasn't sure. And it was right on the estuary of the Severn River, this village, at the very bottom of a forested gorge, Niall had assured her. Its climate would be detached in some way or another, a self-perpetuating system. She suspected he wanted to take the story of this isolated weather back to McWilliams.

She stands up and walks across the room to the painting and looks at the black plastic plaque beneath it, hoping to discover its title. But only the artist's name is printed there: Kenneth Lochhead. "Kenneth Lochhead," she whispers. The Scottish name suggests lakes, rocks, and ominous skies, and yet the mural she is in front of right now looks like a dusky riverbank rather than a lake. There is the long stretch of it, and the people gathered at the shoreline, as if waiting for some kind of a water-related flotilla, a procession of royal watercraft, a ceremonial advance. Or are they witnessing a retreat? Yes, something is moving away from them. They watch this withdrawal, whatever it is, with great dispassion, neutral in the face of their own powerlessness.

"My brother might be near there," Niall had added, almost as an afterthought. Then he had quoted Drake: "'There must be a beginning of any great matter, but continuing unto the end until it be thoroughly finished yields the true glory.'"

"And what is that?" she wondered.

"Self-congratulation," he had said.

Getting there was complicated. She took a train to Dublin, a boat to Holyhead. Then she boarded a series of further trains, secondary and tertiary lines, eventually halting at a sizable town where she hired a cab. Then there was the approach to the village; a wooded lane that back-switched into the deeply forested ravine at the bottom of which stood seven or eight structures, all of them ancient, beside an embankment or burn. The inn, which had been the house in which Drake was rumoured to have lived, was large and almost empty in this off-season, and the hall she walked to the riverside room Niall had rented was uncarpeted and echoing. And there was no river, anyway, the whole waterfront having been dammed up to provide the bed for the same railway that she had travelled on to get there.

The river moved along at the bottom of the opposite side of the embankment, as she discovered while taking a walk that led her through a tunnel and to its edge. It was indeed an estuary, and the tide was out. She wanted to romanticize the estuary but found herself more concerned with mud. It was everywhere, a particular kind of mud that lived half of its life underwater and clung to her shoes.

When Niall arrived the following morning, they removed each other's clothes and made love on the high, lumpy bed. Sun came in through the white cotton curtains and she could hear children playing in the lane below, laughing and calling to one another. They were ravenous and ordered lunch in the room, then walked outside, climbing the steep slopes of the ravine and looking across the expanse of water. Trains passed by on the narrow-gauge railway. He was glad there were trains, he had insisted when she said there might be noise. It made it all seem more real to him. That she could take his arm, could lean toward him out of doors, was to her an unimaginable luxury. She knew she loved him.

On the afternoon of the second day, he began to withdraw. What was it, what was wrong? she had asked. He said it was nothing and told her to stop worrying and imagining things. This hurt her. She watched him, watched his face, waited for him to turn toward her, to at least tell her what was on his mind. For weeks afterwards she would recall his profile, the sternness of his expression, and the dimming down of his mood.

He had fallen silent. There was no talk of Francis Drake or even of the weather, which remained calm and bright. She chattered on, her voice filling the room in a way that made her despise herself. Drake, she said, could only have loved the weather in this spot. What would he tell McWilliams? Perhaps, she ventured, Drake would have written about weather in all the other places he had been. Tropical storms, for instance. Maybe McWilliams would like to think about Drake's memories of storms. Niall had told her Drake spelled storms with an "e" at the end. "There blew up a mighty storme," she said to him, emphasizing the "e" so it sounded like an "a." Past tense, she added when he didn't look at her or smile.

He turned toward the window then, as if looking out at the sky, but she knew he was not looking out, would retain no memory of the arrangement of clouds. "I can't tell McWilliams about being here," he said. "He is very fond of Susan." He turned back to look at her. "My wife," he added.

Tam said nothing. She didn't need to be reminded that Susan was his wife.

"I have to go," he said. "I have to look for Kieran. He's here. Somewhere in the mid-north. He's found work in the construction of a motorway." Someone, some Irishman on a building site, had told him this in London. She imagined Niall, picking through the rubble, the noise of the machinery all around him, looking for his brother, then speaking to this other labourer. It was as if his brother might have been smashed by the rubble or run over by the machinery. She thought of her own father's firm, and the building of motorways.

"I can't be in this country and not look for my brother," Niall had said. Defensively, she thought, as if she had always been trying to talk him out of it. "I just can't do that. They say he's drinking, living rough."

"He's not a child," she told him. "It's possible he wants that life."

"Don't tell me what my brother wants," he said, sudden anger in his voice. "Absolutely no one could want that life."

He opened his case, began to collect his things.

"It's my doing," he said flatly, "all of it."

"How could it be, Niall?" She recalled him using words such as *fault* and *loss* in relation to his brother. Lost him completely, he had said.

"No," he said now, "you can't understand. It is my fault."

"You don't want to be with me," she said. "I can understand *that*."

"Oh, I want to be with you," he said. The anger had not left his voice, but his expression was open, torn. "It's my brother I am talking about. But I want to be with you. And that is my fault as well."

After he left, she sat paralyzed in the room. She could not go outside, could not walk again on the paths where they had been together, a sky over them rather than a roof. All the other relationships she had had in her life, her current acquaintanceships, the people in the village near where she lived, and her warmly remembered friendships from her flying days dimmed, then receded. Even the pure memory of Teddy, sealed in place and preserved by death, felt neither reliable nor retrievable. Hers was a half-life, thin, almost empty, not large enough to claim ownership of this terrible sense of loss. She tried to conjure this rogue brother, wanted to position him on the map she was constantly revising in her mind, the map of Niall's character. But she hadn't enough information to make sense of this preoccupation.

She could not look at the unmade bed. Exclusion was everywhere. Outside, small trains on the narrow-gauge railway approached, whistled, and moved into the distance. Even these small, cheerful machines, one of which she would ride to leave this place, seemed remote.

A faint greyness is entering the air outside the window of the terminal, a moist dawn attempting to make its way through the fog. She must have slept, though she has no real belief in this, and is almost certain she had been in a state of dazed vigilance all night. The number of passengers in the lounge has thinned. There is a woman stretched on a bench opposite to hers, another feeding a baby on the other side of the room, and a large, silent family of what appear to be Irish immigrants on the two banquettes to her left. The children, who had been noisily active for most of the previous day, have now collapsed into various attitudes of sleep, lying against one another like a heap of puppies.

She rises and walks to the counter, where one tired-looking employee is seated on a stool with his back leaning against the wall. When she asks, he tells her that it is unlikely the atmosphere will clear anytime soon. She could get a hotel room, he says, just on the other side of the parking lot. They would call her there when the aircraft is ready to leave. Most of the other passengers have done this already, and there would still be enough hours, he conjectures, for sleep. He intends to go home himself, he says, and catch some shut-eye.

She is surprised by what sounds like an Irish inflection in his speech, but she hasn't the heart or strength to remark on it. "Maybe I'll do that," she says. She asks about a place to eat.

The restaurant should be open for breakfast now, the employee tells her. It's over there, just to the right of *Flight and Its Allergies*. When she registers confusion, he says that the mural, which was really called *Flight and Its Allegories*, had been dubbed *Flight and Its Allergies* by the staff at the airport. "We can't make head nor tail of it," he says. "If I were you, I would visit the Constellation for breakfast before bedding down."

"The Constellation," she repeats. She looks out the window where the airliner sits, motionless, unlit, obscured by the mist. Orion slips into her mind.

The man points to the far side of the terminal where filigreed screens of carved wood form a long dividing wall, then smiles. "Not the aircraft, the restaurant," he says.

She has a faint memory of someone telling her that Newfoundlanders were mostly Irish. And sure enough, the light, sharp consonant at the end of the word *restaurant* recalled the sound of Niall's own voice when he said words such as *constant* or *trust*.

KIERAN'S BODY HAD CHANGED INTO THAT OF A young man, and his mind had acquired more knowledge and therefore a more complicated way of thinking. The bicycle, however, was a source of comfort in that it could be relied upon to stay more or less the same. Kieran knew every sound it made under any condition, how the tires purred on a good road, hissed in grass on a hillside too wet and steep, really, to be negotiated, rattled when descending a stony mountain track. Some days, when he had been riding for a good length of time, the turning of the speed-blurred wheels beneath him seemed to be an extension of his own body, as if the bicycle had become an essential fifth limb. He went out riding in any kind of weather: a day without speed was for him a day when his self felt heavy and encumbered, as if he were trying to walk through slowly churning, waist-high water. And he feared that, unless he moved forward, his mother would begin to speak to him from that water.

Swiftness of passage was a species of intimacy to him. He could bring to mind what he had observed of the hawthorn, sally, and holly bushes of the hedgerows more easily than the bark of the one apple tree outside Gerry-Annie's house. He knew the incline and descent of the most obscure roads and tracks of his parish. Later, in the quiet of Annie's cottage, he could call to mind everything he had seen in the small theatres of roadside windows: a torn curtain, a plaster saint, a china figurine, a face. A change of flowers in a vase or the absence of a toy car from the ledge of a stranger's window thirty miles away were more vivid to him than a shining new oilcloth placed by Annie on the familiar table where he took his meals each day.

When Niall finished his seemingly endless university education, Annie would say, he would become a weatherman like his father. Reports of his successes were sent back frequently from Dublin, and Kieran would hear about these, mostly from Annie, who still cleaned and occasionally cooked for his father, and now and then from his father himself. Niall had joined every athletic team, apparently, often becoming captain. And he had scored hundreds of winning goals, according to Annie. His father called him a natural athlete and said he had known this right from the beginning. The minute the lad stepped out and onto the field, he said. Kieran, who had understood since infancy that physical prowess was Niall's territory, would therefore have never dared to approach the game. Still, he knew the football jargon, more or less. The fencing was more confusing, and he was surprised when he learned that this involved a sword and a mask, believing until then that the activity could have applied only to the penning of sheep. Once he was made aware, he often pictured his brother with his face disguised and a weapon in his hand.

Kieran saw less and less of his father, though he still made one or two obligatory Sunday visits, and now and then his father came up into the hills on a sunny Saturday. Gerry-Annie was always delighted by these events. She brought out the good teapot, cups, and saucers she and Gerry had been given as a wedding present and made a quantity of sandwiches. She'd cut a few roses from the bush near the door and place them on the table. And, when all was ready, she took off her apron, the only time apart from preparing to go to Mass that she was seen to do this in her own kitchen.

Kieran's father would accept a glass of whiskey from the bottle kept in the dresser, and after the ceremonial raising of the glass and the first sip, Annie loved to be told about the weather balloons that his father had launched twice daily at the observatory when he was still working and how it was that they were able to send information back.

"Is it the same balloon, over and over, then?" she once asked. She didn't really believe that a floating object could telegraph the news of distant winds and assumed, therefore, that it must report back to headquarters.

"No, Annie, we use a different one each time."

"But isn't that a terrible waste, and times so bad?"

"You may be right about the waste, but we need a new one each time, as not a single one ever returns."

"Perhaps if you held on to a string, you could pull them back."

"There isn't a string long enough, Annie. And the measurements are taken with the theodolite." She loved this word and afterwards often repeated her suggestion so that she could hear it again.

"Theodolite," she would say with awe, as if hearing the name of the instrument for the first time.

Kieran often thought about how smoothly Niall had entered the adult world, almost as if he had never been a child, or even a youngster like himself. True, there was that gap of almost a decade between them and those early years before Kieran was born when his brother would have been small and living alone with their parents. But now he'd been gone long enough that the city had established itself in his attitudes and in his clothing. He didn't look at all like the young men Kieran worked with. His stance was different than theirs, and his attitudes and speech. While his brother was polite and well spoken, even his apparent kindness was foreign and sometimes unreadable to Kieran, though he sensed, now and then, that Niall was trying to reach him in some way or another.

Once, Kieran took Niall out to see the bicycles that were still, all these years later, being kept in the cow byre. Many of the tires were flat and rust now coated the spokes and rims of the wheels.

"It's odd, her in there always talking to our father about waste," Niall said about Annie, "and these out here unused in the byre."

"She honestly believes that those who left them will come back to claim them." The sound of spring lambs calling for their mothers could be heard coming from the valley as they turned from the bicycles and stepped outside. "But I know the truth," Kieran said, pulling the rough door shut behind him and fastening it with a dark iron bolt. "I've met fellows about to emigrate. They swear they will come back. But they hardly ever do. Mostly they go to London or Liverpool and get stuck there." He walked to the side of the byre and pointed to one, then another of the cottages visible in the fields below them. "Or they go to New York. One went from there," he said, "and all three from there."

"But they'd be making money on the building sites," Niall said, "and they could use that to come home."

Kieran regarded his brother with amazement. It was obvious that he had no knowledge of what the country people were up against. "They send the money home," he told Niall. "There's hundreds in the hills that wouldn't make it through the winter if they hadn't a son or nephew abroad working on the sites."

Niall shook his head. "A pity, that," he said, "and a bloody shame. They ought to be given a chance, those boys. A fighting chance for a life of their own."

"It's not possible," Kieran insisted, "not with the way things are."

Niall dismissed this. "I don't accept that," he told his brother. "Anything is possible if you want it badly enough."

Much later Niall would tell Tam about these times at Annie's cottage. Listening to his brother talk about people so far from his own experience was both surprising and comforting to him, in that it made his brother – this stranger who had come to know other strangers – more vital to him. "As if I might come to know him," he said.

"But I closed the conversations down somehow," he admitted. "I thought I was more knowledgeable than him. And, of course, he sensed that." He paused. "And he withdrew."

In the midst of tight, mannered, and increasingly infrequent Sunday afternoons in the house in town, Niall told her, while the parlour slowly darkened between them, or later, at the evening table with their father, he had come to feel the distance between himself and his brother. All talk was halting and formal and never initiated by Kieran, who seemed both wild and restrained and as palpably suspicious as a fox. Sometimes the quietness in the room was so filled with tension Niall almost wished for the return of his brother's tantrums, anything to break through the forced calm of the board games they played with their father, and then the awkward, silent meal, a shepherd's pie most often, prepared by Gerry-Annie on Friday to be heated up later.

Years before, when Kieran had begun to attend the Derriana School, the conversation had sometimes centred on this, his father asking what he was studying and whether or not he liked his teacher. But these questions had brought only monosyllabic answers from Kieran, and it wasn't until Niall mentioned the bicycle that any expression at all had come into the boy's face. Once, Kieran had become almost animated as he talked about the replacement of a bicycle chain: what it had cost and how much easier the cycling had become once this was accomplished, that and the purchase of the light that was affixed to the handlebars and that guided his evening return to the dark hills behind the town. In subsequent years Niall would try to convince himself that he had not mentioned his own bicycling to his younger brother because he had wanted Kieran to have something that was his alone. And his own bike in Dublin, he told Tam, would have been so much better outfitted; how could he have spoken of it? "Kieran was so bloody proud of that one tin light," he said.

Lying in bed later in the night, Niall had sometimes thought about this light moving steadily upwards like a star rising through the trees of Carhan Wood and appearing at the top of the small mountain they called Garrane. He had held in his mind until he slept this one small, travelling candle, the most lonely and tentative flicker of light that he could imagine, in spite of knowing that Kieran would have entered Gerry-Annie's lane less than twenty minutes after leaving the house and a full hour before he himself had gone to bed. It was in this way, he would say to Tam later, he had come to understand that he missed his brother and that some part of him wished the younger boy could stay home, even though he himself was almost always in Dublin. He had not discussed the boy's absence or even his brief Sunday presence with his father, and knew he would never do so, in the same way that, once his mother was gone, her name was rarely mentioned. Oddly, it was Kieran who had once slipped the word *Mother* into a silence at the table. "Mother says," he had begun. Then he had stopped, as if he hadn't been aware that he was speaking in company. Niall had felt a shadow of discomfort move through him. He resented the younger boy suddenly using the word *Mother*. And he was shaken by the spectrum of possibilities in that unfinished sentence.

Up in the hills at Gerry-Annie's, this young man, this stranger-brother whose voice had taken on the soft accent of the country people with whom he lived, had tried to describe the plight of a workmate who had, indeed, returned from America. "The only one I ever heard about, came back," he said, "was Brian from Garreiny, far back in near Lough Iskanamacteery. They say he came home because his mother was dying of a broken heart." He had kicked a pebble with his boot. "It's a dark place back in there with the mountains so close to one another," he said, explaining the mother who had needed her son to return. "The roads are never dry, even with three full days of sun in summer."

Both brothers had fallen silent again, at the reference to the mother. But within that silence Niall came to understand that, unlike the angry, sad younger brother he had lost, this quiet labourer was someone with a discrete set of experiences that he could seldom share. He was aware as well that the landscape they were looking at – a landscape that he, Niall, had never taken the trouble to learn – was now, and would likely permanently be, his brother's geography.

In the middle of Easter week two years later while Kieran was painting window frames, he paused to open a fresh can, then realized he needed to go into the house to fetch a knife. As he walked back outside with the tool in his hand, he caught sight of his brother at the curve in the road, and beside him, not his father, but a stranger, a woman, in a blue skirt and what appeared to be a yellow blouse of some sort. On top of her head was a wealth of wavy dark hair, lifting in the wind. Niall was not looking at the house as he approached but rather at this woman to whom he seemed to be explaining something, moving his arms as if he were demonstrating an expanse of space or a length of time. The girl, for Kieran could see now that she was not a woman but a girl, walked with her arms crossed and her head down, obviously taking very seriously whatever it was Niall had to say. For the first time in months, Kieran heard his mother's whisper coming from somewhere very far away, but he couldn't make out what she was saying. He put the knife in his back pocket, picked up the paint can and the brush, and moved quickly around to the rear of the house, the shyness in him about the girl with his brother rising in his blood.

Because the weather was so glorious, he had ridden the bicycle for three hours that morning, down to Waterville and along to Ballinskelligs, over the mountain and down into Port Magee, then swiftly back again because he had promised to paint the window frames. But now he wished more than anything that he was back on the bike again, heading up and over the rough road to Port Magee or in the opposite direction, over the Coomakista Pass and along the coast to Sneem. While he stood behind the cottage he heard the girl laugh as she and Niall came up the lane. It was unlike any sound he had ever heard before, and his mother was whispering about it, though vaguely, and in the new language she had that was barely comprehensible to him. And then he heard his brother laugh in a way that was full of happiness. He realized that he himself rarely laughed, even when his workmates teased or joked with him, and he wondered now about the origins of this spontaneous expression. The word *delight* came into his mind.

He opened the can of paint and began to work on the outside trim of the window, through which he could see Gerry-Annie's one table, and while he was working he saw Niall enter the dim interior, with the girl stepping lightly behind him. He could hear Gerry-Annie's effusive welcome and the bustling noises that always accompanied her greetings. "Is it yourself then, Niall," she was saying, "home from the city?" And then to the girl. "Welcome, welcome, Susan, to the parish of Dromid, to the townland of Garrane, and to the house of Gerry-Annie. What a treat on this bright day. Now, where has your brother got to? I'll just step out a moment to find him."

Kieran dropped the brush, bent down to retrieve it, then stood and looked through the window. The girl was near the table, near him, close to the window glass, but her face was turned away from the light. He could see it though, her shadowed face, and suddenly it was as if everything he had ever wanted was in the way her eyes were looking at his brother. Niall sat down at the end of the table and the girl walked up behind him and placed her hand on his shoulder. Niall with "his Susan" in Gerry-Annie's kitchen, and the way the girl's hand had settled, white against the dark of his brother's shirt, and the warm yellow of her own sleeve, her arm inside it reaching for his brother's shoulder. Kieran wanted that quiet touch, that connection for himself.

Susan. He allowed his inner voice to taste her name.

Annie was near him now, telling him to come inside. But he could hardly hear her. His mother was whispering something that was both an echo and a premonition, and the sound was coming from somewhere deep in the valley. As Annie spoke behind him, the girl turned toward the window and, for one moment only, her eyes met his, her expression frank and open, a smile beginning to visit her mouth. He turned then and ran to the byre, rattled the bolt, pushed open the door, grabbed hold of the bicycle, and swung his leg over the cross-bar. Soon he was on the road that climbed up and into the mountains, attempting to rise swiftly away from everything that was confused and changing inside him. There was no accounting for the combination of sorrow and panic that pumped through his heart, no accounting for his mother's distant whispered cautions. From that moment on, the girl's face would burn in his mind.

That night at supper he was both silent and ravenous while Gerry-Annie talked. She asked him to explain his absence and what had got into him to cavort off like that, with his brother bringing his sweetheart up from town to meet him. "You know who she is, Kieran," she was saying, "the jeweller's daughter down in the town. She went away to school, so you might not have seen her, but we all know who she is. She would be younger than Niall by some years, I'm thinking, but then wasn't I myself eleven years younger than my own Gerry. I'd have thought you might have wanted to meet her, she and Niall being so thick."

And when he didn't answer, she asked him why he felt that he had to eat his potato and her potato and all the bread in the basket. When he remained unresponsive, she began to speak again, as he knew that she would, about the girl.

He learned then that she was the daughter of the same jeweller whose shop window he had often passed as a child walking on the street with his mother. He could recall now the way his mother had stopped by that window, her body swaying slightly, while she looked intently, but also somehow impassively, through the glass to the bright-coloured stones and gold and silver. He would watch her profile at such moments, and recalled now her fine white skin and perfect eyebrow, an atmosphere of trance around her. Finally she would sigh, as if dissatisfied by what she had seen, and turn away. Remembering this, he could hear the rustle of his mother's clothing as she began to walk again. He realized that they had never stepped inside the jewellery shop, that its small objects had been only a pause in the gravity that pulled his mother farther down the street under the shadow thrown by the large church and through the door of the chemist's shop. There was a bell on that door, and that bell was strangely ringing in his own mind here at Gerry-Annie's table, along with his mother's whispers, her warnings sent to him in words he could no longer comprehend.

Then he remembered something else. There had been unusual objects in that window: plates and goblets that, to his mind, would never hold food or water. He recalled thinking they were woven somehow, as if they were made out of rope, and yet something rarer than rope, a property closer to lace, or the crocheted edges of the pillow slips on the beds of the house and the cloths that covered the tables. There were brooches as well, made in the same way. "Belleek," his mother had said one day when he asked, her soft voice trailing over the word so that the last syllable was prolonged, then completed finally by the delicate cut of the "k." He had thought she meant bleak, that bowls and plates punctuated by so many holes had a bleak hopelessness about them. They would hold nothing, he had concluded, and would be useless, in spite of their beauty.

It was one of his workmates who told him where the girl lived. While explaining where his own farm was located, he said the words "You pass by the jeweller's house," and Kieran heard this, though the words were not addressed to him. Even more taciturn than usual with a shovel in his hands, Kieran nevertheless heard himself shout down the line of labourers, "And where is that then, your place?"

"Near Carhan Bridge, first road to the right, then up a bit," the young man said. "The jeweller's is farther up the mountain, after you leave the woods, and we are the next lane that leaves the road, after his."

They were building a stone wall to surround the rose garden on the church grounds, just down the street from his father's house. But he had not told his father that he was working in the town, though he would know by now, as Gerry-Annie would have said something about it when she went there in the afternoon to clean. And tonight, in all probability, she would tell him that his father wanted him to come by for tea after work the next day. He did not know if he could do this, his shyness and fear about the girl having extended in an extreme way to include the possibility of his father, or anyone for that matter, talking about her. And then there would be the talk about Niall, his various Gaelic football triumphs – even a miraculous all-Ireland final in the stadium at Croke Park – and how he had top score three years running in science. The wonder of Niall's many victories, how he already had a job waiting for him at the weather station, his father would want to talk about all that. The trophies Niall had won would be shining in the window facing the street, and that picture of him, panting after a game and holding one of the trophies, would be smiling down from the wall. No, he could not do it.

He had seen the girl touch Niall, and he had seen him accept that touch as if it were nothing out of the ordinary. This confident brother of his hadn't even looked up in the midst of such a miracle. In this way Kieran knew that her touch was something familiar to Niall. He shivered as he thought about this and dug the shovel deeper into the earth, imagining that white hand, the shock of it coming to rest on his own shoulder.

He could see the painted green cross on the sign that hung from the outer wall of the chemist's shop each time he straightened up after digging for a spell. Some other man in a white coat was in there now. He had no idea who; he had never been back. But each time he looked at the sign his mother's voice became active, coming from the past now, and so far away, it was as if each word she attempted to say was freighted with such effort that the whisper was more like keening or a long-exhaled sob full of breath and blurred syllables.

TAM HAS EATEN BACON AND EGGS, AND THICK SLABS of bread, and has returned to the waiting room feeling more alert. Nothing in the atmosphere beyond the glass has changed, however.

Walking to the window she sees that a hint of sunlight might be yellowing the fog. Ghost air, she thinks, wanting it to at least move and separate, take some kind, any kind of form. A few other tired-looking passengers have returned to the lounge and sit reading or staring into space. There is no one now behind the ticket desk, and the aircraft beyond the glass still stands as if abandoned, as if it will never fly anywhere ever again. Now the yellowish light fades and an opalescent greyness settles over the aircraft until the outline of the tip of one wing disappears and the large bulk of the fuselage blurs. She wishes she could include this beast in her love of aircraft, but nothing in her stirs as she looks at it. Grounded though it may be, no real drama can be associated with it.

The figures in the painting are coming in and out of focus as she stares at them: the man with the pie, the man with the white banner, that woman who put her in mind of her nan. There is a blue figure drawn in profile just below the powerful, banner-waving man who occupies the central portion of the mural. It has been possible to ignore this small person until now because of the hugeness of the man above, his laying claim to the space around him, and the way his athletic waving arms sweep everyone else out of the way, keeping the pace, his own pace. The victor, she thinks. "The victor, that's me," Niall had said, the bitterness palpable in his voice. "I swept him out of the way. I didn't even give him his one small moment."

They had been sitting beside the window, watching the late-afternoon light pour down the mountain. He had wept then. She had never seen him weep before and she was frightened by the suddenness of this emotion. And she knew, she *knew* he would never weep for her. The memory of some of her own tearful nights returns to her; nights when she had walked alone, back and forth in her cottage, certain that what they had between them could never be sustained, knowing all the while that this was the cheapest kind of melodrama, hating herself and her weakness. She had lived through the war. She knew very well that tragedy could assume dimensions of appalling magnitude. And yet there she had been, safe in that country cottage, behaving like a spoiled child who had been denied ownership of something that had never been, would never be, hers. She had no entitlement to the loss she felt, and has none to the loss she feels.

And still, in spite of this realization, the pain returns and her eyes fill. She wants a cigarette, but when she pulls the pack out of her bag it is empty.

—

Each summer there had been a carpet of montbretia, a vividly orange, lilylike flower, on either side of the lane that led to the cottage, making a ceremonial border for any arrivals. When she had asked about these flowers early on, the neighbours had told her that the plants were not native, had been introduced to the region in an Englishman's garden, a garden from which they had escaped. Once they were free, they had flourished, and by August each year, they filled hedgerows, untended fields, and all graveyards, and, in combination with the pink of the foxgloves, gave an exotic southern feel to a territory dominated mostly by bog and scant pastures. Once when she pointed to the montbretia, Niall told her he didn't approve of invasive species. He had laughed then, and embraced her, another variant of invasive species.

They had been together so infrequently and with such difficulty, and yet the idea of him had surrounded the past few years like a damp climate, the air thick with it, so that everything she did or said or thought in his absence seemed to her muted and pale, although he would have known none of this. Near him she had had the sense that she was emerging, sometimes with such swiftness that she had been taken aback by the space her body occupied in a room, the range of her gestures, and the startling sound of her own voice, the joy in it. Afterwards she would wonder if it would have been wiser to be more restrained, less actively delighted. Still, it was her reaction to him, the emergence of a more vital self in his presence, that had made her believe he was essential. But now she wanted to believe he was not essential, any more than the abandoned cottage or the small grey car, whose trunk she had slammed shut for the last time, was essential. She could leave it all behind.

During the blank periods that followed Niall's withdrawals, she would sometimes try to develop a case against this attachment, which offered only the part of the path where she stood, its pebbles and surrounding foliage, and not a life in what she let herself see as the bright fields beyond. Nothing about her girlhood or young adulthood could have predicted such an impossible absorption in her – a trap really, and one of her own making. But despite this, the future had marched, anyway, into what there had been between them until her own stubborn resilience had begun to seem like a resolution of a kind.

He had walked in and out of her life, fully realized, cohesive, then collapsing into his several disparate parts. She recalls the familiar pattern of his retreats, the purposeful way he collected his things, buttoned his shirt, pushed his arms into his coat sleeves. Once, she had asked him why he had always seemed so eager to leave her, withdrawing so casually, so cheerfully, as if they might have been meeting again in the evening or the following day. He would step back into the crowded river of his life, the science of his work, his family, while for days afterwards she would keep the hours she had spent with him near at hand, looking for gemstones, then later searching for flaws.

Each episode of the mural bleeds into its neighbour's territory, she thinks: there are no disparate parts. She assumes that this fluidity, if that was what she should call it, must have been part of the artist's intention. Composition, she remembers, from an art class at school. The composition of her own life has been altered, with the difficulties of romance dominant and everything else in shadow. And here she is fully halted in the midst of trying to fix that, as if fate were reluctant, in the end, to endorse her attempts to restore balance.

For a few moments she pictures the artist who has painted this mural that has been her companion for more than twenty-four hours. Kenneth Lochhead — a tall man, she suspects, a man fully in control of the long, narrow world he has created on the wall. How satisfying it must have been to see it emerge, fully realized, to know that you have made permanent these departures and arrivals. But would it have served as an antidote to whatever may have been troubling him at the time, if there in fact had been anything troubling him at the time? She doubts this. There is no balm in Gilead.

GENTLEMAN

A dozen years before he began to work on the mural, and a few years after the war he had been too young to participate in, Kenneth had left his colonial country and drifted south for an American education. He had spent his childhood years in the company of borrowed Victorian monuments and borrowed English architecture and responded immediately to the brazenly individualistic city of Philadelphia, where he had been accepted into the Academy of Fine Arts. He was barely out of adolescence, and was as restless and jittery as the streets he began to explore as soon as he arrived. Having become immersed in this busy geography, all his previous notions about art were shaken out of him. Now he wanted his work to be tough, reckless, under construction. There was always the noise of something being built in this city. It beat up against the walls of the school all day and muscled its way into his dreams at night. He loved this, wanted to throw himself into the pulsing heart of it.

And then he met Harding. Sturdy, almost corpulent, and well into late middle age, this teacher had walked into the first mural class with a black-and-white reproduction of Ambrogio Lorenzetti's *Allegory of Good Government* in his hands and had tacked it up on a bulletin board on the back wall of the studio. "This has remained in the hearts of men," he told his eleven students, "because of the importance of its subject and the beauty of its execution. But it has also remained because it is fixed in place in every way it is possible to be fixed in place."

Kenneth looked at the men riding the dignified, high-stepping horses: their plumed hats and belted tunics. A falcon perched on the hand of one of them suggested privilege, class. In spite of their relatively small scale, they occupied the top of the picture plane, as they would have done in life.

"This is a procession," the teacher was saying, "not a parade. This is distinguished by its firm placement in time. And the landscape itself is an eternal landscape. It will never change in its relation to the town."

Kenneth looked at the walls of the miniature city, its gates and towers. It seemed to him that the town sat self-importantly in its surroundings, and everything else was diminished in the face of it.

"This is a mural," Harding continued, "not a painting. It is integral to the architecture it occupies. It is not meant to be loaned, traded, sold, or in any other way moved from place to place. It will always be seen under the influence of the light in which it was painted. No market, good or bad, no *government* can affect its value. It was always, and will always, be of value." He unrolled another black-and-white reproduction and tacked it into place on the board. "And this is its twin," he said, "the opposite wall. This is the *Allegory of Bad Government*."

Kenneth was more excited by this picture: its dark tones and storm clouds, its vividly painted devils. Here there was grave, democratic drama, drama that affected both lords and peasants.

The teacher stepped back now and turned to look at the class. "You," he said, "all of you will no doubt by now have a heard a great deal about abstraction, about non-objectivity in art, and about how that is the coming thing. Be that as it may, in this class, I will be teaching you about the panorama, about the pageant. There are others here who will instruct you concerning the parade, but in this class we will study persistence." He walked over to a metal machine that was placed on a work table and flicked a switch at the back of it. A large yellow square of light appeared on the studio wall. As he fumbled with a glass slide, he told one of the students to turn out the lights and another to pull down the green shades that were rolled at the top of the windows. For a moment the room was dark and grey, and then a crowd of softly coloured people appeared on the wall; pale, opaque, alive with vulnerability. "And now for Piero," Harding said. "Now for the master."

He said nothing while he showed the five glass slides, paused, and then showed them again, finishing with a scene where two groups of slim, elegant young adults were surrounded by foliage on the left and enclosed by architecture on the right. There was something poignant, Kenneth thought, about the curve of the women's necks and the folds in the drapery of their long cloaks. But it was the expression on the face of the central man under the arch in the right of the picture that he was drawn to. It was disturbingly tender, caught in a moment of inexplicable helplessness. "What kind of an artist could capture such transience, such fragility, in something as fixed as a mural?" the teacher was saying. "It is something we must learn if we are to paint murals; how to make fragility – be it benign or manipulative – how to make a moment, a series of such moments, how to make that, and the human life that beats there, permanent."

Not much later Kenneth would learn that Harding himself had designed and painted murals in the 1930s, when the government's Works Progress Administration had hired artists to paint the walls of public buildings. And after he learned this, he would go to the North Philadelphia Station Post Office to take a look at the two works he knew Harding had done there. The bigger mural was soft in colour and seemed to be pregnant with the same kind of dusty sunlight that fell through the upper windows of the public room that held it. Roads swerved up and out of the composition in the right corner and plunged like waterfalls out of the bottom at the left. Horses, men, pieces of parchment, then paper, a wagon filled with parcels. Lone men bent over letters as if worshipping the handwriting of a distant loved one, a woman clasping an envelope to her breast. Clouds, weather, winter. Horses stumbling through snow. All of the cumbersome, necessary machinery, and all of the difficulty of human communication. In the centre there was a large figure standing alone, his expression one of exhaustion; the entire story, whatever it might be, hanging heavily in the account book he held in his hand.

On the wall to the left of the postage counter was the other mural. Smaller, darker, and even more captivating, it depicted miners walking to work. Here there was the movement and vitality, the angry tension of men trapped by industry. Kenneth moved as close as possible to the surface so that he could determine exactly how his teacher had applied the paint, and how he had used light and shadow to bring out the men's expressions, their collective anger. He read the title on the plaque. *Anthracite Coal*, it said. The miners and the superstructure of the mine appeared to all be a part of the same river, almost as if the crowd had a liquid life of its own. A sluice of movement flowed around the architectural structures, the head frame of the mine, columns of miners going to and coming from work.

When Kenneth spoke to Harding about the second mural, the teacher said that he himself had been more satisfied with it. "More important than the big one," he said, "less historical." The WPA had given the artists a list of subjects appropriate for public consumption, he told Kenneth. "We all tried to break away from those prescriptions, eventually," he said. "My God, man, half the country was spending the day standing in breadlines! We needed to get hold of our own subjects."

He began to walk away. Then he turned back. "We all want to believe that we are originals," he said.

Kenneth began his classwork with a scene from the Eddy match factory, which stood on the edge of a river near his home. With faint pencil lines and geometric washes of water-colour, he blocked out the composition on a long, narrow piece of paper. The group of men approaching the factory was just a vague grey column at this point, the shape of it echoing the curve of the river below. But he would somehow put the anger into the next version. He didn't know how, but he was determined to do it.

By early the next week Kenneth was working on a thin plywood panel, three feet long and one foot high. The factory itself had become a solid geometric cube reminiscent of Piero della Francesca, and not unlike the head frame of the mine in the second mural. Harding, making his rounds, stopped behind him for the space of several minutes but said nothing. By the end of the following week Kenneth had painted the factory, the smokestack above it, and he had attempted to catch the anger, as Harding had done, in the gestures of the men, the set of their shoulders, and in the line of their strong, bent necks. Then he began to render the exqui-site light he had intentionally memorized, as best he could, while he stood in front of the post office murals. He was pleased with the tenacity of his own visual memory, and with the results.

Later that week, Harding stopped for a considerable time behind Kenneth's easel. Then he put his hand on his student's shoulder. "Let's go for a drink after," he said. "There is a long, sad story that I want to tell you."

The bar was dark and empty, apart from the bartender, who sat on a stool beneath a shelf filled with glassware and who was looking intently at a small radio from which came the faint noise of a sports event. Behind his teacher's head Kenneth could see that a green light hanging over a pool table was moving slightly in an unnoticed draught, though the air of the place seemed stale and trapped.

After they had removed their coats, Harding went twice to the bar, returning with four pints of draft beer. He reached forward and put his hand on Kenneth's arm when the younger man removed some bills from his wallet. "No," he said. "It's on me. And it's going to take some time." He swallowed a substantial amount from one glass, then sat back in his chair.

"Why am I telling you this?" he asked.

Kenneth knew he was not required to respond.

"Well," the teacher said, "mostly I suppose it is because you are not painting your mural, you are painting my mural."

Kenneth was mortified, realizing there was truth in the statement. "I didn't mean . . ." he began.

"And it's not that I haven't seen this before," Harding interjected into Kenneth's not very strong protestations, "I have seen this *many* times before. The thing is that I have not seen an attempt that is this successful. At least not with the appropriation of my own style *and* my own subject matter. Appropriating both style and subject matter requires a brilliant species of skill. And that species of skill I've only seen once before . . . and it didn't involve my work. But it did involve me."

Kenneth wished he were anywhere but in this bar in the company of this man. He had no idea what to say. Should he apologize? He was filling up with shame. He could feel the colour of it squeezing out of his heart and darkening his neck and face.

"A form of counterfeiting, I suppose, but not quite the same. As a matter of fact, during the war I got to know a counterfeiter." Harding smiled. "A great guy, actually . . . a wonderful guy. And very generous." He began to unbutton his old tweed jacket. "But I am talking about something different here, more serious." He looked around the room and leaned toward Kenneth in a conspiratorial manner. "I've never told anyone about this," he said, "and I am counting on you not to tell anyone else, and I firmly believe, though I don't know you at all, that I *can* count on that. You have a prairie boy's honest face, in spite of what you've been up to."

"I'm from Ottawa," Kenneth said, "but you can count on me anyway. And I was only trying to – "

The older man silenced his student with a wave of his hand. "When I was younger I was in love with a woman who was married to another painter." He fumbled in his pocket and produced a pack of cigarettes. "She still is. And, as you may or may not know, so am I. Married, that is, though not to another painter." He shifted in his chair. "Thankfully," he added.

"I am not going to tell you her husband's name, but be assured you would recognize it if I did. She is not unknown, either, for her early work. There was something between them about her doing better, but I could never really get her to talk about it. Still, this was several years ago, and it, our affair, had gone on for three years before that. A good deal of that kind of stuff in this world." Harding drew a circle in the air with his left hand. "But this was the real thing. I was in love with her and she knew it. And I knew how she felt about me, though we very seldom talked about that. We were both very attached to our families, and we knew that too. We *did* talk about that." Harding was silent for a moment. "It was agonizing," he said. He looked directly at Kenneth from beneath the two messy nests of his eyebrows. "Never, if you can possibly avoid it, get involved in something like this." A fat worm of ash fell from his cigarette, rather emphatically, Kenneth thought. "The trouble is," he continued, "you can't avoid it. It's like a chronic, debilitating disease, something that arrives in the night. It can't be cured. Only managed. For a while. In our case it was a long while."

He had continued to see this woman, Harding confessed, through waves of guilt, anxiety, paranoia, jealousy, desire, joy, and unceasing pain on both their parts. They had tried to stop, several times, without success, and the pain of that was unceasing as well. "She and I were painting a lot and exhibiting fairly constantly at the time and we would be at the same openings – sometimes our work was in the same group show. We didn't sell much, either of us, but we always submitted our paintings to juried exhibitions, and more often than not they were accepted. At the time" – he cleared his throat – "her husband's work was rarely, if ever, included." Harding slid an empty glass to the edge of the table. "I have to confess I was not entirely unhappy about that." He paused. "But *she* was – and I hated this – she was unhappy about that and, as I was to discover, *he* was distraught." Harding began to work on the second glass of beer. "I was to discover how much, how completely, only later, and in the craziest of ways." He smashed his cigarette into an ashtray.

"You never, ever know in these things, you never know what it is that will come along to end it. And, believe me, there is a part of you that is always, *always* looking for some event, some overriding circumstance or a betrayal, that will do the job. Let me assure you, this is the thing you most fear and at the same time the thing you most long for. What you don't imagine is whatever ends it will be something you never could have thought of. Still, as the bard said, 'All's well that ends.'"

"All's well that ends well," Kenneth corrected earnestly.

Harding was silent for a bit, seemingly absorbed by fingering the buttons on his tweed jacket. Then he looked up. "You've heard of the painter Alexander Gentleman? Active around the turn of the century?"

Kenneth shook his head.

"I thought not. But you should have. Someday perhaps he'll get his due, but so far, no luck. Night scenes, mostly, sometimes interiors, often involving water in some way or another, seen from a window or, if they are landscapes, there is always a pier or another point of embarkation. Sometimes there are scenes in badly lit bars not unlike this one. But even if you can't see the water you always sense it is there, just beyond the door, vast and unreliable. These are not large paintings, and there are only two or three of them in public collections, but they are important in ways I can barely describe. They draw you in and in. Then they inhabit you." He paused. "Completely. And the figures in them" – he searched his pockets for matches – "the couples in these paintings are caught just on the edge of something. They are turning toward each other. Or" – he struck a match, then blew it out – "they are turning away. And even if there is only one figure in the painting, the sense of relationship is palpable."

"So you have only seen one or two of these?"

"No . . . no. Many more than that. I knew Gentleman. God! What a name! A ridiculous name for anyone, never mind for such a dark painter! I knew him when he was very old. He lived in a basement: not far from here, actually. One day, just walking down the street, I came across him. His arms were full of his paintings and he was heading for a trash barrel. As I said, he was old, talking to himself. But it was drink, I could smell it, not dementia. I walked him, and his paintings, back to his basement, which was full, absolutely full, of these remarkable works, which, as I was to discover, he flatly refused to sell, even to show. I stacked the pictures he was aiming to throw away in a corner. By the time I left he was snoring. I went back two days later. He didn't recognize me, but he let me in anyway when I said I wanted to see the paintings. This time he was completely lucid, completely sober. A binge drinker, so the drunkenness came and went." Harding lifted his glass. "Unlike some of us regulars."

Having said this, Harding walked over to the bar and returned with two more pints. He pointed to Kenneth's only partly finished first glass. "Drink up," he said, placing the full glasses on the table.

He sat down. Kenneth noticed that his teacher's overcoat had slipped from the back of the chair to the floor, but he said nothing.

"I offered to buy a couple of the paintings, though where I thought I would get the money at that stage God only knows. He refused. But he wanted me to talk about the ones I had chosen. He wanted me to tell him a story about what was going on between the man and the woman in the paintings, was adamant. She has this anger in her – I remember saying that to him – she is torn apart. This about a woman serenely looking out a window toward water while a man sits far from her gazing at the wall, He is addicted to her, I said, and he resents this. Pain – no, hopelessness – is everywhere. I never talk this way, by the way, never. But on I went. They are both, I said, searching for a betrayal on the part of the other and yet they are fused together in some impossible way. It wasn't long before I was describing my most intimate moments with the woman, the joy of those moments, and then the awful chill that followed. The ambivalence, the wanting it to end, and then the terrible fear that it would." Harding slapped his palm on the table. "Never, I tell you, never get involved . . ." He turned his hand over and examined the palm. "But I've already said that," he added quietly.

"So time passed. And she and I painted in our separate studios and showed in group exhibitions. Once or twice these events took place in another city and we were able to spend the night together, which only made things worse. Afterwards I could feel myself withdrawing, wanting to ignore her. It could be I was hoping she would leave me because it was clear I wasn't going to be able to destroy this on my own, though it was also clear that I was trying to do just that. Sometimes she would go cold for a time, not answer her door when I arrived at her studio, stay out of my way when we found ourselves in the same places. But she would turn toward me eventually and there would be this wash of over-whelming relief, and things would be clean between us, for a while.

"I was beside myself nine-tenths of the time and my work reflected this in the best of all possible ways. Now there's an irony," he said. There were times when he wondered if the whole thing had been designed to keep him raw and fierce for his work in the studio. Still, he dismissed this as nonsense. "At that point," he said, "I wanted to believe I would do my best work if I could someday achieve peace of mind."

"Did you ever?" Kenneth asked.

"Achieve peace of mind? Yes," he said, wrapping both hands, one atop the other, around the glass. "Yes, and what a featureless, boring landscape *that* is."

He had begun to take the woman along when he went to visit Gentleman. The old boy really took to her, he said, even allowing her to photograph half a dozen pieces, something that Harding knew would never have happened had he himself been making the request. They brought groceries and sometimes liquor to the reclusive painter. "We had no notion of where he got the little bit of money in his possession and doubted that he was feeding himself in any regular sort of way," he said. "She would bring along some cheese and bread and would heat a can of soup when we were there. And he would eat it. He took to her, as I said. And she, for her part, was absolutely entranced, as was I, by the pictures."

"You must have tried to get him a show somewhere."

"That would have been impossible. There was nothing anyone, even her, could say or do to convince him the work should be shown. He simply refused, sometimes quite impatiently. 'You two,' he would say, 'understand nothing about the personal. You can't make a circus out of the personal; you can't make a song and dance out of it. These are my *personal* possessions. This is my *personal* property.' Eventually she stopped even mentioning it. I would bring it up and she would glance at me with this disapproving look. Still, we enjoyed our visits with him. And it gave us something to talk about during our times together: a sort of joint project. Care and nurturing. That sort of thing."

All of this had been a weird sort of comfort to them, he added, providing what seemed like a steadiness of purpose to their relationship, almost as if the old man had been their child, someone valuable and fragile whom they shared and protected. It had almost looked as if they were happy for a while.

Harding's face darkened. "On our last visit to that basement together, Gentleman mentioned her husband. Where is your man today? he asked. And there was something about his tone that made me realize that she had brought him, had brought her husband, into this world I thought belonged only to us. We had so little, you see. I thought we had so little beyond our own painting and showing, beyond our own uneasy entanglement. And then this. She had so deliberately, so thoughtlessly, allowed her husband into this odd little piece of world I thought I had given to her. Her alone."

Kenneth was confused. Couldn't quite see how that would matter. "What did you do?" he asked.

"I was furious, stormed out of the basement. Just left her there. What had been taken from me, I realized, was this peculiar kind of hope, a hope that I had barely acknowledged to myself and never to her."

"And that ended it."

"You would think so," Harding said, but no, it hadn't been the end. Just the beginning of the end. She had come to his studio a few days later, and had asked why she shouldn't allow her husband, who was interested, apparently, and wanted to meet Gentleman, to see the work. He'd looked at the photographs, after all, and he pestered her to see the real thing. This encounter with Gentleman had lifted her husband's spirits in some way or another. And that, according to her, was a good thing. "There was no reasonable answer to this, of course," Harding said. "But for ten minutes or so, while she was explaining this to me, I thought – and it is the only time in my life that I have felt this way about a woman – I thought I might strike her. I hated everything about myself at that moment. Everything. There was no generosity in me. None. The truth was, I didn't want anything about her life without me to be better in any way. I wanted her to be suffering my absence, not worrying about whether or not her husband was happy, or worse, trying to make him happy, even though I was busily making my own wife happy as much as I could. But it didn't end. Not then. Not yet." He took another mouthful of his drink and touched Kenneth's glass. "I expect you to drink at least two glasses of beer," he said.

Kenneth dutifully raised his glass and looked across the table at his teacher. Even in the face of this confession, he was having trouble picturing Harding as a younger man, one filled with conflict, passion.

In the end they had had one more year. "I couldn't bear it that she was visiting Gentleman with her husband, but I couldn't stop her either. And I still couldn't stop us, so I withdrew completely from Gentleman and never, believe me, never said a word about it, or about him – or about his work again." He began to toy with a salt shaker on the table. "And neither," he said, "did she. Not a word."

Kenneth was starting to pay attention to the pint in front of him. He was wondering how a human body managed to absorb such a quantity of liquid.

"And then came the New York show," Harding said, "the show in which all three of us participated. Her husband, I mean. And her. And me. There were two other painters in this show as well. She hadn't told me that her husband would be among us, and of course I resented this. I didn't want him to be real, you see, wanted him to continue playing the role I had invented for him, that role of the invisible man, the mediocre artist and lacklustre mate. I could cope with the notion that she had two men in her life, but not two painters. I had everyone's roles so neatly defined. And – have I said this? – I loved, I love my wife, had absolutely no intention of leaving her."

Everything about his reaction, he admitted, was unfair – his deception concerning his own wife, the way he wanted the other woman's undivided attention, his cavalier, dismissive attitude toward her husband's work.

"I had seen her husband's stuff before, you see, and knew there wasn't much in it. So I was able to ignore it. Frankly, I didn't even believe he would be able to see how extraordinary Gentleman was. That's the story I told myself about all that, about him, when I allowed myself to think about it at all, which was as seldom as possible."

Kenneth swallowed several mouthfuls of beer while Harding watched. "Good," the teacher said, "More. No? You sure? Okay." He leaned over and picked his coat up off the floor. Kenneth wondered if the session were over. But Harding turned, arranged the garment on the back of the chair, and resumed. "The trip to New York on the bus was hell. They sat together, naturally, but I was alone, hunched in the back of the bus. Strange word, *hunch*, in that it applies to premonition as well as to position, as if you are crouching in the face of some anticipated attack." He suddenly straightened in his chair and cocked his head toward the bar and the radio that was playing there. "Touchdown for the Steelers," he said. "My wife is a football fan. I can take it or leave it."

His wife had given up on openings years before, he said. "It's not that she isn't interested in my work – she is – but all the social niceties, the chat and pretension: she finds it intolerable. She'd had enough of that early on." He paused. "And she wasn't wrong about that either, just in case you are wondering. She was dead right. But that is another conversation."

"So you went to New York," Kenneth said, beginning to feel the alcohol now. It had numbed the embarrassment and opened him to the story.

"Yes. The show was called 'Five Painters from Pennsylvania.' It was in some kind of public building, a library or community centre or something. It was curated by one of the bigger museums, but someone had decided that this city museum should move into the community somehow. I suppose bringing in the Pennsylvanians, a bunch of painters from the provinces, had something to do with that. I barely remember what it was all about because of what happened next."

Kenneth waited, sliding the glass in his hand back and forth on the table.

"I saw his paintings, her husband's new paintings, is what happened." Harding was still gazing in the direction of the bar.

"Yes . . . and?"

"They were brilliant! Stunning! The people there when we arrived, they were all gathered on his side of the room."

"But you said . . ."

"I know, I know. But he had changed completely, or at least his work had. Suddenly the paintings were luxuriant and inclusive, though oddly vacant as well. I still think, though, that I may have been – no, *she* and I may have been – the only ones there who could see this odd vacancy." Harding massaged his forehead with his free hand, then leaned back in his chair. "No matter," he continued. "The certainty with which the paint was applied, the surface texture, was so galvanizing it was as if no one could turn away from it. That's the only thing I can say. The pictures were galvanizing! They leapt off the canvas and entered the room! Collectors were swooping down on them. Critics were discussing them – there were only about ten paintings in all – but there would be half a dozen major articles in subsequent weeks." And six months later the husband had had a one-man show at the Rehn Gallery with, Kenneth assumed, more and more of this extraordinary work. Harding had never looked at anything the husband did again. "Too painful. And the rest was, as they say, history. Everyone who had known him before, and had known his work before, was astonished," Harding said. "And it *was* astonishing. The trouble was, none of it was his."

Kenneth was beginning to catch on. "He had stolen Gentleman's paintings."

Harding was silent for a bit. Then he shook himself out of that. "No. Nothing that simple. He had stolen the tone – I almost want to say the soul of Gentleman's paintings. He had stolen his colour scheme, his brushwork, even his ability to portray vulnerability. His subjects, too, though he had changed those subjects just enough that they had become his own subjects. And I knew, I knew, goddammit, he had been spending the previous couple of years absorbing everything he could about Gentleman's tone and touch, his layering, his use of light and his rendering of the absence of light. And she and I were the only people who would ever know." During the first few minutes of his triumph, Harding could see the husband change before his eyes from someone who was timid and unsure into an artist fully in control of the work he now allowed himself to believe he had created all on his own. "I could tell that in those few moments everything about Gentleman was being erased from his mind."

"And you didn't say anything."

"What could I do? I was in love with her. And I could see it in her – she was glowing – she wanted this triumph for him as much as he wanted it for himself."

"But I thought . . ."

Harding was not listening. "It's that overwhelming desire for the spoils of talent that makes things like this possible. You must never, ever want another artist's vision," he told Kenneth, "no matter how large or how small that vision might be, no matter where the appropriation takes you. No

matter what rooms it allows you entry into, what kind of
fame it garners. Because, even if you are a moral person, if
the wanting starts to own you, you will finally succumb to it
and, mark my words, you will decide to commit the crime.
And no real good can come of it." Harding crumpled an
empty cigarette package in his fist. "The making of art isn't
all that important, you know, in the larger scheme of things."

Kenneth did not believe this, vowed silently that he would
never believe this. Art was everything. There was nothing
larger.

Harding, who had been leaning forward, making his
point, collapsed back into his chair. "She and I exchanged
one long look at the opening, and during that look we
acknowledged that I knew how the paintings happened and
that I would never say a word about this to anyone. I can't
tell you how shattering . . ." He was looking away now, not
meeting Kenneth's gaze. "And, she and I, we never spoke or
saw each other privately again." There had been no final
act; they both had known it was over. Harding had seen
how much she loved her husband. And he had also seen that
this burglary was not the act of a single person, it was an
act of love on her part: they were in it together. "Except for
one thing," he said. Harding and the husband had exchanged
a look as well. "Maybe this was only my own distorted lens
at work," Harding said to Kenneth, "but it appeared to me
that he was sneering, as if these pictures were acts of
revenge. As if," he said, "by completing them he had stolen
everyone's talent and dismissed the whole idea of the

importance of original work. Gentleman's original work, my original work, and, worst of all, hers. It was a tragedy. For him, she would forget all about us, about Gentleman, all about herself."

Harding was slowly shaking his head.

"And Gentleman? You must have seen him, talked to him."

"I went back to see him one more time. But by then he was fully lost, dying. He *did* die not much later. It would have been cruel to tell him, and anyway, I doubted he would believe me – there were times, late at night, when I didn't even believe myself. And what could anyone have done?" Whatever the case, he, Gentleman, had succeeded in destroying much of his own work by then, though a couple of the smaller paintings had escaped – who knows how, maybe he himself arranged it, though Harding doubted this – to public galleries.

Harding stood now and put on his overcoat. Then he sat down again. Kenneth zipped up his own jacket, which he had never taken off. He realized he'd been poised for flight ever since they entered the bar. Harding placed his hands on the arms of his chair as if to rise again, but then he hesitated. "Over the years," he said, "I've wondered if I dissolved for her as thoroughly as she dissolved for me. I expect that's likely the case. And perhaps that's what she wanted all along. Maybe she wanted something that would simply cancel me out. She had handed everything that we were together to her husband, all the power of that. And as I said, when they – no, he – when he erased Gentleman, and her, he erased me." He stood again and tied his plaid scarf around his neck. "And perhaps – it certainly looked that way to me that night – perhaps that's what she always wanted."

More than a decade later, working on the Gander mural, Kenneth held Harding in his mind, a constant presence and a necessary absence. Even what the teacher had taught him, about the distribution of lights and darks, about weighting and composition, had to be remembered and then discarded by him. The piece would explore speed and stasis without ever coming down on the side of one or the other, without making judgments. It would only be the children who would hold an opinion, and it would be an opinion so mysterious it might simply be a certainty about the persistence of mystery. Wisdom without judgment.

THE ESSENTIAL

—

R oads had become everything to Kieran.

There were the roads leading to the town and they had their own enchantments. On them he would see cottages inhabited by those he felt now were his own people, those who worked every day on the land and who rose before dawn on Wednesdays to take animals to the market. Sometimes very early he would come upon the odd hermit, who had night-walked down into the town to drink in a public house and was now sleeping under a hedgerow in the first light, fuchsia hanging above him like drops of sacred blood, a stone for a pillow.

There were other roads that coaxed his bicycle into the mountains: green roads flanked by deserted villages or villages where a single old woman held stubbornly on, with one cow, dependent on a son or nephew to call up to her to replace a rusted gutter, or to deliver supplies of flour, turf, and tea, her whole world one of memories, ghosts, and weather. In her would be the names of places where people had not lived for generations and the sense of ancient bones, those of the victims of the famine and those of the old monks who chose solitude in such isolated locations. There was one old woman who told Kieran she was the keeper of the nearby Killeen, an ancient burial place for unbaptized children. It was situated in the stony, sloping field next to her cottage and she had come, over the years, to believe that the lumpy ground of the place owned her in some important way. Slowly, slowly, she told Kieran, she was giving names to the unnamed children who slept there, and gradually they had come to her to tell her the ways in which they had died. One at time they came to her, she said, "in all their beauty." She had rocked them in her arms. She had sung lullabies to them, and sometimes they had sung back to her, melodies so pure only the Old Ones could receive them. By this he knew she was one of the Old Ones. And he was not. "Be careful of my babies," she called to him as he cycled away, past the Killeen. "Don't startle their sleep."

And then there were the roads that led to the headlands: Bray Head, Hog's Head, and Bolus. It was at the opening to the latter that he met the poet of the peninsula – "the one essential teacher that we all need and that some of us are lucky enough to find," Niall had said to Tam when he spoke to her about this. It was McWilliams for him, he told her, and a man called Michael Kirby for his brother.

Kieran had cycled on a road that seemed to be a funnel of gravity into the village of Ballinskelligs faster than even he would have thought possible, crashing down the potholed road from Killeen Leacht, over the main road and then onto a smaller road beside what had been a modest landlord's demesne, its stone wall slipping by his shoulder smooth as a long grey eel. Behind that wall, Annie had told him, was a man in a small, new cottage, one who was using the burnt-out manor house as a barn for his tractor. Gerry and his mountain-talking mates, she confided, had burnt that house, and she had a terrible aversion to it as a result, and had forbidden Kieran to do even as much as look over the wall for fear of reprisal. "But *I* didn't burn the house, Annie," he had said to her reasonably enough. "The Black and Tans don't ask you that when they come to get you," she had replied. "But there are no more of them here now," he had told her, only to be greeted with a look indicating that the innocent of the earth rarely go unpunished.

But, notwithstanding his curiosity, he sped by the entrance on this late September morning, in love with his own need to cover ground. He might have turned down to the Tra, the beach that extended for miles at this point and that was made of sand hard enough that horses could be ridden on it and bicycles could travel smoothly over it, but it was the road and the land he wanted on this day, not the water.

There was a light fog gathering that thickened as he crossed a bog, so that when Kieran flew through the hamlet of Dungeagan, the houses were softened by mist. Two miles later, entering the quiet townland of Ballinskelligs, he came to a halt at a nest of narrow tracks. He wanted to be out at the very end of things, the limits of the headland, but it was

unclear how he was to proceed, so he stopped and, still strad-
dling the bicycle, lit a cigarette – a new and secret pleasure –
and wondered why he had never come here before. The girl
stepped back into his mind, but he pushed her image away.
She came to him again, however, and he heard himself whisper her name, in a prayerful kind of way. He was immediately
embarrassed by this, as if his brother or his father, or worse,
the girl herself, might have heard, and he turned his attention
forcibly to the decision before him.

He knew about the road that rose above the cliffs and
skirted the headland, so he determined to follow the track
that curved up into the haze, and had placed one foot on the
pedal when he heard a male voice behind him. "I'd have that
bicycle for myself," the voice said, "if you weren't so obviously fond of it." Kieran turned to see a very tall, dark-haired
figure approaching him.

The man was broad-shouldered, with long, muscular
arms. His carriage was straight and slim, almost graceful, but
even his most casual movements suggested an extreme physical strength, a deliberate sort of energy, which was startling
on such a soft day. He wore a blue jumper, which matched his
eyes, one that was knitted in a traditional pattern common to
the region. On his feet was a pair of large, well-worn, but still
firmly intact leather boots. His hand when he offered it was
rough and clean. "Michael Kirby," the man said.

Kieran threw his cigarette on the ground, uncomfortable
suddenly about having been caught with it in his hand. The
man scooped it up, placed it between his lips, and drew deeply

on it. "Ah, tobacco," he said, "I gave it up over a decade ago. That which one has abandoned always tastes sweeter." He dropped the cigarette and crushed it under his boot. "I know who you are and have been expecting you. Did Davey tell you about me?"

"No," said Kieran tentatively, "he did not."

"Well, he told me a great deal about you."

Kieran was taken aback by this. He had seen the tailor only infrequently, but once recently, all right, when it was clear that his coat sleeves hung only to his elbows and that a new garment was a necessity. I thought I was supposed to be buried in this thing, he had said to Annie while he attempted unsuccessfully to pull the two sides of it across his expanded ribcage. She allowed that she was appalled by the extent to which he had grown and had sent him off alone on the bicycle to visit the tailor's house.

"He said quite a lot about wheels," the man continued, "and a not inconsiderable amount about velocity as well. And here you are, with two wheels under you, though not as much velocity as I had anticipated." Mr. Kirby settled himself down on the nearby stone wall. "I suppose the velocity will come to you like. You are built for it, I'd say." He looked Kieran over. "Small and wiry."

Kieran smarted at the word *small*. He was already eighteen and hadn't grown as much as he'd wanted.

"You may still grow perpendicularly," Kirby said, as if reading Kieran's mind. "But you are far too high-strung to grow horizontally. I myself grew, perpendicularly, six more inches after the age of eighteen. My mother had to give me regular doses of onion syrup to slow the growing down or who knows where it might have ended."

Kieran smiled, taking hope from the story.

Kirby continued, "I am a fisherman and, as a result, I have four hundred and twenty-three different kinds of skies in my head." He tapped his skull for effect. "And I am a poet . . . but only when I am thinking in Irish. When I am thinking in English I am a fisherman and a painter, though admittedly I have not painted anything yet. I will, however, and when I do, I will paint all those skies."

"You have that many," Kieran said.

"All decent fishermen have those skies," Kirby assured him, "because of survival. The skies not only tell you what the weather is . . . they tell you what it will be and that, my friend, is much more important. I would recommend that you gather at least a hundred or so skies yourself because of the bicycle, on which, I predict, you are going to be spending the majority of your time in the next years. One thing those skies have taught me is the value of accurate prediction. I'd have been fish food if it weren't for them. I also have predicted that, although I will desperately want to do so, once I become a painter, I will never paint a nude. Wouldn't you love to paint a nude?"

Kieran was uncertain how to answer this shockingly exciting question. He had never let his imagination roam beyond Susan's yellow blouse and the cloud of her hair. Well, that wasn't quite true, but . . .

"As for the bicycle, I would recommend that you start training in earnest. You should begin with your mind because you are going to need it more than you know. Next Thursday, which the skies tell me will be calm and bright, I will take you out to the Skelligs. You must spend two days out there, alone in a beehive hut, without the bicycle. This will be your starting point. What do you know about the Skelligs?"

Kieran had learned in the school that the Skelligs was the name of the two sacred islands that he had seen rising from the sea a few miles off the end of the peninsula. The master had said that in the sixth century there had been holy men out there living a sparse life in corbelled huts on one of the islands' tallest peaks. Cycling near the shore, Kieran had seen the islands, and each time they had looked like formations entirely different from the ones he had seen a few days or a few weeks before.

"There were monks . . ." Kieran offered.

"Not only monks." Kirby waved the holy men away with his hand for the time being. "Absolutely terrible weather, the sea, the birds of the sea, and down at the edge, the fish of the sea, stones, beehive huts, an oratory, a burial ground, one donkey, which is the only thing you will be riding, as there are absolutely no bicycles. And this donkey has been dead for thirteen centuries, so for you it will be the donkey of the imagination. You will be riding the donkey of the imagination, a very good donkey to ride, I'd say."

"I'm not sure I can go."

"And when I say absolutely terrible weather, I mean terrible in the true sense of the word. Awe-inspiring weather! Great bolts of sun slicing through the clouds, rains that drown, winds that roar and shake the island from within, impenetrable fog – not like this fog" – Kirby swung his arm in the direction Kieran intended to go – "but fog that blinds and deafens and causes that stillness that is the true beginning of velocity, followed by the kind of clarity that causes you to wince."

"I might have to work that day, in town."

"Your father should have completed his training out on Skellig Michael, but I fear he did not. But that man he works with, McWilliams, he knew enough to go out there now and then."

Had his father ever been out to this island? Kieran did not know.

"We must respect the weather station, though," said Kirby, his mind having moved for a moment away from the islands to the shore. "They have those extraordinary balloons that go places we can't go – except on the donkey of the imagination, of course – and see things we cannot see. And then there is McWilliams, who as far as I've heard knows everything about everything. They say he knows about poetry, they say he knows about painting, but that he is completely disinterested in these things unless they relate to weather. And then your own father, who works there, and his extraordinary punctuality. It was him, thirty years ago during the time of the shooting, it was him who had the courage to walk out to the balloon house and to set the balloon free while the fighting was going on in the street above. Such a young man at the time, as well, just starting." Kirby sighed, as if mourning the young man that Kieran's father had once been.

"Yes," said Kieran, remembering his father's dependability, how those balloons had to be launched each day at an exact time, without exceptions. His mother's voice came back to him then, the words suddenly clear. *He launched them even on the day of my death*, his mother whispered, reminding him, *even then. And the day he discovered my death as well.* "Yes, that too," Kieran added, looking away into the fog.

"What too?" asked Kirby.

"Nothing."

"Well, nothing is the right place to start when it is extreme velocity you're after." Kirby stood, ready now to allow the monks into the conversation.

> Humble Anchorites
> Your ravaged cells
> Are prayerless tonight
> But flagstones
> Whisper yet,
> And kittiwakes
> In the cave

"The last verse of a poem I wrote," said Kirby, "but useless without the melodious Irish I wrote it in. Of late, I have been composing poems of farewell to everything I know, animate and inanimate, in event of my death. You look surprised? You are correct: I have no intention of dying anytime soon.

But I have been intimate with so many things, so many, it will take decades for me to give everything its due. I began with the first thing I remembered: a cup that my own children have since used. After that it was a particular flagstone on the floor. We had a flagged floor, you see, many did not. And that flag's still there up at Cill Rialaig, though the rest of the house is in ruins. Nothing ruined about the view out the window, though, and there is a poem about that as well. You would be wise to try some poetry yourself, to say in your mind during the race. The old ones could compose and then memorize twenty thousand lines at a time. I have not yet decided whether you should compose before . . . out on Skellig Michael, for example . . . or during the race. Perhaps both. A dreadful pity that you don't have the Irish. But perhaps this English language serves you better, though *that* is difficult to believe."

Kieran found himself focusing on the man's face, the intensity of his eyes. He knew he himself would not be composing poetry. "What race?" he asked.

Kirby looked surprised. "The Rás Tailteann, of course," he said. "Davey allowed as you're the only one for it, though you've only two years to train. It is a hard thing, the Rás, but you are the only one for it. All around Ireland, you'll cycle, stage by stage. By the time you're fitted up and strong enough for it, the Rás will be in its third year. The first one was a glorious free-for-all with the boys from Tipperary quarrelling with the boys from Mayo, and everyone quarrelling with the Ulster Constabulary in the North. But the third Rás will be more settled-like, more dignified. And it is important that you win."

Kieran was silent, not knowing what to make of this. He had never thought about winning anything.

"With that in mind, I make an appointment with you to meet me at the pier Thursday next, seven in the morning, and we will set out. You must get Gerry-Annie to pack enough bread and cheese, some apples as well" – he laughed – "for the donkey."

Kieran remained silent, not wishing to verbally comply. And yet he knew he had already decided to go.

"But Tadhg out on the end there" – Kirby gestured once again toward the road Kieran had chosen – "will have more advice to give you on this and various other important subjects. He is a great one for the advice, Tadhg is, being the last old man of Europe and all, as he'll undoubtedly tell you himself. Off you go then, off to Bolus Head. Stop by the collapsed Anchorite site on the way, if you can find it. There are some huts there looking toward the sea, and a little chapel as well, though it is all just piles of stone now." He looked toward the west. "And once you get up there far enough, you'll come to a green road you'll want to take for the view of the Skelligs that can be had from there. There is an abandoned barracks as well." Kirby paused. "In fact, you won't be able to take that road, now that I think of it. Its gate will almost certainly be closed against you."

Kieran sat on the leather seat of his bicycle and Michael Kirby gave him a push as he headed up the hill in the mist. As he drove his feet into the pedals, he heard Kirby call after him. "No one has been able to get it open," he shouted, "no one." And then as if an afterthought, "Until Thursday."

This is what Kieran could not see as the road under his wheels rose through the haze toward the top of the headland. He could not see Ballinskelligs Bay, or Horse Island curving like a smile in its centre, or the old castle walls on a smaller island near the shore. He could not see the ruined abbey or the many graves that surrounded it, the cliffs that stood angry and dark, and the inlets that narrowed toward hidden sea caves. He passed between the few huddled houses of Cill Rialaig, where the sound of soft Irish voices and the smell of turf mingled with the crunch of his wheels on loose stones. A little farther up, he slipped by large shadows in the shape of gables: the ruins of a previous Cill Rialaig, whose citizens, years before, had walked away; driven mad, some said, by the wind. Minutes later the shape of a small National School was evident. The yard, which hugged the road, was filled with the singing racket of children out for recess. As he pedalled past, the sound of the master's hand-bell was in the air and the children fell silent.

When he rounded a bend that took him higher again, the fog began to thin. Kieran could now pick out the features of the landscape on either side of him, though he could still not see the ocean, which, though breathing noisily below, remained invisible. The dark exclamation mark of a standing stone in a downward-sloping field caught his attention, and then another, several yards away. He stopped, dismounted, leaned the bicycle against a wall, and climbed the stone stile into the site.

He had always avoided such places. The death of his mother was knit into his memory of visiting St. Brendan's Well on Valentia. And yet, these stones before him now seemed benign. He half expected his mother would speak to him here, but she did not. Instead it was the girl who came into his mind. *Leave a token now*, she said, *leave a love token*. He pictured her in his brother's arms and was angered by the persistence of her image, as if she were pestering him in some way or another. Still, fumbling in his pocket he found the shell of a snail he had picked from Gerry-Annie's wall the previous day, and he placed this on the oratory steps. Sensing, as he did so, how foolish he would seem to the girl, could she see him doing this, he quickly left the place and remounted his bicycle.

Alone on the road Kieran considered the mysterious third Rás, how the fact of training for it was emerging from the mist and tapping him on the shoulder, what Kirby had said; the conviction in him! It was as if Kirby had been intimate with him for years and was certain of exactly what it was he should do. He looked down at the bicycle, and as he did, a flicker of what he would later come to know as ambition moved through his nervous system. But the sensation was so foreign to him he couldn't say precisely what it was. Only that he was happiest when he was on the bike with the road gliding under him.

As he moved upwards and away from the Anchorite ruins, the fog lifted sufficiently so that he could see the end of the headland. One arm of the road bent to the left and ended at a small farm, the shape of the house only faintly visible through the fog along with the lines of ancient and irregular fields filled with the soft, pale smudges of sheep. Just in advance of this, the green road Michael Kirby had spoken of climbed to the height of land where the barracks squatted against the sky, a vaguely rectangular shape. Kieran predicted that the view from there could not be had on such a misty day. Another cloud of mist crept between him and the road. And then he heard the voices, tender, sorrowful, an old man and an old woman speaking Irish.

They appeared before him, emerging from the atmosphere as if at the end of a long journey. In English, the woman said, "I've hurt my hand and my heart trying to do it, and I cannot. And he says that he cannot."

"I cannot," the man said, turning to the fence that fronted the green road. "And she cannot either." He fingered his wife's shawl affectionately.

Kieran did not know how to respond. "Cannot what?" he asked.

"Cannot open the gate," said the man. "It has been sealed shut forever by winds and rains. And haven't I cattle up there going astray, right at the very end of Europe? And me, the final old man of Europe, unable to reach them, unable to go to the edge, unable to herd my own kine. There's a pity in that." He shook his head sadly. "I might, for all they know, have gone to Chicago, there's that much separation between me and them."

"One might have calved," said the woman.

"Yes, there might be a calf. Or one might have died over the winter. It's a terrible thing not to know the condition of your own small herd. They are *some* beautiful, those cattle."

Kieran dropped his bicycle on the road and sprinted toward the gate. There was this fierce desire in him to rescue the man's cattle. "I will climb the fence and bring them down to you."

"Ah no," said the man, "it's myself they know. They, being the final cattle of Europe, out there on the farthest western edge of everything and all, would never permit themselves to be driven by any other."

Kieran was grasping the gate so tightly he could feel the roughness of it pressing into his palm.

"I live down there," the old man continued, throwing his arm behind him toward the houselike form that Kieran had previously noticed, two fields from the road, "and those cattle know that. My name is Tadhg and I live with my wife, Tadhg-Sheila" — he bowed ceremoniously in her direction — "and those cattle know her as well. Those cattle want nothing to change; I can assure you of that. And they are lonely for me, by now, those cattle. No stranger could console them. They've been waiting for a terrible amount of time." He sighed. His wife bent her head and examined the hand she had hurt, wincing as she did so.

Kieran had never felt strong. He was small, but some said, Kirby had said it, wiry. Suddenly, in the face of the couple's sorrow, there was this eager potency in him. He grasped a large stone at the side of the road, ran to the gate, and, lifting his arms over his head, pounded the orange-coloured latch for what could have been minutes or could have been hours: he would never be able to accurately say later. At last the bolt fractured and the gate sprang open.

The woman let out a cry, whether from gladness or from shock Kieran could not decide.

Then she began to sing, or to pray, in Irish.

The man walked toward him with his hands in the air, jubilant. "What you have done for us! What you have *done* for us! I thank you! My wife thanks you. The beautiful final cattle of Europe thank you! The last pasture at the very end of Europe thanks you!"

Kieran was silent. Opening the gate had taken more strength than cycling Ballagh Oisin Pass at full speed, and he was gasping for air.

"I have some advice for you, boy" said Tadhg. "At Puck Fair in Killorglin, there is the day of the gathering, the day of the fair, and the day of the scattering. Far too many think it is the day of the fair that is most important, and they will tell you that over and over. But Tadhg has been placed on this road to tell you that, in your life, there will never be anything more important than the day of the gathering. The anticipation, the training, the goal! The day of the fair is nothing but a pale ghost announcing the day of the scattering. If I could, I would be your coach and we would prolong the day of the gathering as long as we could, and postpone, as far as possible, the day of the fair. But didn't you open the very gate that keeps me here on this road where I am saying this? And now don't I and my darling" – he touched his wife's shawl again – "have to pass through it to greet our kine, the final few cattle of Europe that have been expecting us for so long? Goodbye my liberator," he said, "the race is yours to do with what you will." He took his wife's arm and they began to climb the road. Just before they disappeared from view Tadhg turned back to Kieran, who was still recovering from the exertion necessary to move the gate. "What a fine coach I would have made, being a man with advice and all," he called back to him, "but there is no time for that now. In my absence I appoint Michael Kirby. He'll do the job well."

The following week, Kieran met Kirby at Ballinskelligs Pier. Gerry-Annie had been skeptical when he told her where he was going, and didn't hold back expressing her concern. "And you complaining about going to the church," she said, "suddenly wanting to make this pilgrimage! It doesn't seem likely to me with you wanting to be on the roads day after day and that bicycle under you. You'll have no bicycle out there on the holy island. And you'll catch your death, or be blown right off the top of it into the waves, most likely – it's happened before, you know." Still, she packed some bread for him, a bit of ham, and several hunks of cheese. She also placed a candle in the bag, along with a small tin containing matches. He would not tell her about the race, though it had settled in his mind. It was only the girl, really, the thought of her waiting for him at its glorious conclusion, that made him want to do it. Or so he thought. He was still innocent of his own peculiar determination.

The day was not as fine as Kirby's skies had predicted. When Kieran pointed this out, hoping for a reprieve, Kirby said that it was very fine indeed in relation to what he might encounter on the island. And because there was next to no wind, landing would be achievable without his much-loved boat being smashed to kindling on the rocks. While the boat heaved and dove with the swell on the journey across, Kirby identified sea birds, demanded that Kieran do the same, mildly berating him when he could not do so. How was it possible he did not even know a gannet when he saw one? The heads of seals appeared beside the boat, a staring crowd filled with curiosity. "No fish today," Kirby called to them.

Then he turned to Kieran. "While you are there it would be good for your legs if you ran up and down the six hundred steps a dozen times a day. And don't complain about it either, not even to yourself. Be grateful that you didn't have to build the six hundred steps. Be grateful that those monks were such good engineers that you don't even have to *repair* the six hundred steps these thirteen hundred years after they built them. And once you have achieved gratitude, it might be a very good idea if you thought about the other things you have to be grateful for, starting with your heart and breath. Blood and oxygen. And where does that blood and oxygen go? To your muscles, of course. Be grateful for the well-engineered steps whose existence and persistence are sending buckets of blood and windstorms full of oxygen to those muscles. And don't forget your bones. The cage of your ribs that holds everything together, the long bones of your legs that carry your muscles around, and this bone" – Kirby knocked on his skull – "beautifully designed to take care of the most important muscle of them all. Use that muscle when you are running." Kirby leaned forward and tapped Kieran's forehead. "You'll need it to pay attention when the steps are slippery with rain, and you'll need it when it is not raining to reflect upon all the other things you have to be grateful for. That and the naming; I want you to be able to name everything, animate and inanimate, that you cycle past, and be grateful for most of it, and outraged at that which no sane man could be grateful for. What's that bird, by the way? You don't know, of course. Well, you will when I am finished with you. For now you must be grateful, first and foremost, that you are alive at this time and with the proper age on you, with muscles, brain, bone, blood and oxygen, and the desire in you to win this race."

The islands grew in size at the bow of the boat, rising and falling with the waves. The Great Skellig was a dark and intractable triangle. The Lesser Skellig was white with birds – gannets and puffins – so plentiful that the rocks were all but invisible. When Kieran turned his face toward the land, the green-and-brown seam of shoreline tilted back and forth. It was as if the mountains were weighing heavily on one side, then on the other. Then the Great Skellig, very large now, threw its shadow into the boat.

"Here, take the motor," Kirby said. He staggered toward the bow of the boat then, still standing, legs apart, bent over to unspool a coil of rope. "Watch the colours deepen," he commanded, throwing one arm up toward the island. He explained that as you drew nearer, the various shades of colour always intensified; purples and blues on dark days, deep greens and silvers when there was sun.

After Kirby had deposited him on the flat slab of rock that served as the island's quay and had floated away, Kieran stood for a long while watching the birds from the Lesser Skellig lift and fall in the air like white ash and listening to their other-worldly cries. His mother came to him, then but he found that he did not want to hear her when he was so close to the sea, so he began to climb the six hundred steps, easing into a trot, once he was certain of the stability of the rock beneath his shoes. By the time he reached the island's Anchorite site, a chapel and a group of corbelled huts, at the summit, the wind had picked up and he feared it would begin to rain.

But although the day grew darker and colder, no rain fell. As Kirby had instructed, he spent the remainder of the day running up and down the steps, panting and sweating on the way up and terrified that he might lose his footing on the way down, wondering all the while what it was about the man, and about himself, that made him so willing to do what he said. At the end of one last climb he passed through the wall that surrounded the Anchorite site, trotted by the few standing stones of its graveyard, and collapsed with his back to a corbelled stone hut.

The wind came again, stronger than before, a living presence in the dusk, and full of sound. At one point, while Kieran was eating some of the food Annie had put in his satchel, he was certain he could hear the rocks above him rattling, and he thought the hut might collapse, killing him and making his burial site like those of the famine graves he had seen with Donal in the mountains. Finally, the weather became bad enough that he decided to crawl inside.

He could see nothing; the darkness was so total he felt that it might choke or drown him. Eventually, after touching the interior walls of the hut for assurance, he curled on his side and fell into a vacancy so complete he was in the same position when he awakened at dawn the following day.

He came to know almost everything on the island. Small pink flowers, the different kinds of droppings from various sea birds, the stones in the monks' graveyard, particular paving stones, and the way the steps curved around outcroppings of rocks, the grass of the place called Christ's Saddle where the donkey had been.

Late in the afternoon of the second day it began to rain, and great sheets of grey mist climbed the cliffs. He took shelter in the hut, shivering now with cold and knowing he could never achieve comfort. Then he remembered the candle and the tin of matches and he pulled them both from his pouch. The lit candle filled the conical interior with its glow and brought tears to his eyes. He had rarely been so moved.

When he said the word *flame* out loud, there was emotion in his voice. He was grateful for this flame, and he was grateful for the sound of his own voice. When he blew the candle out and lay down on the flags with his eyes closed, he could see the flame's after-image. He let the thoughts of the girl enter him then, without resistance. He was grateful for this as well.

A month or so later, in mid-October, after a particularly gruelling session with Michael Kirby, Kieran revisited the place where he had met Tadhg.

The days were not as long now. There was no longer light in the sky after supper. Kirby had insisted that before sunset Kieran run from the wall near where they met down to the pier and back – a distance of one mile – ten times, while making every effort not to even think about the bicycle. Down the hill, up the hill. "Forget all about the bicycle. Believe your mind and your body are the only things you've got," Kirby shouted whenever Kieran was in view. "Because they are the only things you have got. There is no swiftly moving bicycle without your brain and heart driving it. Rid your mind of machinery! Take all those spokes and wheels and fenders to the mental midden and drop them in. When you finish I want you to describe the remaining wildflowers of the season growing in the hedgerows. Those hedgerows are going to be your neighbours in the race. You'd best get to know them in all seasons."

Wildflowers. Kieran wondered as he ran if the girl knew about such things, and concluded that she would of course.

By the tenth lap he had the blossoms in his mind, one for each run. "A stack of dark pink horns!" he told Kirby while gasping for air, "purple bells, something like white stars, a tall white thing with pins sticking out of it, small pink lanterns hanging down, a little fuzzy ball with sharp leaves, a clump of violet-coloured flowers on a long stem, four yellow petals above a feathery leaf, a yellow button with one white star around it, a rubbery thing with little yellow flowers."

Years later, working with a pickaxe to destroy some hedgerows in England so that a motorway could proceed a mile farther through farms and fields, he would remember the roads of southwest Kerry and wonder if they were still as alive as they had been, still filled with such abundance and disarray.

"Foxglove, harebell, lesser stitchwort, pipewort, St. Debeoc's heath, sea holly, self-heal, tormentil, chamomile, wall pepper," said Kirby. "You've spotted a lot of plants that heal, and that's a good thing. I predict you are going to be needing a lot of healing one way or another."

Kieran smiled at Kirby, mounted the bicycle, and wheeled away. Turning impulsively at the spot where the roads forked, he pedalled up toward the headland. It was a late afternoon of unusual calm: the lowness of the light was such that the edge of Hog's Head opposite was crisp and bright, and the soft shapes of the islands were mirrored in the bay. Cill Rialaig, when he passed it, was alive with children running outdoors, and the ruined houses of the abandoned Old Cill Rialaig stood stark and vacant against a deep blue sky. Farther along, the reflection of the lowering sun shone in each of the school's roadside windows. A man shearing a sheep in a field nearby waved to him. He returned the greeting, rounded a bend, and wheeled past the now open gate and the green road that rose behind it toward the place where he had seen the shape of Tadhg's house in the fog, but he came to a halt once the cottage swung into view.

Everything about the structure was green; even the panes of cracked glass in the windows were covered with an emerald mould. The thatch of the roof was barely visible under the grass and weeds that grew in it among a wealth of tall deep-pink flowers that Kieran now knew were called foxgloves. Moss covered the fieldstone walls. The chimney had collapsed, and lay, a mass of soot-covered plaster and stone, in the west side of the bramble-filled yard beside the remains of a tin roof that must have at one time surmounted the shed or cow byre that occupied the corner of an adjacent field.

Kieran stood looking at the cottage, one foot on the ground, the other still resting on the left pedal of the bicycle. No one, he knew, had lived in this house for many years: the fact of absence was palpable even in the twisted rhododendron bush in the yard. The few blossoms that in spite of obvious neglect had struggled into bloom in May now hung sodden and inert. No woman had picked them to place in a jar near the hearth. No woman and no man had moved in or out of this broken door for years.

It was as if, at this moment, the present and eternity came to him simultaneously and the strangeness of this shook him. He couldn't find it in himself to approach the cottage, but neither could he turn away. His limbs felt heavy, immovable, and for a moment or two he believed he might abide in this place forever, that he had been abandoned by time. Then a light breeze feathered the grass between him and the cottage and broke apart the perfect reflection of the headland far below in the bay, and he knew why he had come to Tadhg's door.

He had had a question. The day of the gathering. What did it look like exactly, and how long did it last? Was it a moment or a season . . . perhaps a lifetime? He looked below him across the fields and down to the sea. There were waves approaching the rocks. From this distance they appeared to be so gentle, moving one after the other in a leisurely fashion toward the cliffs, where they broke apart throwing plumes of graceful spray, like the white silent fireworks he had seen at Puck Fair. Behind him, where he knew the green road out to the end began its ascent, he heard the creak of the gate he had opened moving back and forth in the air.

HALLS OF DEPARTURE

N iall had walked into her life from the road, looking for
that same telephone that would become so central to
what did or did not happen between them. She had seen him
through the window, squatting beside a troublesome wheel,
his bicycle lying like a large wounded bird on the gravel.
She had seen him squint upwards to see if there was a telephone wire heading from a pole to her house. He was not
the first traveller to spot that wire, telephones being so rare
in the parish. After he had righted the bicycle and leaned it
against the wall beside her gate, he had walked across her
grass and she heard his knock. "Sorry to trouble you," he
said when she opened the door. She would always remember
that line: *Sorry to trouble you.* "I'm from Cahersiveen," he
added. He nodded in the direction of the bicycle. "I'm afraid
I need to make a call."

"No trouble," she said, holding the door open and
moving to one side so that he could come in.

His wife, he reported after the call, would come to collect him in a Vauxhall not unlike the one that sat in her own lane, but blue not grey. While they waited for her to arrive, there was some awkward talk between them, mostly about the sad condition of the road. In the midst of this, he said he would go outside to remove the back wheel so the bicycle could be put in the boot of the car. Then moving toward the door, he spotted the sailor's valentine and had asked about it. She explained Teddy's grandparents and, conjecturing — she supposed by her accent — that she was on holiday, he'd asked if her husband was out enjoying the mountains or maybe fishing.

"No," she said, embarrassed. "He's dead. He died some time ago."

"Oh," he had said, "sorry."

"Yes," she had said. "I am as well."

"I suppose," he'd said, "it would be better for me to be outside where my wife can see me."

She agreed, though she knew it would take his wife at least another twenty minutes to arrive.

He had stood in the yard, waiting, sometimes walking up to the road and back again, while Tam intermittently watched him through the window. At one point she saw him bend over to yank a weed from the garden. Now and then he examined the sky above the mountains, as if he thought he might be rescued by airplane. The sun came out and he removed his corduroy jacket, hanging it on the branch of her one hawthorn tree. She had thought him a slim man but realized now that his upper body was strongly built, his shoulders thick

with the muscles of an athlete. There was tenseness as well in
his posture, which was that of a man about to engage in a
series of actions involving tests of strength or skill. Or so
Tam thought, watching him pace, his gait measured and firm.

When the blue Vauxhall stopped on the road beside her
lane, he turned back to the window and waved, mouthing the
words *thank you*, his hand surprisingly large and white at the
end of the dark woollen sleeve of the jumper he had been
wearing under the jacket. Then he had turned his attention to
the bicycle and the boot. Tam could see the grey silhouette of
a figure at the wheel, the shape of the hair gathered at the
back of the head, but nothing more.

It wasn't until nearly nightfall that she noticed the jacket
moving in the wind at the end of the branch and she stepped
outside to collect it. The weather had changed; there would
be rain, and the wind would most likely increase.

Back in the house she began a number of chores. The
ashes needed to be cleaned from the hearth and then taken
outside and scattered in the wind, and a new load of turf
needed to be brought in from the shed. Teddy's grandmother's two brass candlesticks had to be attended to, the wax
removed and their surfaces polished. After this, several letters needed to be finished, one in particular to her mother.
This was a monthly duty, in which she referred to changes in
the landscape or weather, and described one of the few dinner
parties held by the remaining Anglo-Irish in the vicinity in
order to make her parents believe, not entirely incorrectly,
that she had some kind of a life there.

While she was ironing two cotton blouses she had removed from the line out back, she decided he would be back for the jacket soon. He would cycle down the road, then dismount, and approach her door as if the ordinary events of the afternoon had been a rehearsal for something grand and solemn. She registered the oddness of such notions but was aware also of an ominous ability to wait being born in her. Not patience, exactly, there would be too much difficulty for that, but the kind of waiting that would be chronic and painful and yet without any real solidity to back it up. She hung the jacket on a hook behind her front door, and then, before she knew what she was doing, she was running her hands up and down the coarse woollen fabric of its two sleeves.

How lonely it had all been, she thinks now, this inexplicable attachment based on little encouragement from the object of her loyalty, and next to no information about how he himself might have explained his own entry into her arms. Yes, practically everything about his need for her, if that's what it was, was left up to wild conjecture, or to a state of dismal rumination in which she interpreted him over and over. She had developed narrative after narrative during the time when they were not together, which was, she had to admit, most of the time. Even his character underwent transformative scrutiny: he was a philanderer, he was distancing himself from the passion he had for his wife, he knew about the bolter in her, Tam, and the athlete in him was challenged by the game of making her want to stay. He was using her to put his marriage at risk so that he himself would value this marriage more and want to remain in it. He was weak; not strong enough to take the action necessary to achieve what he really wanted, which was her. Yes, on occasion, she had been vain enough to believe he was in love with her, though her own suspicions in the face of all the alternative explanations she invented frequently overrode that belief. He was too Irish to leave his marriage. He was too Irish to remain faithful in his marriage. She was an escape for him, a pleasant recreational activity, one he was unlikely to have to take responsibility for.

Still, the way he had, almost seamlessly, entered her life, bringing the bicycle right inside her door that next weekend so that no one would know where he was, the vulnerability of his expression, and his voice saying the word *please* when he reached for her, the fact that she had known he would return, had shaken her in a way that nothing had in the past. Everyone she had ever been had been available to him; the small girl under the stairs, the young woman in the cockpit with Orion above the propeller, the woman with one sugar bowl rescued from rubble in her hands, the unhappy wife, the reasonable and in truth vaguely happy partner of the innocent Teddy. And then there was the woman she became when Niall himself had begun to come to her door, a woman no longer fully young, no longer a prey to expectations, and then suddenly filled with a crippling sort of passion combined with an uneasy, ceaseless longing. Nothing in her wanted to withdraw as she had always wanted to withdraw. Some other self was born, one she did not fully approve of but was powerless to keep at bay. She wanted him. She wanted much more of him. He took her breath away.

Yes, he had taken her breath away until all the selves she delivered into his embrace had in the end greyed, disintegrated, and become unreachable. In no time at all her world had narrowed to such an extent that everything in her small house was associated only with him: the table where he had taken a brief meal with her, the bed where they had lain together, the floorboards that had felt his step, the now dreadful telephone.

She would force herself to stop waiting. She had had a belly full of it: that, and the awful realization that if she stopped waiting she would be accepting the full knowledge of abandonment. Because not for one moment did she believe that in spite of her sudden departure from Ireland, it was he, not she, who had been abandoned.

In the shadowy areas of the mural there were small, muted figures of indeterminate sex, ones who seemed bewildered by their own lack of importance. They were darkened by foliage or dwarfed by large central characters bent on forward momentum, change and achievement. And yet, it was one of these lesser beings, on the far right, who was the only player in the scene examining the sky, engaged, it seemed to her, in the science of prediction. Like Niall, she decided. Always awake to the circumstances of weather, perhaps wisely knowing that no one could control anything, really. He had no expectations in that regard, no sense that things might be managed differently.

"This could be so destructive," he had told her more than once. "And I've already caused too much damage."

That photograph of a grinning boy astride a bicycle. That darkened profile of the woman in the Vauxhall.

What time was it there exactly? she wonders, shifting her gaze from one international clock to another. Two a.m., she sees, noticing the time in London. He would be sleeping, sleeping it off, whatever it was. She wishes it were morning there instead, because she always knew, without being told, that the beginning of the day was when he thought of her. He would open his eyes and she would fall into his mind. She was sure of this. Later, events that had nothing to do with her would demand his attention and cancel her out. How childish she had been, wanting him to think of her. How ridiculous and painful.

Why had she clung to something that was both so tormenting and so unchangeable when any other woman, even the women she had been in the past, would have ended it years ago and gotten on with life? She was, she had been, an adapter: there was never a situation so surprising or demanding that she couldn't adjust to it in an even-minded way. She had, after all, flown forty-seven different kinds of aircraft during the war, as she had constantly reminded him. There was always a first time and, now and then, an only time. She recalls standing in the grass looking up at a twin-engine Hudson towering above her, monstrous really, like a large grey whale eager to return to an ocean of air. She had never even been near anything of this size, and yet the confidence was so deep in her then, the question of whether or not she could pilot it never entered her mind. She had been filled, instead, with a pure delight in the face of an overwhelming and new piece of machinery. In the cockpit she had opened the instruction manual and read a few pages. Then she had fired up the engine and taken off, sitting on her parachute in order to have a better view through the windscreen. The next day there would have been a Bristol Blenheim or an Avro Anson. Sometimes Spits or Hurricanes. She remembers flying as if in formation on one occasion, moving together like the migrating birds she sees now in the painting, toward a common destination. But there is no information on this wall about where the destination was, what it looked like. How could she, one of those previously forceful birds, find herself so essentially adrift?

ONCE, IN THE MIDST OF HIS TRAVELS, KENNETH found himself in an Italian border town, which, like Koblenz, sat at the site of the confluence of two rivers, but unlike Koblenz was positioned at the centre of the seven surrounding valleys that flung themselves out from the centre of town as if they were the wings of an enormous pinwheel. The train that Kenneth travelled on had plunged into these valleys and eventually straight through the heart of one of the mountains that stood on either side of them, taking him to a place he had not intended to visit.

Boarding a train in Switzerland, he had asked in French for a ticket to Siena. Either because of his lack of skill with the language or perhaps because of the ticket clerk's wandering attention, his fare, he discovered, once he had taken a seat, would take him only as far as an Italian border town at the end of a long tunnel. He had been bewildered by the tunnel, and began almost immediately to feel claustrophobic. The rough blackened rock that hurtled by, the faintly lit acid yellow of the interior lights of the carriage, had him thinking that this might be how a passage to the underworld would unfold – without warning, fed by speed and noise, and disturbingly man-made.

After that clanking half-hour in the company of moist, hard darkness, the industrial town where the porter insisted he disembark surprised him with such brisk vitality and piercing, slippery light that it was difficult to believe that, in spite of its obvious age, the place had been constructed with anything other than metal. Scissors and knives were evidently manufactured here, judging by the contents of the shop windows, along with an array of gleaming sharp objects that could only have been surgical or dental in nature. There were windows filled with mirrors as well, which added to the glare, and shop fronts that displayed stainless-steel cooking utensils. One store he would always remember sold nothing but tongs (some suspiciously forceps-like) and what he eventually decided were clappers for a variety of bells. Eyeglasses were also apparently a feature of the economy, and they filled the windows of several stores, standing row on row on their own delicate silvered frames, staring out like a flock of bewitched birds. The refracted luminosity of the various objects was such that Kenneth was blinded by after-images as he walked away and moved through the shining streets, as if these metal objects were flying before him, as if they were *all* birds of some sort.

A café in such surroundings was difficult to find, but eventually he came across what appeared to be a sort of ice-cream parlour, where the cacophony of spoons assaulting glass was like a badly organized symphony of xylophones. Still, he decided to sit for a while in order to get his bearings. He ordered a lemon sorbetto, and while he was sampling it, he became aware of the couple next to him. Quiet, and absorbed by each other, they were speaking, when they spoke, in English. The girl talked more than the young man she was addressing, and looked with great intensity at her companion's profile. He, for his part, remained, were it not for the anxiety that was evident in his posture, almost aloof, turning to her only briefly, in order to monosyllabically answer the questions she might have put to him. Kenneth could catch only the odd word but felt instinctively that the two had chosen this unlikely town as a destination where they could meet privately and unobserved.

The girl had long, straight reddish hair that fell over her forehead, and nervous hands, one of which moved toward the young man's sleeve as she spoke. He kept looking anxiously toward the crowds passing on the street, as if expecting at any moment to glimpse a posse bent on pursuing him. After a few moments, the girl fell back in her seat and lowered her eyes. She did not look up when the waiter appeared with the bill, nor when, after paying, her companion rose to leave. The young man walked then to the other side of the table and placed his hand quite gently on her shoulder, and she stood and walked away with him.

A small, quite ordinary drama, but one that resonated with Kenneth, who had been more than once ill at ease when he was with a woman he was particularly drawn to. Sometimes the shyness he felt was so extreme he had found himself wanting to escape from a liaison he himself had gone to some lengths to arrange. He put a handful of coins on the table and dived into the crowd, using the distant flame of the girl's hair as a guide. He could not have said why he was following this couple, not yet knowing that prurience was present in his character. When, a few blocks later, the couple disappeared into a small hotel called La Vetreria, Kenneth also entered the establishment and walked up to the front desk to ask for a room.

He did not see the couple again that day, but later the next afternoon, when he was out walking through the streets, he spotted them across the way. The electricity that had been such a part of the young man's demeanour seemed now to have bled into the crowd. The streets were filled with other young men talking animatedly in groups, some of them carrying pennants, all of them walking quickly in the direction of the stadium walls that were visible above the shops of town. Kenneth gradually understood that some kind of significant game was about to take place.

He returned to the hotel and ate alone in the surprisingly empty dining room, climbing the stairs to his room after the three waiters went to gather around a small radio at the end of the hall. He could hear the semi-hysterical Italian sportscaster and the noise of the crowd as he climbed the stairs.

Past midnight he was awakened by the sound of cheering and the singing of songs, and he rummaged for his binoculars in his bag. Then he walked to the window and watched the action in the streets. Men were embracing and gesturing, then bursting into song. He had never seen or heard such collective joy, and it moved him enough that he felt tears sting his eyes. Then his lens picked up one dark-haired man standing, apparently unnoticed by the throng, with a flag larger than himself, swinging the cloth from side to side over his head, his whole body moving with the fabric. Kenneth decided that this was the young man from the café, though he couldn't be sure. Was it that he wanted to be free of the tyranny of the relationship and had left his girl alone in their room? Kenneth did not question why he needed to believe this, but all night long he dreamt that he could hear the red-haired woman weeping, alone in a distant room, and that the sound of this was a long, smoke-coloured ribbon winding down the hall and slipping under his door.

The next morning he walked past the glittering shop windows to the train station – an imposing building built of stone – to buy a ticket to Siena and its feast of art. After he had paid his fare and scrutinized the ticket to ensure that the correct destination was printed on it, he turned just in time to see the couple from the café walk through one of the arches of the entrance. They were heading for the Hall of Departures and he again followed them. The young man had a light blue canvas bag, likely belonging to the girl, slung over his shoulder, and when he paused to look at the boards on which the trains were listed, she once again reached for his sleeve. He swung toward her then, saying something sharp that caused her to withdraw. She walked behind him, head down, as they approached the quays.

On the platform the young man jerked his head in the direction of a particular coach, and after the girl had climbed the metal steps, he lifted the bag up to her. She smiled but his expression remained impassive. She spoke, but as far as Kenneth could tell the young man did not reply. He spun around instead, as if impatient to be elsewhere, and began to move hurriedly away. It was pity that Kenneth felt for the girl then, and a sudden urge to console her.

But he returned to the Hall of Departures, bought a cappuccino at a kiosk, and sat down on a bench, wondering about the girl's journey, whether it would take her through the same dank and raucous obscurity that had preceded his own arrival and whether, if this were so, she would be able to bear it, having been so coldly dismissed. He recalled girls he no longer walked with or, from this distance, wrote to, and felt suddenly ashamed. There could be a kind of cruelty about departure, he thought, but as he had recently learned, there could also be blindness and confusion connected to arrival. He put the paper cup on the floor beside him and looked across the room. On a bench near the wall sat the young man. He was leaning forward with his arms resting on his thighs and his hands gathered together in one tight fist in front of his knees. His expression was open, torn – almost desperate. It was as if, Kenneth thought, he was astonished by his own grief.

Years later Kenneth would place this young man at the centre of the mural, his idea of him having so firmly fused with the image of the soccer celebrant that, as he painted, he forgot altogether that he had never really known if this were so. He clothed him in white satin, transforming him into an Atlas, pinned by his own weight to the ground, yet absorbed by the sky and holding a white banner pierced by metallic, streamlined bird-machines. Kenneth would never be able to say whether this central figure was attempting to invent flight or signalling to those who already had. His virility would be earthbound, yet he and the sail would summon the ether. Just behind this Titan's right ankle Kenneth placed the girl, a shadowed doll, an annulled memory. She would be almost but not quite unnoticeable. She would hold all of the sorrow in the picture in her small, nervous hands while her partner, unknowingly, waved the white drapery of surrender.

KIERAN BECAME WHAT KIRBY CALLED A SWIFT terror on the bicycle and could, with ease, meet Kirby by the Ballinskelligs pier in the morning, receive instructions, ride over the now very familiar pass of Ballagh Oisin, fifteen miles from the sea, through Killorglin, over the Laune River, thence to Tralee, a further fifteen miles, then all around the dozens of miles of the Dingle Peninsula, ascending and descending Brandon Mountain, speeding along the coast to Bray Head, over to Dingle Town, back through Castlemaine, then along the extraordinarily beautiful coast of his own Iveragh, sailing at dusk down to the pier – sometimes with his feet arrogantly placed on the handle grips – where Kirby would be standing, watch in hand.

Good, Kirby would say, but not good enough.

On one of these days Kieran arrived five minutes early and Kirby allowed that he was impressed. "But not overly impressed," he said, raising one hand in a cautionary manner, "not impressed enough. There is something we need to talk about. Tell me everything you know about potholes," he said.

Two months before, Kieran had blown a tire when he encountered a pothole on the flat stretch of bog that provided an otherwise leisurely and joyful ride through inviting open country after the effort of Ballagh Oisin. "There's that devil of a one after the pass," he said.

"Ah yes," said Kirby, "Oisin's pothole, and a legendary one at that. You are aware, I dare say, that that pothole was what conveyed Oisin to the land of Tír na NÓg. They say if you fall right into that one, there is nothing for it but to be gone for three hundred years. A very dangerous pothole indeed but not dangerous now for you as you know it is there, which, apparently, Oisin did not. Still, there are potholes all over this island and you must become intimate with them all before you join the Rás."

This was impossible and Kieran knew it.

"This is impossible, you will say to me," Kirby continued, "but let me remind you that intimacy comes in many different forms. Think of women. I am of the opinion that we may be at our most intimate stage with them when we have not yet even spoken to them, when we are still riding the donkey of the imagination, though headed, admittedly, in their direction."

The girl flared up in Kieran's mind. He remembered that when he was looking through the window, he could see the way the sun touched her long eyelashes. He recalled the faint blue shadow at her temple and the slight rise of her upper lip. There was one intriguing mole just above her collarbone. "Yes?" he said uncertainly.

"The future," Kirby continued, "is the geography with which we are sometimes most intimate, having gone over every version of it inch by inch in our minds. We spend inordinate amounts of time anticipating it, picturing it, trying to control it, measuring it, taking it apart and reassembling it. When we are preparing food, we are preparing for the future. When we are travelling, we are travelling into the future. When we wake in the morning, we step onto the floor and into the future. When I begin to compose a poem, I do so because in the future, I imagine, there will be this wonderful poem. When I look at the sky, I do so because of future weather. Prediction is one of our most natural states of intimate concentration; it is our conversation – our argument, on occasion – with the future. Look at those men like your father up there at the weather station arguing with the future. You must learn to predict potholes beyond the legendary potholes, the one you already know and others I will tell you about. Do you have a pencil and a piece of paper?"

Kieran did not.

"Then we must go up to my house to get one, because you will need to take some notes."

Kirby stood in the parlour. The importance of the lecture, he said, merited such formal surroundings. He told Kieran about the potholes of County Tipperary, the specifics of potholes on roads that ran by the rivers of Clare. Potholes in bog country, he explained, were of an entirely different nature; deeper, and more likely to shift from one day to the next. "Shape-changers," he said. He spoke of the angry potholes of County Galway with their mouths of stone. Be wary, he warned, of the deceptive potholes of County Dublin. "They have macadamized roads there," he said, "and because of this, a rider can become too confident of a smooth surface." In County Cork, he confided, they have every kind of pothole that God can create. Those Cork holes, he maintained, were the kind of potholes that lay in wait for you like dogs hiding in a bush near the ends of lanes they are bound and determined to protect. "You never see them," he warned, "until they catch you by the pant leg." He could not speak about the North, he said, they being British potholes, but Kieran should be cautious indeed around that territory. "They have potholes, I'd say, like landmines, up there, veritable craters waiting for a cyclist from the south."

The idea of the North was not something Kieran had thought about. "Surely," he said, "the Rás would not really go there, would it?"

It had been a particular point of honour, Kirby insisted, for the Rás to penetrate the border at some time or another on one of the northern stages. During the inaugural Rás, he reminded him, the boys had carried the Irish flag with them, weaving in and out, through the six counties, and there had been much comment upon it by Orangemen and the Royal Ulster Constabulary. Quite a fracas had ensued, and these detours had been discouraged since.

Kirby rose from his chair after the pothole lecture and walked toward one of the two shelves of books on either side of the hearth. "This," he said, handing a dark leather volume to Kieran, "is what you must read to understand the formation and persistence of potholes."

Kieran looked at the spine. *Geology of Ireland*, it read.

"Different rocks, different soils, give birth to varying potholes. Know what's under you when you are riding. Remember the Ice Age, that fractional inching forward of everything you think is stable. Learn how water affects what's under you. And never forget: everything, even hard stone, is moving slightly at all times." The truth was, Kirby insisted, you could count on absolutely nothing. What began as a barely noticeable crack could blossom overnight into a gigantic sinkhole that could swallow you and your bicycle in one gulp.

Kieran hadn't wanted to mention the irrefutable fact that he had never once seen Kirby on a bicycle, had never even heard of him riding at any time, but he couldn't help himself. "How do you know all this?" he asked now. "Have you ridden on these roads?"

Kirby looked surprised. "Of course not," he said, "I am a fisherman. The only things I have ridden are the waves."

"So how do you know then?"

Kirby looked out the window of his house and up the road that climbed to Bolus Head. "The donkey of the imagination," he said, "can travel anywhere." Then he began to recite. "To a Pothole," he began,

> O gaping mouth, O teeth of stone
> Hiding in the path of those who go
> Down from their fields to town

Wagon spiller, interrupter of wheels
On roads that speed a shining bike along
Between the mountains

Under which you lurk
With your lapful of yesterday's rain
And your shoes full of yesterday's dirt

—

A few days later, when a late-afternoon mist slid down the mountain and crept up to the windows, Kieran decided he would ask Gerry-Annie about Tadhg, having been too uncertain of what he had seen to bring the subject to Michael Kirby's attention. The way the old couple had emerged from the fog, the feeling of sorrow attached to them, and his own sudden strength in relation to the impassable gate – all of this was still vivid in his mind.

"Do you know one called Tadhg out on Bolus?" he asked her.

"I do, Kieran. I did." She was sitting by the hearth in a wooden chair with arms. It had a cushion on the seat and at the back, and arms on the sides, and was considered by her to be the height of luxury. The furniture in the room, all made out back by Gerry's own grandfather, was dark around them, and concrete under their feet approached and withdrew depending upon the strength of the fire. "He, and Sheila, whom he married," Annie continued. "They were people my own parents knew well. She died first, you know, and then him a year or so later. It was said he was found seated at the table with a knife and fork in his hands and no life in him. My mother said he was a terrible one for the food, always wanting something to eat at any time of the day or night. And then cautious about the fire, only allowing two or three pieces of turf a day – even in cold weather. He was always afraid," Annie told Kieran, "that his turf stack wouldn't last the winter, but he'd eat all the food in the house until there was nothing left and nowhere to get more."

"So they are dead." Kieran tried to run this fact through his mind.

"Yes, dead a good while, I'd say."

"But I opened a hard gate for them. They wanted it opened and I did that."

Annie sighed. "You would of course," she said, unsurprised. "You are a good boy and you would do that for them. You would have to let Tadhg into a field, as he was so fond of his cows." She pushed a strand of grey hair behind one ear, then folded her hands in her lap. "He was a great one for advice when he was alive, particularly on the subjects of grass and how to make a green field for the grass of two cows when it had all gone to rushes and furze and gorse. Oh, the fields Tadhg had! So ancient you couldn't say what manner of man had built the walls. Not a corner on the lot of them. All sort of round, or like the shape of that platter." She pointed to an oval of blue and white perched atop the dresser. "And the names on those fields: *Watery Meadow, The Slope of the Lightning, Swift Dog*

Field, The Field of the Flying Cow. I suppose those fields are there yet." She paused. "Are you listening to me, Kieran?"

He moved his chair and it made a scraping noise. An affirmative sound came out of his mouth, but he wasn't listening. Not really. He was thinking about the day of the gathering, the day of the scattering. He was trying to fit his mind into a thin place where Tadhg and his wife would be alive and dead at the same time, holding on to the day of the gathering for an unimaginable amount of time. Perhaps they had clung to the day of the gathering for so long the entrance to the fair was denied to them. Had he done them a favour when he had smashed open that rusted bolt? He remembered as well that the mist that enveloped them as they moved out toward the edge was bone-coloured, not the same white mist he had ridden through to get to the spot. *The day of the fair is nothing but a thin ghost announcing the day of the scattering.* He remembered Tadhg saying that. *The day of the scattering* could only mean the end of everything.

"Oh, and I recall now the names of some fields Gerry's father had," Annie said. "*The Hollow of the Little Saints, The Bed of the Lost Girl, The Haggard* . . ."

"Who was she," he asked, "this lost girl?"

Annie thought a while. "Someone from far-off, I think they said." A piece of burnt turf fell softly through the grate and flame sprang from the place where it broke. "She had walked a long, long way, perhaps running from something, or maybe just one who had lost her way, and she lay down, I expect, to die in that field."

"And Gerry knew her then." Kieran was picturing this lost girl. She was ancient and alive at the same time.

"No he did not. Nor his father, or his grandfather. She came from another time. A time before."

How beautiful that would have been, Kieran thought, a girl lying spent and pale with the green grass around her, her hair a dark cloud beneath her head, and the sound of the flocks coming across the fields in the evening. All strength gone and only submission left behind. He would have caught her on the edge of that and coaxed her back. Come here to me, he would have whispered, lifting her in his arms. Or he would have lain with her until his warmth bled into her and she opened her liquid eyes. It was Niall's girl he was thinking of. She was the one he saw in his mind lying in that field. He would nurse her back with milk, as though she were an infant.

That night he dreamt of Susan again as he had done on other nights since he had seen her. Sometimes in these dreams, though she had been herself, she had spoken with his mother's own voice, admonishing him for not answering her call or for letting his attention drift. But this time she was like the girl who had come to Donal in the mountains, the girl whom Donal had lost to Africa. There was a river of sheep moving around her and flowing down the slope, and the stars were as strong as they had been on the night Donal had spoken of his own lost girl. Her skin was pure and glowing in an apparent absence of light, and grace was everywhere.

He woke the following morning recalling his workmate's words concerning the house where Susan lived, its position on the wooded hill that rose up behind the streets of the town, and he knew he must go there, believing that even the walls that surrounded her might have something to teach him. As he walked through the cottage and out into the faint beginnings of dawn he could hear Gerry-Annie snoring gently in her room behind the hearth. The light rain was soft on his face, and the crust of bread he had snatched as he passed the table was moist in his mouth. He swung his leg over the bicycle and set out, allowing gravity to pull him down toward the dreaming town. Soon he was standing on the pedals, propelling the bicycle up the incline through Carhan Wood. The rain had stopped and the low sun silvered the road and the holly bushes in the hedgerows. As he passed gate after gate, one dog after another announced his presence. They were answered in turn by those in the valley below. He had forgotten about the dogs: the ones that lay waiting in ditches, the ones who ran down lanes, those who sat in the yard with their backs turned and appeared to pay no attention to him at all except for the barking.

In the end, as he came closer to where she lived, he merely slowed down in the vicinity of the two concrete gateposts that flanked the entrance to her lane, proceeding a mile or two farther along the road, as if he were going to the house of his workmate. He came to the end of the public road and a farm gate closed against him, and the sorrow of Tadhg, his separation from his beautiful cattle, touched him on the shoulder. The dogs had quieted now, but all courage had nevertheless fallen from him, leaving only the sorrow. There was nothing for it, he concluded, but to turn around and go down into the town, where he was still working on the sidewalks. When he passed the lane again, he allowed himself to look at the house he knew was hers, and as he did so, he saw the light above the door go cold and he vowed he would never return to the place.

AMERICA

—

T am herself had never sought anyone, not even Niall, at least not outwardly. In fact, she was almost always the one being searched for, almost pursued. She wonders now if she had encouraged this, had somehow constructed a self that would be just out of reach. Plans to hunt her down and bring her to her senses were often being conceived of by adults during her childhood and early womanhood. Had she sometimes disappeared in hopes of being found? Is that what she was unconsciously hoping for now, that Niall, the great seeker, would begin to search for her?

He had insisted that he had begun to look for his brother almost by accident during a trip to London a few years after Kieran disappeared. No one, not his father, not Gerry-Annie, knew where Kieran had gone, and no one had heard from him since. "A sad situation altogether," Annie had apparently said. "He didn't even take his bicycle."

She worried that he might have gone north to join the Provos, this being after the Rás and all the desperate politics she was certain had ridden alongside it, but neither Niall nor his father thought that was likely. "He doesn't have a taste for politics," Niall's father had maintained. "It wouldn't be like him at all."

Tam recalls Niall imitating Annie's country intonations while he was speaking about his brother being gone. "Oh I hope he hasn't gone and joined the fighting men and been killed," he'd said in a high, womanish voice, throwing his hands in the air. "I've been like a mother to him!" She also remembers how he caught himself in the midst of that, and had apologized, saying that Annie was a treasure and that he shouldn't be making light. He told her that Annie couldn't understand why Kieran hadn't taken the bicycle with him, why he had left it leaning against the wall, and had disappeared some time in the night. She couldn't understand why he hadn't wakened her to say goodbye. "This was a devastating loss for her," Niall said.

Niall hadn't wanted to go to the conference, as it involved crossing the channel in February and he was a man who had known seasickness. But McWilliams had other matters to attend to and asked him specially to stand in for him. "While you are there," the older man had said, "take another few days and see the place. Go see the John Constable oil studies of skies. They are in the Victoria and Albert Museum. No serious climatologist should miss them. That infinite variety."

It was while walking back to his hotel after looking at the Constables that Niall heard Irish being spoken near a worksite, and, in a halting approximation of that language, he asked one of the men where he was from. The man, hardly more than a boy, answered in English, said he was from Clare, a farm near Shanavogh.

Was there no work on the farm? Niall wanted to know.

"Plenty of work," the lad answered. "But no money." The young labourer's hands, resting on the shovel, were plum-coloured in the cold. "There's loads of us Irish boys over here, all sending money home. There's thousands of us."

Niall recalled Kieran telling him about the bicycles at Annie's wall, how it was discovered they had all belonged to those who had left for England or America. No wonder Kieran had left the Purple Hornet at that spot.

"Any Kerrymen?" he had asked.

"God love us," said the young man. "The Kerrymen are as thick on the ground as a snowfall after Christmas."

Niall continued then, knowing chances were slim. "Would you know my brother then, a man called Kieran Riordan?"

The young man thought a bit, then shook his head. "No," he said, "I'd say I do not."

An older man standing nearby suddenly entered the conversation. "You mean the Wheel."

Niall had no reply for that. "What do you mean, the Wheel?" he asked.

"Damned if I know," the man said, "it was a name he wanted for himself, evidently, or one the other boys gave him. But I saw he was Riordan. I saw that name once on a pay packet in his hand, and I know he was from South Kerry, as I am myself. We worked in the same gang here in this city. But he's gone, since, to the Motorways in the north, and a good while back at that."

Much later Niall would think about the chances of having stopped at that precise site the moment he did, the strangeness of having all of Constable's clouds still navigating through his mind while talking to the one man in a city of millions who knew something about where his brother was. "Motorways," he said.

"So they say." The man pushed his shovel into the hole where he had been digging. As he walked away, Niall turned and called out to him, "Is there more than one motorway?"

"There's to be a whole cartload of them," the labourer shouted back.

And so began his interest in motorways. Niall told Tam that McWilliams had been bewildered and amused by this obsession, motorways being the one subject he knew nothing about, although, he conjectured, there was no doubt that climatologists were involved in the planning stages of these speed-tracks, as he called them. What falls from the skies and blows around the surfaces, McWilliams was never tired of reminding those near him, affects absolutely everything.

One day McWilliams arrived at the station with news of the Preston Bypass. Eight and a half miles and a half a dozen bridges, he told Niall, just to avoid Preston. What made the place such an anathema that all this effort was put into not going near it? Pity the poor farmer, he'd said, whose house or byre was in the way. It was to have been finished months ago, but the weather – he'd laughed then – the weather had apparently got in the way.

But the worksite around Preston had yielded nothing more than vague rumours when McWilliams had consulted the climatologist hired by the contractor. Some of these rumours were dire. The Wheel had tumbled from a bridge, or had been run over by one of the large noisy machines that ground back and forth in the vicinity. He had stolen a bicycle and ridden north to Scotland, where he had fallen into extreme drinking because of the easy availability of the malts. He had lost his wages in a poker game and had murdered the winner and was now mouldering in an English jailhouse. And at last, finally, someone said that Kieran Riordan had been banned from work on future motorways – the crime that pre-cipitated this was not specified – and had gone to America.

Motorways, thinks Tam now, not for the first time. The mysterious brother might have worked on sites controlled by her father. "Everything you pull out of the earth needs to be taken somewhere else." She remembers her father saying this, or something to this effect. She thinks of the demolished village. "Anything that moves forward, anything at all pro-gressive, leaves something raw and wounded behind it. Look at America." Had he said that too? Or was this observation simply her own inner voice, instructing her?

America. It was possible that Kieran had passed through this airport.

When Niall went to New York that July of 1958, a full summer front had arrived in the city. The air was hot and still, saturated with humidity, and yet there was not a trace of rain in the forecast. He had never experienced, never even predicted, weather like this, and for the first few days it stunned him. All he could do was sleep, naked, on the sagging bed beside the open window of the fifth-storey hotel room he had rented in lower Manhattan. His dreams were laced with travelling, and discomfort. Sometimes his brother appeared, diving from Culloo Rock. Sometimes he dove with him. There was no sense of danger until he woke, full of panic, believing his brother was dead. And then he remembered it was his mother, not his brother, who had died at that spot.

An old schoolmate, now a plumber in New York who had recently gone home when he heard that his mother was dying, had been the reason for Niall making the trip. The poor fellow had been too late to see the mother alive, arriving just in time for the funeral, which Niall had attended with his wife and almost everyone else in town. It was in the midst of the drinking that followed that the man had touched Niall's arm. "I saw your brother," he had said, "one day on the Bowery when I was on a job. And I was surprised to see him there, it being so far from anywhere the Irish might be boarding." The man had paused, as if deciding whether or not to continue. "He was in a bad way," he said. "He was sleeping rough or, now and then, in what he called Cage Hotels. I remembered this because of the oddness of the name, Cage Hotel."

Cage Hotel. Niall had mentally filed this name.

"On the Bowery," the man said. "The last place, believe me, you'd ever want to be."

Niall had told a few people where he was going, but not why. This private quest seemed more filled with ambivalence, secrecy, and guilt than any clandestine love affair, and that may very well have been why, Tam would later conjecture, the lover in him grew cold when he was preparing to search for Kieran. It was as if he could manage only one system of deceit at a time. Only McWilliams knew the truth of it, or the part of the truth that involved Niall's anguish over what might have become of his brother. "Don't give up on the hope," he said more than once. "You at least know your brother is not dead. You may very well find him. And then, with any luck, you can bring him home."

Something we Irish were always attempting to do, Niall thought. We are always trying to bring people home.

And so McWilliams became a willing partner, passing on information about conferences and talks in London, and then, later, about new theories he had heard Americans were developing. Niall would visit the Department of Climatology at Columbia. Then, as McWilliams had suggested, he would make the eighteen-mile journey out to the recently established Lamont Geological Observatory at Palisades, where core samples from the bottom of the ocean were being examined for clues concerning shifts in sea currents. Yes, he would do this, but when he had fulfilled these obligations he would begin the search again, for it was the search that had really brought him to New York.

On his fourth day in the hotel, he woke before the summer dawn had broken, knowing it would be already ten in the morning in Ireland. Tam walked into his mind then, as she often did at this time of the day, and opened her arms to him, but he pushed even the thought of her away. The puzzle of that connection, the mystery, could not erase the shadows that he felt were moving through the streets of this city to meet him.

He walked out of the hotel, up Orchard Street, and took the first left at Hester. The humidity had survived the night and had preserved the city's smells so that he came to believe that the odours of garbage and exhaust fumes were being absorbed by his skin. He walked four blocks along Hester until he reached the Bowery, then turned right on this thoroughfare.

He felt immediately that he had entered a grim geography. Brick walls appeared porous and insubstantial, as if they had been submerged for several decades, as if when touched they would turn to powder in the hand. On the sidewalks, angled against walls or collapsed near doorways, grey shapes shifted or remained entirely still. It was the sound of retching that caused him to realize that these shapes, slowly becoming three-dimensional in a faintly increasing morning light, were human. A hand grabbed his ankle and he shook his leg violently to free himself from the grasp. He heard the man's voice but not the specifics of the plea. There was the smell of urine and vomit, a line of soot-covered broken windows by his elbow, and the crunch of broken glass under his feet. No colony of lepers could have affected him more. He was dizzy with disgust, but determined to proceed. When the next arm reached for his trouser leg, he bent over and said "Cage Hotel" in the direction of the face that emerged from an unsavoury mop of damp cloth, but the figure shuddered and turned away.

Once the sun was fully up, the coughing began, the coughing and the almost continual retching. He thought of the dogs in his Irish town, how one of them would bark and then another and another, a contagion of sound. It occurred to him now, dogs were more sanitary. He despised himself for the thought, but there it was, present in his mind, refusing to be banished. By now he had covered one side of the street and was about to cross, to make a similar tour of the sidewalk opposite. His level of distress was so high he believed for a moment that pandemonium might break out at any moment, this in spite of the fact that nothing about the bodies that lay like dark boulders in the seams of the streetscape suggested an aptitude for pandemonium. He remembered Gerry-Annie talking about the famine, how she'd heard that the men and women walking down from the mountains in search of the Ballagh Workhouse had died in such numbers on their journey that the roads were made impassable because of the piles of corpses. Families, she'd said, would huddle together when they were dying, children lying atop their parents, their arms and legs braided together so they could never be separated.

A man a half a block away was using both arms to attempt to push himself into a seated position. Having achieved this by the time Niall reached him, he swung a mostly empty bottle in Niall's direction. "Want some?" he asked.

"Cage Hotel?" Niall asked. At least this one appeared to be alive.

"Cage Hotel," the man repeated.

"Yes."

The man was swallowing what was left in the bottle. When he was finished, he looked at the label for several seconds as if trying to memorize the name of an unfamiliar fine wine. Then he opened his fist and let the bottle fall to the sidewalk, where it did not break but rolled instead at a sedate pace into the gutter. "Which one?" the man said.

"The *Cage* Hotel," Niall repeated.

"They are all cages." The man opened his arms as if to embrace the street.

"But . . . why would . . . ?"

"Rooms with wire mesh ceilings." The man removed a stained cap and ran his fingers through a substantial mop of hair oiled by sweat. "Ventilation," he said. "Lets the air through, smells also, and sounds. I prefer plein air." He looked at his crumpled trousers on the sidewalk. "Outside," he translated, "fresh air."

Niall said his brother's name. Then his nickname. "Kieran the Wheel," he said.

"You're Irish," the man said. "A Paddy. Magnificent drunks, the Paddies."

"Do you know him?"

"Maybe," the man said. "Probably I do, if he's been here any time at all. He could be in any one of the cages, but even if he is, he'll be out here soon enough. Or he might be on the street right now. Depends on the day's work."

Niall wanted to know about the day's work.

The man gave Niall a look that suggested he had never met anyone quite so thick. "Drinking," he said, "and begging," he added, holding out his hand.

Niall pulled an American dollar bill from his wallet, placed it in the man's palm, then turned and walked away.

He hadn't covered a half a block before the man was calling him. "Hey, Paddy," he shouted, "he's probably dead, anyway, whoever he is. Most of us are."

SOURCE

———

The summer of 1954 was uncharacteristically dry and bright, but times were lean and work was scarce for the kind of casual labourer Kieran had become. As he had done for the past several years, he spent an August week booleying in the mountains with Donal the sheep farmer, whose hair was turning toward grey now but who was no less strong on the climb to the highest pastures and no less nimble on the rocks.

For the first time Tim the Sky did not venture out to greet them when they came to his elevated fields. He had died the previous winter, and the dog, the Cloud, had died shortly thereafter. Of grief, Donal said.

"Those things Tim saw and that the Cloud saw with him will never happen again," Donal told Kieran. "Remember them, and remember the parts of the heaven he pointed to when he spoke: the heaven above Knocknagrapple, the heaven above Drung. And remember the way the Cloud moved when he was leaping up the mountain to greet us." Ean, who had been running wildly searching behind boulders, circling the house, and scratching at the door, now sat with his head lowered and his back to them. "It's a terrible disappointment to him," Donal said, looking with fondness at his dog, "not to have the Cloud among us."

Tim's house appeared to Kieran to be dissolving into the textured surface of the mountain, the way houses did in this district when they knew they would never be lived in again. Sometimes, even though you were aware of its existence, it was difficult to spot the house at all among the rocks and the ferns. And then, quite unexpectedly, a particular slant of light would make Tim's green door shine as if it had been painted only minutes before.

"It is the past's way of saying goodbye," Donal said when Kieran remarked on this. "A sudden gleaming and then the dimming down. It will speak to us quite a few times like that now," he said, "and then next year, only once or twice. By the third year it will be as if it has never spoken at all, though we'll never forget it, or Tim in it, nor the Cloud either."

It was like that in the mountains, Kieran thought. Very often features of the landscape would appear and disappear. Sometimes it seemed that Michael Kirby's insistence that he remember each detail of every road he cycled was an impossible demand, for what was revealed by the low light of a particular mountain morning might be removed the next afternoon by shadow or by mist. He had once ridden for days back and forth on a long stretch of a rough bóithrín, searching for a small grotto that he was certain he had seen the previous week, and that eluded him for more than a year, returning when he was looking for something else altogether.

In the early autumn, for two slightly madcap weeks, Kieran cycled from house to house with Davey the tailor, who had added house-painting to his array of skills, tailoring being so seldom in demand in what Davey called "the ongoing scarcity." During this period, as they stood on their ladders, Davey insisted that Kieran learn all the emigration songs that he, Davey, knew, shouting them from one gable end to another. The title of each song begin with the word *Leaving* and was followed by the name of an abandoned townland, or sometimes mountains, lakes, or rivers, so that you had "Leaving Cappanagroun," or "Leaving Cillin Liath," or, in the case of rivers, "Leaving the Cummeragh Side," or "Leaving the Banks of the Carhan." The songs were splendidly long, and each of their verses was filled with sorrow. Some verses did nothing but list the people, places, and occasions their composers knew they would never encounter again: crossroad dances, peat fires, mothers and fathers, baby sisters, walks to market, mass in the church, views of the bay. Other verses detailed the terrors of the long journey by ship in surprisingly vivid detail, storms holding a particular place of honour.

"And how's that bicycle training up?" Davey asked once while they were eating lunch between bouts of singing and painting. He jerked his thumb in the direction of the Purple Hornet, which was lying near them in the grass. "Is it faster now that it has thousands of country miles in its bones? We're counting on it to win the Rás. In the spring, I think I recall Michael saying. Less than a year now." He threw a crust to a flock of robins that had gathered in the vicinity the moment they knew he was there. "I saw you down there in the town a couple of months ago when this year's Rás came through."

"Mm," said Kieran, nodding, his mouth full of Annie's bread. The riders had proven themselves to be both a thrill and a disappointment. The cyclists, when they had appeared, had been like a colourful ribbon in a strong wind, almost all of them there and gone before his mind could grasp what it had seen.

"They were all in a tight group," he said to Davey. "Except for the one lad who came along after."

"Ah yes," said Davey philosophically, "the Red Lantern, I heard they call the one holding up the rear."

Kieran had been troubled by the last rider, had felt pity for him. He had also felt a wave of dread come over him as he glimpsed the exhaustion in the boy's passing face.

Davey stood and his birds flew away. "That's a fierce lonely place to be, all right," he said, as if sensing Kieran's thoughts. "Fierce lonely. But it is an experience you will never have, that's one thing certain. No fear of that."

Fierce lonely, thought Kieran. It was true that he was becoming more confident about the Rás. But *fierce lonely* described the rest of his life very well.

For ten days that previous June, before he had gone out to work with Donal, Kieran had managed to find a job in the town installing concrete footpaths. The hours of light were long enough that he and the men he worked with had started at six in the morning and did not lay down tools until eleven o'clock at night. Annie told Kieran it was madness to work like that all day, then cycle back to her in the dark, though for years now he had had a light on the bicycle, and enough training in him that a ride like that would have been a trifle. But he had agreed during this time to stay with his father in the house he had left as a child. Now his brother was home for a stretch and Kieran thought he might see the girl; that Niall might bring her to the house and he might glimpse her.

His father had not seen Niall since Christmas, though his brother's time had been so taken up with Susan that he had spent most of his holiday in the house on the hill with her and her parents. Annie said it was cruel, Mr. Riordan being alone like that during the time around the holidays, and she had insisted that Kieran go into the town every second day during the season to be with his father. As always, she had cooked the Christmas dinner for the house and had stayed to eat at the long dining room table. Susan was at the table as well; her and her dark hair and her presence had made Kieran peculiarly aware of his own chewing, the way he held his fork. Once she had asked him a direct question and the fact of her looking at him had caused him to feel so uncomfortable he hadn't been able to grasp what she said and had merely mumbled something in reply. The entire meal was an agony, but even so he wanted to see her again.

It was unlikely, Kieran's hours being what they were, that this would happen during these ten days in summer, but even the faint possibility, though it filled him with a mixture of dread and longing, was enough. While he was behind the shovel, however, he would not allow himself to look up to the wooded hill where he knew her house was visible – startling and white, shining among dark trees – or down the street to her father's shop, where sometimes, he had heard, she stood behind the counter. Instead he concentrated on the concrete covering the footpaths with a smooth, wet paste.

During his breaks, Kieran visited the various shops he had become fond of as a child, each one a small theatre in itself, its proprietor surrounded by the bright colours of what was on offer – be that tools in the hardware, or candy or cabbages at the grocer's – and a monologue ready to be delivered on any subject relevant to the day. Kieran, being taciturn himself, took pleasure in these adamant revelations of character and opinion, often political but sometimes social in nature, in that they provided him with something like company, and demanded only a nod of his head in return. He avoided the jeweller's shop, however. He could not make an active move toward Susan; any encounter would have to be determined by chance. And what would he have said standing there in his muck-covered overalls in such an establishment, the bell on the door jingling behind him, his clumsiness evident, and no accomplishment in him? He had seen her on the street once or twice heading toward or moving away from the shop. Always there was the same response in him, the panic, the thrill. One time she stood entirely still on the street, looking for something in the bag she carried, her beautiful head bent, completely absorbed in the search. He thought he would die with his shovel in his hand if she didn't find it, whatever it was, and disappear out of his view.

For the first five days in the house he saw no one but his father, who would be up early in the morning. Niall, having graduated in science from University College Dublin, was working for a stretch at the station before entering graduate studies in meteorology in the fall. But not yet being responsible for the balloons, his workday started somewhat later, and Kieran had seen little of him.

His father, however, would talk about Niall, how McWilliams had taken a shine to him, and about how Niall seemed to have a temperament well suited to the work. The young man would go, uncomplaining, out to the instruments in all kinds of weather to read the graphs, his father said. And being one for the trees, he had arranged to have six sycamores, identical to those at observatories in Britain and on the continent, planted on the grounds so that the effects of climate on vegetation might be compared all over Europe. This study was called phenology, his father said, something new that few scientists knew anything about, and McWilliams was impressed that Niall would bring the knowledge of something like this with him to the station. Listening to all this, Kieran wanted to ask about the girl whom he feared Niall was going to marry. But his father never mentioned her, and he hadn't the courage, really, to raise the subject himself.

Late on the sixth day, Kieran entered the house quietly, as he always did at night, not wanting to waken his father. He closed the door softly behind him, took off his shoes, and walked to the parlour. They were there, side by side on the sofa – neither had heard him enter the room – and the girl was in his brother's arms. Her cardigan and her blouse lay on the cushions beside them and Kieran stared at these garments for what seemed to him a long period of time before letting his eyes move to the cream of her bare arms and her breasts, and when he did he was certain that the girl's gaze met his with an understanding of his suffering. Then she gasped and Niall twisted toward where he stood in the doorway. Kieran moved away and stumbled up the stairs. He was trembling as he undressed for the night. Both his mother and the chemist were speaking in his mind now, but he couldn't see them, the girl's look and the paleness of her skin crowding every other image out of his mind.

Kieran descended the stairs the following morning. It was not quite dawn. Certain parts of the room were coming into focus, the table, and the tap that hung over the sink, but the corner where Niall stood was dark enough that Kieran did not notice him until it was too late to withdraw. "I was waiting for you," Niall said. "I thought we should talk."

Kieran said nothing. The stove was on and there was a smell of something spilled on the burner, smouldering in an unwholesome way.

"I am in love with Susan," Niall told him. "We are to be married next year. You could stand up for me," he said. "You're my brother, and that is what is supposed to happen, what you are supposed to do."

The window over the sink was open. Kieran could hear birdsong and the strident, impudent calling of a crow. *Now, now, now*, the bird seemed to say. He wanted to ask his brother how he had arranged such miraculous impossibilities, the betrothal, the removal of a blouse, but there were no words attached to the questions in his mind. He wanted to inquire about being near a girl like that, how to gain the necessary permission to savour each aspect of her. To look at her, to hear her voice, and to know that what she was saying was meant only for you, to be able to touch her: all this was so foreign to him he could barely believe he was in any way related to his brother. He heard his father stirring in the room above, lonely and distanced, beginning another day. "Did she say she would marry you?" he asked. His voice was thick and hoarse, and for the first time he realized how seldom he used it.

"Yes," said Niall, "yes, she did." He was pouring boiling water from a kettle into the teapot. Steam clouded his hands.

"And about last night," he said, not turning toward Kieran, "she is not that sort of girl." She had gone home, he added, shortly after, filled with mortification. He had tried to walk her back, but she wouldn't let him. He, Kieran, should forget about the whole incident.

"Will *you* forget it?" Kieran asked.

Niall pulled out a chair and sat down at the table with his cup. He had left the teapot on the counter, however, and the cup remained empty. "Of course," he said. "We will all three act like it never happened."

"But it will happen again," said Kieran. The kitchen was filling with light. The pain he felt was laced with anger. He was looking at his brother's hands on the cup.

"Not like that," said Niall.

The next night Kieran cycled back to Gerry-Annie's in the dark, unwilling to return to the house that felt tainted now with all the disarray of its various relationships. He knew that the hardship of caring for someone was the way that caring insisted on punching through the skin of even the most ordinary day. It was a dark, moonless night, but he did not lean forward to turn on the bicycle's light, preferring only to smell and then identify the drowsing herds and flocks behind the walls on either side of him, and to feel the road rising under his wheels.

Kirby had told him to do this not two months ago, this unlit night-riding, maintaining that it was the only way to coax the other senses to compete with sight. "The only way to give the other senses a fighting chance," he had said. He told Kieran that he must learn to hear the road's surface when he was riding, so that the road could speak to him, and that he must remain attentive to the way the surface of the road made itself known by shaking the handlebars and the seat. The scent of things was important as well: the vegetation in the hedgerows, the dung in the passing fields, the newly cut hay. "You must smell the peat in the bog," he said, "and then the smoke of peat fires that tells you when you are approaching villages and towns."

His father and his brother had been too close at hand. He wanted to cycle out of the range and the scent of them.

In late September, his training began to intensify. He would need to withdraw completely, he would have to embrace the unfamiliar, live alone, and become intimate with discomfort. The wild part of his nature would be made available to him now, in a more organized way. He wanted to be able to summon it, the power of it, during the stages of the race. He knew he would no longer stand on the edge of wildness or have that wildness come spinning out of him in the midst of tantrum, as it had when he was a child. From now on, Kirby would be his only adviser, and he would approach even him less and less, as he became more and more reliant on aloofness. The training would be everything, he realized, and he would emerge from the effort and pain of it rinsed clean, and ready to present himself to the Rás, and then, triumphant, to the girl his brother said he was going to marry.

"The question now," said Kirby, "is where you will decide to go for the retreat part of your training. Have you any money saved?"

Kieran was looking at the inside of Kirby's boat, a jungle of nets, sinkers, and floats. He couldn't meet the older man's gaze, this fisherman, this poet who knew everything, it would seem, about him. He sensed that Kirby was aware he had seen the girl, parts of her he had no business to have seen. He believed that Kirby apprehended that there wasn't anything now he could look at that did not bring thoughts of her with it. Even the bicycle, vehicle of escape, had become connected to her. The desire for privacy was deepening in him.

"Well, you're the only one who will be riding the bicycle," Kirby was saying, "so you won't be able to take me along, except in your mind of course." He dragged some new netting to the edge of the pier, jumped into the boat, and pulled the nets after him. "You're very quiet this morning," he said. When Kieran didn't answer, he told him that he himself had gone through an uncharacteristically quiet period when as a very young man he was in America for one year. "A sort of linguistic withdrawal came over me," he said, climbing out of the boat and back onto the pier. "I was in Canada, in fact, working for a French farmer on the St. Lawrence River. He spoke no English, but even if he had, I'd have had no conversation to give him."

There was a barrel full of skate near where they stood. "Why Keating even bothers with that mess is a mystery," Kirby said, plunging his hand into the stringy soup of it, then taking it out again and wiping it on his trousers. "The starving could not be persuaded to eat it, I'd say. He says he sells it for cat food, but even cats have more sense than to eat the likes of that."

"I have a little money saved," Kieran said.

"Good," said Kirby, "good. But can you build a hut? Do you know anything at all about wattled shelter?"

Kieran did not answer, and Kirby went on. "That farmer," said Kirby, "the one in Canada, he never really spoke to me, but he was suspicious, I'll tell you that. He had some kind of idea I was going to steal his boat, and the thing was, he wasn't wrong." Kirby seated himself on a coil of rope near the edge of the pier. Kieran sat down beside him, legs dangling over the edge. He would have to leave the man, but not yet.

"So every night he put the oars in a locked shed. I was hoping to go to New York, you see. I'd cousins there I'd never seen, but I had their addresses. They were all working on sky-scrapers, way up, halfway to heaven. They'd get me some kind of work, I had decided. Anything was better than this suspicious farmer. I knew New York was somewhere south of where I was, somewhere on the other side of that river. I wanted that boat to get me across. The farmer had some kind of lumbering operation going in the winter and had me load-ing logs onto sleighs that were to be drawn by horses over the snow toward some sawmill. I never knew where. When the ice went out of the river in spring I knew what to do. So I waited until a night with a moon, then I took two brooms from the barn and rowed myself across the river with those."

Kirby gently punched Kieran's shoulder, as if to awaken him. "You'll have to be resourceful yourself, with the bicycle during the eight days of the Rás. There may be times on some stage of it or another where you have to tie the machine together with string or elastic bands. You may be required to steal the wheels from a baby buggy or a seat from a passing tractor, you'll have crashed that often. You'll have your team-mates of course, and they will be helpful to you and you to them. But in the end it is the inner resourcefulness that matters, the inner problem-solver."

Teammates? This was the first time Kirby had ever raised the subject. Kieran knew about the cycling clubs of Kerry but had always assumed that when he approached the Rás he would do so as an individual.

"The Kerry team, of course," Kirby said when Kieran asked. "You've been up this county's mountains and along its rivers and strands, you've walked with its sheep and gotten to know its dogs. You've even been out on the seas of it. And you've come to understand its country people in a way few of its town boys have. You would want to be part of the team. Or you will want to be part of the team, two months from now, once the period of retreat is over. By then you will have trained twelve hours a day and you'll have your confidence up. You never had much in the way of conversation, but what you had will come back to you after the period of retreat. And perhaps a little more, I'd say."

Kirby was studying Kieran's face. "It will be better with the girl too, whoever she might be," he said gently, "if you take some time apart from the world; if you devote yourself fully to the training."

Kieran said nothing. He didn't want Kirby knowing the way the girl inhabited him. The image of his brother with Susan, his hands on her white skin, flared in his mind, but he pushed it away. He stood up, wanting to be gone.

"Before you go," Kirby said, "promise me you'll come down to me eight weeks from today. Come down to me from wherever it is you decide to retreat to. By then I'll have all the information about the team. The manager is Sean Corkery, if I'm not mistaken. And he's out of Killorglin. You'll be a fine climber for them, that's one thing certain. They'll be climbers themselves, all of them being Kerrymen, but they'll not be like you."

"No, they'll not be like me," said Kieran, dreading the camaraderie and all the talking, remembering Niall and his teammates from the football who had sometimes been around the house when he was a child. "I'll not join a team," he said. Even Kirby would not be able to coax him out of his recalcitrance. It was to be his race, his alone.

Kirby was looking at him in the quizzical way that he had, his eyebrows slanting toward his nose. Then he sighed and turned away. "You're likely right," he finally said. "I see nothing of the collaborator in you; you've no time for relationships. I'm sure you can enter as an individual if you like."

Kieran said nothing, so Kirby returned to the subject of the hut. "The wattle is easy," he told Kieran. "It takes a long time, but it is a simple task. You put poles in the ground in a rectangle, then basket-weave sally branches around them. Don't forget to leave a space for the doorway. But most important is the daub; you must cover the outer walls with it once you are finished with the wattle. Mud, straw, water, and a great quantity of the most important ingredient of all."

Kieran shrugged.

"Animal dung," said Kirby. "You have to mix prodigious quantities of it into the mud and straw and water. Hardly anybody," he said, "understands how essential shit is to holding things together."

KIERAN WALKED TO THE END OF KIRBY'S PIER, THEN swung his leg over his bicycle and rode into the hills, the individual in him, he believed, safe from the complications of others. Climbing, he was alert to the details of the passing road. It was the most beautiful time of the afternoon, late, practically evening, and the stones of the hedgerows caught the light and held it in a way they never did earlier in the day. He moved now in an almost leisurely way, hugging the left side of the road so close to the warmth of the walls he could put out his hand and let it brush the firm leaves of ivy and holly. He passed the wrought-iron grill of a closed gate with a sign marking Dromid Burial Grounds. Twenty yards or so beyond it there was a stile, giving an easier entrance to the site than the latched gate. He had passed the graveyard often, and others like it: there was Sugreana Burial Grounds very near Gerry-Annie's and he sailed past it almost every day, but he would never stop to explore.

The top step of the stile shone, and beyond it he glimpsed a blue skirt. This slight break in the wall, and then this pennant of blue, caught his attention as he wheeled slowly past. Not visiting graveyards had always been as natural to him as sleep or water. He had always refused to stop there, or even to slow down: his awareness of any kind of gathering of the dead was too much like a promise he never intended to keep. There were ghosts enough in him without that. He knew his father went to the grave in the town, had seen him walking along the Main Street in spring with tulips and daffodils in his grasp. His brother, he suspected, would have been now and then at his father's side, if his brother was at home for a time from the city. But he himself had never gone, would never go.

Ahead of him the mountains were brown velvet. He slowed the bicycle, stopped, then turned around and climbed over the stile.

She had a brown jumper over her blue dress, likely because of the wind. "Hello, Kieran," she said.

The sound of his name in her mouth.

"Why are you here?" he heard himself say.

"For my brother," she told him. "He died as a one-year-old baby. Sometimes . . ." She glanced away from him.

"Yes," he said.

She was still not looking at him.

"I know," he said. And then he wondered why he said it, for he knew nothing at all beyond the way her hair was moving in the wind at the back of her head. And then there was her face, and her eyes not looking at him.

"You came on your bicycle," she said, "for your mother."

"No," he said quickly. He didn't want his mother in his mind. Not now. Then suddenly understanding, he wanted to tell her his mother was buried in the town, and as he thought this he could hear again the sound of the first fistful of earth hitting the oaken coffin. He could see the open ditch of the grave where they had put her.

"Why then?" she asked.

"I don't know," he said truthfully. Everything in him wanted to touch her and he was trying to evict the feeling. This was not the chance encounter he had been imagining, but it was a chance.

He fought with his mind for something to say. "You make those baskets," he said, "out of china."

"Yes," she said, surprised, almost laughing, "I do, I did, but only one or two a season anymore. Now I just make brooches. They are easier. And I like to paint the flowers."

She was so mild in her answers to him that he thought she would not have been felt around the house when she was a child, not in the way that he himself, with his sessions of rage, had been felt around his own house. The speech of the country people had entered the cadence of his own thoughts, he realized, knowing that a phrase like *felt around the house* would have been their way of expressing what he was thinking. He would not say this out loud, to her.

"I made half a dozen baskets," she said, "when I was younger. And only very small ones. But it's my father who has made most of them, and all the larger ones. He went to the north one summer to learn how. And later he taught me when I asked."

He was aware that this was a famine burial ground: most of the graves were unmarked, or marked only by the roughest of broken pieces of local stone. Only the tombs around them were large and important-looking, and her family's plot was one of these. There was a flat stone slab resting on four short pillars, with the names of long-dead relations inscribed on its surface. She had brought flowers and put them in front of the child's small headstone, which was situated near one of the pillars.

"There's still one, though," he said. "A small basket. I saw it in the window. It had a flower."

"Yes," she said, smiling. "It never sold."

He knew his mother's grave was toward the west corner of the town graveyard, near the ruin of the Penal Church that was now just a pile of rocks. He had stood in that location when she had been lowered into the ground, though he had never been back to it. A headstone would have been placed there long since, and he imagined it would be modest, not calling attention to itself. "An accident," the priest had said, allowing her to be buried there.

"It looks like a bed," he said of her family's tomb. Then he immediately wished he had not said it.

She laughed at that, however. He focused on the glass jar full of small pink roses she had left near the baby's stone.

"Someone way back," she said, "someone in the family liked this view. Or we would have been in the town as well."

The land sloped down at a steep angle from the edge of the graveyard's far wall, then flattened out into an expansive floor of bog, long strips of which had been recently worked. And then there were the hills beyond, with irregular bright fields climbing up them. He wondered what it would be like to have a baby in the house and then to have that baby gone from it. She had been perhaps the same number of years older than this baby as Niall was older than him. He looked across the wide valley and saw that her house, a white pebble in a vast green pasture, was just visible above Carhan Wood. "And you can see your house from here," he said, realizing, after he said it, that he had revealed that he knew where she lived.

"Yes," she said, squinting in the direction of the hill opposite. "Perhaps that's why, after all.

"Are you still working on the footpaths?" she asked, and the memory of coming into the house from work that night took hold of him so that he thought he might not be able to answer.

"No," he said finally, "not anymore."

She became quiet then, as if she understood his embarrassment and recalled her own part in it.

There had been rosary beads hanging from the little concrete cross on the top of the child's grave. The string had broken and some of the beads were on the ground beside the spot where she had put the flowers. For a moment he could think of nothing sadder than that broken piece of string.

"I like the look of that small basket," he said. And then, "When I was smaller my mother told me baskets like that were called Belleek. I thought she said bleak."

She laughed wonderfully at that, and he felt himself brighten, knowing he had in some way pleased her.

"I should go now," she said.

"Yes," he said, and then: "The baby, did he have a name?"

"Kieran," she told him. "His name was Kieran."

"My own name," he said, surprised.

She nodded. "Yes," she said.

"I'll be leaving the parish soon," he said. "I am going on a sort of retreat where I'll be by myself for some time." He was amazed that he had told her this.

"Are you going to Lough Derg?" she asked. "Are you making a pilgrimage?"

"No," he said. "It's not like that."

"My mother went to Lough Derg once after the baby died. She was gone for three days." She looked troubled by this distant memory. "And three nights," she added.

He did not know what to say to this.

After a few more moments of silence, she spoke again. "I am glad that we came across each other here," she said, "that we were able to speak to each other a little."

She turned then and walked toward the stile. He watched as she climbed the two steps, her white hand against the dark stones of the wall, steadying herself. He continued to watch as she walked away from him down the road, the blue flame of her skirt visible at times, then hidden by the hedgerows. Over and over like that until she went round a corner and passed out of his view. He thought she was like a piece of blue paper being blown down the road.

When he could no longer see her, he ran the conversation in all its brevity again and again through his mind. She had been kind to him, even after what he had seen; she had not run away and she had not dismissed him. Kind to him. And once he had let that thought settle, to his discomfort he began to weep, an act so unfamiliar to him it seemed to have come from a place far enough away he couldn't name it. Tears had never been a part of the tantrums, never even part of his sorrow. He wiped the moisture from his face with the heels of his hands, then sat down on a nearby headstone and wept some more, coughing with the effort of it.

She had not mentioned Niall. Not once. And he believed that that had been a kindness as well. It seemed significant to him that it was she whom he had spoken to just when he was on the edge of the retreat: the unlikely chance of it feeling to him like the working of a powerful destiny. He would be able to take more of her, that blue skirt, and the way she had said his name, with him into his aloneness. He would be able to take her infant brother as well, something large and important he now knew about her. The graveyard was alive with the small orange lilies he knew as montbretia. He left a fistful of them on the baby's grave before he climbed the stile where her foot had been, mounted his bicycle, and rode away.

—

Kieran woke in the night knowing the place where he should spend the months ahead. He could almost see it in the dark, the way it would be.

At dawn he dressed and tied together a bundle of extra clothing, leaving two sleeves of a shirt hanging so he could knot them at the front of his neck when he was on the bicycle. He had a satchel as well, which he now removed from a nail on the wall so that he could fill it with food from the kitchen. A few moments later, helping himself to apples, potatoes, biscuits, and one tin cooking pot, he experienced a pang of guilt, and decided to leave a message on the calendar beside the door, it being the only paper in the house. *Gone on retreat*, he wrote. *Back in two months.* He knew Gerry-Annie would puzzle over this, knowing him to be the farthest thing from religious, but this was all he could muster at the moment, never having been one for explanations. And he was anxious now to be gone.

He had ridden on recent weekends all over County Cork, along its coastlines and deep inland, looking for the right spot, and while he could justify the hundreds of miles of searching as part of the training, he was not satisfied by anything he had seen. There was a pastoral feel to this neighbouring county, probably like the English countryside, he thought. What he felt was that it wasn't wild enough for him, too cultivated and kept. While he moved smoothly through the better maintained roads near Georgian houses, he sensed an absence of privacy on the land. And he would need isolation. He had hoped to find something near the cycle track he had heard about at Banteer in North Cork, but once he had laid eyes on the track itself, it seemed pointless to him to circle round and round on a flat surface – what could be gained by that? And the surrounding fields spoke to him of lushness and domesticity. It wasn't what he wanted.

The sky was a dusty plum colour when he stepped outside and was whitening toward the east. He recalled the morning when he had cycled past Susan's house, the discomfort of that, though no one had seen him. But now that he had spoken with her, he recognized the desire to repeat that small journey, as if she might welcome him. But he pushed the notion aside and pointed the bicycle in the opposite direction, then pedalled off on the familiar route he had taken each morning, years before, to school, passing through Island Boy and Killeen Leacht, heading for Derriana Lough. Everything was still, as if dreaming. Nothing paid him any mind. Even the windows of the school seemed withdrawn and muted, uninteresting to the young man he had become. The lake when he reached it was so still the adjacent hillside was crisply mirrored there, an upside-down world.

As he began the ascent up and away from the water's edge, he could feel the energy flowing from his torso to his legs and the pleasure of this sensation travelling the arteries that branched into his arms and along his spine, the electric physicality of the effort. The road, a track really, became rougher once he left Coomavoher behind, and the few cabins he passed were vacant and had been so, it appeared, for a number of years. The roofs were gone but the chimneys still surmounted open hearths. He could have chosen a small, empty structure, roofed it with wattles, and set up housekeeping, but he had a mind to build his own shelter in a place where no one had done so before, and he would stick to that. He knew the place, having been there once or twice when he was younger, and the memory of it had come to him in the night and had claimed him.

The track came to an abrupt end at a small stream that cut in front of him, then leapt over the edge of the steep hillside, heading for the lake below. He dismounted and began to walk the bicycle along the bank on a path made by mountain sheep. The land had flattened out here, but he was aware of the subtle incline that allowed the water to travel at considerable speed over a bed of stones. He was high enough now that when he turned to gaze down at Derriana Lough, it appeared to have the same dimensions as the basin of water he washed with, mornings at Gerry-Annie's house. It wasn't long before he reached Tooreenbog Lough, the first of five lakes that climbed up the mountain like jewels on a necklace, each one smaller than the one before, beaded together by the thread of the stream and knotted by a succession of diminutive water-falls, not one of which was taller than his shoulder. Around him, nothing but high bog lands, heather, and sedge grass, and a few brave foraging sheep. He walked by Lough Adoolig toward the farther lakes that no one, ancient or otherwise, had ever bothered to name, coming at last, after a final water-fall no higher than his handlebars, to the small shield of water that was the source.

The entire watercourse, a miracle of geography, was available to him now. He could see the path of the stream, lined at its lower leg by oak trees before it entered Derriana

Lough. The dark perimeter of this opened at its western edge to the narrow Cummeragh River, which made its way past the tailor's house, then moved sinuously down a long valley until it reached Lough Curran six miles away. And then there was the estuary where that lake narrowed and the water fanned out through marshlands into the Ballinskelligs Bay and the sea. The arm of Hog's Head on the left, and the arm of Bolus Head on the right. It was a tremendous view: seven lakes and the sea, the irregular fields, the old walls, and the strips of harvested bogs drawn on the landscape by the labours of men long dead. He thought of Tadhg, the last old man of Europe, of his wife, out there at the final reach of Bolus Head, but he knew there were no ghosts here where he planned to build his hut. Perhaps his own ghost sometime in the future, but no ghosts now.

He leaned the bicycle against the one small oak that had somehow rooted in this windswept place, knowing that its trunk would be the corner post for his hut. He removed the axe he had strapped to his crossbar, walked down the slope toward the fourth lake, where he had noted a grove of sallies, perfect in height for wattles, then brought back two bundles of these on his return, using the thicker pieces for upright posts that he pounded into the ground at two-foot intervals with the blunt end of the axe. After some thought, he decided that he would make the dwelling eight feet long and six feet wide, leaving two feet of open space in the east wall for a doorway. Then he began to weave the thinner sally branches back and forth between the posts, and the walls began to grow. Sometimes the wattles broke. Experimenting, he found that if he twisted the sally branches with two hands when he came to a corner, the fibres would give rather than snap. It wasn't until the walls were about three feet high that he realized he was using a method of weaving similar to what Susan must have used when making her Belleek baskets. He felt this connected the two of them in some way and was warmed by this.

By the end of the next day the walls were up. He could have finished them more quickly, but he knew he needed to continue his cycling so as not to lose strength in his legs. The following morning he set out on a hundred-mile ride, tearing down into the valley, pleased about the climbs he would have to make once he reached the bottom. On his return trip he removed timber and tin sheeting from the roof of a disused cow byre and, when he had pocketed all the nails he could pull from the timber by hand, tied the materials messily together, attached the end of the rope to the bicycle, and pushed the vehicle and all that trailed behind it up toward the last of the lakes. He had made the south wall of the building taller than the north by about eighteen inches so that his roof, when he had it in place, would have enough of an incline that the rain would run off. One of the vacant cottages had a clay pot on the top of its chimney, and he would cut a hole for that in the tin in order to have a decent flue, and a small chimney of his own, when he needed to make an indoor fire.

After the roof was up he began to make the daub, which was easier than he had thought it might be, because of the non-stop defecating of a flock of nearby sheep. He used the dry ends of rushes for the straw, there was plenty of mud in the vicinity, and water was everywhere. Once he had added the dung, he beat the mixture with his boots in a kind of joyful dance until it reached the right consistency, then applied the resulting paste to the wattled walls one handful at a time, while the sheep watched him with a bemused curiosity. The child in him loved the process, and the next morning, when he saw the walls had hardened, he was ridiculous with pride.

He thought it would be good to do some off-bicycle training as well to increase the strength of his torso and arms, and remembered an article he had furtively read in a magazine he had seen in a shop in the town while the shopkeeper was serving a bevy of customers. The men pictured in the black-and-white photos were jumping with muscles, having apparently made use of the barbells advertised here and there in the pages. He determined to make himself a set of these with the materials at hand. A bough, three inches in diameter, was lying to the side of the oak tree, having been torn most likely from the trunk by a gale the previous winter. He seized this and chopped at the branch end until he had a strong pole about five feet long. Then he sought and found two stones, each the size of a man's head. These he tied to each end of the bough with the rope, but they slipped from their rigging no matter the knots he employed. Eventually he bought some wire in a hardware store in town and that, along with the rope, did the trick.

While he lifted the barbells early each morning, under varying degrees of rain, or on the few fully clear days, he thought about what he would call the unnamed lakes. Or he thought about Susan, how she would feel about his new strength, whether or not she would notice the fine cut of him when he won the Rás. And him a single rider. Independent. *Unique*, he liked to think, savouring the sound of the word. He would never be part of a team.

He eventually decided on Wattle Lake for the name of the fourth lake because he had used the sally branches near its shore for his shelter. The third lake was round and pleasant and he wanted to call it Gerry-Annie Lake, feeling that was the least he could do for the other mother he had so abruptly left behind. But his own lake, the smallest, his neighbour, was more complicated. He knew it better than the other two, was beginning to learn its moods. It was fully black at some moments, but then he would look again and it would be gleaming under the touch of light or a shift of wind. At the remotest point of it you could see the continually spreading hand of the source. Each day, just after dawn, there was a heron that flew slowly and with great dignity up the valley, then settled down to fish in the lake's shallows near the source, paying no attention to the animal with long arms and three heads that he, Kieran, became when he was lifting his makeshift barbells. For a time, he considered that the nearby water should be called Heron Lake, or Source Lake, but the names never really took. It was the girl making herself felt in his mind, how she would still be sleeping at this early hour. While he prepared his body for her, and for the Rás, she would be dreaming, her hair spreading across the pasture of the pillow like the dark fingers of the source. There was that field Gerry-Annie had told him about. He wondered if he would call this water the Lake of the Dreaming Girl, but as he became more intimate with it, he settled on the Lake of the Dreaming. He would be the only one that would know what the dreaming meant.

THE CORNER THAT SHE TURNED

——

Kenneth had found he wanted some sunlight in the right-hand side of the picture. The piece, he decided, had unwittingly become a night journey, and should be completed by a blazing zone of morning arrival; a redemption of gold after a dusky departure. There would be nothing dubious in this region, only clarity and luminescence. Everything would bloom. Everyone's arms would be open. He had almost finished, could see the full composition now. Still, as the afternoon shadows moved across the tile floor of the unfinished passenger lounge in which he painted, a memory from the last part of his own travels settled in his mind.

He had wakened in a European room he didn't recognize. Sunlight was moving in yellow bars through the slats of the shutters, then scattering, like bright, shivering amoebae, across the walls and over the ceiling. Barely awake, he had watched this, wondering where the light would have settled had it not been trapped in a room, and then the room's shadowed furniture began to take shape, and he recalled his arrival at the hotel the night before, and the journey that led to the arrival, and finally the reason he was there. This was where they were going to meet.

The train had been crowded and hot and, after leaving Milan, it had passed through one dispiriting industrial town after another. He had had trouble believing that the still lake and the quiet mountain scenery she had described could be anywhere near this part of the country, but eventually the window beside him blackened until all he could see in it was the reflection of his own face, and he knew they were leaving the more populated part of the north. Some teenaged boys got onboard at one stop or another, rough, jostling one another, and paying loud, gleeful attention to him. But still he had looked out and into the darkness, and toward the intermittent faraway lights that must have come from isolated farmhouses, or the traces of villages climbing up a slope.

An hour later, after stepping off the train at the tiny station at Orta, he had walked through badly lit, shuttered streets toward the faint sound of lake water splashing against what he imagined was a stone abutment or pier. The hotel, she had said, was on the lake, and she hoped they would have a view. There were mountains all around the lake, she said, and a monastery on an island that could be reached by a ferry that shuttled back and forth all through the day. He had had a sense of neither mountain nor monastery as he approached the broken sign over the hotel's door, only this slight breathing sound of lake water that he could hear right now in the room, though the windows remained closed.

He had taken the room for three nights, using up a considerable amount of his remaining cash to do so, as she had been uncertain when she could get away, whether a Wednesday or a Thursday would be possible. He was anxious to see her, believing he was in love in a way he had never been before, though he knew that she was not free and that any thought of a future was a thought that must be banished from his mind. He was too inexperienced and uncertain to even conjecture how she might have felt about him, so he had flung himself into the circular wholeness of being completely alone in love. Everything he saw, even something as simple as an abandoned flower on a sidewalk, or a dead bird near a lamppost, was examined by him in the light of this innerness that was both exhilarating and disturbing, though not yet as painful as he would have expected.

He had met her at an art opening in Milan. She spoke some English; they had fallen into a conversation about the contemporary Italian painter Giorgio Morandi, and at the conclusion of this she had touched his arm and had asked him how long he would be staying in the city. Her husband owned three or four galleries in the city, and as Ken soon came to discover, she was often left alone in these narrow places, which were more like long halls than rooms, in order to keep an eye on the paintings and talk to potential clients.

She was beautiful in an unusual way, with dark brows and lashes, and almost white blond hair. It was this hair that he would look for through the glass of one gallery or another once he began to seek her out in what had progressed from being a cautious to a fervent way. Her hair, he thought, was like a lamp in an otherwise dark room. Her English was good, but not good enough for him always to be able to grasp what she was saying on the telephone, if he was lucky enough to find a telephone in working order, which was seldom the case in Italy. In the galleries, however, he could read, or thought he could read, her expression. And then there was the physical way she had of searching for the correct English term, twisting her arms and torso as if the phrase were lodged somewhere deep inside her and must be released from her mouth, like the banderoles he had seen emerging from the mouths of saints in fourteenth-century Italian pictures. He was moved by this. He did not know her age, but assumed she was older than he was, and knew her to be more sophisticated.

Once it was clear that they would become lovers, he had checked out of the hotel where he was staying and had rented a room for a full month in spite of the fact that he had intended to stay for only a week in Milan. Soon, though, she had begun to talk about the lake and the mountains, and he came to understand she wanted a more romantic setting. There was a hotel in Orta, she told him, a hotel on the lake. They could have one, maybe two days there. There were some small shrines in the hills that she wanted to show him, and some stations of the cross. They were peasant art, she said, but art nonetheless, and charming in their way. She wanted him to see them. They could take a small train from Orta, up into the mountains, stopping every ten miles at villages along the way. Some of the villages would have the chapels of the penitents. Yes, she had told him, when he asked, there were Penitenti Bianchi and Penitenti Negri. Or there had been, back in the fifteenth century. And sometimes, even now, there were processions, but not at this time of year, which was early autumn.

He rose from his bed and walked across the wooden floor to one of the windows, where he struggled for a bit with the metal clasp that held the shutters in place. Finally the shutters sprang open and the room was flooded with a kind of shocking and beautiful light that revealed mountains, sparkling lake, and pilgrims waiting patiently for the ferry to the monastery island outside, but also cracks in plaster, dust motes, crumpled papers, coins from his emptied pockets, and yesterday's breakfast crumbs between the floorboards inside. Among the crumpled papers was a schedule of trains, and as he picked this up and smoothed it out on a table beside the bed, he realized that he had no idea which of the three trains she would take from Milan. He would have to be at the station, therefore, for each arrival, unless she arrived on the first. At the moment this thin piece of paper with its tiny, practically unreadable black type was more significant to him than the magnificent view. There was no morning train, but there were two in the afternoon, and the one he himself had arrived on near midnight. Today was Wednesday. He hoped she would be at the station just after noon.

He waited for the first train with eagerness. There would be the exquisite pleasure of lovemaking in the afternoon, followed by the novelty of lovemaking at night, something they had not yet experienced, at least together. There would be long, earnest conversations, with her struggling to find the correct English words. She would wear a nightdress, an Italian nightdress, and he would slip the straps from her shoulders. He found he could not sit still while he waited, so he walked back and forth between the two benches in the station. And then, when the station came to feel too confining, he paced back and forth on the quay. When the train arrived and she was not on it, he walked around and around the exterior walls of the station, worried that he might have somehow missed her.

After about ten minutes of this he wandered back into the town.

Everywhere he went there was the sense of the lake, though often he could not see it. Occasionally the sound of the ferry's horn reached him, announcing the departure of another boatload of pilgrims. He did not want to take this ferry, though he had no idea why. He ate a plate of spaghetti at an outdoor table in a town square and drank two glasses of faintly bitter red wine. Then, with nothing to do until the four o'clock from Milan, he decided to take a look inside the church, the door of which was open, revealing a velvet black interior, as if there were absolutely nothing inside but a limitless void.

As always in such places, there were murals on the walls depicting obscure religious subjects, many parts of which were missing because of repairs over the centuries, or because, if the painting was a Virgin or a Crucifixion, thousands of hands had touched whatever regions of the paintings were within human reach. It was interesting to him that such damage could be caused by worship. He was thinking about this when he heard a scuttling noise and then the sound of a galvanized pail scraping across stone flags.

At the front of the church, an old woman, dressed entirely in black, was washing the choir stalls, bending toward the pail, wringing out her cloth, then moving her arm in a slow circular motion over the surface of the wood. In spite of her bent back and her squat form, there was grace in her movements and the kind of absorption that spoke to him of tenderness and devotion. She hadn't noticed him at all, or if she had, she was paying him no mind, and he realized she would take this attentiveness with her to each aspect of the church she was required to clean. Kenneth was struck by this, and years later, working on the Gander mural, she would come to mind. The combination of discrete courtesy toward and rapt engagement with the surface she was working on would be something he would discover in himself when the brush-strokes on the wall were going well.

She was not on the four o'clock train. Kenneth returned to the hotel and lay down on the bed that had been made up in such a ludicrously perfect fashion it looked as if no one had slept in it. Not anyone. Not ever. By now the sun was on the other side of the hotel and the room had become sober and remote, like the rooms behind braided ropes he had seen in famous houses all over Europe – rooms in which famous people had slept or died, or both.

He swung his legs around so that he was seated, cross-legged, looking at the headboard, an elaborately carved affair with rosettes, garlands, and two small angels, one on either side. He remembered a song his mother used to sing to him about angels guarding a sleeping child, and it occurred to him that his mother would hardly have approved of the adventure he was about to undertake, though likely not until tomorrow, he conjectured, though he still intended to meet the midnight train, just in case. In the meantime, he would draw the bed, the wardrobe, and perhaps make a watercolour of the view out the window.

As expected, she had not been on the night train, and the next morning he woke quite early with the amoebae swimming on the upper wall rather than on the ceiling, and the word *arrival* repeating itself in his mind. Unless she arrived on the first train there was not going to be time for more than one chapel in the mountains. Even if she did arrive on the one o'clock train, they would have to depart almost immediately for the mountains in order to get up there and back before sundown. This small journey could be rehearsed by him in the course of the morning so that he would at least know where they would be going, and valuable time would not be wasted hunting for shrines. He bought a sweet bun in a pastry shop that had opened early in the square. It seemed suddenly miraculous to him that there were people all over the world who were willing to rise in the dark to bake morning bread: what sense of vocation drove them to do this? Thinking such thoughts, he headed for the station. Coffee would have to wait.

Ten o'clock found him staring at a mural in a Chapel of the Black Penitents. He had had to ask a stranger on the train about the whereabouts of the chapel, and though the woman had looked at him oddly when he had done so, she had asked someone else, who in turn asked the conductor. An incomprehensible conversation erupted – somewhat argumentative, Kenneth thought – during which several village names, or at least what he assumed were village names, were bandied about until one was agreed on and written down on a scrap of paper. *Bozano*, it read.

The villages were reasonably close together, and the train stopped at regular short intervals. Trontano was reached in just over half an hour. After he left the train Kenneth was required to ask once again about the chapel and wondered at this point why he had not inquired after the White Penitents, believing, perhaps inaccurately, that it might have been a more benign question. This notion was reinforced when he read the soiled piece of paper on a table near the entrance of the chapel that explained, in rough English, that the black penitents had been called upon to attend funerals and other unhappy events and that they had sometimes worn dark cloaks with skeletons embroidered on the back and skulls on the hood. The mural he was looking at was a crude depiction of the seven deadly sins with gluttony riding on a pig, and sloth taking the shape of a fat, slumbering man. Two naked lovers, tied back to back and surrounded by flames, represented lust. To Kenneth's surprise, the couple looked not at all desperate, as if they had discovered something amusingly arousing about the position they found themselves in even in the midst of their eternal predicament. There was a slightly sour smell of old candle wax and perhaps stale incense in the chapel, and Kenneth was not unhappy to leave it for the open air.

He arrived back in Orta just before the one o'clock train from Milan, and was once again disappointed and by now angry and hurt, convinced, suddenly, that she was not coming at all, had never intended to meet him, and had sent him off on this journey to get him out of her white blond hair. He walked sullenly back into the town until he reached a narrow street where he could hear the nearby lake but could not see it, and where he had noticed there was a bar. Here he settled outdoors at a rusted tin table, ordered a small carafe of red wine and, tired by now of pasta, a plate of antipasto as an act of defiance.

In the next twenty-four hours Kenneth would come to a full understanding about waiting and its sister, hope, how even as you lie in an empty bed at two o'clock in the morning, even when the room you have rented is yours for only three more morning hours, hope will still cross the room to meet you, if only to keep you turning on the spit. You argue her away from you only to discover that some semblance of her remains in the shadows where the light of the lamps doesn't quite reach, or just behind a door where a knock might be heard at any moment. There is also a suggestion of hope in the breathing sounds of a body of water that you have never properly looked at, or a departing ferry you have never taken.

There would be no water in the Gander mural, not even a hint of water, though all who looked at it would have crossed, or would be about to cross, an ocean. The figures on the wall would always be landlocked, perhaps listening to the sound of water they could not see. Landlocked and waiting, always waiting, for the arrival of something, or someone they were never going to meet again.

Painting the bright sun-drenched sky of arrival, Kenneth realized that the woman from Milan would always be the absence on this waiting room wall, the pale, curving path strewn with leaves, the vacancy of a deep blue, limitless night. It was a decade later, and he was in Gander,

Newfoundland, and yet he suddenly recognized her atmosphere in such things, though he hadn't thought of her for years, and could not even fully remember her name. Yes, she was there in the mural, the one significant event that never happened. The path that hope had walked and the corner that she turned.

———

It was *his* place, Niall had often reminded her, his peninsula. He had known these winds, this rain since infancy, he told her: he, the expert of weather. What was an English toff like her doing there anyway? He would smile then, laugh, but behind this apparent playfulness she could feel something else, something that wanted her gone from there.

Without a multi-generational history she could never actually be a part of the surroundings. "It's in the genes," he told her. She could imagine she was happy here, but that was all it would be. Imagination. "You English are only here for the view," he said once. "There's no reality in it."

There was nothing to keep her there, he insisted with the playfulness gone from his voice, and one day, if she was smart, she would realize this and vanish in the night. She was fortunate she had that former husband somewhere, and a father, who provided her with an unearned income. Otherwise, she would never have been able to stay.

"You people," he said. "You people never have to work for a living."

He himself worked with the landscape, he explained; he interpreted and recorded its moods. I own this, he might just as well have said. And you are an interloper.

"Well, Mister Weather," she said, "sometimes I think that you're just a front blowing through. And maybe this isn't just the first time. Maybe I'm part of a repeating pattern. Who is next? Someone else who is only here for the view?"

He had turned toward her then, his face white with anger. "What do you want from me, Tamara?"

"Please," she said, "please just tell me something, anything about who you are, what you feel. Are you happy, Niall, are you ever really happy? How am I supposed to know you? You tell me nothing."

"I'm happy," he said. "Maybe there is nothing to tell and it is only you who imagines that there is."

"I want more of you," she said. "How can there be anything so wrong with that?"

He became fiercely protective of his wife at times like this, her innocence, her loyalty, as if any act of self-revelation on his part was a further betrayal of her. He became overtly expressive of the terrible thing he was doing to her. Tam believed he wanted her to be conscious of this as well, her part in it. She wouldn't say it, wouldn't ask, and what does your wife do, exactly? How does she work for a living? She would not defend her own role, whatever that was. There would be no explanations coming from her about how it was she came to be there with him in her arms. She would not remind him that it was he who knocked on her door or called her in the mornings. And she would not bring Teddy into the argument, would not point out that she came as a partner into this world of his.

Feigning kindness suddenly, a hand on her arm, he said, and not for the first time, "You should make a life, a family of your own."

She could feel her age when he talked like this, the passage of time and the arc of the relationship. Her age and his own and the weight of the secret they held between them.

"I love this cottage," she told him. "I love that mountain," she said, pointing out a window. "And that one. I know the names of every dog from here to the pass." She wanted him to believe it was the landscape and everything else that was alive in it that held her, not him. "The people here know me," she said. "I have been in their kitchens." Which, she might have added, was more than he could say, wheeling out here from the town with a profession under his arm and a feeling of superiority in his mind.

He had never wanted his life to be like this, he began again. He had never wanted to harm his innocent wife. He had not been looking for this, he said, insinuating that somehow she *had* been looking and had sized him up and hunted him down and had remained, stubborn, demanding, insisting that he appear. And then, as if out of concern for her, he told her she was missing her real life, that there was a life she was owned by and that this life was going on across the channel, without her. As if there was a drama somewhere, in hiatus, the stage set, waiting for her to walk on so the curtain could go up. As if she had wickedly abandoned everything, which, though she would never admit it, she almost had.

"This *is* my life," she told him. "I know the people in the town shops. I know how the grass grows in the middle of the road." Her drawings lay on the table in the next room, but she couldn't bring herself to cite them. If he chose to dismiss them, she would not argue.

"Can't you see how good your life would be?" he said. "Think of the country house weekends. All those drawing rooms, the children home from the right kind of schools for a day or two, servants in the hall. You could stop drawing the planes and concentrate entirely on wildflowers. The English love wildflowers, I've been told."

"Don't," she said. "Just don't."

"Why don't you see it would be so much better for you, Tam?" he said. This from a man who only an hour before had been so intimately encircled by her the walls of their bodies had seemed to dissolve. "Better for all of us," he said, hell-bent on bringing his wife right into the room.

After a session like this she would storm through the three rooms of her empty cottage, weeping, unable to contain the rage and desire. She would pull out the old photos of Teddy and wilfully try to mourn him, but she knew her tears were not for that boy who had never caused her grief and only for the man who had, who did. She wanted Niall to come back to console her. She wanted to slap his face. She wanted his hand between her legs and his mouth on her breast in the angriest of ways. She wanted to break the unspoken contract that was between them, the one she had been forced to accept without ever being apprised of the terms. She wanted to tear the power out of him, to humiliate him. She wanted to watch him through the window, locked out of her house, her life, begging to be allowed back in.

She made a series of plans, attempting to resurrect the woman she had been before all this had entered her life. She crumpled up the botanical drawings and began to draw nothing but the planes, and when she found she could no longer do this from memory, she went to the library in Killorglin and borrowed a book entitled *Aircraft of the War* and traced the black-and-white photographs in it. She made alarmingly expensive phone calls to men she had known in the past, once even going so far as to invite one of these men, whom she had tracked to New York, to visit when she found he was miraculously unattached and planning, he said, a trip to Ireland, only to have to cancel the invitation with improbable excuses. Once she adopted a feral cat, named it Noxious, and spent hours trying to coax it out from behind the dresser. It came to her only when there was food in her hand, then seized its dinner, and retreated hissing.

"Christ, Nox," she said to it, "even you!"

She went outside at night and circumnavigated the cottage in the dark, stumbling over uneven ground, anger and sorrow arguing in her head, looking in her own windows at the warmth of her own pointless domesticity as if she were a

voyeur of her own life. There was her bed with its eider-
down, there was her table. A vase filled with silly wildflowers
collected three days ago when she knew he would be arriving.
There was the chair where she sat and read or looked at the
book about aircraft. Tilting her head as far back as it could
go, she staggered back and forth while gazing into the hard,
cold sky, the darkly seductive dome above her, stars they
would never see together, blocked out at earth level by the
ebony shapes of the mountains, until she crashed into the
cottage wall outside her bedroom window. There was her
long nightgown hanging on the back of the door, looking just
like her ghost, no, her corpse. And near it a calendar full of
empty days, askew on the wall.

She let the cat go back to the wild.

Who was he, anyway, this mild-mannered weatherman
who hadn't the courage even to break with her? Why were
certain gestures and expressions of his so essential to her?
Why even now did she want to stretch out at his side? If only
she *could* leave. But she had lost her bearings. Her instruments were lying to her. She would not be able to make her
way, even with familiar territory under her, toward any kind
of landing strip. She traced several more planes, so furiously
her pencil tore the onionskin on which she worked.

When she slept at times like this, the dismantled village of
her childhood came back to her in dreams. Sometimes Teddy
strolled by, but only as he had been when he was a child.
Sometimes her nan stood firmly in her path, holding a cardigan in her hands and scolding. Never her parents, and rarely

Edgeworth Hall. It was the old people of the village who were most present in the dreams, walking through their vanished streets with baskets over their arms, their ancient Biblical names – Obadiah, Rachel, Kaziah, Eber – suddenly available to her, though she was certain she had forgotten them. Her father had torn their houses down and scattered them to the winds.

Niall was trying to displace her. It was as if he had eviction on his mind. Had there been thatch rather than slate on her roof he would set it on fire. He would bring in the battering ram and smash down her walls, force her out into the open, all for the convenience of an uncomplicated life. She recalled his hands in her hair, the smell of him, the physical fact of him, and the betrayal she felt in the face of everything that had passed between them at such moments. It was unbearable. She would have to leave; she was certain of this.

She stared at the phone that squatted mute and malicious on her desk. At times like this it would remain silent for over a week, once for ten full days. Sometime during these silences she would stop weeping, and the anger would float away like a cloud of mist rising up one of the mountains, then evaporating into the ether, and the terrible distance would set in. She was apart from her life, separated from her self. Her self would go into the town to shop. Her self would go for long walks down the road, but she, Tam, was nowhere to be seen. She had disappeared. She was floating overhead, unreachable. Even the dogs whose names she knew did not approach her but simply watched her walk by. She was a familiar stranger, not dangerous enough to bark at, but unworthy of engagement.

On some morning or another in the midst of this, she would awake to a clear day, walk outside on the wet grass in bare feet, and be able to actually hear the animals in the fields or the sound of a distant tractor. She would turn on the radio and listen with some interest to the news, then sit at her desk and begin to add colour to the Spitfire she had traced days before. She would brush her hair, apply a bit of makeup, and gaze in the mirror with some admiration at the self she began to recognize again, knowing that this would be a day when he would call. Each piece of cutlery, the dishes on the shelves, the deep wells of the windows – all of this was possible again. The sentimental sailor's valentine on the wall, the simple hearth with its glowing lump of turf, the delicately painted flower on her morning teacup, a blue willow plate, all of this in attendance under a dust cloth in her hand. When his call came, she would answer it after the second ring.

And then there was the last time, the final time, the time that all the other times had been a rehearsal for.

She could barely recall what she had said, except that the word *hope* had been tossed around by her in the most futile of ways. Give me something to hope for, she had said, or something to that effect. Give me something to look forward to.

He had been pacing back and forth in the room, preparing to leave her again. "The only thing we can hope for is that this — whatever it is — will evaporate in the night," he said, "that we will no longer want it."

"All right," she said, "I will work toward that."

"Good," he said, "that will be best. I will work toward that too."

She softened then, but only briefly. "Can't we just talk about it?" She had been pleading, and she knew it. And she hated this in herself.

"No," he said. "I won't talk about it anymore." He stopped moving, turned toward her. "I won't do it, Tamara. Not ever again."

"You are saying never."

"Yes," he said, "that's what I am saying."

"Not even if . . ."

"Not even then."

Once, a few years back, she had decided to join the people of Cloomcartha, farmers and their families, on an annual trek over two mountains on the old butter roads and the tracks only the keepers of mountain sheep knew. On the other side they were to meet the few remaining inhabitants, a couple of old bachelors and their dogs and pasture animals, in Gloragh, a collection of rough cottages deep in an unvisited valley. She had been charmed by the idea of this, the sense of inclusion. Speaking to him about it, she had laughed and said she might get lost. "If you do get lost," he said, "I'll have to come to look for you."

He would not say that now.

"You can leave," she said. She was standing with her arms crossed and something unidentifiable roaring in her head. "I think you should leave, Niall. Now."

But he did not leave. Instead he crossed the room toward her and pulled her roughly into his arms. The desire had come again then, ferocious and with a mind of its own, and she felt herself rising to meet it, encouraging it, as they wrestled each other toward the bed. "This is the way it is, Tamara," he said. "This is all we can hope for."

Afterwards they had lain bathed in sweat, silently facing each other and soberly looking into each other's faces. Then, without a word, he had risen and walked naked around the room, picking up his clothing and hers, sorting the garments and placing them on two separate chairs. He said nothing. But as he dressed to leave, he turned back to her and began finally to talk.

That night she circumnavigated her house under a partial moon. Then she stood motionless at the end of the drive until the lights of the mountain farmsteads went out one by one. Later she twisted in the sheets: the pain terrible in every kind of way. By morning that frail possibility of going forward with what they had been to each other, that fragile light, had been put out.

The next day the wind shrieked and hail tossed itself against the glass of the bedroom window. But by afternoon, a square of sunlight moved steadily across the floor, then inched up the fireplace wall. The phone was silent all through the daylight hours. Then the darkness came again.

The next morning she dressed and began to pack. By noon she had called the airlines and had booked the flight. There was that man in New York, though she had no clear memory of him, only that he had survived his missions, and that he had taken to her. There was the publisher, and the illustrations for the warplane books. There might be some kind of life in that. She didn't know, but she was convinced that everything here in the Iveragh had been annulled.

Nitall had opened himself to her; a river of speech had flowed out of him. And then he had firmly closed everything down. "I want no part of it," he had said.

The majority of her life has been swallowed by waiting, she thinks now. *He took your life*, her inner voice says, but even as it says this she knows how extreme the thought is. And yet, here she is, still waiting. She, who has flown every kind of questionable warplane, sits here waiting at the end of the second day, waiting for the most domestic of aircraft, grounded by fog. She thinks of Niall here in this very room, on his way back from New York, waiting while a plane, destined to return him to Ireland, refuelled. He had not found his brother, would never find him, and would not recover from his loss: the injured brother, the brother with a heart large enough to be broken.

No amount of speed or distance can change what is unchangeable. It really doesn't matter whether the fog clears, whether the journey is interrupted, or whether it is ever resumed. The brother is probably dead by now. She will never have a child. Her father will continue to destroy the English landscape. She will continue to trace obsolete machines on paper, the remnants of her previous life. And the man with the white waving banner in the mural, the one with all the power? He will completely adopt his own father's quiet, ordinary life.

She asked Niall once about meteorological predictions: how accurate were they when all was said and done? The good weather, he had told her, the high pressure systems, sometimes change their minds and drift off to other zones. "But you can count on the gales," he had said, "the storms. The bad weather arrives right on time."

BELLEEK

———

After three or four weeks of training and isolation near the lakes, Kieran turned his attention to the condition and maintenance of the bicycle, his beloved Purple Hornet. It would need gears, he felt sure, and this worried him, but his knowledge of mechanics was scant, and Kirby had said nothing to him about this. Kieran had often polished "the Hornet" and, on occasion, he had sanded and painted it – always the same dark purple. He had replaced its seat and its wheel guards. (Kirby had always raised his eyebrows in admiration whenever these overhauls had taken place.) He, Kieran, couldn't count the number of chains and tires that had come and gone over the years, and once or twice, when he had been feeling flush after a good spell of work, he had bought a new wheel. But in his heart he feared that gears couldn't be added to a bike as old as his was. There was the bicycle store in Killarney, where he had purchased the tires and wheels, but he had kept his conversations there short. Even the thought of asking about gears humiliated him. It was likely every other cyclist in the country knew perfectly well you couldn't put new gears on an old bike. It sounded like something people would say: "You can't put new gears on an old bike."

As it turned out, you *could* put new gears, three speeds of them, on an old bike. The man in the Killarney cycle shop was firm on this, you *could*, but you would have to have the money necessary to buy those gears and then you would have to pay for the fitting of them. The amount was more than Kieran's depleted savings could provide, although he had been very stringent with his cash and had taken to hunting rabbits with snares he had made with wire, rather than buying meat at the butcher's in town. They tasted well enough roasted over the spit he made for the fire, but their screams when they were captured put him in mind of a child being murdered in the night and caused him distress. Sometimes his mother spoke after the screaming subsided and only a faint whimpering remained. He knew he would have to become a labourer again for three weeks or so. He would have to get a job somewhere, and apart from evenings and weekends, the training would have to be maintained by cycling back and forth to the place of employment.

As if reading his thoughts, the man in the shop told him that word had it that the railway was hiring for the repairs on the trestle bridge that crossed the mouth of Valentia River just at the edge of Cahersiveen. "Perhaps the strength of you," he said, "would be what might make them want to take you on so late in the day, the work having already begun and all." He should ride over there now and see if there was use for one as tough as he appeared to be. "And the climbing," he said, "would be good for the legs of a cyclist training for the Rás."

Why did he think he was training for the Rás? Kieran wanted to know.

Hadn't Michael Kirby himself told the man so. He'll be in here for the gears, Kieran will, Kirby had apparently said, once he figures out that he has to have them, though God alone knows where he'll get the money. In his opinion, the man continued, God himself had injured that trestle just so Kieran could work on it. "Get over there and start climbing. And tell them John Kelly from Killarney Cycles sent you. We're counting on you here for the glory of the county."

"I won't join the team," said Kieran. "I'll be in it as an independent."

"That may be," John Kelly answered, "but if you win, the team will claim you in the end."

Kieran liked the work on the trestle, the climbing, and the heaviness of the winching. With no fear of heights, he became almost immediately fond of hanging by a rope over the slow, muscular progression of the river, or of watching the same river develop opaque bars of light when the sun shone between the slats that held the rails in place. He could see the whole town from there, the mountain behind it where Susan's house was, and he believed he could even pick out the shop window behind which he knew she would be standing at the counter, her head bent or her face turned, perhaps, toward the light and the view that would include the trestle he stood on. Sometimes, if he held the shop window in his gaze long enough, he imagined he could see the little basket she had made with its one flower, still unsold, and on display, though he knew this was impossible.

Even when he had made enough money for the gears, he continued to work on the trestle. He was determined to stop eating the rabbits and wanted to buy some meat from a butcher. Certainly he would need more cash for the months ahead when he would return to Gerry-Annie's. It was a point of pride with him now that he would pay his own board, and he intended to buy a pair of boots for Annie, ones that he knew she wanted. They had fur around the ankles and were made of rubber so that her feet would remain dry on her walks in and out of town to clean for his father. There was a red umbrella as well that he had seen her eyeing in the window of Mary Margaret's shop. He liked to think of her telling his father that it was he, Kieran, who had bought these items for her, and pictured how the old man would shake his head in amazement at what his son could provide.

The work was completed finally, and he and the other workers took down the scaffolding and collected their last pay packets from the temporary railway office that they then also dismantled. The Purple Hornet, beautifully fitted with its new gears, waited at the wall of the road, as alert as a dog in the presence of sheep and, to his mind, as full of anticipation of an important task about to be undertaken. It was November. There were only five more months before the Rás, and they

would be months of rain and storm; often he would be training, he knew, in the very teeth of the gales that would soon
begin to cartwheel in from the Atlantic. At Christmas his
brother would come again, home from Dublin, but he didn't
want to think about any of that, liking the notion of the girl
alone with her father in the shop and then later in the evening
with both her parents in the house above.

There would be the evening fires at Gerry-Annie's for
him, and food he had bought himself boiling over them. There
would be the books that Kirby had given him to read and long
sleeps taken in the hours of full blackness, night after night
until the days came longer again and the Rás grew even nearer.
He wanted the dark season, the company of Gerry-Annie, and
the punishing rides through the calamitous weather. But first
there was something he knew he had to do.

He had brought his only good shirt and one pair of decent
shoes with him that last morning to the trestle, stopping by
Gerry-Annie's to collect them on his way to work. Annie said
nothing about his absence, though he saw the look of relief on
her face as he walked through the door. She wondered out loud
if he was going to a funeral, as she had never known him to
voluntarily take that shirt down from its hook on the wall. He
smiled at that observation but didn't explain. "Perhaps I'm
thinking of going to Mass," he joked.

"You could wait till the roof was slated before that would
happen," she said.

After he had finished work, he walked behind one of the
abutments of the trestle and removed his boots and changed

his shirt. The shoes were a bit small, so he took off his socks as well, while light and shadow from the river simmered on the concrete he leaned against. His trousers were spattered with paint from the trestle and mud from the road, but he was hoping that only the top half of him would be observed, that and maybe a glimpse of the shoes as he entered. Once he was on the bicycle the shoes felt uncertain and slippery on the pedals, but despite this he was on the main street of the town in minutes.

He pushed the bicycle into a rack in front of the bank and walked beside the church until he came to the spot where he knew he must cross. Here he paused, trying to will his heart to stop beating so insistently, and wondering if he should turn back. There was the glass of the shop front, full now of silver and pearls, some of the jewellery hanging from black velvet, the rest positioned on the satin floor of the bay window. And then the small basket, the colour of cream, with its one mauve flower and the two perfect pale green leaves. He had come this far. He had taken the shirt from the hook on Gerry-Annie's wall and put on his good shoes. To turn back now would be a kind of defeat, he told himself. So he walked in his uncomfortable shoes across the street, opened the door to what seemed to him to be a cacophony of bells, and entered the shop.

She looked up then and said his name with surprise. Her wonderful hair was pulled back and her face was lit on one side only by the sunlight coming in through the window. He could see her father at the rear of the store seated on a stool and bent over something on a table under a strong light. The man looked briefly up at the sound of the bells, but soon turned his attention back to whatever he was examining.

"What brings you here?" Susan was asking, a pleasant, courteous tone in her voice.

Kieran wanted to tell her that she had brought him here, the thought of her strong in him night after night. "I've come from the trestle," was all he could manage. "The work on it is finished."

"Oh," she said. "I didn't know you were working there above."

"Yes," he said. "One month now."

"Niall never said in his letters."

The mention of his brother troubled him, that and the sudden thought of letters between them. "Niall wouldn't have known," he said.

There was a display case in front of her, like a glass sepulchre from a fairy tale, and in it the bright stones of the rings looked harsh and significant. On top of it her two hands were nervously, yet almost imperceptibly, moving. Kieran felt that the silence between them was enormous and that he hadn't the tools to break it. The ringing of the telephone at the back of the shop startled him, and then there was her father's voice speaking about the time of a delivery.

"I've come for the basket," Kieran said. He could hear the father, still talking in the back.

She glanced up at him, with a blank look that gradually moved toward comprehension. The cool courtesy left her

demeanour, and she became visibly shy, as if he had asked her
a question so intimate it could not be answered.

Her father hung up the phone and the silence came again.

"My own basket?" she eventually asked, in a voice so soft
Kieran could barely hear it.

"Yes," he said, "in the window."

She walked out from behind the glass counter and crossed
to the front of the store, where she bent at the waist and
reached into the light to grasp the small object. She returned
with it in her hand, saying that it would be dusty from being
on display for such a long time.

"I don't mind," he told her. His blood was booming in
his ears. He could barely hear his own voice and was concerned that he might have spoken too loudly, might have
even shouted. "It doesn't matter," he added as quietly as he
could.

She returned to her place behind the counter and placed
the basket on top of the display case. Then she took a thin
piece of cardboard from what must have been a shelf near her
feet, folded it into the shape of a box, and filled it with tissue
paper that she also took from the same mysterious spot. As
she placed the basket in the little nest she had made for it, her
hands shook slightly. He would remember this trembling,
and would interpret it over and over.

"What were you after from the window, Susie?" her
father called from the back of the shop.

"It's just my little basket," she answered, "that Kieran
here wants to buy."

"He'll be wanting that basket for a girl, I'd say," the father said, laughing.

Kieran placed some money on the glass counter and Susan took it and offered him some change from the cash register.

"This is good, Susie," the father called again. "Now you'll have to be making another."

"Would you like me to put a bow on it," she asked Kieran, "if it is for a girl?"

"There is no girl," he said quietly, "it's for myself." And then, with a great stab of courage, "It's because of you."

She looked at him quizzically, and he looked back at her for as long as he could bear it. Then, when he turned his face away, she did something astonishing. She put her hand briefly on his, where it rested on the box. "Thank you," she whispered.

The bell that announced his departure from the shop rang in his mind all the way back into the hills. That and an after-image of her hands. The trembling. And then the warmth of the palm when she placed it over the roughness of his knuckles.

The following dawn he rode into the town with a card made from the basket's box in his jacket pocket. On it he had pencilled a map of where he was hidden, above Derriana Lough. He had drawn small wavelets on the lake so that she would know it was water, and had written the word *stream* alongside the line he had made for the watercourse that joined the five lakes. By the time he was making the road into the town he was running out of space and so he put an arrow there with the word *town* at the end of it in case she was confused. Then he turned the cardboard over and, having no envelope, wrote her name on the back of it. In the middle of the map he had printed the word *please*, just that, *please*, but had then thought better of this, and had tried to erase it with the dried-out rubber at the end of his pencil. The result was an unsightly smudge covering the word *please*, which was still visible if one looked closely enough. He drew a line through the word, as if to cancel such an audacious request, but in the end this looked too severe to him, almost discourteous, and when he tried to erase the line, he made a hole in the cardboard and cursed himself for doing so. A messy job all in all, and slipping it under the door of the jewellery shop was a great and terrifying risk, but one he knew he could not prevent himself from taking. He had been warning himself against it all night long. But by the first light he had lost the argument.

It was his last week at the hut, and the loss of it would now be magnified by the fact that it had become the only place where he could imagine her coming to him. Donal's story all those years ago, the poem he had said on the mountain under the stars, had bitten deep into Kieran. *I came unto him / the sheep were gathered by him.* Over and over again since that night, his mind had painted the picture of a girl climbing a slope toward him with a whole valley behind her and the sea beyond. Her eyes would be down on the path until she saw him, and her stride would be measured and purposeful. It had always been like that, he decided. Even before he knew Susan, he had had a thousand prompts for the moment.

When he caught first sight of her early on his last Sunday afternoon in the place, his heart recognized the picture she made stepping from rock to rock on the edge of Wattle Lake. Even though she had not yet reached him, it was as if they were old lovers now, with just a faint shyness, like ripples in the water, and the rest of it calm, reflective. There would be little talk between them, he knew, and there would be no resolution. He would have to search for her over and over again. All through his life there would be this distance. But now, where he stood, with two lakes between them, he could see her coming closer and closer.

He waited until she had reached the Lake of the Dreaming and had raised her eyes to his. Then he moved toward her. "Come here to me," he said.

THE RÁS

——

She has slept again, this time lying full out on a banquette. The faux-leather upholstery is stuck to her cheek on this third morning so that she feels she is peeling a part of herself from the surface as she rises to a seated position. She had succumbed to the bar in the evening, along with a few other Irish passengers, and in their company she had drunk a full bottle of wine so that she is now thirsty and disorientated. She hadn't gone to the hotel. Remembering a tale about Ferry Command, how the crew of the first transatlantic aircraft during the war had spent their Gander nights in a railcar on a siding near the runway, she had felt that succumbing to a real bed in a comfortable room would be, in some mysterious way, an admission of defeat. But now she has to admit she longs for a bath: the immersion and the heat.

It is only when she looks toward the mural that she realizes it is the sunlight that must have wakened her, the same sunlight that is raking across the picture. The oranges and yellows have intensified, and the expressions on the faces of the children appear to have altered in this changed light.

When she glances out the window, she sees that there are two airliners: the one that brought her here and another, both of them gleaming and wholesome, beyond the plate glass. Healthy, she thinks. Those are healthy planes. Now she notices that the waiting room is full of fresh passengers. The employee she had spoken to yesterday had been correct in his predictions. "This fog will clear off by morning," he had said, his pronunciation so similar to Niall's, "I can feel it." He had consulted a paper on the counter. "And the Shannon flight from New York is scheduled to arrive on time." She can barely believe that she has managed to sleep through the arrival of the second Constellation, amazed that the noise of it would not have wakened her. Perhaps it taxied up to the terminal while she was talking, while she was talking with the loquacious Irish. Someone, speaking about the Easter Uprising, had used the word *penultimate*, and she had immediately thought of Niall.

It was he who had taught her the meaning of the word, using it in relation to a gale that had ripped a half-dozen slate tiles from the roof. "This is the penultimate gale of the winter," he had said, explaining that there would in all likelihood be one more. Would *ultimate* be the correct word to describe their last moments together? she wonders now. She doubts this. The word suggests some kind of victory. "The victor, that's me all right," he had said, his voice filled with bitterness and loss.

She had been surprised when he had begun to speak while he was preparing to leave, having been so often silent after conflict, or after love. With his back to her and one arm in a shirt, he said, "You insist you want to know something more about me. So here it is: my brother and I were in a race together." He turned toward her and sat down on the bed where she still lay. "We were in a race together, just before I was to be married." He put his other arm into a sleeve but had not buttoned the shirt. "Neither of us knew the other would be there. But Susan," he said. "Susan knew. She knew and she told neither of us. Had I known . . . had I known the damage."

He had stood, walked over to the mirror that hung above her chest of drawers, and raked his hands through his hair. Once, a year or so before, when he had caught her looking at her own reflection in this same mirror, he had told her that his mother had spent good deal of time studying her face in an oval mirror that had hung on her bedroom wall. "Not in a vain way," he had said, "but more as if she was trying to come to an understanding of her own character." That mirror had vanished shortly after her death, he told her. "My father must have taken it down."

"What sort of race was it?" she asked him.

"The Rás Tailteann," he told her as he walked back to her bedside. "I had been training the previous year in Dublin, was on the Dublin team, and eventually became captain. I knew Kieran was mad for his bicycle, but I never knew, never dreamt, what it could mean to him. I never thought . . . well . . . I wouldn't have believed that he could have entered something that organized. Who could have known it?"

He walked to the chair where his clothing lay, put his trousers on, returned, and sat again near her on the bed. His shirt remained open. Beneath it was the flannel undershirt he always wore. Because of the damp, he had told her. There was something so ordinary and touching about that garment, a leftover habit, she always thought, from his childhood. "I couldn't believe the cut of him," he said. "He was practically unrecognizable. The arms on him! The legs! He had increased in size — you would think that was impossible, but he had. I hadn't laid eyes on him for months, not since Christmas, though some people had seen him here and there and had reported the sightings to my father. He'd already begun to disappear, you see, and had been gone for a couple of months in the autumn. No one, my father said, knew where he was sleeping, what he was doing. Maybe Gerry-Annie. He came back to her for the winter, you see . . ." He paused and bent over to pull on his socks, then straightened and gazed out the window. "His face when he saw me!" he said.

"He must just have been surprised," Tam said.

"No, yes, of course he was surprised. There I was, captain of the Dublin team. He was surprised, but that was not the look I saw. Something dark and unidentifiable came over his face. I had lifted my hand and was about to walk over to him, and then that look. It stopped me in my tracks, though it wasn't until much later that I knew what his face — what that look was telling me."

Tam wanted to know what he thought the look meant, but she was afraid he would close down if she questioned him too much. "He would have been on the Kerry team," she said instead, leading him gently forward.

"Kerry claimed him ultimately, yes, but he rode as an independent. I didn't think a man like him would ever be in Dublin for any reason, much less for the beginning of a bicycle race. He knew nothing of cities. But he would have ridden up on his bicycle, which had, I couldn't help but notice, new gears."

He explained that he himself had stayed out late the night before drinking with his mates and there was the thin air of a hangover around him the morning of the start. "There were all these patriotic speeches delivered in Irish by the organizers," he told Tam. "They were insisting that we were all riding for the unification of Ireland: something larger than ourselves to work toward, something to keep us all going. They kept saying we were the new Fiana, the new warriors — it wouldn't be like that now, I shouldn't think, but the Rás itself was only in its third year at the time, and there was still a lot of politics mixed up in it. It's a cruel thing, a race like that: sometimes you *do* need something larger than the self at work; sometimes you'd be working for the team, or the county, or the glorification of Ireland or whatever. But mostly it's personal, though at the time I believed there was nothing personal, no real personal aspiration in me. I was a natural athlete, I knew that, but that ability seemed completely neutral. I rarely even thought about it. In many ways it meant nothing to me. Nothing."

Not nothing, Tam thought. She knew the competitive side of his nature. Often he would clock the time it took him to ride to her house, and would tell her about his speed on one occasion or another. But she would not contradict him now. "The ability or the race?"

"Either . . . neither."

A silence entered the room. Niall was holding one shoe, and his expression was pensive and faraway. Outside there was the full calm that sometimes follows the cessation of rain. Drops of moisture beaded the clothesline but the glass of the window was dry. Tam wanted him to come back to her. She touched his arm. He straightened his spine, looked at her, and began talking again.

He recalled very little about the start of the Rás, he told her, beyond glimpses of his brother, hunched over his bike and, Niall said, "with a fierceness in him you could feel twenty yards away." The city fell behind them and the roads twisted toward one horizon or another. "One hundred plus miles, Dublin to Wexford," he told her.

There had been wind that day, and rain. The macadamized surfaces were slippery, and mud from those that were not macadamized was thrown into your eyes and nostrils. The jerseys they all wore became saturated and sagged heavily down onto their thighs. There was no hope of drying your clothes in the places . . . mostly private homes . . . where they were billeted at night, so that you knew that you would be taking the dampness of County Dublin and County Wexford with you the following day to Kilkenny. "The only hope," said Niall, "was to wear the wretched articles of clothing at the bar in the evenings where there might be a fire. We called the evening drinks the Night Stages and found that powerfully amusing."

Why was that amusing? Tam wanted to know. He told her then about how the race was divided into eight stages. "A series of punishing distances," he said. "Like stations of the cross."

The nightly sessions in the bar were an antidote of sorts to the day's suffering and, he added, an acknowledgement of more to come. "That first night I didn't see my brother in any of the bars I walked into," he said. "And the following day I didn't see him at all."

He had thought that Kieran might have dropped out some time early during the second stage; the going was bad and he himself was suffering, vomiting more than once from the exertion. But by the time he reached Waterford, there was talk of Kieran among the cyclists. It was said he had crashed near a bridge just the other side of Dungarvan and that the bicycle was so ruined he had thrown it in a ditch and had stolen an under-geared specimen from a local farm-yard, catching up with the bunch an hour later. He was a galloper, they said, and had broken away from the pack on this ordinary bicycle, sprinting up the hill and disappearing into the distance. But, at the end of that second day, when Niall himself looked up from the chain he had been attend-ing to in Kilkenny's main square, he saw Kieran sail down the main street on the undamaged bicycle he had referred to as the Purple Hornet. He sensed something then about his brother that he had never suspected before. Kieran, he realized, would be spoken of and interpreted during the course of this race, and perhaps elsewhere as well. His silences and distances would inspire fantasy. Stories would be told about him, theories would be developed. Later that night, one of his teammates told him that Kieran was billeted nowhere, had refused to be billeted. "He apparently wanted to sleep outside on the edge of town," Niall told Tam, something about night air, a beneficial change in the ozone that he was said to have claimed would occur when sunlight absented itself from oxygen.

"That was nonsense, of course," Niall said to Tam. "There was no science in it. But the boys were all for believing it. Some of them would have slept outside themselves were it not for the rain. They referred to Kieran as 'the Independent,' or 'the Individual.' They didn't even know he was a Kerryman and I didn't say he was my brother."

Tam leaned forward and put her hand on the back of his bent neck. "Oh, Niall," she said.

"I met a girl in Kilkenny," he said, not looking at her, "at a dancehall in the town. Sheila, I think . . . No, it was Siobhan. The girls were out in force, of course, once there was a pack of young men available. She had long fair hair, and I remember thinking it was wonderful, this hair of hers. We danced a few times and we shared a couple of pints. She said her uncle was driving one of the support vehicles – the Broom Wagon, they called it – and that she would arrange to go along for the remainder of the Rás and would look out for me." Niall shook his head, remembering. "I was flattered by her attentions, that was all. And I was already engaged by then. Still, I didn't discourage her."

"The Broom Wagon." Tam had laughed.

"It's what they called it," Niall explained, "this van that collected all the wrecks, swept them up, and some of the broken cyclists as well. And there were more of those than you might think, broken bicycles and their riders." The Broom Wagon had ridden behind the vehicle carrying the spares.

"A good fifteen percent of the riders lost their bikes. But, in spite of what the boys believed, even in the face of all evidence to the contrary, Kieran had not lost his bike. Not yet."

By the third stage, from Kilkenny to Clonakilty, Niall's body had adjusted and his muscles knew what was expected of them. "And for the first time it was a day of full sun," he said. "The hills were long and gentle, invigorating climbs followed by full pleasure on the way down." He had stayed with the bunch, though he knew he had the strength in him for a breakaway or two. For the first time he enjoyed the countryside, even leapt off his bicycle to shake the hands of spectators at Thomastown, knowing he could easily catch up. His jersey had finally dried, and his muscles and heart and brain were synchronized to such an extent that the whole hundred-mile stage felt like an act of grace, a courtly dance. Full of benevolence, he encouraged teammates who were feeling the heat, and let one or two of them shelter in his wake.

"Normally the team shelters the captain," he told Tam, "but I was feeling so confident I wanted to return the favour." Without the slipstream created by those around you, the going was hard, he said. Wind friction could slow you down considerably. "And I was not unaware that my brother, being a solitary rider and all, had no one to shelter him." He paused, and Tam saw him redden with emotion. "And, yes, that gave me satisfaction," he said.

Six miles out from Clonakilty he had decided to move ahead and had begun to accelerate, breaking away from the Dublin team. Breathing deeply, his body almost parallel with the crossbar, he tightened his thighs and pumped his legs furiously. Passing through the village of Ballinascarty, he lost all sense of the machine, as if the bicycle had become an extension of his limbs, as if it had become flesh itself. The feeling was almost sexual – everything was fluid and ringing and empty of language, the body having taken over from the mind. He left the team behind, and then the bunch, leaning into corners, and jamming his feet into the pedals on inclines. The deepest, farthest cells of his body, even his hair and nails, felt as if they were ignited by oxygen and heated by blood. When he reached Clonakilty he yelled involuntarily, the noise from his throat snapping him upright and throwing his head back as he crossed the finish line of the stage.

Five minutes later, while he was sluicing the remaining water from his bottle over his head, he was told that the Independent had won the stage, and had arrived a half an hour earlier without one other cyclist anywhere near him. "I could feel the change happening in me then," he told Tam. "I didn't know what the change was, but I could feel something emotional, something almost primal, happening to me. I didn't want him to have won the stage. It was all wrong, had never been like this. He was never the one to succeed. He was somebody apart."

He glanced in Tam's direction, but she knew he didn't really see her. She had become a vessel into which he was pouring this canticle, she thought, and a flicker of resentment lit a portion of the gratitude she had felt when he had begun to actually talk to her. And then his face opened and anger came into it. "This was not ordinary competitiveness," he said, curling one hand into a fist and encircling it with the other. "This was something I had never felt before, a complete change of climate . . . to be defeated by him. I was the wondrous Niall, the brilliant, accomplished older brother." He scrubbed his face as if attempting to remove all expression. "In the life that I had lived until that moment, this was the way it was. I had no familiarity with the alternative."

That night he had danced again with Siobhan but had drunk no alcohol, wanting nothing to interfere with the following day's performance. Even this girl in his arms was alive with rumours concerning the Independent: how he had trained with the best coach in Ireland, how he had fed himself on cow's blood and sheep's milk, and had lifted weights in travelling circuses. Niall had laughed hearing these things, and then he had kissed her, wanting to distract her from the subject. But even so, she went on. It was said that he had no home, was a wild boy who had grown up among the last standing oaks of Glencar. He had climbed, they said, Carrantuohil Mountain three times each week from the time he could walk, even in the wildest winds. In fact, as an infant he had learned how to walk on the slopes of that mountain. There was much speculation about how this wonder would ride on the following day, the fourth stage, when the cyclists would head into the hard hills of Kerry, and finish in Tralee.

"I knew I couldn't let him defeat me there," Niall said, "so I left the night stage early, determined to sleep profoundly in preparation." The girl had wanted him to stay, but he wouldn't do it. "There would be my father, watching when we went through Killorglin, you see, and my fiancée. Yes, Susan would be watching. I couldn't let her see me losing. Whoever prevailed in the mountains would be called the King of the Hills and would be given the corresponding jersey."

"And your brother," Tam asked. "You hadn't seen him again?"

Niall had not yet seen him, and did not want to see him, he said. He wanted to stay out of his way.

"The next day dawned fair," Niall said. "The roads were dry and I made a good start." Staying with the bunch as far as Bantry, he barely felt the effort, even on the inclines, and he was confident that he had a sizable reserve of strength for the mountains and gaps of his home county. He was a meteorologist. He could read the skies and be prepared for the upcoming weather in a way that no one else would be prepared. There would be a kind of choreography about his attacks and breakaways in his home county. He could take the King of the Hills, he believed, with strength and pleasure. All year, training in Dublin, he had been looking forward to this stage.

Then he saw his brother. The yellow jersey he now wore was a blaze of colour on his back, a flame. "It was like a bog fire, that jersey," he said. "Just when you thought you had quenched it, it flared up again, somewhere in your line of vision. And Kieran would be wearing that jersey when we passed through the Gap of Dunloe, and not much later my father would see that." He paused. "And Susan," he added.

"He crashed on a bridge near Glengarriff, Kieran did," he said. "I saw him there with the ruined purple bicycle and I could see the pain coming out of him, feel it, as I sped by, though I was unsure whether or not the pain was physical." Niall stood now and walked across the room, where he sat down on a chair facing the bed. "There was nothing in me," he admitted to her, looking at the floor, "that wanted to stop for him. I hadn't even the charity for that. Relief is what I felt. Whatever the outcome of the day, I was certain that my brother would never catch up now, on the unfamiliar spare machine that would be given to him."

"The pack left the main road after Kenmare and cycled into the mountains of Kerry. I remember feeling a kind of wild joy at the sight of these mountains, knowing I was ready for them and equal to any rise in elevation. Every kind of weather you could imagine was in those skies above," he said. "I tried to tell myself it was like I was chasing cloud formations, trying to outdistance bursts of rain, or keeping up with one particular shaft of sun. It was a powerful experience, as though the mountains themselves were giving me everything they had. The wind was at my back, and I plunged into blade after blade of piercing light. I remember whispering over and over, I am home, I am home." His face darkened. "And I remember trying to stop myself from thinking, these mountains aren't mine, they are Kieran's."

Kieran had passed him after what had been, for Niall, an ecstatic ride through the Gap of Dunloe. "Quite near here," he said, gesturing toward the window and everything outside of it, "just before we got to Beaufort. He gave me a look that I believed was filled with contempt, having manoeuvred the spare bike so that he was right beside me for at least thirty seconds. By then I couldn't bear the look of that jersey on him. I was damned if I was going to give him the King of the Hills as well."

He told her how he had intentionally summoned mental images of every victory he had won, gaining strength from the memory of these blazing precedents. He recalled the beaming confidence with which he had posed for photographs with trophies in his hands, the entitlement of being carried through the streets on the shoulders of teammates, glories in the sports fields of the university. Imagining them as platoons of an army bent on his defence, he revisited triumph after triumph, working back through time until he reached the games of his teen years, and then the games of his early youth, where his mother and younger brother would be standing on the edge of the field, watching him win. He revised the way his mother's hand had rested on his brother's shoulder in these pictures and replaced it with her raised arm pointing in his direction. The Dublin team sheltered him when they could keep up and shouted encouragement from behind him when they could not. By the time he reached Killorglin, he was well in the lead and could recognize his father's cheer in the crowd, having heard it in his mind over and over on the approach. Kieran had fallen behind him, but not so far behind him that when Niall looked for his father in the gathering he couldn't see that the older man was gazing in astonishment, not at him, but at his younger brother and the jersey on his younger brother's back. And beside his father, he glimpsed Susan, her eyes on Kieran, an unreadable look on her beautiful face.

"It was fury that drove me into Tralee," Niall said, "with Kieran and the Kerry team, which had now moved close to him, on me like a pack of hounds."

"Did you get what you wanted then?" Tam asked. She felt she was with him in this race.

"Yes," Niall admitted. "Yes I did. I was King of the Hills. But it meant nothing to me."

"But you were the victor in Tralee." She believed this was what he wanted her to say.

Niall fell silent. Then he spoke. "The victor, that's me all right," he said. "I swept him out of the way. I didn't even give him his one small moment." He turned away in the chair, hiding his face in one hand. Tam quickly wrapped a sheet around her body, slid out of the bed, and crossed the room to him.

"It's all right," he said, barely responding to her embrace. "I'm sorry." He rose from the chair then and, with his back

to her, walked to the window, and she returned to her place
on the bed.

He had gone to the Munster Tavern in Tralee minutes after
his arrival in that town, and had to be tracked down by the
organizers for the King of the Hills presentation, which
then took place alongside the bar with drinks in hand. He
had not gone back to his billet for dinner but had eaten fish
and chips instead in this establishment, with Siobhan across
the table from him, smoking cigarettes and leaning forward
now and then to run her fingers down the front of his King
of the Hills polka-dot jersey. "It was a ridiculous garment,"
he said to Tam, "something a child might have worn . . . or a
clown . . . but I was happy enough to have it on me then. Ah,
the night stages . . . you could be sure there was plenty of
drama in those as well after the circus of the day, lots of talk.
I was told that the Independent had dislocated his shoulder
in the crash but had ridden like a goddamned miracle nonetheless, having been told that he was still in the overall lead.
He was seeing the doctor, they said. Siobhan was mightily
impressed with this information. But how relaxed I was
once I heard this, figuring Kieran wouldn't be in the running the following day."

He danced again that night with Siobhan, he said, the
competitiveness in him and his blood up because of the alcohol. At one point he pushed her into a booth where he tried
to get his hands under her sweater and up her skirt. Tam

could see him leaning forward, his advances toward the girl: Siobhan would allow this for a few minutes, then shove him away, lighting a cigarette, and telling him not to be an animal. He would bend toward her then, and gently remove the cigarette from her lips, placing it in an ashtray on the table. Then he would kiss her long and slow, waiting for several seconds before slipping his tongue between her teeth.

Niall, seated once again in the chair, shifted his weight from one hip to the other, then looked directly at Tam. "I didn't even know he was in the bar until he shoved me up against the wall. 'Susan,' he was shouting, 'you've nothing at all in your heart for her!' And all this with a dislocated shoulder, mind you! It occurred to me a few years ago that he might have been persuaded not to finish the race because of his injury if it hadn't been for that night stage and him seeing me kissing that girl. Rage in the midst of sport, as I'd come to know, is a narcotic. It deadens pain. Or at least the physical pain."

Kieran had spat in Niall's face before letting him go. He then slammed out of the silenced bar, everything happening so quickly there was no time for Niall to respond. Niall wiped his face with his polka-dotted sleeve, his fierce energy of the earlier evening settling into a cold fury. Gradually he registered the stunned puzzlement on his teammates' faces. "Was that your fiancée's brother?" one of them had asked him. That was the moment when he finally confessed. "No," he had said, "that was *my* brother."

This revelation did nothing to abate the rumours concerning the Independent. It was said that there was a dark blood feud between the brothers of each generation of the Cahersiveen Riordans going back to Norman times, when one member of the tribe had betrayed another in battle. It was also said that there was traveller blood in the family, and it was this that caused the youngest boy in each generation to "go wild," to run away to the mountains as soon as he could walk to be suckled by feral goats. It was said that the blood feud would, in each generation, be played out by a test of skills, a fiddling or piping contest during famine times when the men would have been weak from hunger, but most often by a sporting event: foot races, hurling, or Gaelic football. It was hinted that the feral boy was the one destined to win and that nothing, not even physical injury, could stop that destiny from running its course.

Niall, who in the past would have been amused by such nonsense, was instead fully inflamed by what was related to him, with a smirking expression, by the girl who now had heard he was "promised" and was showing disdain for him and other "cheaters" of his ilk. She told him it was also being said that, generation after generation, the two brothers would love the same woman, and only one of them, therefore, would marry. Often, she added, one brother killed the other brother in a terrible barroom brawl concerning the woman in question.

The following day during the fifth stage, with panorama after panorama of the lush fertile landscapes of County Limerick opening before him, Niall rode like some kind of madman, pushing his limits beyond what he thought he could

bear, relishing the awareness of pain in the face of the im-
munity to pain brought about by his rage. He recalled his
brother's tantrums, those terrible explosions that tore apart his
early domestic life, and in full knowledge of the real story, he
began to blame his brother for his mother's death. It could
only have been the chaos caused by this difficult child that
had led her into the arms of adultery and drugs, he decided.
He allowed everything about the horrors of his brother's
birth to present itself to his mind, the memory as sharp and
blinding as a knife in the sun. *He broke her in half, he broke her
in half,* he chanted through clenched teeth while climbing the
long, subtle, yet exhausting slopes of the region. He was
determined never to look back, not even once, during the
stage. Still, there were times he believed he could smell
Kieran's breath and could feel the heat of it on the back of his
polka-dot jersey. Once or twice he thought he could hear his
brother shouting Susan's name, even her middle name, Ann.
How did he know this? What had the two of them plotted
while he was in Dublin? The memory surfaced of the night
Kieran had interrupted him just when he had managed to
remove Susan's blouse. How long had he been standing
there? How many times had he stood there before? And the
panting of him now at his back! Had this disturbed bastard
been following him all along, clocking his every move? And
all the time keeping such distance from him.

There were crowds lining the grimy streets of Limerick
City as the pack tore through that town, a colourful mass of
hair, eyes, and cloth smeared against dark factory walls,

making an infernal noise and gesturing wildly. The shouting and clapping sounded like jeering to Niall, and he found himself wondering how they knew that he, a champion, had been defeated by his faulty little brother. Keeping his head down, not wanting to show his face, he watched raindrops from a sudden cloudburst shudder along his crossbar, one following another, two colliding, then fusing, and the unnerving thought came into his mind that were he and his brother to crash together in this race, they might actually become one. A two-faced monster, he whispered, and, having taken such a notion out of his brain and into speech, he thought he might be going mad. He had forgotten to drink, he then realized, was becoming dehydrated and confused. After that he paid close attention to his water bottle, through the gentle Silvermine Mountains, and into Nenagh, though even the act of swallowing was difficult, and the cylindrical bottle strange and foreign in his hand.

He won the stage by four seconds, but knew his brother was there at the finish, in the small clutch of cyclists that had arrived at his heels. Dropping the bike, he did not turn around but staggered instead across the town square to a fountain, where he immersed his head in cold water, trying to drown out images of his brother and cool the tantrums that he could feel rising in his own heart, as if he was the one who had owned them all along.

The Independent was, of course, still in the lead; Siobhan had told him this later that evening, he explained. Even though he himself was stage winner and King of the Hills, the Wild

Wonder, as they now called him in the Broom Wagon, had gained so much time in that half-hour on the second stage that he had kept the yellow jersey, and was likely to keep it forever. His brother was said to be fully exempt from pain, she told Niall. Having been on hand when the Broom Wagon attempted to patch up Kieran's shoulder after the crash, she could attest to this. He puts it somewhere else, she announced, or at least that's what he said. He puts it on the tops of the mountains or in a cloud ... somewhere where it won't bother him. Some man called Michael Kirby had taught him how to do this. Rumour had it that this Kirby was a magnificent sports coach, could transform anyone into an athlete, and had been the making of Olympic runners Pat O'Callaghan and Ronnie Delany, and that while working in America in his youth, he had been in on the training of Jack Dempsey.

"I knew Michael Kirby," Niall said to Tam. "He was a fisherman, and full of weather lore – some of it surprisingly accurate. I knew he was friendly with my brother, but I didn't know he was that essential teacher, and even had I known, I never could have guessed that he would coach." He shook his head. "He is my father's age, an older man then and almost an old man now."

"Did you ever think about asking him where your brother is?" Tam said. "He might just know."

Niall dismissed her suggestion, shaking his head again and moving his arm as if tossing her words out of the way. "Then the next stage was Nenagh to Castlebar," he continued. Overnight it had become unusually warm and there was full sun on the riders all day. "You cursed the rain," Niall said, "but let me tell you, you longed for it when it wasn't there and it was the sun around you all the time. By noon you were chewing the handlebars."

There were a number of ways to become dehydrated, but sun turned out to be the most unpleasant of the lot. There were reflections, refractions, and sun-blindness to contend with, and shimmering mirages in the distance. At one point Niall thought the road ahead was quivering with an oil fire and had braked involuntarily, skidding into a fall, other riders missing him by fractions of inches. Both he and the bike were unharmed, and in minutes he was back in his seat, but his brother had taken the lead when he was down, or so he believed: by now he was unsure whether the yellow jersey was sun-ghost or human. The first dozen or so racers got caught up with a funeral just outside of Killimore. Taking their caps off out of respect, they pushed aggressively through the mourners only to be stopped down the road by a dozen untended cows. The herd trotted for a quarter of a mile in front of the cyclists in an infuriatingly insolent manner before decamping casually down a farm lane.

These interruptions, frustrating though they may have been, had allowed Niall to recuperate from his hallucinatory state and had put new wind in his sails. He stopped only once more that day, to fill his water bottle, and afterwards felt the old euphoria enter his nervous system on the long stretch through the Burran and into Castlebar. In the end he had won the stage by nine seconds. He discovered his brother had kept the jersey, however, having ridden beside him into the town, just before pulling ahead. They did not speak on arrival, Kieran walking off before Niall had a chance to catch his breath. "I watched him move away," he told Tam. "His upper body was tilted toward the right. He was nursing that shoulder, the shoulder and the pain he was supposedly unable to feel. I allowed myself to feel some sympathy for him then, but the determination had got into me and wouldn't let go, so I pushed the feeling aside and went, instead, to look for the girl."

She was not to be found, however. Having relatives in Castlebar, her uncle had no doubt insisted she should spend the evening and the night with them. The billets that night were crowded, and Niall and his teammates were sleeping two and three to a bed. But no one wanted to search out a tavern; the length of the Rás was beginning to alter the notion of sleep. They all longed for it and retired early.

Still, the talk about the Independent continued. He was out there in the dark, one of the men said sleepily, seeking out herbs for controlling pain. He had exercises he knew, taught to Dempsey by Kirby, for overcoming injury and staying the course. No dislocation, not even a fracture, could stop him, he had been that tightly wound by his coach. Wasn't he just like a boxer, staggering back after an almost knockout, even more eager to continue the fight? Furthermore, it was said that he had dismounted his bicycle and had said five "Hail Marys" with the mourners on the road, making up the time lost with hardly any effort at all. "He's my goddamned brother," Niall had hissed in the dark of the room, "there's nothing you can tell me about him. He's not a stranger."

But he *was* a stranger. What did he know of him, really, beyond sporadic visits to Gerry-Annie's and then those grim, tense evenings with their father? He'd had no idea that aspiration could have made an appearance in his character, no idea that he would appoint himself as a protector of Susan. Was his brother, in some cruel joke, trying to get back at him for a series of imaginary misdemeanours? Was that what this was all about?

The seventh stage was the easiest, shorter by several miles, and covering a terrain of relative flatness. Niall flew off into the dawn of the sombre day, the spray from the previous night's rain rising on either side of him like silken, transparent wings. The anger had dimmed somewhat and his confidence was back. He finished the one-hundred-and-twenty-mile stretch and arrived well ahead of the pack in Sligo, having averaged thirty miles an hour and with plenty of time ahead of him for both recuperation and recreation. He hadn't seen Kieran in the course of the ride, and Niall felt in his bones that the injury must be causing him to lag behind. He knew his stage victories were unearned: there was no way that Kieran could have kept up after days of pain. But he relished them nonetheless and swaggered into the tavern in the evening, certain he was the hero of the day.

It wasn't long, however, before he was told that the Wild Wonder had come in only six minutes after him, and was still overall race leader. This worried him, but he firmly believed that Kieran would flag on the last stage, which was to be the longest at one hundred and fifty miles. It was said that he was eating nothing at all except what he could catch or find in the nearby woods, and while Niall didn't quite believe this, he suspected that the pain would have diminished his appetite and that, on a stage as long as the one that would present itself the following day, Kieran was bound to get the "hunger knock," the crippling fatigue that had taken many a rider out in the past. He also knew there came a time when exhaustion or pain stopped the body from absorbing nourishment even when meals had been taken. Limited food would ensure the knock's arrival. With this in mind, Niall had eaten two dinners that night; one at the billet and another in the tavern, with an extra bowl of local potatoes thrown into the bargain. By now he wanted to sleep with the blond Siobhan, but there was no privacy to be had, and anyway, the unsatisfied lust would cause a kind of ferocity in him the following day, as he knew well from the playing fields of the past. Susan came into his mind then, and he recalled that she would be in Dublin for the finish, standing with two fathers, her own and his.

"I wondered," Niall said, "why I hadn't thought of this before." He stood and began to walk back and forth on the carpet at the end of the bed.

"About the two fathers?"

"No," he said, walking to the window and back, "not them. I wondered why" – he stopped and gave her a sidelong look – "I rarely thought of Susan at all."

Tam wanted him to sit down again. There was something in this pacing that suggested he was about to leave. He was developing a bit of a stoop, she realized, and for the first time was aware that he would someday become an older man. "Come here," she said, laying her hand on the bed.

He sat back down in the chair, however, and she was hurt by this small refusal. "It's true, though. I never thought of her," he continued. "There were others in the Rás who carried on about their girls. I believed I just wasn't the type to wear my heart on my sleeve. Now I wonder if I had a heart at all."

"Of course you . . ." Tam began. She couldn't finish the sentence. She couldn't use the word *heart* with the whole room between them and the memory of their earlier words so fresh in her mind. She sat up instead and opened her arms. "Come closer, Niall," she said. "Come over here and . . ."

He was not listening, not responding to her. "You have no idea what kind of condition Kieran was in the following morning," he said. "He came to the start with the Kerry team manager – a man I knew and still know – guiding him, practically carrying him, and it was clear he barely knew what was happening. His pallor was bad, wrong, and, though I wasn't close enough to see, I knew his eyes would be unfocused. This manager and another fellow from the Kerry team literally lifted him onto the bicycle." Niall shifted in his chair and cleared his throat. "Then with two others holding the bike, they placed his hands on the bars and strapped his feet to the pedals. I remember thinking, They want him now, they want him badly, and I remember feeling the unfairness of this, the appropriation. Though I never would have admitted this, I admired his stance as an independent, and some part of me wanted him to keep that. And now here were these men claiming him, as though he had always been theirs. He was nobody's. Not mine. Not theirs. And their insistence that he continue in his condition was cruel: I wanted to believe that. They had encouraged me to join the Kerry team at one point, you know, but I was all Dublin by then, a spoiled, educated toff who wanted nothing to do with my home county. It was bloody cruel what they wanted from him, and I believed, and enjoyed believing, there was no way he could provide. Still, when they shoved him off, he rode like the wind."

Niall had bided his time on the first half of the stage, stopping often to fill his bottle or to gulp down a sandwich. The weather was unsettled but cooperative, raining just when you thought you couldn't stand the sun, and shining when the rain had weighted you down, drying out the jersey you were wearing, polka dot or otherwise. Then, to his utter amazement, Kieran and his yellow jersey passed him just outside Mullingar. The crowd in that town had been howling for the Independent — by now the news of this wonder had preceded him and no doubt was part of what spurred him on. "But, in truth, it was the support of the Kerry team that did it," Niall said, "those boys from Castleisland, or Milltown, or Glenbeigh. Only farmhands or butcher's boys; spalpeens, some of them. They were surrounding him, cutting the force of the air around him in half, sometimes leaning toward him in order to speak . . . one of them even laid a steadying hand on Kieran's shoulder. It was as if they were all in an exclusive club that no one was going to be able to break into. And all of this, mind you, in a life-threatening zone of speed."

The sight of his brother being so tenderly ministered to had lit a kind of fire in Niall's mind. "I barely remember the rest of the Rás," he said to Tam, "only that, hours later, when I gained on him, and then passed him, he was riding by the wall, not paying attention to the boys in the team who were still doing their best to protect him, but looking at the goddamned wall, as if he wanted to find a bird's nest in the hedgerows, or a snail between the stones. Then suddenly he was up on the pedals and making a breakaway. An ignorant way to ride. But that was my last rational thought. After that I had no access to my own brain. It was like I had left my body, was watching myself on the bicycle from somewhere else, as if I were a spectator, or my own ghost, or overhead in a balloon. And then, soon, the streets of Dublin – those crowds – and after the finish I was down on my back with my father and Susan's father pouring water over me, telling me I had won the stage."

"Won the stage," he said to Tam, "but not the Rás."

"I was familiar with being carried on other men's shoulders. I had won four stages in a row, they told me as they hoisted me along the street. No one had ever done that before. No one would ever do that again. But who is Rás leader? I eventually managed to blurt out. I should have known the answer. The front runners always win. And then my father, one of the men holding me, said the words. 'Your brother,' he said. 'Your brother is Rás leader.'"

The men had put him down at the place where his brother was lying. A double victory for the Riordans, they had said, and his father had said this with them. "And there was Susan with Kieran's head in her lap. He was barely conscious and she was weeping, weeping and gently touching his ruined shoulder. I'm certain I heard him say four words to her. *You are mine now*, he said. I'm sure I heard him say this. A trite and romantic thing to say, right out of a penny novelette! And the blind innocence of the statement, and of the man who made it! The stupid sincerity! I was appalled by it – by him – felt he had no right to this ludicrous innocence and sincerity. And the Kerry team around him, and each member of it looking on and listening with tears in his eyes. The inane sentimentality of these people," he said, gesturing toward the window as if one could see the Kerry team, gathered together in a nearby field.

"The medics were on him then, and he was taken away, and Susan stood and squared her shoulders. I'm sure of this too. She actually braced herself. And then she came to me. As if she knew, she *knew* who she belonged to, she walked over to me."

"Of course she would have been sorry for your brother's injury," Tam said.

Niall was on his feet now, fully dressed and ready to leave her cottage. "You would think that," he said, "but it was not so. She loved him, you see, and he her. I fully understood in that moment what had driven my brother throughout the race. It wasn't rage that deadened the pain; it was this love between them, that sincerity and innocence. He must have believed that after winning, once he was a victor, she would come to him. But she hadn't in her the courage for that. And I claimed her, I *claimed* her. I had no love at all, for anyone. All I had was this insistence on winning. She asked, only once, if I thought it was the best thing, this marriage. But I insisted on it. And, afterwards, he left the country. He left the country and never came back. There's no glory here, no quantity of newspaper stories – and there were plenty of those, you can be sure – that can save you from emigration. Not if you are a man like him, a man of the hills, a man from the mountains, a man full of sincerity and innocence. What else could he do?" Niall looked out the window for a moment and then turned back to Tam. "What else would he have wanted to do? I'd taken everything from him."

Tam, naked in the sheet she had wrapped around herself, felt vulnerable and exposed in the presence of this man who was dressed for other rooms, other relationships. She wanted him to cross the room, place a hand on her bare shoulder. He had opened this whole disturbing chapter of his life to her, and yet they were still somehow apart. He would not permit her to console him. "She could have refused you," she said softly.

Niall did not turn toward her. "What kind of a life could he have given her, this 'Wild Wonder'? And," he said again, "I insisted on it."

Tam could barely speak. "You love her then."

He looked at her for what seemed a long time. "Have you understood none of this?" he said. "I'm a waster, Tamara, I waste things. I waste people. I deplete them. I have never troubled myself to know the value of anyone, anything, not my own abilities, my own good fortune, my family, Susan. The small magical brother I was given was worth ten of me, and I utterly disregarded him."

"But for me . . ." she said, looking away as if ashamed by what she was about to reveal, "you transform every room you walk into. It's never been like this with anyone. It is impossible for me to let it go."

He was silent, his face so disclosed and pained she found it difficult to hold the gaze. Then he lowered his eyes and shook his head. "No," he said. "You've misunderstood. This — you and me — this is the only time I've come close to anything like that. And I cannot replicate the kind of sentiment I saw that day in Kieran. I don't have it in me. Nothing about this is ever going to be redeemable, Tamara. And I can tell you now I want no part of it."

"That can't be true," she began, "because we would never . . ."

But he was striding out of the room, through the kitchen. The sound of his footsteps ceased for a few seconds. Then she heard the front door opening, and she knew he had walked away.

MORNING

—

The building had been finished around him as he worked. There had been a symphony of drills, hammers, electric saws, always in his ears, shrieking or staccato against the tiny brushstrokes the tempera demanded. The workmen, joking with him, sometimes throwing eggs, or the shells of eggs that littered the floor beneath the scaffolding he stood on, were good men, and hard workers, as Kenneth had come to know. One of them had come up with the mock title *Flight and Its Allergies*, and he had joined in the hilarity that ensued among them. They had joked with him, and one or two, genuinely curious, had asked him questions while he painted one figure or another. They had also coaxed him into bars after work — had even, on occasion, invited him home for supper. As the weeks passed, Kenneth thought about his own family, his separation from them. It would be good to be back.

It had taken him three months to complete the thirty-six four-by-six-foot panels that would join together, like a huge puzzle, to form the immense mural. The last thing he painted, on the final morning, was a third apple – airborne – tossed by a child juggler. The apples were like tiny planets, and the child, otherwise small and unexceptional, gained power through his manipulation of them. Kenneth had to break one last egg to paint this, and as he passed it from hand to hand, letting the white drain to the floor, and allowing the clean yolk to settle in his palm, he looked at this boy – his serene, confident expression, the three apples aloft, the face calm with the knowledge that they would be kept in the air indefinitely. While Kenneth mixed the yolk with the warm shades of ground pigment, he remembered the critic telling him to keep things on the picture plane flat, two-dimensional, and he smiled as the apple became spherical under his brush. When he could imagine the weight of it in his hand, he knew he was finished. Then he began to toss brushes, palettes, and pigments down to the floor below. There was a drill shrieking somewhere in the building. The clatter his tools made on landing must have been drowned out by its noise.

Kenneth figured he had broken five thousand eggs, more or less, in the making of the mural, and each time he broke the shell, he thought of the critic's head, the smooth baldness of the top of it. Humpty-Dumpty, he thought, this wall, and the wall of cultural fashion that could keep you out, for a while, until the great fall. By now he knew that fashion always fell, it failed and fell. He was happy to be free of it. And as he used the shell to separate the white from the yolk, he thought about Harding, a man who had never made use of egg tempera. He wondered what had become of him. And the woman Harding had loved, whether she had ever painted again, and whether or not he himself would ever come across a painting by Gentleman. The girl in Germany, the couple in Italy, floated by, a sense of them here and there in the mural. These narratives fought for space in his mind. But the mural itself, he knew, was divorced from narrative. As it should be, he whispered to himself, as it should be. *Flight and Its Allegories*.

Once he was on the ground, he rifled through a canvas sack until he found the camera he was looking for, a Brownie Starflex, with six exposures still available. He shot the mural from left to right. Then he walked across the full length of the half-tiled floor. This was the last exposure and it would make the mural look incredibly small, like a two-inch-long piece of ribbon with an unreadable pattern on it. But he wanted to show its proportions to a friend and, in any case, the more professional pictures would be taken later, after he was gone, when the mural had begun to live its own independent life in the presence of an audience.

For months now there had been noise, the workmen's power tools and, in the odd moments when those were silent, the roar of the planes arriving and departing at the old, soon-to-be-abandoned terminal. He had seen the passengers, through the plate glass of the windows, rivers of them, pouring down the steps that were pushed up to airliners, then flowing darkly across the tarmac. What would they make of *Flight and Its Allegories*? Would they be struck by it? Or would they simply pass it by, preoccupied by the mysteries of their individual lives as they walked forward or waited in the lounge? He was not unaware that public art could be – and often was – ignored. Still, what pleasure he had taken in the making of it.

He hauled the canvas sack full of brushes and pigment out to the old grey car, a junker he had bought four months ago from a fisherman. He hoped this vehicle would be reliable for another couple of days, long enough to get him to Channel-Port aux Basques. He had not arrived and would not be departing by air, and for the first time he became aware of the irony of this. There would be the drive across this huge, wild island, the ferry that would connect him with the mainland train, then days of train travel to the centre of his vast country. He would leave the car at the port, to be towed, stolen, or junked. He would step onto the ferry. Quite possibly, he would never return.

Five or six years later Kenneth would pick up a newspaper to discover that there were fewer and fewer planes landing at Gander Airport. Larger aircraft with jet engines were now over-flying the "Crossroads of the World" – and its beautiful new terminal – on most transatlantic flights, as there was no longer any need to stop and refuel. A picture of the empty passenger lounge would be placed beside the article. In it Kenneth would be able to see a corner of the mural, but the shot would be so grainy and unfocused, the figures would be unreadable.

But now, during the drive across Newfoundland, the Italian lakeside town of Orta was present in his mind, the ferry he had never taken, and the meeting that had not taken place. But he was finished with waiting now; he would leave that to the passengers, those who were adrift and pausing on their journey from one set of travels to another.

THERE HAD BEEN TIMES WHEN SHE HAD FELT THAT Niall and his embraces had been forced upon her in some way. Not that he had forced his way into her world so much, but she had assumed that the person she had been when he walked through her door, the person she would be all through their long, sporadic, and fragile communion, had been all but powerless in the face of him and the way he filled a room. Lack of certainty, ambivalence, impossibility, and no hope whatsoever of resolution had all been sidestepped by her, sometimes completely ignored. It had been as if she had been running away from any reliable version of herself. And yet now she finds herself thoroughly caught in the most unreliable version of all.

She looks up and sees a small female figure placed in the far right of the mural's picture frame, lost in the shadows of dense foliage, a bouquet of something that is not quite floral in her hands. Oddly bridal, Tam thinks, though there is no veil and the woman is painted in brunette colours, not just her hair and eyes, but also her brown clothing, her shoes. And yet, in spite of her entanglement in pale shadows, in spite of the stillness of her pose, she appears to be emerging. She seems about to step away from her partner, a diminutive male figure, more emphatically situated in dense vegetation and shaded more intensely by greys and blacks. She would step forward, he would step back, or she would step back and he forward, whatever the dance they might be performing.

And now this sudden choice: two planes, two Constellations gleaming on the tarmac, one heading for New York, the other destined for Shannon.

She visualizes her small house, empty now of the life she has lived in it, with no lamps lit and a cold hearth. Sometimes a downdraft from the chimney might touch a curtain, but otherwise there would be no breath at all in the room. "Dark houses," one of the neighbours had said about a clutch of stones that had once been four or five cottages at the end of the road. "Dark houses," the old man had said. "We don't like that kind of thing near us." *Near us*, Tam thinks now. *Dark houses*.

Beyond the windows, there would be drenched fields and tarry bogs slowly succumbing to the bruise-coloured dusk of an autumn afternoon. So beautiful really, and so strangely gratifying. She herself has seen, has been moved by such things, moved by the muscular weather and the departing light. The day could start fair and by early afternoon a gale of increasing ferocity might be twisting the two trees in the yard. You never knew how the weather was going to present itself or what your own reaction would be in the face of it. And occasionally there had been a man with her, a man who had predicted this weather and who would be preparing to leave. But she had known, essentially, she has to admit she had known, that he would always come back. The phone would ring, and the dance would begin again. Then there would be that heron, lifting out of the marsh, wind under its wings and the pull of a nest near the lake. "Desperate trouble," Niall had said, "you could step into desperate trouble from something like this." The dance. And then the lament.

She looks at the mural, moving her head from left to right, taking in the full brunt of it in the rich, low morning light. She allows its chaos and its odd calm to enter her mind. Some of the figures are so emplaced they seemed to be wholly defined by the act of absolute arrival. Others are caught in the process of moving away. And far back in the trees, rendered in shades of grey, one or two appear to be poised on the edge of full disappearance.

She thinks of Niall's mother, her final desperate step. Had that walk into air and darkness been a comfort or a declaration of full despair? How had her face looked to her that last day in the oval that was her mirror? Did she waver, even for a moment, when her love for the two boys presented itself, as it must have done? She couldn't have foreseen what would become of her youngest son, how he would collapse into the nightmare of rage. And she wouldn't have known that the other, older boy would be unable to recognize his own fragility in the face of her defection. And yet in him, from then on, Tam now understands, there had always been hesitation and curtailment.

For one moment she pictures the artist finishing up, descending from the scaffold, stepping back, and looking at the long sweep of what he had done. Something would have struck him then, a sense of loss: the knowledge of an ending. How intimate he would have been with the skin of the wall, with every square inch of it. For months maybe, the way he touched and changed that surface would have been the only real relationship in his life. Still, he would have collected his brushes and his paints. He would have climbed down from the scaffolding. And then he would have had to walk away.

Year after year she had feared that each meeting would be their last. That they would be spent, or were already spent and not admitting it. But still they met, and still the flesh leapt to life, as if an essential transfusion were taking place. Whatever complicated collection of moods she had amassed during their time apart would be swept aside like an irrelevant detritus in a swollen river, drowned by engagement and communion. And afterwards she was elated or filled with grief. She could never predict which.

Then, after years of restraint, the relationship had slipped over an unacknowledged edge and quietly deepened for her so that everything they had missed – a child, shared sleep, the comfort of morning rooms – began to feel like possessions wrenched unfairly from her rather than those she had never owned. It was as if they had made grave errors of judgment, she and Niall, and the grief – for her – was almost unmanageable. Alone she composed the perfect sentences she would never say to him about this, sentences about how she couldn't bear to watch him walk away one more time, or the horror of suspecting that when all was said and done, he had decided against her in some crucial way. Still, he had always returned, and when he returned, there had always been those moments of joy. "This mystery," he had said once. She remembers him saying that.

She opens her handbag and searches for her ticket and her chequebook. When she finds them, she stands and moves away from the bench. At the counter, the man with Niall's accent is absorbed by other travellers. There would be a new schedule for the day that is clarifying beyond the windows, a new list of passengers. The silver skin of the two waiting planes is something she is familiar with, that and the almost-erotic desire to board one of them and to own the hand that operates the controls. Barely imagined and never to be real-ized, the life in New York fades and withdraws, and she knows, suddenly, that Niall's mercurial brother is not in that city. He is alive somewhere, with his own peculiar history active in his mind. The long narrative Niall had presented to her was not finished, not yet. "It's not finished yet," she wants to say to Niall now, "not any of it. And there is no fault, no blame."

The passenger who had been standing in front of her moves to one side. When she places her hand on the counter, the ticket agent looks up. "Shannon," she says.

HE PEDALLED ALONG THE ROAD FROM CAHERSIVEEN, past the birthplace of Daniel O'Connell, the Great Liberator, over the Fertha River at the bridge at Carhan, then past the lichen-yellowed ruins of the old workhouse at Ballagh. The road began to rise slightly now, but Kieran barely noticed; each indentation and every hint of elevation was so familiar to him that the features of the road's surface might have been extensions of his own body. A glimpse of the painted iron gates of the long-gone landlord's house and splashes of pink, the surviving roses from the landlord's abandoned gardens. And then to his right, the empty Gothic window of the church ruins, fragile over the potent shadow thrown by its own darkened walls. And all around it, the undulations of the burial ground, and those teeth of stone, unembellished markers for the graves of the poor.

It was the gable end of the house he saw first, still painted blue, the shape of the chimney with some of its plaster gone and the stones showing, two orange chimney pots, strangely new-looking, but with no turf smoke moving out of them and over the valley. There had never been a lane — except the one that led back to the five fields Gerry O'Connell had built — and the grass had always grown right up to Gerry-Annie's stoop.

This grass was long now, and once he dismounted from the bicycle, it began to soak his shoes. The red paint he himself had put there years ago had peeled and faded, and the door was slightly ajar. Not knowing what to do or how to let his new self enter, he came to a halt in front of the threshold. He had torn in and out of this door as a boy but now hesitated to announce the man he had become. He saw that the white paint on the window trim was missing in most places, and he thought he would fix that in a day or two. He hadn't yet noticed that one of the panes of glass was smashed on the ground beside him.

With the flat of his hand he pushed on the door, but it didn't budge, so he used his shoulder to nudge it open, then stepped over the weed-choked threshold and into the room. So familiar were the shapes around him it took him some time to realize that the interior had changed, though Gerry-Annie's belongings were everywhere in the room. Her kettle sat in the ashes of her fire, the iron bar from which it had hung having rusted and collapsed. The pattern on the oil-cloth that covered her table was indistinguishable, furred by dust. Two cups and saucers sat on the table, similarly coated, and one was broken, likely by visiting sheep who had defecated, he was beginning to find, all over the concrete floor. In places the rising damp had removed the upper coat of paint from the blue-grey walls, revealing surprisingly vibrant colours that must have come from the time of Annie's youth, when Gerry himself had still been alive.

A breeze was moving through the window by way of the missing pane he now took note of, and Gerry-Annie's disintegrating lace curtains moved with it. One of the curtains was stirring near his elbow and he caught it in his hand and held it there. He was moved even by something as simple as Annie's stitches holding up the hem. But it was her two coats hanging beside the door that shook him; the one for everyday, and the one with the lambswool collar for Mass, a pair of shoes and a set of fur-topped galoshes neatly placed beneath. Each coat was cocooned in a shroud of pale spider webs, and each was like Gerry-Annie's ghost standing near the wall. More than anything else it was the thickness of the webs that made him come to realize how long she had been gone.

He found himself in the adjacent room staring at her bed. The quilt she had made from scraps given to her by Davey the tailor was there and one pillow, its slip much stained by leakage from the roof. He glanced at the Sacred Heart still hanging above the headboard, opaque under the dusty glass of the frame, and for a minute he thought he might want to say a prayer, as he knew she would have liked that. But the moment passed. What good had all that been to her in the end with no one left even to clear the most intimate of her belongings from her empty house? He hoped, however, that a proper Mass had been said for her and that some neighbours, at least, had stood by her grave.

Walking back into the room, he realized he had planned nothing beyond this reunion with his childhood, the child he had been and the woman who had loved that child, and now he did not know what to do. He had slept outdoors for most of the previous three months and that, plus illness and the drink, had altered his appearance, made him look even more the vagrant than he already was, though he rarely thought of this, having little access to mirrors. But now he wondered. Had Annie been sitting near the fire, would she have recognized him as he drew near to her? Without her, there was no avenue of approach to the boy he had been, no way of keeping that boy alive. He couldn't remember how she had survived, procured the meat for the stew, the bread for the table, or, beyond the tailor's skill and his own father's generosity, provided the clothes for his back, even shoes, for he had never gone barefoot except in summer. The tailor must be gone as well. He remembered him as an old man, in spite of his vitality, his expertise with the violin given to his grandfather, allegedly by a landlord, the way the birds had dived in through the door, stood on his knee while he fed them, then flown out again.

The cow byre's tin roof was loose on the boards and rattling in the wind, but it had held enough of the rain at bay that the spade and scythe he found beneath it were not rusted through. Neither were the bicycles, all twelve of them, though some had fallen and seemed to be clutching at one another on the earthen floor. He turned away from these, shaking his head and remembering.

"Gerry's spade, Gerry's scythe," he heard himself say, touching each object in turn and saying out loud the name of a man he had never known beyond the desperate role described by Annie in her stories about him. There was a metal pail as well, with only one small perforation in the bottom, and this he took out to the pump, where he moved the handle up and down. He was listening to the crow-call sounds of the pump's inner workings with such concentration that he was startled when the water gushed into the pail and onto the ground beside it. It seemed like the beginning of something to him, life bubbling out of the earth, and he took some heart from it, and from the small tin cup still hanging from the spout.

His mouth remembered the taste of the water as he drank.

By mid-afternoon, having found Gerry-Annie's broom behind the door standing handle end down so that the bristles were not bent, he had swept all evidence of sheep from the room and had thrown four pailfuls of water across the floor. It seemed neither the paint nor the concrete had deteriorated, and an ox-blood red colour emerged after the third pail. He found a filthy rag near the fireplace, washed it under the pump, and began to wipe the dust from the table's oilcloth, which revealed itself to be decorated with the fishing scenes he remembered liking as a boy, and then, after carefully removing the dishes from the open shelves of the dresser, he took them outside. Five minutes later, washing the dishes in the pail, he admitted to himself that, even without Gerry-Annie's warm presence, he had come home.

By evening he had found a pitchfork, removed the old grey straw and the mice nests from Gerry-Annie's bed, scrubbed

the headboard and slats with the cloth, and had surrepti-
tiously borrowed fresh, dry straw from of one of the small
stooks he had taken note of in a nearby field. He had one
candle with him in his pack, and this he lit as the darkness
deepened, recalling gratitude. Then he removed a bundle of
torn cloth and began to carefully unwind it until a small
Belleek basket emerged. This he placed on a shelf near the
bed, where he knew he would see it when he woke. He pulled
a frayed blanket from the bottom of his pack, wrapped himself up, and settled into the place beside the wall that had held
his child's body in the past when, for those brief, but vividly
recalled first few weeks, he had slept with the comforting
plump warmth of Gerry-Annie beside him, lest, she'd said,
there was some kind of fracas in the night.

Just before he closed his eyes, he thought, as always, of
his brother, simply because the habit of thinking about him
had outlived the anger that had first accompanied those
thoughts. He'd go to the weather station, he decided, maybe
not tomorrow but soon. Blood, he thought, but in relation to
their being siblings: there was not the whisper of a feud left
in him. He would be able to separate now the girl he had
loved from the woman who, for years now, would have been
his brother's wife.

He awakened in full dark to the sound of animal hooves and
soft lowing accompanied by quiet laughter and speech; girls
bringing cattle down from the mountains to the morning

market in Cahersiveen. Annie told him she herself had performed this task, each week, from the time she could walk until she married. It was a struggle at first, she had told him, to keep up with her older sisters. But she'd wanted to do it, and so they'd let her come along.

He recalled then the miraculous Rás Tailteann, how the last old man of Europe and his wife had been there to celebrate him at the finish, and beside them his mother, insubstantial but radiant with no warnings on her smiling mouth. Michael Kirby, the actual, with his fist in the air, Davey the tailor, Donal from the mountains, Gerry-Annie herself, his own father all present, all cheering him on. And Susan as the girl she had been, how he had collapsed toward her, how they had fallen together then, and fallen apart.

And now, the light of a lantern beam on the wall, the sound of a switch brushing an animal's flank, the music of old Irish words carried on a girl's breath: all of this enveloped him as he lay in the dark with the light of one star reaching him through a hole in the roof. It was these things that made him come to know it was morning, and that the day about to break was Wednesday.

ACKNOWLEDGEMENTS

———

This book is a work of fiction: all characters, situations, relationships, and sometimes settings are products of the imagination or have been worked on and transformed by the imagination. There were several instances when I felt I needed to keep the actual name of the person whose life had contributed to the makeup of the character I was creating, mostly because I wanted to honour the person in question. This was especially true of the Canadian artist Kenneth Lochhead, whose mural *Flight and Its Allegories* remains a fascinating fixture in Gander International Airport in Newfoundland. But it is also true in the case of the poet, fisherman, and Gaelic scholar Michael Kirby, whom I had the great privilege of coming to know in Ballinskelligs, Ireland, in the 1990s. The verse on page 230 is from his book *Skelligside* (Lilliput Press, 1990). His bicycle coaching is an act of my imagination. The meteorologist, McWilliams, is partly based on the *Irish Times'* extraordinarily gifted weather forecaster and writer of weather lore, Brendan McWilliams. Alas, I never met Brendan McWilliams, but I was — and remain — a great admirer of his *Weather Eye on Literature*, and *The Illustrated Weather Eye*, the beautiful book his wife, Anne McWilliams, compiled after his much-too-early death.

There is one reference to the fabulous farmer, footballer, and folklorist Padraig O'Connell. He will have to look carefully to find it.

Significant sections of this book could not have been written had I not come across the highly engaging and brilliantly researched volume by Tom Daly entitled *The Rás*, published in 2003 by The Collins Press, Cork, Ireland. I owe Mr. Daly a great debt for providing the factual details concerning this demanding and delightful Irish sporting event. I am also indebted to Ted Fraser for conversation, and especially for his beautifully written and insightful *Garden of Light*, the important catalogue that accompanied the 2005 Kenneth Lochhead retrospective. *Turner in Germany* by Cecilia Powell (Tate Gallery Publications, 1996) was also a source. Bill Terry in Sechelt, British Columbia, was extremely helpful and more inspiring than he knew when he shared a family story, and Noreen O'Sullivan in the Cahersiveen Library helped me track down some of the places associated with that story. In Gander, the librarian Pat Parsons was both welcoming and instructive, as was the staff at the University of Regina Archives where Kenneth Lochhead's papers are housed.

A few patient people read and commented on the manuscript in its early stages. Among them I would particularly like to thank Joanne Lochhead for her warmth and generosity, Marilyn Dickson for sharing her expertise concerning aircraft and female aviators, Michael Phillips for his charity, and Mieke Bevelander for listening. As always, thanks to the copyeditor, Heather Sangster, for her sharp eye and her wisdom as she unearthed mistakes, factual and otherwise, and to Lynn Schellenberg, who read and carefully corrected the proofs. I am extremely grateful to both, as well as to Kendra Ward for making things circulate among us all. I was extremely gratified by Ileene Smith of Farrar, Straus and Giroux and Juliet Mabey at Oneworld Publications in the U.K. responding as enthusiastically as they did to the manuscript.

Enormous gratitude goes to Ellen Levine for her long-term affection and for her brilliant expertise.

Finally, and as always, I would like to thank my publisher and editor, Ellen Seligman, for her loving attention to this book and all the others, and for a sustaining friendship that has enhanced my writing and my life for thirty years.